PERFORMING SHAKESPEARE
IN THE AGE OF EMPIRE

During the nineteenth century the performance of Shakespeare's plays contributed significantly to the creation of a sense of British nationhood at home and the extension of her influence overseas, not only in her own empire but also in North America and Europe. This was achieved through the enterprise of the commercial theatre rather than state subsidy and institutions. Britain had no National Theatre, but Shakespeare's plays were performed up and down the land from the fashionable West End to the suburbs of the capital and the expanding industrial conurbations to the north. British actors also travelled the world to perform Shakespeare's plays, while foreign actors regarded success in London as the ultimate seal of approval. In this book Richard Foulkes explores the political and social uses of Shakespeare through the nineteenth and into the twentieth century and the movement from the business of Shakespeare as an enterprise to that of enshrinement as a cultural icon.

With the prospect of the tercentenary of Shakespeare's death in 1916 the campaign for a Shakespeare Memorial National Theatre gathered pace. This was promoted as a benefit to the whole English-speaking world and the equal of the state theatres of Europe, but it fell victim to the outbreak of war, which coincided with a decline in traditional Shakespeare and exposed the nation's lack of any institutional stage.

The achievements of leading Shakespearian actors, managers and directors, not only from Britain (Macready, Phelps, Irving, Tree and Granville Barker), but also Europe (Saxe-Meiningen, Modjeska, Bernhardt, Salvini) and North America (Forrest, Cushman, Aldridge and Booth), are set in the context of national and international events, alternative forms of patronage and the forces of nationhood and imperialism to reveal the intricate and fascinating story of the performance of Shakespeare's plays across the globe during this period of apparently limitless British ascendancy.

PERFORMING SHAKESPEARE IN THE AGE OF EMPIRE

RICHARD FOULKES

CAMBRIDGE
UNIVERSITY PRESS

PUBLISHED BY THE PRESS SYNDICATE OF THE UNIVERSITY OF CAMBRIDGE
The Pitt Building, Trumpington Street, Cambridge, United Kingdom

CAMBRIDGE UNIVERSITY PRESS
The Edinburgh Building, Cambridge CB2 2RU, UK
40 West 20th Street, New York, NY 10011-4211, USA
477 Williamstown Road, Port Melbourne, VIC 3207, Australia
Ruiz de Alarcón 13, 28014 Madrid, Spain
Dock House, The Waterfront, Cape Town 8001, South Africa

http://www.cambridge.org

First published 2002

Printed in the United Kingdom at the University Press, Cambridge

Typeface Baskerville Monotype 11/12.5 pt.   *System* LATEX 2ε   [TB]

A catalogue record for this book is available from the British Library

Library of Congress Cataloguing in Publication data
Foulkes, Richard.
Performing Shakespeare in the age of empire / Richard Foulkes.
p.   cm.
Includes bibliographical references and index.
ISBN 0 521 63022 3
1. Shakespeare, William, 1564–1616 – Stage history – 1800–1950.   2. Shakespeare,
William, 1564–1616 – Stage history – Great Britain.   3. Shakespeare, William,
1564–1616 – Stage history – North America.   4. Shakespeare, William, 1564–1616 – Stage
history – Europe.   5. Theater – Great Britain – History – 19th century.   6. Theater – Great
Britain – History – 20th century.   7. Theater – History – 19th century.
8. Theater – History – 20th century.   I. Title.
PR3099.F68 2002
792.9'5'09034 – dc21   2001037957

ISBN 0 521 63022 3 hardback

To the contributors to Shakespeare and the Victorian Stage *and the memory of Gareth Lloyd Evans and J. C. Trewin*

Contents

Illustrations

I am grateful to the University of Leicester Reprographic Unit for processing illustrations 1, 3, 4, 6, 7, 9 and 10.

Acknowledgements

The performance of Shakespeare's plays in the nineteenth and early twentieth centuries has been an abiding interest of mine stretching back long before the comparatively short period which I have spent directly on this book. My debts and thanks extend over three decades, in the case of some libraries – for instance – unto the second and third generation of librarians.

My immediate acknowledgements begin with the University of Leicester for granting me study leave and the Arts and Humanities Research Board for an award under the Research Leave Scheme. The British Academy – not for the first time – provided funds for research in Britain and the United States. As a result I was able to work in the following libraries to whose staff I am indebted: the Folger Shakespeare Library, the Harvard Theatre Collection, the Shakespeare Centre Library, the Shakespeare Birthplace Trust Record Office, the Shakespeare Institute, the Shubert Archive, New York, the University of Bristol Theatre Collection, Manchester Central Library and the British Library. I should also include the University of Leicester Library and the H. A. Jones Theatre Collection at the University Centre, Northampton.

I gratefully acknowledge the gracious permission of Her Majesty Queen Elizabeth II for the use of material from the Royal Photographic Collection and the Royal Archives.

I have benefited from the assistance of: Dr Katharine Brisbane, Miss Pamela Clark, John Cunningham, Charles Edwards, Dr Peter Fawcett, Nicole Fayard, Professor Werner Habicht, Professor Peter Holland, Emeritus Professor H. A. Jones, the Venerable T. Hughie Jones, Kaori Kobayashi, Anthony Meredith, Professor J. R. Mulryne, Professor Michael Patterson, Miss Pat Perkins, Sheila Rosenberg, Professor John Stokes and Roger Warren.

I greatly appreciate the support and encouragement of my colleagues in the Department of English at the University of Leicester.

Dr Victoria Cooper, Commissioning Editor for Drama at Cambridge University Press, has brought her customary enthusiasm and commitment to the volume.

I am grateful to my family for their understanding attitude towards my absorption in Victorian Shakespeare, especially to my wife, Christine, who has lovingly sustained me through the processes involved in bringing this book to completion.

Introduction

The theme of this book is that Shakespeare's cultural pre-eminence, nationally and internationally, during the period 1832 to 1916 was based on the performance of his plays. Recent studies of Shakespeare's elevation to the status of national icon by Gary Taylor (*Reinventing Shakespeare* 1990), Michael Dobson (*The Making of a National Poet* 1992) and Jonathan Bate (*Shakespearean Constitutions* 1989, *The Genius of Shakespeare* 1997) have not concerned themselves greatly with the stage. Yet it is a truth universally acknowledged that Shakespeare was a consummate man of the theatre, immersed in its practicalities as well as its arts, sensitive to its socially diverse audience and alert to the verdict of the box office. His plays were the product of his unique genius and the theatrical conditions in which he worked. His genius inevitably assured his place in the nation's artistic pantheon, but his roots in popular theatre ensured his place on the stage until almost the end of the period under review.

Whilst not denying the instances of royal, aristocratic and civic patronage, it is nevertheless true to say that historically the basis upon which the British theatre operated was commercial. Britain's monarchs did not erect grandiose court theatres, its governments did not aggrandise themselves with imposing state theatres and its municipalities did not minister to their citizens through the medium of subsidised theatres. Not that the theatre lay outside the sphere of official regulations. The warrants issued to Thomas Killigrew and William Davenant on 21 August 1660 by King Charles II were perpetuated by the monopolies enjoyed by Covent Garden and Drury Lane, not the least important aspect of which was their exclusive right over the performance of Shakespeare's plays in the capital. Successive managers of the patent theatres fell under the obligation to perform the plays of the national dramatist, but without the state subventions enjoyed by their continental counterparts. In 1832 the spirit of reform reached the patent theatres with the recommendation of the parliamentary Select Committee that the monopoly be abolished, though it took until 1843 for this to happen. The abolition of the patent theatres' monopoly was consistent with other anti-restrictive reforms in trade, politics and so on, but voices (Edward Bulwer Lytton, W. J. Fox amongst them) were raised arguing that the state should assume responsibilities for the recreation of the people (particularly the poor) including the establishment of a National Theatre. This suggestion fell on deaf ears and instead of being privileged by enshrinement (or incarceration) in a national institution, Shakespeare had to take his chance in the knockabout world of commercial entertainment.

This outcome was not the result of formal debate or political policy making, but rather a reflection of the prevailing attitudes of the day. Theatre managers, like the electorate as a whole, were to be enfranchised, in their case with the freedom to perform Shakespeare's plays on an equal footing. In the event there was an explosion of Shakespeare from lowly suburban theatres such as Sadler's Wells and Shoreditch to the West End and the court itself; his plays were staged with the vigour, imagination and taste which characterised so much Victorian endeavour. Whether this would have happened if a discrete, specialist institution had been set up charged with the performance of the classics – Shakespeare in particular – can only be a matter of speculation, but it can certainly be asserted that one of the great strengths of the Victorian stage was that it did not segregate actors, audiences and theatres into the legitimate and the illegitimate, the highbrow and lowbrow.

The situation was characterised by the royal family. Queen Victoria's tastes were decidedly catholic, ranging from circuses to Charles Kean's Shakespeare revivals. Prince Albert was more earnest, quizzing Macready about his text for *As You Like It* and looking to the court theatres of Germany for examples of patronage, but he never overlooked the importance of the entertainment available to the population at large. The couple's eldest daughter Princess Victoria, the future Empress (albeit briefly) of Germany, was in her father's mould, whereas, in this respect if in little else, their eldest son, the future King Edward VII, was closer to his mother, devoting himself to the sheer enjoyment of the theatre in all its diversity throughout his adult life. After her husband's death in 1861 Queen Victoria completely renounced the stage for over twenty years, so it was the Prince of Wales who set the tone which, when it came to Shakespeare, ranged from diplomatic (visiting foreign companies) to personal (Mrs Langtry as Rosalind) connections. Kaiser Wilhelm II's theatre-going was in marked contrast to his English cousin's; he maintained an impressive, though rather moribund, court theatre and made it a principle never to attend public playhouses.

Although the British theatre was not beholden to the state for funds, its members nevertheless sought out a quasi-official role. At the beginning of Queen Victoria's reign the stage had been held in low esteem and its leaders seized any opportunity to contribute to national events as a means of elevating their own status and that of their profession. Shakespeare was of course their ace card, which they were only too willing to play at a royal wedding or diplomatic occasion. By the end of the nineteenth century the theatre's fortunes had been transformed, with many leading actors drawn into at least the fringes of the Marlborough House set and Henry Irving's knighthood in 1895 spurring on the ambitions of his peers. For an actor with such ambitions, services to the national dramatist, especially as a diplomatic initiative or contribution to some national event such as a coronation, were particularly apt. Accordingly the performance of Shakespeare's plays featured in the marriage ceremony of Princess Victoria, the coronations of Edward VII and George V, visits by members of the German royal house and – less propitiously – conflicts such as the Boer War.

British actors had long ventured overseas in the search for new audiences, but this process was given added momentum by the colonial expansion of the nineteenth century and the improvement in land (trains) and sea (steam) transport. Although personal advancement (status and money) was their principal driving force, these actors were inevitably implicated in the spread of British hegemony. This could be both an advantage and a disadvantage depending on their destination and the time of their visit. Macready's arrival in the United States in 1848 coincided with a build-up of anti-British feeling, whereas on all of his eight North American tours Henry Irving seized the opportunity to strengthen bonds between the two nations. Throughout the English-speaking world Shakespeare was the playwright whose plays audiences wanted to see, no doubt in some cases because of patriotic and sentimental attachments, but above all because of their sheer entertainment value: the action-packed plots, the legendary yet recognisably human characters, the rich humour, the lofty tragedy, the sensational murders, spine-chilling apparitions and breathtaking battles as well of course as the incomparable language, which was becoming the official and everyday tongue of peoples of very different linguistic and cultural backgrounds. In India the students who flocked to Shakespeare may have been encouraged by the principles enshrined in Macaulay's 'Minute of 2 February 1835' on Indian Education, but English actors invariably testified to the enthusiasm and responsiveness of audiences in the sub-continent and indeed further east.

British actors travelling these enormous distances to perform Shakespeare obviously incurred substantial costs during the long (weeks, months) journeys, but such was the demand at their destination(s) that their outlay was usually (handsomely) recompensed. Even if successive British governments had been minded to do so it is inconceivable that they could have organised the export of Shakespeare on this scale. When the Comédie-Française visited London in 1879, Matthew Arnold sent up the cry '*organise the theatre!*' but those countries which did subsidise the theatre made little impact on the world stage. Corneille, Racine, Goethe, even Molière, as products of a different tradition and system, shared little of Shakespeare's popular appeal.

Instead non-English speaking actors turned to Shakespeare. Naturally many came to London in search of the ultimate imprimatur on their work, as Americans such as Edwin Forrest, Charlotte Cushman, Edwin Booth, Mary Anderson and others did. Helena Modjeska from Poland, Madame Ristori, Salvini and Rossi from Italy, Sarah Bernhardt – having deserted the Comédie-Française – and the Duke of Saxe-Meiningen's company all converged on London, but they also took Shakespeare to audiences across the globe. Modjeska, who did learn English, enjoyed enormous popularity performing Shakespeare in America, but so too did Salvini who always performed in Italian, though sometimes with an Italian-speaking company and sometimes with an English-speaking company. Actors of many different native tongues became adept at these bi-lingual performances of Shakespeare. That they could do so was testimony not only to their own skills, but also to Shakespeare's common currency in the profession across the world and the savvy of their audiences.

This global Shakespearian network was a powerful force for the exchange of technique in both acting and stage practice. Macready, who was influenced by Talma, was Charlotte Cushman's model. The French actor Charles Fechter helped to revolutionise English Shakespearian acting. Originating in Manchester, Charles Calvert's *Henry V* traversed America and the southern hemisphere. The Duke of Saxe-Meiningen, who had been impressed by the productions of Charles Kean and Samuel Phelps, in turn made a strong impact on Henry Irving, Frank Benson and Beerbohm Tree. The ever-eclectic Beerbohm Tree travelled widely, absorbing ideas from Max Reinhardt in Germany and the combined talents of Edward Gordon Craig and Constantin Stanislavski in Moscow, as well as venturing to Hollywood to film *Macbeth* with D. W. Griffith.

For many, Shakespeare was nothing less than a passport to freedom. Ira Aldrich, though the most celebrated, was by no means the only black

American actor to make a successful career performing Shakespeare in Europe, in his case being a particular favourite in Russia and Poland, where he died. Conversely Helena Modjeska had escaped the, for her, repressive situation in Poland and after decades as an international star died in California.

Although Shakespeare had written for a theatre from which they were notably absent the performance of his plays in the nineteenth century afforded extensive opportunities to women. Modjeska, Ristori and Bernhardt took absolute control of their own fortunes, as did Charlotte Cushman and (more briefly) Mary Anderson, in all of whom aspects of Henry James's international diva, Miriam Rooth in *The Tragic Muse*, can be detected. Ellen Kean, Ellen Terry, Adelaide Calvert and even Madge Kendal and Lillah McCarthy pursued their Shakespearian careers for the most part in consort with a male partner, but they were also active in a managerial capacity, as were Sarah Lane, Lillie Langtry, Annie Horniman, Lilian Baylis and Lena Ashwell.

Lena Ashwell pioneered the provision of entertainment, including Shakespeare's plays, at the front during the First World War. This was a profoundly alien outcome for Shakespeare who for so long had embodied the spirit of freedom and internationalism through the performance of his plays. And yet throughout the nineteenth century and more markedly during the early twentieth century the spectre of national rivalry had lurked alongside that between individual actors. So colossal was Shakespeare's achievement that it seemed to be too great for one nation alone. Britain was of course only too glad to share her most famous son proprietorially, but this did not always satisfy rival claimants. In America for instance Edwin Forrest voiced the view that he and his countrymen, many of whom after all were of the same stock as the English bard, could claim him as their own and from Germany the cry of 'unser Shakespeare' arose ever louder.

My attempt to pursue Shakespeare across the stages of the globe over almost a century is of course fraught with difficulties and pitfalls. I make no claim to have produced a comprehensive history of Shakespearian production worldwide during those years, though readers should gain a reasonably full picture of the main developments in Britain at least. I am acutely aware of the problem of contextualisation across such a broad canvas, but hope that my summaries will be of benefit to those unfamiliar with (that aspect of) the subject without irritating (too much) those who are.

The hero as actor: William Charles Macready

THOMAS CARLYLE

On 12 May 1840 Thomas Carlyle delivered his lecture 'The Hero As Poet: Dante; Shakespeare', the third of six in his series 'On Heroes, Hero-Worship and the Heroic in History'. In his lecture Carlyle identified what he considered to be Shakespeare's prospects not only in the land of his birth, but also around a world which during the remainder of the century was to become increasingly dominated by the English language. In a key passage Carlyle identified Shakespeare's role at home and abroad:

In spite of the sad state Hero-worship now lies in, consider what this Shakspeare has actually become among us. Which Englishman we ever made, in this land of ours, which million of Englishmen, would we not give-up rather than the Stratford Peasant? There is no regiment of highest Dignitaries that we would sell him for. He is the grandest thing we have yet done. For our honour among foreign nations, as an ornament to our English household, what item is there that we would not rather surrender than him? Consider now, if they asked us, Will you give-up your Indian Empire or your Shakspeare, you English . . . ? (1946, p. 148)

Carlyle's pride in Shakespeare as the greatest 'Englishman we ever made' is proprietorial in an almost timeless way. He identifies Shakespeare as the product of a particular period ('This Elizabethan Era') in the nation's history, but the credit is shared by all his countrymen in perpetuity. The scale of the importance with which Carlyle imbued such a hero is evident from his valuation of 'the Stratford Peasant' above a 'million of Englishmen' or a 'regiment of highest Dignitaries' or 'your Indian Empire'. During the next three-quarters of a century 'the sad state of Hero-worship' was to improve – beyond even Carlyle's aspiration – reaching such heights that a 'million of Englishmen' and more were indeed sacrificed not directly for Shakespeare, but for a patriotic ideal with which he had become indissolubly identified. This was certainly not Carlyle's intention. He perceived that in the case of Shakespeare hero-worship would be a force for peace:

England, before long, this Island of ours, will hold but a small fraction of the English: in America, in New Holland, east and west to the very Antipodes, there will be a Saxondom covering great spaces of the Globe. And now, what is it that can keep all of these together virtually one Nation, so that they do not fall-out and fight, but live at peace, in brotherlike intercourse, helping one another . . . We can fancy him [Shakespeare] as radiant aloft over all the Nations of Englishmen, a thousand years hence. (p. 149)

By the time he delivered his hero-worship lectures, Carlyle had developed strong personal links with the contemporary author whom he would not have been alone in considering to be a candidate for such status: Goethe. In 1824 Carlyle sent a copy of his translation of *Wilhelm Meister*, with its influential critique of *Hamlet*, to the German author, with an accompanying letter and a correspondence ensued over the rest of the decade. Carlyle paid fulsome tribute to Goethe for the help which he had gained from the German author's works in overcoming his own spiritual crisis, but the scope of the letters extended from the benefits which great literature could impart to individuals to those which it could exert between nations. Thus on 20 July 1827 Goethe wrote to Carlyle:

It is obvious that the efforts of the best poets and aesthetic writers of all nations have now for some time been directed towards what is universal in humanity . . . striving to diffuse everywhere some gentleness, we cannot indeed hope that universal peace is being ushered in thereby, but only that inevitable strife will be gradually more restrained, war will become less cruel, and victory less insolent. (Norton ed., 1887, p. 24)

Carlyle reciprocated these sentiments, drawing attention to the 'rapidly progressive . . . study and love of German Literature' in Britain, where 'within the last six years, I should say that the readers of your language have increased tenfold' (p. 85).

In practice the implicit notions of national superiority and cultural hegemony were all too liable to surface in the form of rivalry, sometimes personal but also national, in which the achievements of artists and writers became part of the chauvinist arsenal rather than the instruments of peace.

MONOPOLY

Amongst those present at Carlyle's lecture on Shakespeare was William Charles Macready, the 'Eminent Tragedian', seen to be manager of

Drury Lane Theatre. Ever sensitive about the status of the profession which he had reluctantly joined, when the decline in the fortunes of his actor–manager father placed the law and the church beyond his reach, Macready expressed himself 'disappointed in his [Carlyle's] treatment of the subject', an opinion no doubt conditioned by what the actor took as Carlyle's view 'of managers of playhouses being the most insignificant of human beings' (Toynbee ed., 1912, vol. 2, p. 60). In fact Carlyle had expressed his admiration for Macready's attempts to elevate the contemporary stage in a letter of 12 January 1838, in which, though describing himself as 'an entirely *un*theatrical man', he had expressed his wonder 'at your Herculean task. Proceed in it, prosper in it' (Archer, 1890, pp. 117–18). Carlyle's sentiments were apt, for if Shakespeare was to become the ornament of the English stage, it was upon Macready that the responsibility principally rested.

The status of the two principal London theatres, Covent Garden and Drury Lane, had come under parliamentary scrutiny in 1832 when a Select Committee had been appointed 'to inquire into the LAWS affecting DRAMATIC LITERATURE' (*British Parliamentary Papers, Stage and Theatre I*, 1968). Though the committee's remit extended to authors' copyright and other issues, it was the monopoly of the performance of 'legitimate drama' – principally Shakespeare – enjoyed by Covent Garden and Drury Lane that was most fiercely debated. These two theatres based their claim on the warrants granted by King Charles II to Thomas Killigrew (the King's Company) and Sir William Davenant (the Duke's Company) on 21 August 1660. In due course these companies had taken up residence at Drury Lane and Covent Garden respectively, and, though these theatres had been successively rebuilt, being enlarged each time to accommodate the capital's expanding population, their nineteenth-century managers regarded themselves as the heirs to Killigrew and Davenant and the privileges accorded to them by Charles II.

Charles Kemble, the youngest brother of Sarah Siddons and John Philip Kemble, whose precarious management of Covent Garden had only been salvaged by his daughter Fanny's debut as Juliet in 1829, nevertheless staunchly defended the monopoly, claiming that: 'certain plays . . . cannot be adequately represented without space to do them in; for instance such plays as Coriolanus or Julius Caesar' (p. 45). When asked whether audiences would prefer to see the plays 'as near their own doors as possible', Kemble replied 'I do not believe that there is any demand for it.'

In 1832 Macready had no experience of managing a patent theatre, but he was insistent upon the retention of their privileged status, though when asked how many times he had played Shakespeare during his current engagement of two years at Drury Lane, he was obliged to reply that he had played Macbeth six times, Richard III 'five times, and Hamlet once and the Winter's Tale once' (p. 135). When it was pointed out to him that 'by limiting the performance of Shakespeare to the two great theatres, you leave it to the caprice of the proprietors of those theatres', he replied 'Yes; but they pay for that caprice, and the losses have been very heavy indeed in consequence.' Both Kemble and Macready were invited to make comparison with the Théâtre-Français (Comédie-Française) in Paris, but of course that received a state subvention, something never enjoyed by the English patent companies/theatres. The supporters of the monopoly found themselves in the unenviable position of asserting a privilege without having the means of carrying it out effectively.

Not only were the economic and demographic odds stacked against the patents, but also the very monopoly they were defending had long been more honoured in the breach than the observance. For years minor theatres had resorted to various ruses in order to perform Shakespeare. The most common was some form of music, an extreme case being the performance of *Othello* as a burletta, 'which was accomplished by having a low pianoforte accompaniment, the musician striking a chord once in five minutes – but always so as to be totally inaudible. This was the extent of the musical element distinguishing *Othello* from the dialogue of the regular drama' (Nicholson, 1906, p. 330). Another subterfuge was to perform Shakespeare's plays with different titles: '*Othello* under the title *Is He Jealous?*; *Romeo and Juliet* under the guise of *How to Die for Love*; *Macbeth* as *Murder Will Out*; *The Merchant of Venice* billed as *Diamond cut Diamond*; and *Hamlet* as *Methinks I See My Father*' (Broadbent, 1901, p. 107). Absurd though these instances now seem, they do make the crucial point that Shakespeare was still a dramatist with huge appeal to a 'popular' audience. He could be 'box-office'; otherwise managers would not go to such lengths and risk falling foul of the law to stage his plays. Jane Moody has argued persuasively 'that this process of adaptation began primarily as a legal safeguard but also provided an opportunity to translate Shakespeare for popular consumption' (1994, p. 62 and 2000).

Although the Select Committee's second recommendation was that all London theatres 'should be allowed to exhibit, at their option, the

Legitimate Drama', it was not until 1843 that the necessary legislation was passed. In the interim intrepid managers assumed the responsibility of the patent houses, accepting to varying degrees that the performance of Shakespeare's plays was part of their remit. Alfred Bunn, who did 'not think it compatible with the disposition of this country, that its places of public entertainment should be up held by any grant from Government' (1840, vol. 1, p. 34) nevertheless drew attention to the financial penalties of producing Shakespeare at Drury Lane in the 1835–6 season. The twenty-four Shakespearian appearances by Macready – with 'every possible advantage to back him' – in the lead brought in £4,542, 'a nightly average of £189' compared with Madame Malibran whose sixteen performances in the *Maid of Artois* 'yielded a nightly average of more than £355 . . . Difference per night! – £166' (vol. 2, p. 72). The uneasy partnership between Macready and Bunn was terminated on 29 April 1836, not by the inadequacy of the financial rewards attached to staging Shakespeare, but by the former physically assaulting the latter at the end of Act 3 of *Richard III*.

MACREADY AS MANAGER

Macready set up, in opposition to Bunn, as manager of the other patent house, Covent Garden, issuing on 23 September 1837 his prospectus, which Bunn dismissed as 'this pretty document' (p. 268). In it Macready proclaimed 'his strenuous endeavours *to advance the drama as a branch of national literature and art*' (p. 267), drawing from his rival Bunn his resolve 'to sustain the character [which] Drury Lane has long enjoyed of being the FIRST THEATRE OF THE EMPIRE' (p. 273). Combative as ever, Bunn referred to the acting companies as 'the respective forces' (p. 277) and, the air thick with claims to 'national' and 'empire', battle was duly joined.

One of the causes of the decline of the drama, which the 1832 Select Committee had identified, was 'the absence of Royal encouragement'. Clearly if either (or both) of the patent houses was to achieve the status of a national theatre, the 'encouragement' of the sovereign was very much to be desired. By an apparently propitious synchronism on 20 June 1837, just months before Macready inaugurated his Covent Garden regime, the eighteen-year-old Queen Victoria had succeeded William IV. Furthermore in her prime minister, Lord Melbourne, the young sovereign had a fellow devotee of the theatre with whom, as George Rowell has observed (1978, p. 21), she discussed Shakespeare's plays and contemporary performances of them. Macready did not permit his professed republicanism to stand in the way of his swift application for the royal patronage, record-ing in his diary for 19 August: 'Wrote my memorial to the Queen, re-questing her to let me call the Covent Garden players, "Her Majesty's Company of Performers." Inclosed it in a note to the Lord Chamberlain and sent it' (Toynbee ed., 1912, vol. 1, p. 407). His diary entry for 23 August shows that Macready had received an equivocal reply from the Lord Chamberlain, expressing the queen's interest, respect and admiration, and intimating that, though it might be deemed impractical to accede to his precise request, 'other means might be found of render-ing assistance to his undertaking'. The monarch's response fell short of Macready's hopes (if not his expectations), but he had succeeded in in-troducing at the very outset of the new reign a theme – royal patronage – which was to be not only crucial for the theatre, but also significant for the nation in the ensuing decades.

In the event Macready's management made what William Archer de-scribed as 'but a languid start' (1890, p. 112) with a worthy, but uninspired revival of *The Winter's Tale* (30 September 1837) and during the first year of her reign the queen's patronage was weighted towards Drury Lane, where she relished the performances of Charles Kean. As Hamlet, which she saw on 26 January 1838, the queen found 'his delivery of all the fine long speeches quite beautiful' (Esher ed., 1912, vol. 1, p. 265), but she was even more impressed by his Richard III, which she attended twice (5 February and 1 March), and pronounced 'a *triumph*': 'He [Charles Kean] was dressed exactly like his father [Edmund]' (pp. 271–2). As the queen's comments imply Charles Kean was then very much under the shadow of his famous father, but in time he was to make his mark as a producer of Shakespeare's plays and render his sovereign signal service.

Whatever the immediate attractions of Shakespeare at Drury Lane may have been, at Covent Garden Macready was developing the princi-ples of Shakespearian production, which were to establish his reputation and influence his successors for the rest of the century and beyond. The turning point was his revival of *King Lear* on 25 January 1838. Though the dominance of Nahum Tate's *The History of King Lear* (1681) had of late been somewhat eroded, the Fool was still a notable absentee from the English stage. Macready had originally cast Drinkwater Meadows in the role, but was so apprehensive about the result that he thought 'we should be obliged to omit the part' until George Bartley suggested Priscilla Horton, whom Macready agreed was 'the very person' to per-form 'the sort of fragile, hectic, beautiful-faced, half-idiot-looking boy' that he had in mind (Toynbee ed., 1912, vol. 1, p. 438). Though by no means disinterested, being a member of Macready's coterie, John Forster clearly reflected the approbation of 'the three crowded audiences', which had so far attended *King Lear*, when he wrote his review (*Examiner*, 4 February 1838) in which he discoursed on the importance of the Fool and the beneficial effect on Macready's Lear: 'Mr Macready's Lear, remarkable before for a masterly completeness of conception, is heightened by this introduction of the Fool to a surprising degree. It accords exactly with the view he seeks to present of Lear's character.'

Lord Melbourne was aware of Macready's improvements (though he confused Tate with Cibber) when on 4 February he asked the queen if she had seen *King Lear*: 'It is *King Lear* as Shakespear wrote it; and has not been performed so, since the time of Queen Anne' (pp. 269–70). It was a reflection of the queen's tastes that she did not see *King Lear* until 18 February 1839, by which time Macready was highly indignant about her attendance at rival theatres, especially five visits to Drury Lane at the beginning of 1839 where Van Ambrugh's Lions occupied the historic stage. By then Macready had added another major Shakespearian revival to his credits: *Coriolanus* (12 March 1838). In Forster's view it surpassed all Macready's previous Shakespearian achievements and 'may be esteemed the worthiest tribute to the genius and fame of Shakespeare that has been yet attempted on the English stage' (*Examiner*, 18 March 1838). James Anderson, who played Aufidius to Macready's Caius Marcius, attested to 'the immense success' of Macready's Shakespearian revivals, which the manager refused to exploit by long runs. Instead Macready staged *The Tempest* (13 October 1838), in which – together with Dryden's and Davenant's alterations/additions – he dispensed with the dialogue of the first scene in favour of a spectacular shipwreck, and *Henry V* (10 June 1839), the centrepiece of which was Clarkson Stanfield's scenery, especially his illustrations of Chorus's speeches. Archer considered that with *Coriolanus* 'Macready seems to have anticipated all the Meiningen methods' (1890, p. 115). The hallmarks of this style, which was to dominate the nineteenth-century Shakespearian stage, were large casts, thorough rehearsals and pictorial, historically accurate sets; all of them were conducive to high costs. Without a subsidy, long runs were the only answer, but these Macready eschewed. At a dinner to mark the end of his Covent Garden enterprise, with the Duke of Sussex heading the distinguished assembly, Macready spoke of his hope and intention 'to have left in our theatre the complete series of Shakespeare's acting plays... But "my poverty, and not my will," has compelled me to desist from the attempt' (Toynbee ed., 1912, vol. 2, p. 17).

Macready's rather improbable successors, as what Clifford John Williams has called the 'custodians of the National Drama' (1973, p. 155) at Covent Garden, were gentleman-comedian Charles James Mathews and his wife Madame Vestris, whose early career had been based on her skills as a dancer and singer. Their inheritance was awesome, not only in terms of Macready's achievements, but also in the sheer scale of the undertaking. Mathews compiled 'A Return of all Persons engaged in this Establishment during the Week ending 26th December 1840': the total was 684 (pp. 151–2). Madame Vestris, determined to improve the conduct of the auditorium, closed the upper gallery, thereby making the cheapest seat in the house one shilling and sixpence. This action, hardly designed to promote the patent house as a theatre for all levels of society, provoked the anger of the galleryites, who were finally admitted to a less elevated part of the theatre for their usual price of one shilling. Their presence (and protest) at least showed that there was a demand from the denizens of the cheaper seats for Shakespeare at a patent theatre, but whether Madame Vestris's choice of what she described as 'a long-neglected play of England's immortal bard' (in Appleton, 1974, p. 124) would have been theirs was another matter. *Love's Labour's Lost* (30 September 1839) ran for only nine performances. Its most successful feature had been the sets designed by J. R. Planché, the distinguished antiquarian, and executed by Thomas Grieve, who were reunited for *A Midsummer Night's Dream* (16 November 1840) with Mendelssohn's music (for the first time – Wyndham, 1906, vol. 2, p. 154) and a corps of over seventy dancers. Planché suggested a striking effect based on Oberon's 'Through this house give glimmering light' (Planché, 1901, p. 274), which brought the production to a spellbinding finale:

the entire place seems sparkling with countless hues of light, and the delighted eye passing its thrill of pleasure to the tongue, one exclamation of delight springs from the beholders as down falls the curtain. Take it all together, I do not believe a happier revival ever took place on the stage, than in *The Midsummer Night's Dream*. (E.R.W. in *Theatrical Journal*, 1 May 1841)

Werner Habicht has pointed out that Ludwig Tieck's 1843 Berlin revival of *A Midsummer Night's Dream* 'coincided with the comparable effort of Elizabeth Vestris and Charles Mathews in London' (1996, p. 99). Theodore Martin considered that 'probably no Englishman...was more conversant with the history of the English stage than Tieck' (*Nineteenth Century*, February 1880), a claim substantiated by the German actor's 1817 visit to London during which he attended thirty performances in two months. For *A Midsummer Night's Dream* (Williams, 1990, pp. 183–5) Tieck combined features of the Elizabethan stage and characteristics (lavish choreography, painted scenery and Mendelssohn's music) in common with Madame Vestris's revival. The success and distinction of their *A Midsummer Night's Dream* not withstanding, the Mathews/Vestris Covent Garden management ended in 1842 – even more ignominiously than Macready's – in bankruptcy with Mathews being imprisoned, albeit briefly, for debt.

Though the days of the patent theatres' monopoly were clearly almost over, Macready, encouraged by his coterie (including Dickens, Forster, Bulwer Lytton) took Drury Lane, opening with *The Merchant of Venice* on 27 December 1841, swiftly followed by *The Two Gentlemen of Verona* on 29 December. *The Two Gentlemen of Verona*, like Madame Vestris's revival of *Love's Labour's Lost*, reflected the patent theatre manager's resolve to range beyond the familiar canon and met with little more (twelve performances) success. Indeed given his response to the King of Prussia's selection of *The Two Gentlemen of Verona* – 'I could have wished he had stayed at Windsor or gone to any other theatre, rather than have fixed on such a play' (Toynbee, 1912, vol. 2, p. 155) – it is somewhat surprising that Macready staged the play at all. Sir William Martin had reported from Windsor the king's preference for *Macbeth*, which, though it would have been a much better showcase for Macready personally and Shakespeare on the London stage, could not be prepared in time. So the King of Prussia saw England's eminent tragedian as Valentine at an only moderately well-attended house, which greeted him warmly and in marked contrast to the protocol to which he was accustomed at home: '"one cheer more" was shouted by a person in the pit, and "one cheer more" was accordingly given'. Once ensconced in the royal box:

The king . . . paid the most intense attention, making quite a study of the performance. He had a book with him, with which he followed the actors line by line, and we do not think he could have missed a word of the piece. At the end of the serenade to Sylvia he applauded, as well as at the situation where Valentine rescues Sylvia from Proteus. (*The Times*, 1 February 1842)

On his visit to what *The Times* (29 January 1842) described as one of the 'two national theatres', the King of Prussia had been accompanied by the Chevalier Bunsen, a versatile scholar, who had just become ambassador to Britain. Though hardly a model monarch (indecisive, mystic and eventually insane), King Frederick William IV did set an example to the British crown of royal patronage of the theatre. Like most of his countrymen (and indeed Macready) the king preferred the major tragedies to a minor comedy. The earnestness which Frederick William displayed towards such a slight piece as *The Two Gentlemen of Verona* typified the German approach to Shakespeare, which continued during the reigns of his brother Wilhelm I and Wilhelm's grandson Kaiser Wilhelm II.

Macready's production of *As You Like It* with which he opened his second season on 1 October 1842 was one of his finest achievements. True to his principles, Macready restored the true text, cutting only a modest 387 lines from the total of 2,845 (Shattuck ed., 1962a, Introduction); Charles Marshall as scenic designer provided ten complete settings, seven of them in the Forest of Arden replete with musical birds, sheepfold and babbling stream; and Macready, a suitably melancholy Jaques, led a company of overall talent.

Possibly encouraged by King Frederick William's example and certainly by her husband, Queen Victoria responded positively to Macready's proposal, submitted to George Anson, equerry to Prince Albert, that she should make a state visit to *As You Like It.* On 7 June 1843 Macready 'Received a note from W. Anson, informing me that the Queen would command on Monday, an act of kindness which I felt very much. Sir William Martin called to give me the official intimation' (Toynbee ed., 1912, vol. 2, p. 211). Since Victoria's marriage to Prince Albert, the royal family had been augmented by another theatre-enthusiast, one whose tastes were rather more serious and purposeful than his pleasure-seeking wife's. Thus Macready recorded that when he was introduced to the royal couple after the performance the queen simply 'said she was much pleased and thanked me', but 'Prince Albert asked me if this was not the original play. I told him: "Yes, that we had restored the original text"' (p. 212).

Such was the significance of the queen's command that the *Theatrical Journal* of 17 June 1843 was almost entirely devoted to an account of it. It described Macready's efforts, as Carlyle had done, as 'Herculean' and bemoaned the 'shameful neglect of public patronage and supineness of popular feeling'. The royal presence had attracted an overflowing audience (£606; Downer, 1966, p. 223), Macready having decided against increasing the prices, but 'respectable and well-behaved' they bore 'the almost suffocating heat' and crowding 'cheerfully and patiently'. The more fortunate of them could see: 'The Royal box, an elegant and tasteful fixture, supported by gilded pillars attached to the stage . . . gorgeously fitted up in the form of a tent with hangings of rich crimson falling from the top.' The appearance of the royal party (the queen in black velvet with diamonds and the Garter ribbon and Prince Albert in full military uniform with the Garter ribbon, badge and star) was greeted with 'a tremendous burst of spontaneous applause', which the queen graciously acknowledged. Then the curtain rose on 'no less than three hundred professionals' who gave an enthusiastic rendition of the national anthem, which was greeted 'with cheering and waving hats and handkerchiefs' after which 'the performance of the drama commenced'. For Macready, who had been quick to register the importance of royal patronage, it was too late to rescue his management and the patent theatres as an institution. In July the *Theatrical Journal* reported that 'The two patent national houses are now without tenants' (1 July 1843).

The issue of the *Theatrical Journal* for 24 June 1843 reviewed Macready's Drury Lane season, listing his Shakespearian performances which totalled ninety-eight of ten plays, with twenty-two for *As You Like It* and twenty-six for the other major revival *King John* (Shattuck ed., 1962b). On 24 July Macready went to the Home Office 'and had a conference with Manners Sutton, to whom I complained of the injustice done to myself and the dramatic art by the Bill of Sir J. Graham as it stands. I urged the right of acting Shakespeare being given to the licensed theatres if the patent theatres were unable to act his works' (Toynbee ed., 1912, vol. 2, p. 216). His experience at the two patent houses had led Macready to concede the point of the question posed to him in the 1832 Select Committee. Later that month the *Theatrical Journal* published:

the truthful petition of Mr Macready, the most able, experienced, and influential dramatic artist of our time – in which he boldly remonstrates against the monopoly of the patents attracted to our national theatres, and the absurdity of 'the vested rights' that preclude the performance of Shakespeare within five miles of their locality. Monopoly is the bug-bear of our present government . . . If Shakespeare be, as he is, the most exalted of all our native poets, surely his pure teachings ought to be given in all our dramatic temples throughout the land for the benefit and instruction of all classes; not by confining his intellectual splendour within the limited circle of the few to the utter exclusion of the many. (19 August 1843)[1]

With the passing of the 1843 Theatre Regulation Act, Shakespeare was free.

Three years later in September 1846 Macready himself took an engagement at the Surrey Theatre, formerly a minor, which blazoned its coup: 'First Appearance of the Eminent Tragedian Mr Macready

Mrs Davidge having concluded an Engagement with him for a limited number of nights, at an enormous outlay, is resolved in order to present a series of SHAKSPERIAN TRAGEDIES in the most perfect form, to her Patrons the Public, to spare neither expense, or labour.'[2] Mrs Davidge engaged a strong supporting cast for a repertoire dominated by Shakespeare (*King Lear*, *Macbeth*, *Othello*, *Hamlet*). At the first night (7 September) and the last (7 November) the press described 'the house filled to suffocation' (Knight, 1997, p. 220). Dramatic critics made a direct connection between what they saw at the Surrey (and Sadler's Wells and the Queen's) and recent legislation: 'A remarkable change has taken place of late in the bent of the public taste, as regards the support of legitimate drama in different theatrical localities.' The writer proclaimed it 'a great thing to draw large numbers of the frequenters of a minor theatre together, and show them that there is an entertainment of a far higher class than they have been accustomed to run after, more capable of moving the real feelings, and furnishing them with far more to think about, to their improvement and gratification than the miserable ranting melodramas of the old school'. Undoubtedly this had been the intention behind the 1832 report and the 1843 legislation, but, having noted the enthusiasm and attentiveness of the Surrey audience, the same observer could not help wondering whether he had witnessed Surrey regulars, 'usually [amongst] the noisiest', 'awe[d] into silence and reflection' or 'a totally different class of persons', attracted to the Surrey by prospect of seeing Macready at lower admission prices than in the West End in which legitimate fare was then scarce. He concluded, with more optimism than confidence: 'We are willing to believe it is the first theory.'[3] Whichever was the case, a question had been posed which would recur for years to come: did supposedly 'popular' Shakespeare draw the audiences it intended to, or simply attract the regular, Shakespeare audience to a different venue?

AMERICA

Immediately following Macready's season, the Surrey Theatre hosted the Misses Cushman, Charlotte and her sister Susan, who, opening with their celebrated performances as (respectively) Romeo and Juliet, produced on the audience an 'effect . . . not one whit inferior to that they had made upon those in the more legitimate spheres'.[4] It was appropriate that Macready should be followed by the American actress whom, according to Helena Modjeska, Edwin Forrest called 'Macready in petticoats' (Modjeska, 1910, p. 501). Trained as an opera singer, Charlotte Cushman decided to become an actress on the advice of James Caldwell, manager of the St Charles Theatre in New Orleans where she made her debut as Lady Macbeth in 1836, propitiously on 23 April (Smither, 1944, p. 128). Cushman did not possess a costume for Lady Macbeth, but was able to borrow one from the 'other important house in New Orleans, the French Theatre, [which] often gave *Macbeth* in translation' (Leach, 1970, p. 43). That a young American actress should choose Shakespeare for her debut in a predominantly French city and furthermore be able to borrow the costume for Lady Macbeth from the French Theatre there is eloquent testimony that Shakespeare was occupying an expanding world stage.

Macready and Cushman first appeared together in *Macbeth* at Philadelphia's Chestnut Theatre on 23 October 1843. By his own sparing standards, Macready was almost fulsome in his praise: 'The Miss Cushman who acted Lady Macbeth interested me much. She has to learn her art, but she showed mind and sympathy with me, a novelty so refreshing to me on stage' (Toynbee ed., 1912, vol. 2, p. 230). In the eyes of some there was such a physical similarity (depressed nose, broad brow) between Macready and the mannish Cushman that they might have been brother and sister, but more importantly Cushman consciously set out to adopt Macready's style of acting. Alan S. Downer (1946) identified five schools of acting in the nineteenth century: Kemble, Edmund Kean, Macready, the Prince of Wales's Theatre (Wigan) and Irving, characterising Macready's as an amalgam of Kean and Kemble, combining the intensity of the former with the scholarly approach and declamatory beauty of the latter. Fellow actor Lawrence Barrett wrote that for Cushman 'the revelation of his [Macready's] art fell like a message of revelation' (1889, p. 17) and thereafter she 'followed his example' in seeking 'finer shades of meaning', giving to her Lady Macbeth in particular a 'new intensity'. The cross-influence between English and American actors was a vital feature of the Shakespearian stage in both countries during the nineteenth century.

Macready arranged for Charlotte Cushman to partner him in subsequent engagements during which he gave her his customarily guarded encouragement: 'Note from Miss Cushman . . . I think it is only my duty to myself to be strictly circumspect' (Toynbee ed., 1912, vol. 2, p. 234), but even after their first meeting the American actress had announced: 'I mean to go to England as soon as I can. Macready says I ought to act on an English stage and I will' (Leach, 1970, p. 117).

Macready, who had previously visited America in 1826, was intent upon meeting the republic's most prominent citizens, as his diary entries recording engagements with Longfellow, Charles Sumner and Ralph Waldo Emerson testify. In this he was promoting Carlyle's ideal of an extended 'Saxondom' and indeed doing so with the sage's assistance. On 27 August 1843 Carlyle dispatched letters from Annandale to John Greig of New York and to Emerson in Boston. To the former he wrote: 'No public character in this island has, to my mind, so distinguished himself for honourable demeanour in late years',[5] and to the latter: 'He loves Heroes as few do . . . This Man, presiding over the unstablest, most chaotic province of English things, is the one public man among us who has dared to take his stand on what he understood to be *the truth*, and expect victory from that: he puts to shame our Bishops and Archbishops' (Norton ed., 1883, vol. 2, pp. 33–6).

In Emerson Carlyle had a kindred spirit, not merely an Anglophile but one who in his *Representative Men* (1850) treated 'Shakespeare: Or, The Poet' in very much the Carlylean vein with his emphasis on 'great men', his exploration of the national and religious circumstances surrounding his life, his role as 'the father of German literature' and as the 'poet-priest' which 'the world still wants . . . [as] a reconciler' (Jones ed., 1956, p. 477). In the opinion of Walt Whitman, Carlyle – together with Tennyson and Hugo – was not 'personally friendly or admirant toward America; indeed quite the reverse', because 'they . . . cannot span the vast revolutionary arch thrown by the United States over the centuries, fix'd in the present, launch'd to the endless future' (Stovall ed., 1964, p. 478). Whitman, whose enthusiasm for the Shakespearian performances of Charles Kean, Edwin Forrest, Charlotte Cushman and Edwin Booth in New York in the 1840s is abundantly evident in his 'The Old Bowery A Reminiscence of New York Plays and Acting Fifty Years Ago', reflected elsewhere ('Poetry To-day in America – Shakespeare – The Future') on the necessity for a nation to create its own culture: 'The stamp of entire and finish'd greatness to any nation, to the American Republic among the rest, must be sternly withheld till it has put what it stands for in the blossom of original, first-class poems' (p. 474). Whitman recognised that the United States (then thirty-eight of them) stood 'heirs of a very old estate' (p. 475), but though he looked 'mainly for a great poetry native to us . . . these importations till then will have to be accepted, such as they are, and thankful they are no worse' (p. 478). Emerson and Whitman might be identified with the literary elite, but, as Larry Levine has shown, Shakespeare's plays far from being a highbrow preserve were in performance 'an integral part of . . . popular entertainment in nineteenth-century America' (1988, p. 21). The consequence of Shakespeare's appeal to all classes was that he became the focus of tensions between them, from the deference of the Anglophiles to the counter claims of the nationalists.

This Macready was to discover to his personal cost during his 1848–9 tour in which he became the target of elements in American society which were inflamed by what they perceived as an air of cultural superiority in certain English visitors. Charles Dickens's *American Notes* (1842) and *Martin Chuzzlewit* (1843–4) and Mrs Trollope's earlier *Domestic Manners of the Americans* (1832) had been seized upon to fuel resentment far beyond their actual readership. The tragic Astor Place riots on Thursday 10 April 1849 have been thoroughly chronicled by Alan S. Downer (1966, pp. 299–310), J. C. Trewin (1955, pp. 221–5) and Richard Moody (1958) and form the subject of Richard Nelson's play *Two Shakespearean Actors* (1990). The hostility fomented by Edwin Forrest against Macready resulted in a death toll of seventeen with many others injured. Behind the personal rivalry lay a clash of two cultures. Edwin Forrest, the first American-born actor to achieve star-status, belonged in Lawrence Barrett's opinion to a 'method' (powerful voice and physique) which dated back 'through the Kembles to Betterton and Barton Booth' (1881, p. 4). As an actor Forrest appreciated this tradition and the fact that Shakespeare's plays offered the finest roles in the repertoire, but as a patriotic American he could not regard the theatre of another nation as superior to that of his own. Barrett illustrates the point colourfully. For a performance of *Hamlet* in a small American town towards the end of Forrest's career, the manager, in the absence of more conventional scenery, 'hung two American flags at the stage openings, and these represented drop curtains as well as palace, platform, chamber, and castle'. Forrest determined to show the audience that '"Hamlet" could be played in that foreign frame with none of its powers shorn or weakened, while his own patriotism would stimulate his energies, as his eyes rested on the banners of his native land' (p. 6).

Edwin Forrest was the first major American actor to seek the imprimatur of the London stage for his Shakespearian performances, making his debut at Drury Lane in 1836. Of the reviews which he received, those by John Forster, Macready's associate and friend, laced with what James A. Davies has called 'an edgy mockery' (1983, p. 68), caused most offence. As Davies points out much of Forster's criticism was based on aesthetic principles (upheld by Macready) of unified effect. Thus he wrote of Forrest's Othello 'The performance was made up of an infinite variety of parts, through which there was no unity ... Mr Forrest had no intellectual comprehension of what he was about' (Archer and Lowe eds., 1896, p. 21). Instead of unity of conception and execution Forrest strung together a series of effects. The murder of Desdemona was 'a down-right Old Bailey affair . . . It was full of the falsest seekings for effect' (p. 24). In Lear's great speeches Forrest alternated fierce and tender tones with complete disregard for sense; as Macbeth he indulged in 'violent contortions' aimed to impress the gallery (p. 33) and as Richard III he displayed 'hideous looks and furious gestures, ear-splitting shouts and stage devouring strides', culminating in 'one of the most wretched and melodramatic tricks of the profession':

While Richard fought with Richmond he had provided himself with long and heavy strips of black hair, which were fixed in such a way that they came tumbling over his forehead, eyes, and face, with every barbarous turn and gesture. The princely Plantagenet – he

'Who was born so high
His aiery buildeth in the cedar's top,
And dallies with the wind and scorns the sun' –

was thus accomplished by Mr Forrest in all points of a savage newly caught from out the American backwoods. (p. 41)

Even though Forster's reviews might be construed by his countrymen as critiques of the contrasting acting styles of sophisticated English actors and their American counterparts, that in itself would have been offensive to Forrest, but the disdainful allusions to America, of which the 'backwoods' reference was the most extreme, were bound to incur his personal wrath and patriotic indignation.

When Forrest made his second British tour in 1845–6, Forster's pen was again tainted with vitriol, mocking Forrest's business of scraping his sword against that of Macduff in the final combat until 'an enlightened critic in the gallery shouted out, "That's right! sharpen it"' (Downer, 1966, p. 276). Forster received no encouragement from Macready in writing so derisively about Forrest, but the American, convinced that the English actor was implicated, followed Macready to Edinburgh. There on 2 March 1846 during a performance of *Hamlet* he hissed Macready's favourite piece of business with a handkerchief just before the 'The Mousetrap'. Probably mindful that Forster's criticisms had been directed at his performances, rather than at him personally, Forrest claimed that he was showing disapproval at one aspect of Macready's performance by hissing, just as he would show approval by applauding. John Coleman described the consequences of the incident in characteristically dramatic

terms: 'There can, however be no doubt that that one stupid hiss in
Edinburgh wrecked a great reputation and caused a deplorable calamity'
(1904, vol. 2, p. 350). He went on to say that though Forrest 'retained
his hold on the *oi polloi*', he was 'utterly alienated from the refined and
cultured moiety of his fellow citizens'. Undoubtedly there were social,
as well as personal and national, antagonisms behind this incident and
these were associated with different styles of acting Shakespeare. There
was the thoughtful, refined, restrained style which appealed to the discerning (usually well-to-do) playgoer, and there was the broader, bolder,
even barnstorming style, which appealed to what Coleman dubbed the
oi polloi.

These tensions were certainly evident in New York when Macready began his final American tour with *Macbeth* at the Astor Place on 4 October
1848. As on his previous visit when he had sought out the republic's
'prominent citizens', Macready was taken up by the 'aristocracy', but
amongst the less well-off, who felt threatened by foreign labour of any
kind, there was increasing support for Nativism (Downer, 1966, p. 297).
This was Forrest's natural (and nationalistic) constituency, which he marshalled effectively to harass the English actor. From the outset there were
rumours of hostility towards Macready, but his first performance was
warmly received. Unwisely the English actor made a curtain speech
thanking his audience for having refuted his detractors. The speech was
seized upon as a challenge by a friend of Edwin Forrest, James Oakes,
who produced a lengthy piece in the *Boston Mail* (30 October) alleg-
ing that Macready was responsible for the hostile reception accorded to
Forrest in 1845. The two actors published rival accounts and Macready
began an action against Forrest, who followed him from city to city acting the same roles at rival theatres, as he did in New York. There on
10 May, with mayhem and slaughter surrounding the Astor Place Opera
House, Macready, the true professional, acted on to the bitter end: 'The
death of Macbeth was loudly cheered, and on being lifted up and told
I was called, I went on, and . . . quitted the New York stage amid the
acclamations of those before me' (Toynbee ed., 1912, vol. 2, p. 426).

PARIS

Apart from America, where his early achievements were eclipsed by this
calamitous denouement, the country which Macready visited most often was France. In 1822, as part of a continental tour, which included
Verona and Venice in both of which he experienced the power of the

city's Shakespearian associations, Macready attended performances at the Paris theatres. The great French tragedian Talma was ill then, but when Macready saw him act he was immensely impressed, admiring his unconsciously dignified and graceful attitudes, his flexible and powerful voice, but most significantly (and influentially): 'His object was not to dazzle or surprise by isolated effects: the character was his aim; he put on the man, and was attentive to every minutest trait that might distinguish him' (Pollock ed., 1873, p. 180). In 1822 a troupe of English actors also visited Paris to play Shakespeare in English at the Porte-Saint-Martin, but, as J. J. Jusserand judged, 'the attempt was a premature one' (1899, p. 451). Anti-English feeling following the Napoleonic wars had not subsided. At the opening performance of *Othello* on 31 July the audience threw fruit at the actors and shouted 'Parlez Français' and eventually the military intervened. Following an even worse reception of *The School for Scandal* on 3 August, the company decamped to the Théâtre de la Rue Chantereine where they gave private performances by subscription. There they remained until the beginning of October affording the discerning, though small, audiences the opportunity to see scenes, such as the death of Desdemona, which were excised on the rare occasions when French theatres essayed Shakespeare.

The resistance of the French to Shakespeare was not based only on recent history. The tone had been set by Voltaire, who had been exposed to the native stage during his visit to England. In his *Preface to Brutus: Discourse on Tragedy*, addressed to Lord Bolingbroke (1731), he wrote of his experience seeing *Julius Caesar*: 'I surely do not claim to approve the barbaric irregularities with which it is filled; it is only astonishing that there are not more of them in a work composed in a century of ignorance by a man who did not even know Latin, and who had no teacher but his own genius' (in Le Winter ed., 1976, p. 33). In his own plays and his critical writing Voltaire upheld the rigid interpretation of the classical unities, which had long dominated the French theatre. However the hostility with which the English players had been received in 1822 not withstanding, Voltaire's critique of Shakespeare (Lounsbury, 1902) was being challenged.

Madame de Staël and Charles Nodier had shown the way. Nodier, the first disciple of Romanticism to be admitted to the Académie Française, had written his *Pensées de Shakespeare extraites de ses Ouvrages* at the age of twenty-one in 1801 when hostilities between Britain and France were – temporarily – halted by treaty on 1 October. Monsieur Guizot, author of the essay 'On the Life and Works of Shakespeare', which appeared in

1821 as an introduction to a French edition of the plays, was successively professor of history, ambassador to London (1840), foreign minister and prime minister (1847). Guizot posed the question 'whether Shakespeare's dramatic system is not superior to that of Voltaire' (1852, p. 1). He pointed out that in England in Shakespeare's day 'a theatrical performance' was 'a popular festival' (p. 2) and 'dramatic poetry, therefore, could originate only among the people' (p. 3). Guizot recognised the popular origins of Shakespeare's plays and their innately broad appeal. He analysed *Macbeth* to show what would have been lost had it been written on classical principles: the comic porter, the murder of Lady Macduff and her children and much more besides. These comic and action scenes, which no French dramatist would have included, accounted in large measure for Shakespeare's continuing appeal to mass audiences across the globe during the nineteenth century. As Guizot presciently remarked: 'England will not be the only country indebted to Shakespeare' (p. 141).

In *Racine et Shakespeare* (1823), Stendhal referred to the English players' performances of Shakespeare in 1822. He contrasted the court audiences, for which Racine had written, with the 'new class which had a growing thirst for strong emotions', proposing three reforms: writing in prose, abandoning the unities and making French history the subject matter (1962, p. 7). Stendhal provoked an intense controversy, debating at the Académie Française with its permanent secretary, Monsieur Augier, a staunch classicist and producing further pamphlets including 'What is Romanticism?' Thus when another troupe of English actors arrived in Paris in September 1827, the climate had changed significantly for the better since 1822. The circumstances and significance of this visit have been extensively chronicled from the handsomely illustrated *Souvenirs du Théâtre Anglais à Paris* (see Eddison, 1955) and J.-L. Borgerhoff's *Le Théâtre Anglais à Paris sous la Restauration* (1913) to biographies of those who participated and those who were influenced by them.

The first Shakespearian offering was *Hamlet* on 11 September with Charles Kemble in the lead as he was for *Romeo and Juliet* (with Harriet Smithson) and *Othello*, which followed. The press was generally laudatory (Williamson, 1970, p. 181) and in his daughter Fanny's opinion: 'My father has obtained a most unequivocal success in Paris' (1878, vol. 1, p. 191). Fanny Kemble described the Irish actress Harriet Smithson, her father's Juliet, Desdemona and Ophelia, as 'a young lady with a figure and face of Hibernian beauty, whose superfluous native accent was no drawback to her merits in the esteem of her French audience' (p. 188). If performing to a non-English-speaking audience was a positive benefit for Harriet Smithson, it was evidently no disadvantage to Kemble, who told his daughter that 'in spite of the difficulty of the foreign language . . . his Parisian audience never appeared to him to miss the finer touches or more delicate and refined shades of his acting' (p. 189). Charles Kemble had evidently mastered a style of acting in which pictorial techniques of gesture and expression compensated for the spoken word, which was to be an important accomplishment for Shakespearian actors – with various native tongues – during the coming decades.

Fanny Kemble attributed Harriet Smithson's success to the sympathy aroused by playing heroines who were victims of incidents 'infinitely more startling' (p. 188) than French audiences were used to. In fact the English company had substantially adapted the plays partly in the interests of simplicity, but also in deference to French taste. In *Hamlet*, references to Fortinbras, Ophelia's songs, Hamlet's bawdy and anything at all digressive were cut, but Ophelia's madness and the graveyard scene survived to excite French susceptibilities (Heylen, 1993, pp. 46–7). The effect of Smithson, 'Fair Ophelia' (Raby, 1982), his inspiration and eventually his unhappy wife, on Hector Berlioz was the most extreme outcome of these Shakespearian performances on the Parisian artistic community. Victor Leathers (1959, pp. 86–91) has enumerated the writers, artists and musicians for whom the experience of seeing the English players in Shakespeare was a turning point: Hugo, Alexandre Dumas, Vigny, Musset, Delacroix and of course Berlioz. The English players in Shakespeare had played an important part in blowing away 'the stagnant vapours of neoclassicism' (Hemmings, 1994, p. 185).

Macready, though he had been in Paris in early September 1827, did not act with the company until 7 April 1828 when he played Macbeth, supported by Miss Smithson (less happily cast than previously) and the witches who excited laughter. Greatly admired in Sheridan Knowles's *Virginius*, Macready made way for Edmund Kean, but returned in June and added Hamlet and Othello (tactfully obscuring the murder of Desdemona) to his laurels. Whereas during the opening months of the season the impact of the English actors had been on the artistic community at large, Macready particularly impressed his fellow actors. Alan S. Downer quotes a French critic, who voiced his countrymen's preference for Macready over Charles Kemble and Edmund Kean because of 'his gift of creating emotion . . . being natural without vulgarity, and elegant without affectation' (1966, p. 116). Downer describes the effects of this Paris season on English acting as 'far-reaching', as French actors adopted Macready's realism and a quarter of a century or more later exported it back to England as the new school of naturalistic acting.

When Macready returned to Paris in December 1844 his engagement was as usual on a commercial footing, promoted this time by the London manager John Mitchell, but he was also fulfilling a diplomatic role. In October 1844 the French king, Louis Philippe, had visited Queen Victoria at Windsor, where she had lavishly entertained him and his entourage (including Monsieur Guizot) with banquets, concerts and drives, but not the theatre, probably because – with Macready absent in America – there was nothing of suitable calibre available. In November 1844 *Punch* (vol. 7, p. 247) published a letter, of which it claimed to have been given an exclusive copy, from Queen Victoria to the King of the French 'touching Shakespear in France':

Windsor Castle, Nov. 27th, 1844

My Dear Brother of France,
      Health and greeting! The bearer of this letter is Macready. You doubtless remember on your late visit to our Court, that, among other things, I expressed my regret at the absence of Macready – he was then on his way from America – by which you were denied what I conceive to be one of the highest of all intellectual enjoyments, namely Shakespear finely acted. However, Macready is now with you, and I know you will cherish him . . .
      Your affectionate Sister of England,
                                          Victoria, R.

Elsewhere in the letter 'Queen Victoria' referred to her frequent attendance at Drury Lane during Macready's management, the drama being 'worthy of the best encouragement of an enlightened monarch'; her wish – resisted by Peel – to make Macready a baronet; her admiration for Helen Faucit 'a great favourite of mine' and her desire that her actors should 'not linger in Paris . . . for I assure you I don't well know how I shall get over the time without them'.

Shortly before he left England the Carlyles visited Macready, in Paris he initially had Charles Dickens's company and was soon fêted by the *beau monde*, whom Mrs Trollope had heard 'prate of Shakespeare', but had happily not offended in her *Paris and the Parisians* (1836, p. 102). Though its tone was facetious, *Punch* was not alone in ascribing a diplomatic dimension to Macready's visit; the *Athenaeum* described it as 'the true point of the *entente cordiale*' (28 December 1844). Difficult as ever to please, Macready complained that the Théâtre Italien was 'too large' and the audiences 'too fashionable' (Toynbee ed., 1912, vol. 2, p. 283). *The Times* reported crowded houses consisting of 'the British residents in Paris' and 'the elite of French society' in the ratio of one to two, with many of the latter following the play in French and causing a 'flutter . . . audible throughout the house when it became necessary that a leaf of the work be turned over' (2 January 1845).

Macready's leading lady was Helen Faucit, who had been in his Covent Garden and Drury Lane companies and had for a time become infatuated with him. Typically, Macready had excluded (Archer, 1890, p. 163) most of the plays (except *Romeo and Juliet*) in which Helen Faucit excelled in favour of those which gave him greatest prominence, but nevertheless as her biographer Carol Jones Carlisle has written: 'For Helen Faucit the visit to Paris was an unqualified success' (2000, p. 141). Inevitably Macready was resentful, recording that he had been told 'that *Miss H. Faucit's friends were my enemies*' (Toynbee ed., 1912, vol. 2, p. 283) and, similarly partisan, Theodore Martin, whom Helen Faucit married in 1851, wrote: 'When he [Macready] returned to play in Paris in 1844, this enthusiasm, we remember, had very sensibly cooled' (1906, p. 167). In fact both Macready and Miss Faucit scored personal triumphs, particularly in *Othello* and *Hamlet*, even though proportionately at least the actress did not have a large role in either play.

Particularly contentious in *Othello* were the scenes in Desdemona's bedchamber in which 'l'abandon des usages classiques' (in Juden et Richer, 1962–3, p. 13) was so shocking. The sight of the English actress clad – only – 'en camisole . . . coiffée d'un joli bonnet de nuit orné d'une ruche' in a setting which 'pour l'assistance éclairée, le lit, l'oreiller et le tapis étaient d'une realisme trop bourgeois' (pp. 12–14) was alien indeed. Still to come was 'le vulgaire et terrible breiller [pillow]' in administering which in deference to French susceptibilities Macready 'tire les rideaux du lit au moment ou Othello étouffe Desdémone' (p. 13). Such was the power of the acting that linguistic barriers crumbled as Théophile Gautier observed: 'la réalité que montrent les interpretès de Shakespeare, dépasse la double barrière de la convention et de langue' (p. 21).

There was speculation as to whether King Louis Philippe would select *Othello* or *Hamlet* for the performance at the Tuileries. He chose *Hamlet* and the stage in the Hall of the National Convention was fitted up exactly as at the Ventador. Macready acknowledged that 'it was such a theatre as befitted the king of a great nation', but could not help wondering 'whether great nations ought to have kings' (Toynbee ed., 1912, vol. 1, p. 284). As with the command performance of *As You Like It* at Drury Lane Macready was torn between asserting the dignity due to his profession and resenting

1. *Othello* at the Salle Ventador.

the source from which it came. The contrast between the exuberance displayed at Drury Lane and the strict protocol in Paris was stark. In France (as other English actors were to discover when playing before other heads of state) there was no applause during the performance, such applause as there was only following the monarch's lead.

The occasion was altogether grander than any in which Macready, or any other English actor, had participated at home (or abroad) before. In addition to the king and queen, the princes and princesses, members of the cabinet (including Guizot), who occupied the whole of 'the spacious gallery immediately opposite the stage' (*The Times*, 20 January 1845), in the side boxes were 'the various Ambassadors and Ministers from all the Courts of Europe, with their ladies, the leading members of the Chambers of Peers and Deputies, and all the most distinguished foreigners at present residing in Paris'. All were decked out in their finery: jewels, diamonds, uniform, court dress. Compared with this the English theatre was indeed without honour in its own land. Understandably *The Times* took the view that 'of the performance of the play we are not here called upon to speak', but did observe that 'though the play was somewhat abridged, the scene of the grave-diggers being wholly omitted, it seemed to lose nothing whatever of its interest by the curtailment, and the tragedy went off in the most satisfactory manner. Hamlet . . . was never played by Macready with more spirit and power'. Macready, his own sternest critic, concurred: 'In my mind I never gave such a representation of the part, and without a hand of applause' (Toynbee, 1912, vol. 1, p. 284). Similarly he considered his acting of Macbeth on 6 January 'better than I have ever done before' (p. 282). Far from being an impediment the language barrier was a spur to achievement.

After the performance Mitchell and Macready were presented to the king, who spoke ('in choice English') of having seen *Hamlet* played frequently, most recently by [James] Bennett, enquiring somewhat disconcertingly of Mitchell 'Pray who is Bennett?' (*The Times*, 21 January 1845). The king, whom 'Queen Victoria' in *Punch* had encouraged to award the English actor the Legion of Honour, presented Macready with 'a most splendid poniard, in a still more splendid case'; the blade 'set in gold', it and 'the pure gold case . . . enriched with diamonds and other precious stones'. A few days later Louis Philippe, apprised that the venture had not been as financially rewarding as expected, sent Mitchell 3,000 francs. Without undue delay Macready, who as an actor knew that costume jewellery could be deceptively convincing, submitted the king's gifts to the inspection of his London jeweller, who pronounced the poniard to be silver-gilt and the jewels sham: 'that *shabby dog* – Louis Philippe' (Toynbee ed., 1912, vol. 1, p. 291).

Nevertheless the verdict on Macready's Paris season could be nothing less than positive. *The Times* (20 January 1845) hailed the performance at the Tuileries as 'an event in the history of the two nations which to have foretold a few years ago would have set the prophet down as the idlest of dreamers'. Even if the *rapprochement* which artistes could effect between nations was vulnerable to other forces, that which they forged amongst themselves was more durable. In Macready's case his 'amitié littéraire' with George Sand found expression in her adaptation of *As You Like It*, set in the Faubourg St Germain, with Jaques (Macready's role) transformed into the hero, falling in love with Celia (Ewbank, 1996, p. 134).

Always a reluctant member of the profession, which he led with such distinction, Macready was intent on retiring as early as possible and undertook his American tours with the object of replenishing his funds. When the time came, he was determined that nothing in his career should become him like the leaving it. He undertook an extended series of 'farewell' performances. Bulwer Lytton tried to secure the presence of Prince Albert for the valedictory dinner, but received what Macready regarded as 'the (virtual) refusal of Monsieur le Prince Albert to preside at the dinner projected to me. It is what I anticipated' (Toynbee ed., 1912, vol. 2, p. 486). Despite his indignant tone Macready could hardly have expected any other response. The Prince was simply applying his rule of not presiding at functions in honour of individuals (only at those for institutions). Prince Albert, together with the queen, attended Macready's penultimate performance (King Lear at the Haymarket) on 3 February in order, in the words of his biographer Theodore Martin, 'to testify his respect to the veteran artist' (1882, vol. 2, p. 64).

At the end of his last performance ever – as Macbeth at Drury Lane on 26 February 1851 – Macready delivered a highly charged speech from the stage, speaking of: 'My ambition to establish a theatre, in regard to decorum and taste, worthy of our country, and to have in it the plays of our divine Shakspeare fitly illustrated'; this had been 'frustrated by those whose duty it was . . . to have undertaken the task. But some good seed has yet been sown' (Toynbee ed., 1912, vol. 2, p. 497).

This was no idle boast. Macready had advanced the cause of Shakespeare on both of the fronts identified by his friend Thomas Carlyle. At home he had successively managed both of the patent theatres, setting standards of Shakespearian production – thorough rehearsals, competent company, restoration of the text, pictorial scenery and appropriate costumes – for the rest of the century. Amongst his revivals were two plays, *Henry V* and *As You Like It*, neither of them to the fore at the time, which were to become the most favoured expressions of English national identity. Republican though he claimed to be, Macready recognised the importance of royal patronage and actively sought it. Once he accepted the inevitable demise of the patent theatres he argued for the de-restriction of Shakespeare and personally took an engagement at a former minor theatre. Macready evolved an acting style (drawing on Kemble, Kean and Talma), which was noted for its intense realism and was imitated by actors across the world. Abroad in his three tours of America and his two visits to Paris, Macready succeeded in extending the appreciation for Shakespeare and his works amongst fellow-artistes and the public at large. His unhappy experience in America, though partly caused by personality traits – his own and Forrest's – was indicative of the way in which national and social tensions could find expression in the reaction to the performance of Shakespeare's plays. As complex as any character in the plays in which he appeared, Macready had answered the call of Shakespeare, the theatre and his country with great distinction.

2

Equerries and equestrians: Phelps, Kean and Astley's

SAMUEL PHELPS

The actor who seized upon the opportunity presented by the abolition of the patent theatres' monopoly most promptly and most effectively was Samuel Phelps. Arriving in London in 1837, after an arduous provincial apprenticeship, Phelps spent most of the next five years in Macready's companies at the patent theatres, where he was treated – to his considerable frustration – as both protégé and rival. As an actor Phelps was very much in the Macready mould (intelligent, powerful voice, intensity of feeling though falling short of the transcendent heights of which his mentor was capable). However, when, at the conclusion of his Drury Lane management in 1843, Macready invited Phelps to accompany him to America, the younger actor declined (John Ryder went), opting instead to hazard his future as a manager.

Of all the London theatres that were enfranchised to perform legitimate drama by the passing of the Theatre Regulation Act on 22 August 1843, Sadler's Wells in Islington, an unfashionable suburb three miles north of the West End, was by no means especially promising. Dennis Arundell's description of the period 1838–43 as 'At Low Ebb' (1965, pp. 122–32) is sadly apt for a theatre which had been noted for its aquatic attractions. On Whit Monday (27 May) 1844 Phelps, initially in partnership with Mrs Warner, a powerful actress regarded by some as 'the equal to Charlotte Cushman' (in Mullin ed., 1983, p. 500), launched his enterprise, having previously apprised the residents of Islington about it by means of a printed address. In their address Phelps and Warner referred to their intention that Sadler's Wells should become 'a place for justly representing the works of our great dramatic poets' at a time when the 'National' theatres were failing to do so and 'the law has placed all theatres upon an equal footing of security and respectability' (in Allen, 1971, pp. 82–3). They asserted 'the notion that each separate division of our immense metropolis, with its 2,000,000 of inhabitants, may have its own well-conducted theatre within a reasonable distance of the homes of its patrons' and undertook to 'offer an entertainment selected from the first stock drama in the world', performed by 'a *company* of acknowledged talent... at a price fairly within the habitual means of all'. However, though the new managers were determined that there should be no financial obstacle confronting potential patrons, they were insistent upon the tone which they were setting: 'such an endeavour is not unworthy of the kind of encouragement of the more highly educated and influential classes' for a theatre, which aimed 'at the highest possible refinement, and... the most intellectual class of enjoyment which an audience can receive'. Phelps and Warner were setting themselves the formidable challenge of performing the classics to uncompromising standards in a way which would appeal to local audiences and attract the support of 'the more highly educated' classes from further afield.

By choosing *Macbeth* Phelps gave himself the opportunity to assume for the first time a role particularly associated with Macready, but to stamp it as his own. The *Athenaeum* (1 June 1844) identified a significant difference, characterising Macready's Macbeth as 'so studied in all its parts, and subdued into commonplace by too much artifice', whereas:

The straightforward and right earnest energy of Mr. Phelps's acting, on the contrary, made all present contemplate the business as one of seriousness and reality; while the occasional pathos of his declamation thrilled the heart within many a rude bosom with unwonted emotion. The spectators were visibly agitated, and incapable of resisting the impulse.

Although the *Athenaeum* observed the 'audible exclamations of astonishment [at the new scenery] from the usual visitors in the boxes', of greater interest was the rest of the 'overflowing audience' in a theatre, with a capacity of 2,600 dominated by its large pit (accommodating 1,000 on benches). Though it was natural to him, it seems likely that Phelps had cultivated a straightforward and energetic acting style as most likely to appeal to the 'rude bosoms' of which he knew the Sadler's Wells audience would consist. There is evidence to suggest that not all of that first-night audience were altogether susceptible to the power of the performance. Godfrey Turner, writing on 'Amusements of the English People' (*Nineteenth Century*, December 1877) recalled that 'on the opening night there was a disheartening influence, for the management, in the villainous language of the gallery-folk, whose obsessive oaths, yelled forth at full pitch, rang through the building'. According to Turner, the next day Phelps 'found an old Act of Parliament, in which was a clause expressly meeting his difficulty', copies of which Phelps had printed and distributed around the neighbourhood with the result that by the end of the week Sadler's Wells 'though just as crowded ... was silent to the highest and hindmost bench'.

Phelps's proud record during his eighteen years as manager of Sadler's Wells was chronicled by his nephew W. May Phelps and John Forbes-Robertson (1886). In her chapter 'Phelps and Shakespeare' Shirley Allen (1971) has written of both the actor and the manager and in her chart of 'Shakespearean Performances' has shown that Phelps staged thirty-one of the plays for a total of 1,632 performances (out of 3,472) with *Hamlet, Macbeth* and *The Winter's Tale* accounting for 171, 133 and 137 each (pp. 314–15). In the range of his Shakespearian repertoire, his loyal and talented company, his continuance of Macready's textual restoration, and his harmonious – but restrained – scenery, Phelps made an outstanding and influential contribution to the nineteenth-century Shakespearian theatre.

The nature of his audience, as that for Macready's 1846 season at the Surrey, continues to intrigue theatre historians. A number of reviewers commented upon the audience as well as the performances. In 1857 at *Twelfth Night* Henry Morley observed 'our working-classes in a happy crowd, as orderly as if they were at church, and yet as unrestrained in their enjoyment as if listening to stories told them by their own firesides' (1891, p. 138). In Islington Shakespeare had taken his place in the 'English Household', as advocated by Carlyle: 'Shakespeare spoke home to the heart of the natural man' (Morley, p. 138). Earlier, in 1847 at *Macbeth*, Jonas Levy found: 'the house ... crowded in every part ... the play ... listened to with the greatest attention [by] ... the audience ... drawn from all classes of society and representing every condition of life' (*Lloyd's Weekly London Life*, quoted in W. May Phelps and Forbes-Robertson, 1886, p. 102). Westland Marston confirmed that within the social spectrum: 'he [Phelps] draws to Sadler's Wells intellectual playgoers from all quarters – the West End, the Clubs, and the Inns of Court – and they swear by him' (1890, p. 120). The local clientèle and discerning visitors combined to create a heterogeneous audience united by the power of Shakespeare.

GERMAN VISITS

Amongst those drawn to Sadler's Wells was Theodor Fontane, the German novelist, who in 1855 took up 'employment in London as

co-ordinator of a press agency set up there by the Prussian government' (Jackson ed., 1999, p. xiii). Applying his personal literary gifts
and visitor's perspective Fontane has left an invaluable account of the
London theatre in the 1850s. Naturally Fontane made frequent comparisons between Shakespeare as performed in London and in Germany. He
described Sadler's Wells as 'a people's theatre', at which Mr Phelps, 'the
best Shakespearean actor', provided 'a skilled hand . . . guiding the whole
work' with meagre resources (p. 59). In *Hamlet*, the first play which he saw
at Sadler's Wells in October 1855, Fontane was especially struck by the
interpretation of Polonius, which emphasised his foolishness rather than,
as in Germany, his wisdom. The English audience was in full accord with
the actors, Polonius's admonitions to Ophelia to be on her guard against
Hamlet being 'accompanied throughout by hearty laughter' (p. 61). He
found the effects in the Ghost's scenes, achieved by sliding scenery and
skilful lighting, highly impressive and though he considered Phelps too
old for Hamlet, comparing him unfavourably with Emil Devrient whom
London audiences had seen in the role in 1852, he was impressed by
the duel with Laertes, particularly the ingenuity with which the rapiers
were exchanged. Emphasising humour in (or in Fontane's view imposing
it on) Polonius, making the Ghost truly magical and enacting the duel
with virtuosity, all served to maximise aspects of the play with high
popular appeal.

In *The Tempest* the simple scenic devices for the opening shipwreck
'were so convincing that we think we are in the thick of the storm'
(p. 68) and though he had reservations about Trinculo and Stephano
('two low fellows, drunk for five acts on end'), he was emboldened to suggest 'that we [Germans] must attempt to put these scenes on stage . . . to
make a trial of the public taste' lest 'our refinement may have led our
taste awry. By turns prudish and trivial, we have lost the taste for low
humour' (pp. 69–70). In *Henry IV Part 1* Fontane approved the way in
which Phelps had cut and arranged the text 'so as to make the work
comprehensible and the sequence of events clear' (p. 71) and considered
that 'complete justice was done to the comic side of the play', in accordance with 'the English nation['s] . . . natural gift for comedy' (p. 74).
Even the minor roles were well played and Falstaff (perhaps Phelps's
best role) was, like all the comic characters (Bottom, Malvolio), which he
created, unintentionally funny. When it came to 'the offensive buffoon-
ery . . . with Hotspur's body' Phelps, in contrast to another actor in the
role at the Surrey Theatre, exercised restraint, though: 'The gallery boy
has to have his laugh, and something must be given to him' (p. 75). Thus
Fontane articulated the essence of Phelps's achievement: he brought out

those elements in the plays which appealed to 'a rude bosom', but did so
with taste and discretion, avoiding the excesses of more overtly populist
performers of which, in John Forster's estimation at least, Edwin Forrest
was one. This approach enabled Phelps to score successes with plays
which were little rated in either England or Germany. *The Merry Wives of
Windsor* was 'cheered and applauded from beginning to end' (p. 75); *The
Two Gentlemen of Verona* was 'enjoyed for its own sake' with Launce always
appearing with 'his bull-dog' (p. 77) and in *Coriolanus* the aristocracy and
the mob were 'thoroughly English . . . It was as though these fellows with
their cudgels had been taken from the street, and even if the whole picture was not true to history, it was at least true to *life*. That was the appeal to the audience' (p. 79). This was 'the impulse', which the *Athenaeum*
had identified on the opening night of *Macbeth* and which Phelps succeeded in keeping alive, in preference to a picture 'true to history'
favoured by some of his contemporaries.

By the time Fontane saw *Macbeth* on 21 February 1857, Mrs Warner
was dead and Miss Atkinson appeared opposite Phelps, but this enabled
him to make a point about the hold of tradition on the English theatre:
'she [Miss Atkinson] is only the bearer of an interpretation . . . Such tradition is here regarded as sacrosanct' (p. 84). Concomitant with this
Fontane noted the audience's familiarity with the play and heightened
attention to well-loved passages, which are greeted 'with thunderous applause': 'The actor is not merely encouraged but well nigh *obliged* to
perform the finest passages in a way calculated to please merely the ears
of the gallery, rather than the understanding of a more discriminating
minority' (p. 80). By 1857, his obligations to the gallery seemed to weigh
more heavily on Phelps, whose acting was in any case becoming rather
dated. Curiously two scenes, both commended by Guizot, the porter's
and the murder of Lady Macduff, were not played, but for the witches
Phelps used his customary devices (gauze and lighting) effectively; the
chamber in which Duncan was murdered was located 'very close to
the audience' (just off the right-hand side of the proscenium arch) creating heightened immediacy; the banquet scene presented a crowded
stage in a realistic setting; the sleepwalking scene was rather over lit;
but the crowning glory for the Sadler's Wells audience was the final
fight:

Finally, the combat between Macbeth and Macduff is as brilliant as ever. No
beating of tin shields, no victory offstage, but real, visible hacking at each other,
until to the jubilation of the gallery Macbeth is defeated and the curtain falls.
(p. 87)

Within a few weeks Fontane saw *Macbeth* at the Schauspielhaus in Berlin. In using the Tudor style the director showed a shaky grasp of British history and was not well served by a set painted entirely on canvas (in England the picture at the back of the stage was painted on wood); the extensive stage space was inartistically used; of the Macbeths, Hermann Heinrich acted 'scene by scene, not as a unified whole', as Phelps had done, and Fraulein Heusser could claim 'only very limited praise' and as for Duncan 'luckily' he 'was murdered in the second act' (pp. 87–95). For all its superior resources the results achieved at the Schauspielhaus were inferior to those at Sadler's Wells.

Back in London on 19 January 1858 Fontane attended a unique performance of *Macbeth* as part of the celebrations for the marriage between the Princess Royal (Victoria and Albert's eldest child, Vicky) and Prince Frederick William of Prussia (Pakula, 1996, p. 77). The princess had inherited her parents' enthusiasm for the theatre and delighted in the Windsor Theatricals, inaugurated with a performance of *The Merchant of Venice* at the castle on 28 December 1848 (Chapman ed., 1849; Webster ed., 1849). The Rubens Room, the usual venue for these performances, was inadequate for the 1858 nuptial performance for which a West End venue had to be secured.

Understandably the theatrical profession was delighted that it should play such a prominent part (four evenings, each illustrating 'a separate department of dramatic art' with 'the supremacy of Shakespearian drama being acknowledged by its selection to inaugurate the course', *Era*, 24 January 1858) in an event of national, indeed international, significance. The arrangements reflected the nature of royal patronage. Instead of taking over a London theatre for its own purposes, the royal household delegated Mr Mitchell, who had managed Macready's visit to Paris in 1844–5 and specialised in bringing foreign companies to London, to mount a series of performances at Her Majesty's Theatre in the expectation of royal patronage. Although this smacked of economy, it did mean that ordinary paying customers could attend the performances, which were overshadowed by controversy. Charles Kean, who had directed the Windsor Theatricals since their inception, only received an invitation to appear from Mitchell, not a court official: 'He [Kean] felt that he had been snubbed. Here was the Master of the Revels, the Director of the Windsor Castle theatricals, put aside for a speculating Bond Street book and box seller!' (Scott, 1899, vol. 1, p. 248). Kean declined. He countered by offering his own theatre, the aptly named Princess's, and company, but the space was deemed to be inadequate. Mitchell turned to Phelps and Helen Faucit, both of whom accepted, the latter 'on the condition that it should be without fee or reward' (Martin, 1890).

Mitchell ensured that Her Majesty's Theatre was magnificently decked out for the occasion:

Draperies of pale blue silk cover the panels on all the boxes which are also adorned with flowers. Ten private boxes, including Her Majesty's, have been thrown into one extensive royal box which occupies nearly one whole side of the dress circle, besides which a reception and a banquet room have been fitted up in truly regal state. (*Theatrical Journal*, 27 January 1858)

Whatever the play had been it would have come a poor second to the occasion, but the choice of *Macbeth*, though evidently a favourite of the Prussian royal family, as a prelude to the royal nuptials was bizarre. In the event the royal party 'did not arrive till deep in the second act . . . just when Mr. Phelps had begun the famous dagger soliloquy' (*The Times*, 20 January 1858). Up to then the audience had been craning for sight of the royal arrival and thereafter for glimpses of the queen and her entourage. The press dutifully listed the dignitaries: the King of the Belgians and legions of Germanic princes with their suites (*Illustrated London News*, 23 January 1858). *The Times* supported Charles Kean, but nevertheless expressed sympathy for Phelps: 'How, in the presence of that frigid public, must Mr. Phelps have longed for the hearty Shakespearians of his own district! . . . It is no joke to play tragedy before a *blaze* public, whose whole mind is absorbed by a Royal box.' The *Theatrical Journal* disparaged the audience as 'fashionably-ignorant' (3 February 1858) and 'dastard' (17 February 1858), excepting the occupants of the gallery, the only part of the theatre which the 'dramatically-disposed' could afford at Mitchell's inflated prices. It was not until the concluding rendition of the national anthem by the cast (the actresses now dressed as bridesmaids), soloists and 'M. Benedicts's Vocal Association of 300 voices' (Scott, 1899, vol. 1, p. 166) that the assembly displayed any cohesion or enthusiasm.

No one would have dissented from Fontane's verdict on the performance as 'ill-starred in every respect' (Jackson ed., 1999, p. 111). The theatrical profession was highly indignant that 'the Drama has been recklessly ill-used, and a very bad representation of what it is has been given to Foreign potentates' (*Theatrical Journal*, 17 February 1858) and the *Era*, conscious of German regard for Shakespeare, expressed concern that 'if our illustrious guests were not such competent critics of Shakespeare, and his admirers, we should anticipate no very complimentary opinion would be expressed of the power exercised over his countrymen by our great national poet' (24 January 1858). The performance of *Macbeth* had failed on both of Carlyle's counts. It had not displayed Shakespeare's secure place in 'our English Household' and had done nothing to raise 'our honour among foreign nations'.

Just over a year later, in March 1859, Samuel Phelps took his company of twenty-five complete with costumes and scenery to Germany, where they performed in Berlin, Leipzig and Hamburg in a repertoire of six Shakespearian plays plus Bulwer Lytton's *Richelieu*. Why the cautious and suburban Phelps should have ventured abroad is a matter of speculation. According to John Coleman 'it was alleged [that] he [Phelps] made the visit at the instigation of the Crown Prince and Princess' (1886, p. 229), but the visit was arranged on a commercial basis by Ferdinand Roeder, a theatre agent, and Friedrich Wilhelm Deichmann, director of Berlin's Friedrich-Wilhelmstadisches Theater (Engle and Watermeir, 1972, p. 238), who presumably considered it opportune for an English company to perform in Berlin so soon after the royal marriage. The princess wrote to her mother of her 'intense delight at hearing Shakespeare in English again', but, as 'Mr Phelps is not a favourite actor of mine' (Fulford ed., 1977, p. 172), it seems unlikely that she was directly responsible for the English actor's presence in Germany. In fact during her first year in Germany the princess had been preoccupied with the difficulties attending her introduction into the stiff Prussian court and the – troubled – birth of her first child, the future Kaiser Wilhelm II.

Certainly, as the *Era*'s remarks reflected, in going to Germany Phelps was performing Shakespeare in the country, which most prided itself on its knowledge of and enthusiasm for the English dramatist. In his *Dramatic Notes/Hamburg Dramaturgy*, Lessing extolled the strengths of English drama, making (in numbers 10, 11 and 12) favourable comparisons with Voltaire (ed. Bell, 1890). Goethe's contribution has already been noted. Schlegel in *A Course of Lectures on Dramatic Art and Literature*, delivered in Vienna in 1808, countered the case against Shakespeare and advanced influential arguments for him. He rejected Voltaire's insistence on the unities and dismissed the 'social refinement' which prevailed 'through the whole of French literature and art' (1846, p. 267), celebrating, rather than condemning, the absence in Shakespeare's world of 'that artificial polish which puts an end to everything like free original communication, and subjects all intercourse to the uniformity of certain rules' (p. 349). Like Guizot, whom he probably influenced as he did Madame de Staël, Schlegel showed that the imposition of the unities on *Macbeth* would result in the loss of 'all its sublime significance' (p. 255).

He suggested that 'the trade and navigation which the English carried on with all the four quarters of the world' was conducive to an understanding of 'foreign matters' (p. 348) and reflected on Shakespeare's contrasting appeal in Germany and France, proclaiming: 'Shakespeare is the pride of his nation' (p. 345).

As Simon Williams has written, 'Schlegel's translations revealed in the originals previously unacknowledged aspects of Shakespeare's work' (1986, p. 211): the large casts, the frequent changes of location and the swift transitions from serious to comic. In the theatre Ludwig Tieck and Karl Immermann were in the vanguard, both of them trying to retrieve features of Shakespeare's theatre. Immermann's most notable achievement was *Twelfth Night*, which he staged in a (makeshift) hall with an amateur cast in 1840. As already noted with reference to Madame Vestris's revival of *A Midsummer Night's Dream* at Covent Garden in 1840, Tieck had staged the play in 1843 at the Berlin Royal Theatre to produce 'a compromise between conventional theatre and the non-illusionism of the Elizabethan stage' (p. 215). This production was staged at the invitation of King Frederick William IV (Speaight, 1973, p. 106), not long returned from England and the experience of seeing Macready's production of *The Two Gentlemen of Verona*.

Phelps began his Berlin season with *Othello* on Monday 28 March 1859: 'The house was crowded by the *elite* of the Court and the nobility at present staying in the capital, and the Princess Royal has, we hear, taken a box for the entire representation' (*Era*, 3 April 1859).

The only other English-speaking actor to have performed in Berlin in recent times was Ira Aldridge, the black American whose most celebrated role was Othello, which he performed to acclaim in Germany from 1852 onwards. Phelps's Othello met 'with qualified approval' and was not repeated, but Fontane recorded that the rest of the repertoire enjoyed 'a continual increase in audience numbers up to the end of the series' (Jackson ed., 1999, p. 100). Fontane, who was anxious lest Berliners did not consider that Phelps lived up to his accounts of the English actor, was relieved by the success of *The Merchant of Venice*, *King Lear* and *Macbeth*. Berliners were particularly impressed, rather as the Parisians had been with Macready, by the English actor's ability to express (despite the language barrier) intense emotion, the unity of his conception and his refusal to resort to applause-seeking tricks: 'we never met an unnatural display of art, or a far-fetched effect, seeking only for the hurried . . . applause of the mass (pit)' wrote one critic of Phelps's Lear (reprinted in the *Theatrical Journal* 20 April 1859). As for the productions, the effects (the appearance of the witches – as in a mist – behind a gauze), which had so impressed Fontane in *Macbeth*, worked their magic, but over and above that there was the unity, which Phelps achieved between all the elements of performance to bring out the essence of the play. This was evidently not lost on 'one of the most enthusiastic members of his audience in Berlin . . . the young Duke of Saxe-Meiningen, who dated his own appreciation of the need for ensemble work and meticulous staging to his experience of Phelps's production of *King Lear*' (Richards, 1971, p. 192).

Phelps went on to Leipzig and Hamburg; in the latter he played *King Lear* to 'almost empty benches', despite the city's large – and rich – English population, who were as apathetic about the theatre abroad as they were at home, but nevertheless 'the number of theatrical connoisseurs present made his triumph the greater' ('Dornbusch' reprinted in Phelps and Forbes-Robertson, 1886, p. 243). Despite Phelps's *succès d'éstime* in Berlin, the tour ended on a rather deflated note; not that Queen Victoria would have been surprised, writing as she did to her daughter: 'I am rather ashamed Phelps should be heard at Berlin, but his company I believe is fair enough' (Fulford ed., 1977, p. 172).

A visit by Queen Victoria to Sadler's Wells was broached in the press from time to time. As early as 1844, *Punch* (19 October) published 'a satiric description of Queen Victoria attending Sadler's Wells with King Louis Philippe and presenting Phelps with a cross of the Legion of Honor' (Allen, 1971, p. 94). London had no theatrical venue comparable to the French king's, which as Macready discovered the next year 'befitted the king of a great nation', but perhaps it had something more valuable as this comment by the French critic Augustin Filon unwittingly suggests: 'From 1850 to 1860 the permanent home of Shakespeare was the theatre of Sadler's Wells at Islington. Imagine Corneille exiled to the *Bouffes du Nord*, or, further still, to the *Theatre de Belleville*' (1897, p. 157). In 1853, Douglas Jerrold, again in *Punch*, observed in his review of *A Midsummer Night's Dream*: 'As yet Her Majesty has not journeyed to the Wells; but who knows how soon that "great fairy" may travel thither, to do grace to bully Bottom!' (Phelps and Forbes-Robertson, 1886, p. 130). A letter from Charles Dickens to Phelps the following February (25 February 1854) indicates that the possibility of a royal visit was being seriously pursued: 'I am sorry to inform you that the difficulties in the way of the Queen's coming to Sadler's Wells are insurmountable. But a very just reference is made to you and the theatre in Colonel Phipps's letter' (p. 390).

Although the queen's attendance at Sadler's Wells was out of the question, Phelps had appeared before her at Windsor Castle, in the court

theatricals of which Charles Kean had been director since their inauguration in 1848. George Rowell (1978, p. 47) quotes the Queen's letter of
6 January 1849 to the King of Prussia referring to the assistance afforded
by his representative at the English court, the Chevalier Bunsen, in setting
up what Prince Albert conceived as a counterpart to the court theatres of
Europe 'in an attempt to revive and elevate the English drama which has
greatly deteriorated through the lack of support by Society'. In a profession riven by jealousy the appointment of the relatively undistinguished,
but Eton-educated, Charles Kean caused widespread resentment. In fact
Kean did try to enlist actors from a range of theatres, not just the one with
which he was associated. Even Macready appeared, as Brutus to Kean's
Antony in *Julius Caesar*, and Phelps performed the king in *King Henry IV
Part 1* and Hubert in *King John*. Though Shakespeare was – inevitably –
the most frequently performed dramatist, his tally of thirteen out of the
fifty nights of performance, before Prince Albert's death brought the
venture to a close, was indicative of the royal family's catholic tastes.
Nevertheless into the 1850s, when Phelps had established himself as the
nation's pre-eminent Shakespearian, albeit at his unfashionable theatre
in Islington, voices were raised that he was being slighted by the court.
Douglas Jerrold hailed Phelps's appearance as Henry V, supported by
several members of his Sadler's Wells company, as the breaking of 'The
Great Kean Monopoly' (*Lloyds Weekly Newspaper*, 13 November 1853).
Henry V, though not one of Phelps's greatest successes, was a particularly
apt choice for a performance before the royal family, even in the confined space of the Rubens Room, which imbued the Chorus's lines 'Can
this cockpit hold / The vasty fields of France?' with added resonance.
Amongst the audience were foreign visitors, the Right Honourable W. E.
and Mrs Gladstone, courtiers including Colonel C. B. Phipps, who as
Keeper of the Privy Purse controlled the performances, and of course the
royal family itself, in particular the future King Edward VII for whom
the performance had been especially arranged to celebrate 'the boy's
twelfth birthday' (Lee, 1925, vol. 1, p. 20).

His parents' attentions did not necessarily produce the desired effect
on their eldest son and as Sir Sidney Lee (biographer of Shakespeare,
Queen Victoria and Edward VII) observed: 'But perhaps a surfeit of
Shakespeare in his early theatrical experiences accounts for a marked
diminution of his enthusiasm for the national dramatist as his career
came to a close. A pantomime or a farce proved from the first rather
more attractive' (vol. 1, p. 20). With his sister Vicky there was no such
problem; the future Empress of Germany evinced great enthusiasm for

Shakespeare from an early age, being, like her mother, a staunch admirer of Charles Kean.

CHARLES KEAN

Although he had won Queen Victoria's approval as an actor, Charles Kean had modest managerial credentials when he was appointed director of the Windsor Castle Theatricals in 1848. Kean set about his task with a will, working with Thomas Grieve, the Covent Garden scenic artist, to convert the Rubens Room into a miniature theatre at a cost of £376 14s (Bevan, 1954, p. 160). Over the years the remuneration received by actors performing at court became a matter of dispute, but in the words of 'One of Her Majesty's Servants':

The money paid by the Queen for large theatrical entertainments does not pretend to compensate a manager for his outlay, but, on the other hand, it should not be forgotten that the Royal purse is heavily taxed on these occasions. An army of skilled workpeople are fed and paid at the Castle for days before and after the performance. The theatrical troupe are treated *en prince* when they arrive, and the hospitality shown them is boundless. (*The Private Life of the Queen*, 1898, p. 90)

Compared with the grandeur of the Tuileries and the French king's largesse to Mitchell and Macready, there was an inescapable parsimony about the British monarch's attitude to the theatre, but in 1848 Louis Philippe and his prime minister, Monsieur Guizot, were preoccupied with off-stage drama. Richard Schoch suggests that by establishing the court theatricals – and ceasing to attend opera – in 1848 Queen Victoria 'sought to align the monarchy more closely with her people...as a paralysing fear of revolution gripped her own realm' (1998, p. 127). On the other hand, as George Rowell has pointed out, the choice of Windsor Castle, rather than Buckingham Palace, and the concentration of performances over the Christmas–New Year period 'stresses the family appeal of these performances' (1978, p. 48), another factor in which might have been a secluded location during the Queen's recurrent pregnancies.

Ironically Charles Kean's most ambitious theatrical undertaking to date had been in America, where even in the Mississippi valley the family name – 'Edmund Kean, the elder'[1] – could be exploited to attract an audience. The exploitation this time however was by Charles (the younger) Kean. In 1823 Charles Kemble had staged *King John* at Covent Garden, with costume and set designs by J. R. Planché, creating what is generally regarded as the prototype for the antiquarian revivals which were to dominate the nineteenth-century theatre. Macready, who played Hubert in 1823, was understandably indebted to Kemble when he revived *King John* in 1842, but, as Charles H. Shattuck has shown, examination of Charles Kean's prompt-book reveals 'how nearly he [Kean] followed Macready's text and ground plans', as he did the Macready-Planché costumes and – substantially – Telbin's sets (1962b, pp. 54–5).

King John, which had been preceded in what was intended to be a series of magnificently mounted Shakespearian productions by *Richard III* on 7 January, opened at the Park Theatre, New York on 16 November 1846 'Produced under the Immediate Direction and Superintendence of Mr.Chas.Kean, at a cost and with a degree of Correctness and Splendor, it is believed, hitherto not witnessed in any Theatre'. It had cost 'nearly $12,000' (Carson, 1945, p. 15). The hallmark was 'the UTMOST FIDELITY OF HISTORIC ILLUSION!' in the attainment of which 'no labor or expense has been spared' (Vandenhoff, 1860, pp. 237–9). The scenery was painted 'on upwards of 15,000 square feet of canvas' and 'the costumes' and 'costly armors', 'all from the Authorities named hereafter', totalled '176 in number'. In one scene the stage was populated by 150, amongst whom Mrs Kean, the former Ellen Tree who had married Kean in 1842, as Constance, gave the most impressive performance, adding to the already considerable reputation which she had made on her previous visits to America. *King John* 'ran with some difficulty, to moderate houses, the best of which did not reach $800, for three weeks' (p. 239). New York audiences were resistant to the use of their stage to illustrate – and instruct them about – English history. Although, as Charles H. Shattuck has written, the Keans were 'ultimately frustrated in their endeavor' to produce in America 'a grand series of classic English plays according to principles of historical accuracy', 'their significant contribution to Shakespeare in America was to initiate this typically Victorian staging practice' (1976, p. 106). From his own point of view Kean had gained experience at the Park Theatre, which was to be invaluable to him when he came to set up his own management in London.

Charles Kean did not establish his management (initially with Mr and Mrs Keeley) at the Princess's Theatre in Oxford Street until 1850, by which time he was indebted not so much to the 1843 legislation as to the special advantages accruing from his royal patronage and another of Prince Albert's initiatives: the Great Exhibition.

Kean's biographer, J. W. Cole, described the effect of the Great Exhibition on the nineteen London theatres, whose potential clientele was expanded by the seven million visitors drawn to London during the six months in which it was open. During his, exceptionally long, opening season at the Princess's from 28 September 1850 to 17 October 1851, Kean made a net profit of £7,000 (1859, vol. 2, p. 3). Although the season had opened with *Twelfth Night* Shakespeare had not figured large in the repertoire, but Kean had absorbed two crucial points: the public taste for history at the Great Exhibition, where 'perhaps, on the whole the Medieval Court [prepared by A. W. Pugin], as a department, excited the most general interest' (*Tallis's History and Description of the Crystal Palace*, 1851, vol. 1, p. 227), and the importance of long runs to finance the costs of large-scale Shakespearian productions.

Pre-eminent in the series of Shakespeare's plays which Kean mounted during the 1850s were those about medieval English history. In pursuit of the principle of the 'Utmost Fidelity of Historic Illustration' Kean, who became FSA (Fellow of the Society of Antiquaries) in 1857, consulted scholars, their books, the British Museum, ancient buildings and their contents. An expert team of scene designers and an army of costumiers translated this historical material into accurate stage pictures. In the process the plays were ruthlessly cut and rearranged, though, by way of compensation, Kean often added an 'Historical Episode' in which the protagonists, supported by hundreds of extras, enacted some event which Shakespeare had thought it sufficient merely to describe. Of *Coriolanus* at Sadler's Wells Theodor Fontane wrote: 'if the whole picture was not true to history, it was a least *true to life*' (Jackson ed., 1999, p. 79), but at the Princess's the opposite was the case. The picture was 'true to history', but devoid of the immediacy which was the key to Phelps's success with his Sadler's Wells audiences. Fontane summarised Kean's achievement:

The Shakespeare he offers is a *new* Shakespeare. Great and small must serve him: the archaeologist and the costumier; the British Museum and the pyrotechnist; heraldry, numismatics and the new laws of colour combinations- all are enlisted to overcome the apathy of the educated classes and to make Shakespeare popular again even in higher circles of society. (p. 32)

Thus 'the lack of support by Society', to which Queen Victoria had referred in her letter to the King of Prussia in 1848, had been remedied, as, following the queen's lead, the educated classes flocked to Kean's productions. Amongst them was Charles Dodgson (Lewis Carroll), whose clerical father was utterly opposed to attending theatres, who began his life-long obsession with the stage by seeing *King Henry VIII* at the

Princess's. Though he successfully revived *The Winter's Tale*, *A Midsummer Night's Dream* and *The Tempest*, Kean's foremost achievements were with English history plays set in the Middle Ages. Richard Schoch has proposed that this 'theatrical medievalism – the recovery and transmission of the Middle Ages as a *lived experience* – was a[n] . . . act of nation-building' (1998, p. 18). *Henry V*, which Kean had ceded to Phelps at Windsor in January 1853, enjoyed great popularity at the Princess's where Queen Victoria saw it four times in the spring of 1859, writing to her daughter: 'I wish you could have been with us to see Henry Vth which is quite as fine as your beloved Richard II' (Fulford ed., 1977, p. 172).

KING RICHARD II

It was with *Richard II*, one of the very few Shakespeare plays which Phelps did not stage, that the royal family's enthusiasm for Shakespeare *à la* Kean reached its apogee. Kean's *Richard II* was unique in being performed at Windsor Castle prior to the Princess's Theatre. The performance of 5 February 1857 took place in St George's Hall, where Kean specifically set his Act 5 Scene 4 (Shakespeare's 5.6), thereby achieving as complete authenticity as possible. First used in preference to the Rubens Room in 1855, the long, high, narrow hall with poor acoustics was not well suited to theatrical performance, but came into its own for this occasion. The queen observed: 'It was curious that a Play, in which all my ancestors figured, should just have been performed in St. George's Hall' (in Rowell, 1978, p. 49). The impact on the royal family was manifested in several ways, in the case of the queen by attendance (no doubt accompanied by some of her family) at five performances at the Princess's.

The Princess Royal, a capable artist, produced her own record of *Richard II*. The princess's drawing master was Edward Henry Corbould, who had first exhibited at the Royal Academy in 1835 at the age of twenty. A distinguished watercolourist, Corbould also illustrated works by Chaucer, Spenser and Shakespeare; he was instructor in historical painting to the royal family from 1851 to 1876. Corbould's 'Sketchbook',[2] containing rough drawings of costumes, sets and properties in Kean's productions, is indicative of his own theatrical interests, as are his letters to the actor thanking him for seats or even making the 'occasional slight suggestion' as the 'Historical Painter who looks to the stage as the only place where may be found the living embodiments which his inventive mind so earnestly seeks'.[3] Corbould was contending with the 'inventive mind' of his royal pupil, as he wrote to Kean on 28 March:

The fact is that eight days back The Princess Royal asked me to call and see you and I was expected to express <u>for her</u> – pleasure which HRH had just informed me was beyond the power of language to convey this pleasure was wholly derived from your treatment of Shakespeare and Richard II. The message was equally to you and your wife.

Unfortunately the – easily – harassed Corbould, had been 'so pressed with botherations' that, although the princess had desired him again and again 'to see you and Richard II under prohibition of seeing her face again till I have done so and fully expects I will do so tonight', he had made no attempt to secure a ticket for what was now a sold-out performance and wrote imploringly to Kean to admit him 'into some nook or corner':

I am told that places have been forestalled for at least three weeks in advance . . . The Princess wonders at what she calls my apathy on a subject that occupies her sleeping and waking hours – as she dreams by night and draws by day the endless beauties of your groups & effects – I believe she knows every line poetically and artistically. HRH purposes commencing on Monday a picture to be furnished by 24th May to give to the Queen on her birthday and requires me to procure some of the details of costume for that purpose.[4]

In his attempt to respond – belatedly – to 'the unfathomable delight caused by the whole play' to the princess, Corbould was also admitted to Telbin's studio where he sketched until 'the wearied state of nature' forced him to go home.[5] The princess's drawing of Charles Kean's *King Richard II* was no doubt a much-appreciated birthday present for the Queen. The Princess Royal also thought of her hard-pressed instructor, presenting him with a drawing of The Tournament of Richard II 'signed, inscribed and dated: Osborne, May 1857 for Mr. Corbould' (illustration 2).

As well as a drawing of *Richard II* from her daughter for her birthday, the queen received a specially commissioned set of photographs from her husband for Christmas. The gifts reflected the shared enthusiasm for the play and the giver's particular metier. The meticulous attention to detail and truth to life, which characterised Kean's productions, was symptomatic of the decade in which the Pre-Raphaelites flourished and photography advanced scientifically and artistically. The prospect that his productions could be preserved for posterity by photography would have appealed to Kean and fortunately close to his theatre (73, Oxford Street) at No. 65 there was a photographer, Martin Laroche, who was at the head of his profession, even to the extent of challenging

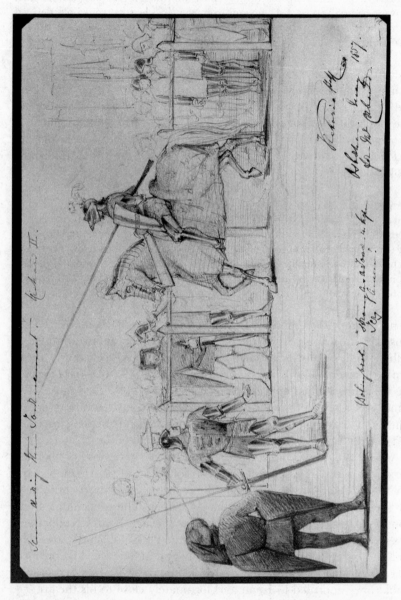

2. 'The Tournament of Richard II' by HRH Princess Victoria.

W. H. Talbot in court.[6] The result was a series of fine photographs, which had considerable commercial potential.

On 24 September 1857, Dr Ernst Becker, Prince Albert's librarian and a founder member of the Photographic Society, received an invoice from Laroche for the considerable sum of £126.[7] This covered six black and white sets of photographs, all of *Richard II*, as was the most expensive item, a set of eighteen 'slightly coloured photographs' at £54 14s, the bulk (£43 3s) of the cost of which was the painstaking retouching of the photographs to match the colours used on stage, a task which Corbould had performed for some photographs of *Macbeth*.[8] When Dr Becker photographed the Queen's Christmas tree on 24 December 1857 the Laroche photographs were on prominent display amongst her other presents (Dimond and Taylor, 1987, p. 80). Also in the Royal Photographic Collection is a remarkable photomontage by Laroche, '263 Portraits of Actors and Actresses' and, in Prince Albert's album of 'Theatrical and Musical Portraits' [cartes-de-visite] the only known photograph of Laroche.[9]

The English royal family was of course uniquely privileged, watching plays about its ancestors performed in a historic royal residence, but it was not, as its European counterparts tended to be, isolated from popular taste. The queen also regularly attended the Princess's and other West End theatres; the photographs which her husband gave to her were commercially produced souvenirs available to any admirer of Kean's production. Though they were consciously setting an example in their patronage of the theatre, the royal couple's enthusiasm, not least for Shakespeare, was genuine and contagious. In financial terms their patronage was modest, but it achieved more for the theatre than a bounty spent either on their own entertainment or on what authority deemed to be beneficial for the populace at large.

There were no performances at Windsor for Christmas 1858 and, though the royal family still patronised his London theatre, Kean was relieved of his duties at court, without the knighthood for which he and Mrs Kean had raised their expectations. Kean's place was taken by William Bodham Donne, the Examiner of Plays in the Lord Chamberlain's office and connected to the Kembles by marriage. On 31 December 1860, Donne wrote to Fanny Kemble: 'Her Majesty has again consigned to me the care of the Windsor pleasures: and the results have as yet been very successful ... We have a brand new stage and proscenium; and I suspect shall have erelong a theatre in Windsor, à la mode de Versailles.'[10] If such a theatre had ever come about, it would have been alien to British tradition, but within a year Prince Albert was dead and royal patronage came to an abrupt end. The erstwhile director of the Windsor Theatricals had already been obliged to seek decidedly more humble patronage.

SUBURBAN STAGES

Writing to Fanny Kemble in May 1861, Donne described the Keans 'drinking of the cup of affliction to the very dregs . . . playing three weeks at the Standard Theatre – in that picturesque region where the Eastern Counties Railway rears its head – and no one went to see them'.[11] Donne's own professional duties now included inspecting those London theatres which, since 1843, had been free to stage Shakespeare in such a way as to appeal to their local clientele. As Clive Barker wrote of Sam and Sarah Lane at the Britannia Theatre in Hoxton: 'The audience want plays, and, perhaps surprisingly, they want Shakespeare' (1971, p. 11).

The Standard Theatre in Shoreditch, the location of James Burbage's Theatre in 1576, had opened in 1837, but was extensively remodelled in 1845 in the wake of the 1843 legislation. James Anderson described his engagement with John Douglass at the Standard in 1853 as 'one of the most brilliant and satisfactory of all my East End arrangements'. The business was so good during the initial three weeks that Anderson stayed on playing 'twenty-three characters in twelve weeks' and clearing 'over £720' (1902, p. 214). Anderson played nine Shakespearian roles including Hamlet, Lear and Prospero, the last with Miss Eliza Terry as Ceres, Miss Seaman as Juno and Miss M. Terry as Iris in a performance which commenced 'with Purcell's celebrated music'.[12] In 1855 Anderson was back with Douglass at the Standard on terms of £60 a week, when Tully and Stammers offered him the title role in *Macbeth* at Drury Lane – 'making a great feature of Lock's music' (p. 228). The managers came to an understanding that Anderson would act three nights a week at each theatre, 'the patrons at the East End . . . would be glad to see their favourite actor going from the Standard to the Lane', but E. T. Smith the lessee 'put a stopper to the proceedings' by reminding Tully and Stammers that their agreement with him was for operatic and musical pieces only (p. 229). Nevertheless the point is made that there were actors, those who might be dubbed 'lesser stars', who worked freely between the East and West End and found in the former audiences with an appetite for Shakespeare.

At the performance (9 April 1856) of *Antony and Cleopatra* which he attended at the Standard, which 'has the lowest status of all the theatres' (Jackson ed., 1999, p. 16), Fontane found himself seated 'between a worker from the docks and a grenadier from the Scottish Fusiliers'. Fontane identified scenes in the play ('the drinking scene . . . reminds him of his own frailty') which the grenadier might find either familiar or stimulating to his imagination. The leads were Henry Marston and Elinor Glyn, and, with the exception of the latter, the whole thing was 'utterly artless and uncouth', but 'the play was sustained by its own strength' and clearly appealed to the audience. The contrast with Germany was more marked than ever: 'in Germany we always treat Shakespeare as something separate, "caviare to the general" . . . We are too refined . . . Shakespeare is a poet for the people, for *every* class of the people'. He concluded by saying that German theatres should take care that their Hamlets were able not only to 'declaim their soliloquies', but also 'fence with a French rapier in the final act' (p. 19). The importance of the duel or fight, which Shakespeare often used as a theatrical climax, at the Standard and theatres like it, is stressed by J. B. Howe. Finding William Creswick, who played Richard III, disinclined to rehearse their fight thoroughly, Howe (Richmond) went home: 'I shut myself in my room and rehearsed it over with a walking stick, making of the towel-horse an imaginary Richard, till I arrived at a satisfactory conclusion that I knew backwards' (1887, p. 139). Howe was rewarded by Creswick's praise as 'the best swordsman he ever fought with', as well as the audience's appreciation.

Another theatre at which Howe appeared over many years was the Britannia in Hoxton. Originating as a saloon, it was enlarged in 1850 by Sam Lane, who ran it until his death in 1871 after which his widow Sarah, who played principal boy in pantomime into her seventies, upheld the family tradition until she died in 1899. Sydney Fairbrother, the Lanes' granddaughter, recalled that: 'When the pantomime season came round, Juliet or Desdemona became the Principal Boy' (1939, p. 29). This principle was even applied to Hamlet. Chance Newton recalled that one of J. B. Howe's rivals in the role was Sophie Miles, a 'Brit.' leading lady 'who was one of the biggest favourites ever known there, or elsewhere' (1927, pp. 188–9). Other Britannia Hamlets included Marie Henderson and Julia Seaman, they and Sophie Miles choosing the role for a benefit performance (Davis ed., 1992, pp. 126, 162 and 188). For Julia Seaman, Hamlet became a regular role (200 performances) on both sides of the Atlantic and W. J. Lawrence described her 'as the first [female] colloquial

Hamlet' who popularised 'the Fechterian concept of the Prince'.[13] Another novelty was what Chance Newton termed this 'Hamlet hotchpotch', which took two forms: six popular actors playing Hamlet one night each at six theatres; and five different Hamlets playing an act each at the same theatre (1927, pp. 193–4).

This approach was also applied to *Richard III* at the Britannia, where three Richards appeared for John Parry's benefit: Thomas Drummond (Acts 1 and 3), Parry 'in imitation of *Edmund Kean (!!!)*' (act 2) and Howe (Acts 4 and 5) (Davis ed., 1992, p. 126). Clearly personal financial gain was the over-riding consideration for a benefit and Shakespeare evidently – with a little ingenuity – fitted the bill. The bard held the same attraction for the Lanes, who were above all an astute business couple (Sam left £60,000; Sarah £126,000). After the abolition of the monopoly – 'the dawn of freedom for the London playhouses' – 'They all now hastened to perform Shakespeare and the classics to their patrons . . . They [the managers] would have given any class of play that meant good business, but Shakespeare was then not only a great attraction, but had the additional merit in their eyes of being free from fees' (Crauford, 1933, p. 230). The 1832 Select Committee's recommendation on copyright had placed contemporary dramatists on a much more secure financial basis, but ironically this added to the attractions of works whose authors were deceased.

The Lanes essentially ran a stock company, but they did occasionally engage visiting attractions. In May 1852 Anderson, on terms of £100 a week, opened in *Coriolanus* 'to a house crammed and jammed from floor to ceiling with an enthusiastic crew' (1902, p. 208), later adding four more Shakespearian roles to his repertoire, having played Caius Marcius four times in the first week. Anderson spent much of the 1850s in America, not only New York and Boston, but also from New Orleans up the Mississippi to Louisville and Cincinnati and across to San Francisco (opening with *Hamlet*), a journey which, there being 'no railway to the Pacific Coast', took a month to complete (p. 246). As English actors traversed America, one particular American actor was obliged to pursue his career on the other side of the ocean, with the Britannia amongst engagements, which took him all over Europe, including Russia. The African Theatre in New York, where Ira Aldridge had begun his career in 1822–3, having been closed down by the authorities, the black actor moved to London where his 1825 engagement at the Royal Coburg included the role which he was to make his own: Othello.

Aldridge found it difficult to break into the West End, so he spent most of his career touring the outer London theatres, the provinces and – from 1852 – Europe, enjoying the patronage of the Duke of Saxe-Meiningen (Mortimer, 1995, p. 67), the Tsar of Russia (his performance in St Petersburg with a German troupe being recorded by Théophile Gautier: Marshall and Stock, 1958, p. 229) and audiences in Constantinople, before dying in Poland, where he was buried with great honour in 1867 (Mortimer, 1996). Aldridge appeared at the Britannia in 1852 and 1857. As Othello he was noted for his naturalness, his vocal felicity and intense pathos. In April 1857 Aldridge played Aaron in his own version of *Titus Andronicus*, from which the excesses of the original had been removed to produce 'a play not only presentable but actually attractive'. Aldridge delineated his own performance 'with judgement and great force of expression':

He rants less than almost any tragedian we know – he makes no vulgar appeal to the gallery, although at such a house as this, the appeal is a tempting one – he is thoroughly natural, easy, and sensible, albeit he has abundance of physique at his command when the exercise of it is required. (*Era*, 26 April 1857)

As Erroll Hall has shown, other black Americans 'moved to England, becoming involuntary exiles from home in order to pursue their love affair with the Shakespearean stage' (1984, p. 17). Morgan Smith was a particular favourite at the suburban theatres, not only as Othello, but also as Richard III, Shylock, Macbeth and 'an especially black Hamlet' (Newton, 1927, p. 207). If the minor theatres had not been legitimised, there would have been a serious shortage of venues for these performers. For Charlotte Cushman the engagement at the Surrey Theatre in 1846 was one of many at London theatres, amongst them the Princess's and the Haymarket. Inevitably she had her imitators as Romeo, Fanny Vining at the Theatre Royal, Marylebone in September 1849 giving 'a fervid impersonation of the impassioned Romeo' with American actors Anna Mowat and E. L. Davenport as Juliet and Mercutio respectively. Davenport proclaimed patriotically that amongst actresses 'C. Cushman can lick all the tragedy ones (heavy), and our little Mowat all the juvenile and comedy ones', but acknowledged that, although 'we can play Shakespeare almost *without* rehearsal', it 'was not so here', partly because of the actors' own professional pride but also because of the extent of 'the stage appointments' (Edgett, 1901, p. 30).

Two theatres which, in their contrasting ways, attracted attention for their 'stage appointments' were the Haymarket and Astley's. Even in the era of the patent theatres' monopoly the Haymarket had enjoyed a partial dispensation. On 27 March 1844, Benjamin Webster, a Shakespeare enthusiast in his own way (Webster, 1969, pp. 66–7), availing himself, as Madame Vestris had done at Covent Garden, of J. R. Planché's expertise, staged *The Taming of the Shrew* in the Elizabethan manner. As with the Vestris/Planché *A Midsummer Night's Dream* four years earlier, affinities with Tieck were discernible. Jan McDonald has identified the main features of the production. It began on a typical painted scene of an inn, changing to the Lord's bedroom 'where the Katharine and Petruchio story is enacted by strolling players made up "so as to give a sort of resemblance to Shakespeare, Ben Jonson and Richard Tarleton"' (1971, p. 160). The precise nature and working of this set are somewhat elusive, but it was based on curtains and screens. Mrs Nisbett was more successful as Katharina than Webster was as Petruchio, but they reappeared in the roles for a further fourteen performances in 1847, when Henry Crabb Robinson expressed his 'more than usual pleasure in seeing *The Taming of the Shrew* according to Shakespeare's text. An imitation of the ancient stage in its simplicity – a curtain and an inscription instead of a scene' (Brown ed., 1966, p. 183).

In contrast to the Haymarket's *The Taming of the Shrew* 'according to Shakespeare's text', at Astley's Amphitheatre Garrick's adaptation *Katharine and Petruchio!* was preferred by its manager William Cooke for his equestrian treatment in January 1857. Astley's had originated in the 1760s, when it was opened as a riding-school and circus by Philip Astley, a former sergeant-major and horse breaker-in. In 1803 Astley's was relocated (to Wych Street), one of nineteen such establishments built (in England, France and Ireland) by Astley for equestrian spectacles. Not surprisingly, Astley, who was a shrewd businessman serving huge public demand, won the approval of Jeremy Bentham, who described Astley's as 'the only theatre in which John Bull really takes delight' (Walbrook, 1926. p. 110). During the 1830s Astley's was managed by Andrew Ducrow, a brilliant – though barely literate – equestrian, whose admirers included Charles Dickens (Johnson ed., 1964, pp. 33–9)[14] and the future Queen Victoria, a great enthusiast of the circus. In 1833 Victoria attended Astley's to see Ducrow (Rowell, 1978, p. 24). Whether or not[15] Victoria attended Astley's as queen, Cooke headed his playbills 'Under the Patronage of Her Most Gracious Majesty the Queen, and H. R. H. Prince Albert' and in 1856, his traditional fare of romantic and military melodrama being in decline, he adopted the 'new course' of 'selecting celebrated works from the general dramatic stock' (*The Times*, 11 February 1857).

Cooke's first choice was *Richard III* (4 August 1856), still heavily indebted to Cibber and re-arranged in three acts with 'modifications . . . so that Horses might be introduced as often as possible'.[16] The result was commended by the critics. For instance the *Illustrated London News* (6 November 1856) was gratified 'that the acting has not been sacrificed to the desire of spectacular display' and went on:

The tragedy is throughout very sensibly performed with little indeed of noise and rant. The lines fall distinctly upon the ear, and the text for the most part is delivered with well-trained discrimination. The performers are evidently emulous to show that they are equal to the task of legitimate drama, and, not wanting in poetic feeling. A highly respectable level has been achieved, and it is satisfactory to add that what was meritorious in the acting was duly appreciated by a numerous audience.

James Holloway performed Richard 'in a most judicious manner, wisely avoiding the tendencies to rant with which the dialogue abounds', introducing 'a poetic spirit' and bringing the audience 'under the influence of a master-mind; and in this way the great purpose of the drama is effectively promoted'.[17]

The achievement of such high standards by the actors and the audience's evident appreciation were entirely in the spirit of the 1843 legislation, but William Cooke 'Ever anxious', as the playbill put it, 'to attend to the suggestions of his patrons' drummed up the equestrian attractions of his 'superb Stud of Highly Trained Horses! Who, from their perfect tuition and judicious arrangement, will impart vigour, and give reality to the many Scenes of Warlike Bearing'. Cooke also extolled the 'COSTUME, SCENERY and DECORATIONS', which in the tradition of Charles Kean, were after designs based on paintings at Hampton Court (Saxon, 1968, p. 157). Again in the tradition of Charles Kean at the Princess's, Cooke introduced a spectacular pageant of Richard's accession to the throne. The influence was not just one way. When Kean staged *Richard II*, the year after Cooke's *Richard III*, he introduced real horses (for Act 1.3 and Richard's and Bolingbroke's – interpolated – entry into London) which were supplied by William Batty, Cooke's landlord (p. 168). Whereas at Kean's theatre the audience's attention might have been directed at the exquisite accoutrements, at Astley's it was Richard's overthrow by Richmond that was most eagerly awaited. The penultimate scene

3. *Richard III* at Astley's Amphitheatre.

(Act 3.6) was 'Bosworth Field THE BATTLE! And Death of "WHITE SURREY"'. At Bosworth Richard, mounted on White Surrey, did battle 'with several opponents, whom he successfully resists, but not without the sacrifice of his noble steed'.[18] Cooke's stud showed the effectiveness of their training by 'the docility' with which 'they retain[ed] the semblance of death, while the swords of Richard and Richmond are clashing over their heads' (Willson Disher, 1937, pp. 214–15). Against 'the impressive picture' of the field of battle 'strewn with bodies, equine and human' (*Illustrated London News*, 6 September 1856), the final combat took place 'in the usual way – with this addition, that Richmond hacks him [Richard] about the neck, until he finishes him and the piece off at the same time'.[19]

The success of *Richard III*, 110 performances in the end, encouraged Cooke to stage more equestrian Shakespeare: *Macbeth* (the attack on Dunsinane and the combat between Macbeth and Macduff were as exciting as they were realistic), the aforementioned *Katharine and Petruchio*, and *Henry IV Part 1*, but without equivalent critical or popular success. During the 1860s the American actress Ada Isaacs Menken, whose attempt at Lady Macbeth in Nashville in 1858 had reduced James E. Murdoch as the Thane to 'a mere prompter in Scotch kilt and tartans' (Mankowitz,

1982, p. 6), drew the crowds as Mazeppa. In March 1870 the veteran Phelps appeared at Astley's (with the Vezins) in *Othello*, but, as *Punch* (24 March 1870) observed, for the first act in Venice 'riding is a rather superfluous accomplishment', though it did make some ingenious suggestions for the introduction of horses into the rest of the play.

From 1843 through the 1850s Shakespeare was a genuinely popular dramatist amongst all levels of English society, from the court at Windsor and the educated classes at the Princess's to Phelps's suburban citadel in Islington and such improbable outposts as the Standard, the 'Brit.' and Astley's. Credit for this burgeoning activity should certainly be given to supporters of the 1832 Select Committee and the 1843 legislation and to the lead given by the royal family; indeed momentum declined markedly after Prince Albert's death in December 1861. But so too did the vitality of the theatre profession with the retirement from management of Charles Kean and Samuel Phelps. During the two decades leading up to the tercentenary of his birth in April 1864, Shakespeare had achieved unprecedented status and popularity on the English stage and beyond.

3

A babel of bardolaters: the 1864 tercentenary

THE GARRICK JUBILEE

It was the great eighteenth-century actor David Garrick who first embarked upon the serious business of celebrating Shakespeare at Stratford-upon-Avon with the Jubilee to mark the bicentenary of the bard's birth held there, belatedly, in September 1769. The idea of commemorating its most famous son had only arisen in Stratford during the construction of a new town hall in 1767, when local lawyer Francis Wheler had what Garrick's biographer Ian McIntyre has described as 'an idea of brilliant simplicity' (1999, p. 412) casting 'his hissing fly over the water' in the form of the suggestion that the actor might donate 'some Ornamental Memorial of their Immortal Townsman [Shakespeare]' to the corporation for their new town hall within which: 'they would be equally pleased to have some Picture of yourself, that the Memory of both may be perpetuated together in that place wch gave him birth & where he still lives in the mind of every Inhabitant'.

Garrick was by no means the first or last ambitious man for whom the prospect of harnessing his own aspirations to present fame and future immortality to Shakespeare's bright star was irresistible. In this respect Garrick was also capturing the spirit of the time. The campaign (by public subscription) for Shakespeare to take his place in Poets' Corner in Westminster Abbey achieved its aim with the unveiling of Flemish sculptor Peter Scheemaker's statue 'to enormous public interest, early in 1741' (Dobson, 1994, p. 141). Dobson postulates that Garrick's aspiration was 'establishing Drury Lane Theatre rather than Westminster Abbey as the rightful home of Shakespeare's spirit' (p. 165). Garrick was certainly zealous in creating as close an identification as possible between himself and Shakespeare to the extent of erecting a 'Temple of Shakespeare' in the grounds of his Hampton estate in 1755. Three years later he installed 'within it a specially commissioned life-size marble statue of

58

Shakespeare, by Louis François Roubiliac, the most important sculptor working in England in the eighteenth century. Garrick's statue was intended to surpass Westminster Abbey's, and by general consent it does. Garrick himself allegedly posed as Shakespeare' (Taylor, 1991, p. 119).

Jonathan Bate has identified 'a complex set of forces' which, 'by about 1760', 'had combined to give Shakespeare an extraordinary preeminence': he had 'penetrated' Westminster Abbey 'the most potent symbol of the established Church'; he had 'furnished' the literary establishment with 'a model of distinctively English (un-French, un-neoclassical) genius'; he was becoming 'a cultural icon' for the expanding literate (but not classically educated) population of both sexes; and certain of his plays were associated with 'key moments in the life of the nation' (*Henry V* in war; *Henry VIII* for coronations). Not only was 'the climate . . . right for his [Garrick's] Bardolatrous projects', but the foundations were being laid for Shakespeare's place in the nineteenth century and beyond.

The progress, setbacks, achievements and disappointments surrounding Garrick's Jubilee have been fully chronicled (Deelman, 1964 and Stochholm, 1964). The initial proposal for 'some Ornamental Memorial' of Shakespeare 'some Picture of yourself' expanded into an ambitious programme of events, which necessitated the construction of a building known as the Rotunda, similar to that built at Ranelagh twenty-seven years earlier. Inevitably costs rose, but the town council, whose original motive had been to get a free statue of Shakespeare from an actor whose own eminence would add a certain lustre to it, was unmoved by Garrick's suggestions that it might underwrite the venture, though some wealthy Stratfordians did make individual contributions. The civic fathers' determination that the present-day citizens of the small Warwickshire town, which happened to be Shakespeare's birthplace, should not be burdened by expenditure disproportionate to their wealth and number set the tone for years to come. So too did a pervasive suspicion amongst the townsfolk of incomers, who were either theatricals, and therefore objects of inured prejudice, or well-to-do, and subject in their own eyes at least to appalling exploitation. Accounts of the extortionate prices charged in the town were undoubtedly embroidered, especially by Garrick's rivals (Samuel Foote claimed to have paid 'nine guineas for six hours sleep' – McIntyre, 1999, p. 422), but Garrick's own proposal in his capacity as 'the Steward' that 'no more shall be taken than a Guinea a Bed' (Deelman, 1964, p. 145) fell on deaf ears.

Unable to affect the nature of man (in the form of the citizens of Stratford), Garrick might have hoped that nature herself would be on his side, but the elements loured upon his efforts. As the Rotunda (octagonal, in wood, with a capacity of one thousand) was being constructed (under the not very effective supervision of Garrick's brother George) near to the Avon, on pretty much the same site as the Memorial Theatre, no one could have foreseen the extent to which the river was to swell during the three days when the building was in use. The first day (Wednesday 6 September) began at '6 o'clock in the Morning, with a grand Discharge of Cannon, Ringing of Bells &c.' (programme in Stochholm, 1964, p. 104). Though everyone (except the stone-deaf) resident in the town had free access to this diversion, the rest of the day's events (a performance of *Judith* in Holy Trinity Church and 'An Ordinary for Gentlemen and Ladies' in the Rotunda) were strictly confined to those who could afford the considerable admission charges. Late in the day persistent drizzle gave way to continuous rain and by the next morning 'The heavy Rains made it impossible' (James Boswell quoted in Stochholm, 1964, p. 68) for the 'PAGEANT of the principal Characters in the inimitable Plays wrote by Shakespeare', which would have given ordinary folk a taste of the events in the Rotunda, to take place, the damage (£5,000 at least, in Deelman, 1964, p. 211) to the costumes, being the decisive factor.

Those privileged with places in the Rotunda were feeling chilly and damp. Garrick himself had awoken with a cold and had been badly cut across his face by the 'perhaps not quite sober' (McIntyre, 1999, p. 426) man entrusted with shaving him. All in all not an auspicious start to the day on which the success of the Jubilee depended and to which Garrick himself was absolutely central as author and performer of 'An Ode upon dedicating a Building, and erecting a Statue, to Shakespeare, at Stratford upon Avon'. After the overture from Thomas Arne and an orchestra and chorus totalling one hundred, the actor, mustering the full power of his personality and professionalism rose, bowed and began:

> To what blest genius of the isle
> Shall Gratitude her tribute pay...?

To which answer came:

> Now swell at once the choral song
> Roll the full tide of harmony along;
> Let Rapture sweep the trembling strings,
> And Fame expanding all her wings,
> With all her trumpet-tongues proclaim,
> The lov'd, rever'd, immortal name!
> SHAKESPEARE! SHAKESPEARE! SHAKESPEARE!

After which the actor turned to the chorus which took up the cry, in subtly modified lines, reaching a crescendo with 'Shakespeare! Shakespeare! Shakespeare!' The audience, stunned by the combination of declamation and singing, was even more impressed by Garrick who, in Christian Deelman's estimation, had given 'the greatest performance of his life' in Stratford that day (1964, pp. 216–17).

There followed a further episode. Earlier in the week several newspapers had published 'An Oration in Honour of Shakespeare', a prose piece, the principal theme of which was that, rather than imitate nature, such were Shakespeare's creative powers that '*He was as another nature*' (Stochholm, 1964, p. 86). It seems doubtful that Garrick was the author of the 'Oration' (Edmund Burke has been suggested) and whether he actually delivered it that day in the Rotunda, but it formed a backcloth to what occurred next. Before and after a piece of music – 'to recollect and adjust your thoughts' – Garrick issued the challenge: 'Now Ladies and Gentlemen will you be pleased to say any Thing *for* or *against* SHAKESPEARE.' To the astonishment of the audience a man seated on an aisle conveniently close, indeed suspiciously so, to the orchestra, made his way on to the stage where he discarded his conventional greatcoat to reveal a suit of startling blue, decorated – fashionably – with silver frogs in the style of a Macaroni or Frenchified fop. He proceeded to denounce Shakespeare as 'a vulgar author' and, after admitting that he did not 'much love his country', wished that 'it would submit to become civilised', the first step being 'never to suffer so execrable a fellow as Shakespeare' (in Stochholm, 1964, pp. 88–9). The speaker, whose true identity as Thomas King, a much-loved Drury Lane actor, was becoming apparent to more and more members of the audience, was countering both the criticisms of Voltaire against Shakespeare and the recent jibes at Garrick. Boswell considered that this 'smart ironical attack' was out of place amongst an assembly of 'enthusiastic Admirers of Shakespeare', all of whom were no doubt in sympathy with Garrick's politely sarcastic riposte: 'I hope we are *not yet refin'd* enough to accept this Gentleman's Proposals for the improving our Theatre, but that we shall Entertain and content ourselves with that Heav'n has sent us in SHAKESPEARE' (p. 91). In countering Voltaire (Garrick had of course written King's speech), in asserting Shakespeare as the author of nature and in claiming him as God's gift to England, Garrick was defining important issues for Shakespeare's forthcoming ascendancy at home and abroad.

Although the heavens continued to deluge Stratford, the 'Race for a *Jubilee Cup*, of 50l. Value' was run on the third day and by 9 pm it was possible to let off the fireworks. The pageant was eventually staged (as part of *The Jubilee or Shakespeare's Garden*) at Drury Lane on 14 October, but perhaps the most important point established by Garrick in 1769 was the precedence of Stratford, the poet's birthplace, over London, the nation's capital, in honouring his name and works.

Garrick hoped that jubilees would become regular events, but it was not until 1820 that local interest was revived, again by a London actor, Charles Mathews, who had been so appalled by the miserable barn in which he had performed in 1814 that he instigated a meeting at the town hall 'to consider the best mode of erecting, in the form of a theatre, a national monument to the immortal memory of Shakespeare' (Mrs A. Mathews, 1838, vol. 3, p. 168). The scheme attracted the support of the vicar and the mayor and Mathews was duly elected president and treasurer with a view to enlisting support from 'every poet, artist and sculptor whom he was fortunate enough to know' (pp. 168–9) and even the King himself. The theatre scheme was diluted into one for a statue, an oft-repeated tactic when the response to an appeal for donations was disappointing, but even then there were those (such as Lord Egremont) who considered Shakespeare 'to be the property of the whole kingdom' and therefore hoped 'that the statue may be placed in the metropolis' (p. 204).

In 1824 the Shakespeare Club was formed in Stratford and three years later it organised its own jubilee. Left to its own devices the town had no doubt that a pageant was the thing and the mayor, accompanied by fifty constables, a military band and Francis Raymond's theatrical company from Northampton dressed as Shakespearian characters, led a procession from Holy Trinity Church to New Place. There in the garden of Shakespeare's one-time home, the mayor formally laid the corner stone of Stratford's first theatre, the construction of which was in fact already well underway (Warwick, 1974, pp. 85–90).

In 1830 the centrepiece was again a pageant, with the young Charles Kean as leading participant, but this time through its own efforts the town had achieved important (indeed the most important) recognition. On 29 March:

The Committee of the Royal Shakespeare Club, having this day received, from the Rt. Honourable ROBERT PEEL, a letter communicating the gratifying intelligence, that HIS MAJESTY THE KING had been graciously pleased to announce his determination of becoming Patron to the Club, and the Festivities intended to be given at the ensuing commemoration of Shakespeare, they lose no time in acquainting you with the important fact, and respectfully soliciting your subscription and interest for that occasion.[1]

Thereafter bills for the pageant proclaimed 'PATRON HIS MOST GRACIOUS MAJESTY THE KING' and drew attention to the significance of the date (23 April) on which it would take place: 'ST GEORGE'S DAY . . . the adopted Birthday of his MAJESTY, and still more celebrated as the Anniversary of the IMMORTAL SHAKSPERE'. A 'holy trinity' was established 'The King, the Poet and the Patron Saint'. In enforcing this identification of Shakespeare with the sovereign and the nation's patron saint, the Stratfordians of 1830 had produced an historic variation on Shakespeare's 'Cry "God for Harry, England and Saint George"'.

Between 1830 and the tercentenary of Shakespeare's birth in 1864, significant progress had been made in promoting his status not only locally, but also nationally. By 1840 scholarly interest in Shakespeare had developed to the extent that a national Shakespeare Society was formed. The leading figure was John Payne Collier, now still principally associated with the notorious forgeries – the 'Perkins Folio' – of which he was accused in the 1850s,[2] but then a respected as well as prolific scholar. Also on the council were Charles Knight, publisher and editor of a popular pictorial edition of Shakespeare, the Revd Alexander Dyce, editor of Shakespeare and many of his contemporaries (Marlowe, Middleton, Webster) and J. O. Halliwell, aged only twenty, but already a bibliophile and Shakespearian (Stavisky, 1969, p. 26). The basis of the Society as conceived by Collier, who became its first director, was 'an organization of several hundred subscribers who would pay a fixed sum, usually a guinea, to receive eight books a year in well-printed, well-bound editions' (Ganzel, 1982, pp. 69–70). In a reversal of common academic experience, the Shakespeare Society had ample members, but a shortage of editors, the reason being that the low subscription rate was underpinned by the officers and editors working without remuneration. Nevertheless the Shakespeare Society published much original material (forty-five volumes) and would probably have continued but for the controversy surrounding Collier which resulted in its disbandment in 1853.

By then Shakespeare's memory had been secured in the form of his birthplace, the sale of which had been advertised in what Sidney Lee described as 'the ungrammatical grandiloquence of the auctioneer, the famous Robins':

It is trusted the feeling of the country will be so evinced that the structure may be secured, hallowed and cherished as a national monument almost as imperishable as the poet's fame. (Lee, 1906, p. 222)

A distinguished committee was formed under the presidency of Lord Morpeth (afterwards the seventh Earl of Carlisle) with Dickens, Macaulay and Lytton as active members. Prince Albert headed the subscription list with £250. Morpeth, who was then Chief Commissioner of Woods and Forests, offered to make his (government) department 'perpetual conservators of the property' (p. 222), but instead the Shakespeare Birthplace Trust was set up. It was natural, therefore, that when the gardens and residence at New Place (Shakespeare's last home) came on to the market in 1861, the same procedure should be followed: a new Shakespeare Fund (with J. O. Halliwell a leading figure), a subscription list again headed by Prince Albert (£100) and the Shakespeare Birthplace Trust taking responsibility for the property. However although not entrusted to the government, Shakespeare properties had been secured by a countrywide subscription, being far beyond the means of Stratford itself, and did therefore represent the whole nation's determination to enshrine Shakespeare's memory.

PLANS FOR 1864

The future of New Place was (ostensibly) the subject of a book entitled *Shakespeare's Home at New Place Stratford-upon-Avon* by the Revd J. C. M. Bellew, one of the most colourful participants in the plans for the impending tercentenary. Leaving Oxford without taking his degree, Bellew, having failed in his attempt to make his way in the theatre, entered holy orders. As preacher at the Bedford Chapel, New Oxford Street, Bellew drew large, fashionable congregations who were impressed by his *voix d'or*, fine – allegedly bleached – white hair and impeccable ecclesiastical millinery. Already familiar in theatrical circles, Bellew later turned his talents to dramatic readings (reputedly earning £1,000 a year from this form of entertainment) which Charles Kemble had initiated at Buckingham Palace before Queen Victoria and Prince Albert with a reading of *Cymbeline* in April 1844 and which was long favoured by those who regarded a visit to the theatre as immoral (Lane, 1870). Bellew, who dedicated his book to the Revd Granville John Granville, vicar of Stratford, was at pains to uphold Shakespeare as 'not only a Great Man, but also a Good Man!' (1863, p. xv) and stressed his loyalty to his hometown; 'instead of residing in London and occasionally visiting Stratford, it may be much nearer the truth to say that he lived the latter years of his life chiefly at New Place, and only visited London . . . when his presence was absolutely necessary' (pp. 217–18).

Bellew devoted the latter part of his book to the 'swiftly approaching' (p. 317) tercentenary. He was utterly contemptuous of Garrick's Jubilee: 'A sillier or more useless exhibition was never witnessed.' The key word was 'useless', which in the mid-nineteenth-century lexicon was a thoroughly pejorative term. Whereas those who attended Garrick's Jubilee aspired to little more than pleasure (hard won in the event), their Victorian counterparts expected a 'practical purpose, and not a frivolous pageant to the memory of the great man' (p. 329). The use(s) to which the expected funds would be put were an important inducement to donors. One purpose, of course given the subject of the book, was 'the laying-out of New Place Gardens and the erection of some monumental structure, commemorative of the purchase and of the 300th celebration of the Poet's Birth'. However such a monument was not to be, as in 1767–9, 'some [useless] Ornamental Memorial', but a structure . . . practically useful for literary purposes, and a benefit to Stratford and the nation' (p. 332). An alternative, which would present 'common ground' was 'the subject of education' (p. 325). Certainly education had increasingly become a matter of public concern during the mid-nineteenth century from reforms at the Universities of Oxford and Cambridge, government Commissions on Education, education for women and the Working Men's Institutes. The expansion of education inevitably led to the formulation of alternatives to classics. As the pre-eminent 'native' author, Shakespeare took his place in the curriculum from 'the learning by heart extracts from good authors' (Marvin ed., 1908, p. 88) to which Matthew Arnold listened in his capacity as H. M. Inspector of Schools to the degree courses in English Literature at University College and King's College, London (see Palmer, 1965 and Bacon ed., 1998). A more specific suggestion from Bellew was 'the completion of the [Royal] Dramatic College' (p. 337), an ambitious scheme combining the housing of retired actors and the education of actors' children for which the profession had secured royal patronage (Foulkes, 1985), and/or endowing 'a few Shakespeare scholarships' there (p. 339). There was no shortage, in Bellew's fertile mind, of purposes to which the proceeds could be put and they all fulfilled his essential requirement of being useful.

Another issue broached by Bellew was the respective roles of Stratford and the capital in the forthcoming event:

That the Tercentenary of his birth should be celebrated in his birth place is a propriety which everyone will recognise; but there is no reason why the people of the Metropolis should not commemorate the occasion, as well as the select few whose time and means will allow them to congregate at Stratford. Such a double celebration seems almost a certainty. (p. 330)

'Such a double celebration' was indeed the certainty which Bellew postulated. He had also identified a significant social consideration by distinguishing between the 'select few', who had the time and money to attend a suitable celebration wherever it was held (as had happened in 1769), and the rest of the population, who in 1864 could not be denied their right to take part and would even (in some cases) assert their own claim on Shakespeare as the 'Poet of the People'.

As predicted by Bellew, tercentenary committees were formed in Stratford and London (Foulkes, 1984). Stratford was fortunate in possessing in Edward Flower a citizen who was equal to the occasion. The Flowers were a distinguished radical family. Edward's father Richard and his uncle Benjamin had founded the outspoken monthly *The Political Register* in 1807; Benjamin's daughters Eliza and Sarah were (respectively) a composer and poet; and Edward himself had spent formative time on his father's settlement in Illinois and at Robert Owen's New Lanark community. Settling in Stratford after his marriage to Selina Greaves of Barford, Flower established a – highly profitable – brewery and devoted himself to local affairs. He had already served as mayor in 1851 and 1852, but 'in anticipation of the "Tercentenary", a numerously signed requisition from the inhabitants was sent to induce him to become Mayor, that he might take a leading part in celebrating the occasion' (*Illustrated London News*, 7 June 1864). The family's involvement in the forthcoming events was chronicled by Sarah Flower, wife of Edward's eldest son Charles and a Martineau by birth, who reported in her first diary entry on the subject in June 1863 that her father-in-law had 'found it hard to come to any agreement' (1964, p. 51) with his fellow celebrants. Although he was the mastermind behind the enterprise, enlisting local worthies such as Lord Leigh of Stoneleigh Abbey, forming committees and engaging staff, Flower could not dictate decisions and he and Lord Leigh were both dismayed when the vote at a County Meeting in May 1863 eventually went in favour of a statue rather than the endowment of university scholarships for pupils from Shakespeare's alma mater, the town's grammar school.

The leadership of the London committee was much more problematical. In addition to the National Shakespeare Fund founded in 1861 by J. O. Halliwell, there was the Urban Club, a gathering of literary and theatrical types founded in 1858 (Jeremiah, 1876), and the aforementioned Royal Dramatic College. Who could unite such diverse ambitions? In his own estimation at least, it was W. Hepworth Dixon, who as a Deputy Commissioner, had been responsible for starting one hundred of the three hundred committees constituted for the Great Exhibition, which seemed to be his exemplar for the tercentenary. Since then Dixon had channelled his energies into travel, authorship (*The Story of Lord Bacon's Life*, 1862), helping the aristocracy organise their archives and editing the *Athenaeum* (1853–69). With J. O. Halliwell and the (very) minor novelist J. Cordy Jeaffreson as joint honorary secretaries, Dixon set about launching the National Shakespeare Committee exploiting his aristocratic connections (two dukes, nine earls, one viscount . . .) and using the *Athenaeum* as its mouthpiece, proclaiming: 'The Committee might be a large one, made to include every sort of celebrity, social, literary and scientific' (30 May 1863). The model of the Great Exhibition is discernible, not least in the stress laid upon royal patronage:

To begin, it is, we think, desirable that whatever is done should be done under the inspiration of a common thought, made visible by the ascertained sanction and adhesion of the one august personage who represents the whole country. The patronage of the Queen, the Presidency of the Prince of Wales, would give to the project of a grand Commemoration the only basis worthy of the name of Shakspeare. (30 May 1863)

Unfortunately the Shakespeare tercentenary found the royal family not only bereft of the member who would have given most enthusiastic support, but also in a state of continuing mourning which militated against active involvement by his widow or any of their children.

The Prince of Wales had taken over his father's duties with the Royal Dramatic College, but that was an existing royal commitment. The letter dated 19 May 1863 Marlborough House from Herbert Fisher, private secretary to the Prince of Wales, to Dr Kingsley, a Stratford medical practitioner then acting as honorary secretary to the tercentenary committee, read: 'I am commanded by The Prince of Wales to say that His Royal Highness feels a disinclination to make an engagement with reference to so distant an event as the proposed Shakespeare Tercentenary Festival.'[3] The want of 'the ascertained sanction and adhesion of the one august personage who represents the whole country' was certainly reflected in the increasingly divisive transactions within and between the two tercentenary committees and exacerbated by the lack of a recognised leader within the theatrical profession.

The Stratford committee tried valiantly to secure the services of Fanny Kemble, Helen Faucit, Ben Webster, Samuel Phelps and Charles Fechter, not one of whom appeared there. The Keans were out of reach in Australia and Macready was in retirement. Although it had appointed Robert Hunter as its paid secretary in September 1863, the Stratford committee considered it needed a London representative to deal with members of the theatrical profession in situ and appointed Bellew, but the result was chaotic, with the two men making conflicting offers to rival actors. Bellew was a great admirer of Charles Fechter, whose conception of Hamlet, according to Edmund Yates, was 'much mellowed and improved under the advice of our other friend Bellew' (1884, vol. 2, p. 6). Although born in London, Fechter was by parentage, upbringing and accent French. He made his debut as Hamlet at the Princess's Theatre on 20 March 1861 (Field, 1882, p. 50). G. H. Lewes considered Fechter 'lymphatic, delicate, handsome, and with his long flaxen curls, quivering, sensitive nostrils, fine eye, and sympathetic voice, perfectly represents the graceful prince' (1875, p. 119). The audience's cry of 'How natural!' could, according to Downer's theory, be traced back to the influence of Macready on French actors, but between Fechter and the actor generally regarded as Macready's heir, Samuel Phelps, there existed the deepest antipathy.

On 7 December 1863 Hunter wrote inviting Phelps to perform at Stratford, but in adding a private letter alluding to Hamlet, Othello and Macbeth, he was almost certainly overstepping the committee's instructions since only five days later Bellew wrote to Flower:

Phelps is a wretched Hamlet, but he is an Englishman. Fechter is a very attractive Hamlet, but he is (as Mr. Phelps called him) 'That bloody Frenchman'! . . .

I believe if we could get him to play Hamlet, he would be an *immense attraction*. Phelps would be none at all. I should say Mr. Phelps never has made any mark in Hamlet; and he is now quite too old.[4]

Fechter protested himself 'trop heureux de feter la naissance de son immortal creatur',[5] whereas Phelps, when eventually apprised that *Cymbeline* was all that was on offer, claimed that he should be 'considered the foremost man in my profession in a demonstration meant to honour Shakespeare' and that 'The Stratford Committee have insulted me by asking any man in this country to play Hamlet on such an occasion without having first offered the character to me.'[6] In the event Fechter withdrew at short notice, causing considerable speculation about his motive, which in his own words was that: 'I find the general public turning against me.'[7]

Even this was not the full extent of the professional and national jealousies encountered by the Stratford committee. Following Phelps's refusal to act in *Cymbeline* the committee secured Helen Faucit's agreement to play Rosalind in *As You Like It*. Her ever-attentive husband, Theodore Martin, busied himself with the details of the arrangement, all of which seemed to be satisfactory until he discovered that the French actress Stella Colas was to perform Juliet in Stratford. This had come about through the initiative of actor George Vining who 'kindly offered to proceed to Paris and ascertain whether Mdlle Stella Colas would consent to personate Juliet in the tragedy which drew such houses in London some months since during the lady's engagement at the Princess's' (*Tallis's Illustrated Life of London*, 23 April 1864). Estimates of Mdlle Colas's talents varied. G. H. Lewes considered her success as 'proof of the deplorable condition of our stage' (1875, p. 115) and exploitation (by manager if not actress) of the taste for French Shakespeare set by Fechter does seem likely. However Mdlle Colas showed commendable sensitivity and diplomacy in her letter of 18 April 1864 to Dr Kingsley:

I am just arrived in London and hear now all that has taken place on the subject of foreigners bearing a prominent part in the public homage to the national poet; also I am told to my great regret that Miss Helen Faucit has resigned her part, in consequence of my performing at Stratford. I hope this last report is not correct, as it would be most painful to me to be in opposition to any English artist, especially one so highly placed.

I beg to assure you, sir, that my only object in accepting this offer, quite unsought for on my part, was to render a service in a time of necessity, and I hope you will do me the justice to make this known to the English public, who have hitherto received me with so warm a welcome.[8]

In its efforts to engage Fechter and Colas the Stratford committee had alienated Phelps and Faucit. Of the four only Colas appeared.

The London committee made no effort to direct the capital's theatres, opting simply to incorporate suitable fare in its programme. Instead it concentrated on enlisting distinguished patrons, who would add lustre and – hopefully – donations to the cause, the principal object of which (as in Stratford) was 'a statue of Shakespeare', with 'any surplus being handed over to the Dramatic College or Shakespeare Fund' (*Athenaeum*, 6 June 1863). In its pursuit of the eminent the London committee became enmeshed in a fierce literary controversy. On 25 April 1863 William

Makepeace Thackeray had been the speaker at the annual Shakespeare dinner of 'Our Club' (a literary group which included Dixon and Jeaffreson). Jeaffreson recorded that as Thackeray left the table the eminent novelist bowed stiffly to him 'whilst Shirley Brooks regarded me with a look of exultation, which I could not at the moment account for' (Jeaffreson, 1894, vol. 1, p. 309). The reason was that Thackeray assumed that Jeaffreson was the author of an unfavourable review of his daughter Anne's novel *The Story of Elizabeth* in that day's issue of the *Athenaeum*. The animosity became so intense that Sir Charles Wentworth Dilke, the proprietor of the *Athenaeum*, lifted the rule of anonymity and the offending author was revealed to be Geraldine Jewsbury. Irrespective of the authorship, Thackeray's hostility towards the *Athenaeum* and its editor was irremediable and inevitably extended towards the National Shakespeare Committee. To persevere with an invitation (repeatedly ignored) to Thackeray to become a vice-president was nothing short of perverse and at the meeting on 8 December Jeaffreson counselled against, but Thackeray's supporters insisted on a vote in which only nine (in some counts thirteen) of the sixty present supported the author's candidature. Thackeray's friends (led by Henry Vizetelly) planned to press his case at the next meeting, but fate intervened for, on the morning of Christmas Eve, the novelist was found dead in his bed and overnight the affair became a matter of life and death. It was certainly Hepworth Dixon's death-knell, tolled by Theodore Martin, and virtually the committee's:

> 'Who killed HA'P'ORTH DIXON?'
> 'Who killed Ha'p'orth Dixon?'
> 'I' said T Martin
> 'Of that I am sartin
> 'I killed Ha'p'orth Dixon . . .'[9]

The London committee, although it produced a programme of events, could not claim to have directly initiated any of them.

THE CELEBRATIONS IN STRATFORD

In Stratford, despite all the difficulties, the scene was set. A splendid wooden Pavilion, capable of accommodating up to 5,000 people for events as diverse as a banquet, concerts, plays and a ball, was erected in Southerns Lane. That year 23 April fell on a Saturday, which, although a working day for many, meant that more people were free to participate than on an ordinary weekday. A proposal by the National Shakespeare Committee for a public holiday came to nought.

The programme began at noon with the president, vice-presidents and committee gathering at the town hall and proceeding 'to inspect the site fixed upon for the erection of the National Memorial, at the Market House, in High Street'.[10] The inclusion of 'National' was a clear signal of the status which Stratford was claiming. Just after two o'clock, as the official party was leaving the town hall for the banquet in the Pavilion an – unscheduled – event occurred, which added an international dimension to the Stratford proceedings, when the mayor received a deputation from Germany. They represented the Hochstift, an organisation, which had purchased the house of Goethe and also 'arranged lectures and other means of instruction for the youth of Germany' (Hunter, 1864, p. 167). In fact the delegation was made up of two distinguished German academics who were resident in England: Professor Max Müller, then Taylorian Professor of Modern Languages at the University of Oxford but also a distinguished Orientalist, and Professor G. W. Leitner, Professor of Arabic at King's College, London.

Apprised of the purport of the visit, the mayor (Edward Flower) 'immediately proceeded to convene the Corporation of Stratford at the Guildhall, and as soon as a sufficient number was present to form a quorum Professor Max Müller said':

Mr. Mayor and gentlemen of the Town Council, the city of Frankfort, the birthplace of Goethe, sends her greeting to the town of Stratford-upon-Avon, the birthplace of Shakespeare . . . When honour was to be done to the memory of Shakespeare, Germany could not be absent; for next to Goethe and Schiller, there is no poet so truly loved by us, so thoroughly our own, as your Shakespeare . . . He has become of ourselves, holding his own place in the history of our literature, applauded in our theatres, and in our cottages studied, known, loved, as far as sounds the German tongue . . . There is many a student in Germany who has learnt English solely in order to read Shakespeare in the original . . . It is from his plays that our young men in Germany form their first ideas of England and the English nation . . . Great nations make great poets; great poets make great nations. Happy the nation that possesses a poet like Shakespeare . . . May England never be ashamed to show to the world that she can love, that she can admire, that she can worship the greatest of her poets. May Shakespeare live on in the love of each generation that grows up in England. May the youth of England long continue to be nursed, to be fed, to be reproved, and judged by his spirit. With that nation, that truly English, because truly Shakespearian nation, the German nation will always be united by the strongest sympathies; for, superadded to their common blood, their common religion, their common battles and victories, they will always have in Shakespeare a common teacher, a common benefactor, a common friend. (Hunter, 1864, pp. 167–70)

Max Müller was eloquently echoing the sentiments of Carlyle as expressed in his correspondence with Goethe and his lecture on Shakespeare: Shakespeare's place not only in the 'English Household', but also 'in our [German] cottages', the indissoluble link between 'great poets' and 'great nations', the pride with which England should show her love for Shakespeare to the world and Shakespeare 'superadded' to other bonds between Germany and England. The address itself laid even greater emphasis on the common heritage of the two nations:

Once, as their blood, so was the language of the nations of the Saxons on this and that side of the German Ocean, the same. Sprung from one stem, two separate branches have developed into a separate and perfect growth . . . Once our country sent to Britain's shores that heroic youth which came as deliverers and established a new Saxon nationality against the invasion of Latin races and influence. Shakespeare's poems, in return, restored to us the mothers' travail of Germania . . . Old Teutonic virtues gained their footing as emancipators and ex-pellers of Latin corruption . . . As England's sons, wherever they be on this globe, so do all Germans thankfully praise the one and only William Shakespeare. May the kindred of blood once more assert its power by uniting into one fellow-feeling all the members of the race of the Saxons on this or that side of every sea. (pp. 170–1)

'Saxondom', which Carlyle had envisaged as embracing English-speaking peoples across the world, had been expanded to include the nation(s) whose language(s) shared the same origins as English and who were equally in thrall to Shakespeare. Germany's contribution to the appreciation of Shakespeare was already impressive as Franz Thimm, publisher and dealer in foreign books at his premises in Brook Street, London, demonstrated in his *Shakespeariana 1564 to 1864 An Account of the Shakespeare Literature of England, Germany and France during Three Centuries with Bibliographical Introductions* (1865), but the tercentenary provided further impetus resulting in the founding of Die Deutsche Shakespeare–Gesellschaft – the German Shakespeare Society (Habicht, 2000).

   The German connection was a recurrent theme of the succession of speakers at the banquet, held in the Pavilion at 3 pm: 'Tickets for the Banquet (including wine) – 21s Spectators (to the Gallery) – 5s'. The committee's president the Earl of Carlisle, who had won prizes for English and Latin verse at Oxford and was in his second term as viceroy of Ireland, drew 'Cheers and laughter' when he said; 'As to Germany,

I believe her boast is that she reveres, and understands, and fathers him even more thoroughly than ourselves' (Hunter, 1864, p. 180). The Earl also drew attention to France where he claimed 'the tone . . . in which Shakespeare is now spoken of and judged' had been reversed since 'the sarcastic armoury of Voltaire' had been targeted at him. In fact the authorities had stepped in to ban a special tercentenary performance of *Hamlet* and excerpts from other plays at the Théâtre de la Porte-Saint-Martin, but Victor Hugo's *William Shakespeare* – 'Shakespeare is the great glory of England . . . The native town of Stratford is an elect place; an eternal light is on that cradle' (1864, p. 305) – reinforced the earl's case.

The opportunities afforded by the Hochstift's address had not been exhausted and in formally presenting it at the banquet Professsor Leitner, like Hugo, stressed the importance of Stratford (implicitly over London): 'The house of Shakespeare is a national property delivered into your trust' (Hunter, 1864, p. 189). He went on to proclaim Germany's dedication to Shakespeare 'our missionaries have proselytised the whole civilised world for him' and to claim that 'in the distribution of national duties the one specially assigned to Germans is the empire over the thought and literary labours of the whole of this globe. Whenever any nation from one pole to the other exhibits dawnings of literary development, German scholars will investigate them [to] . . . the common good of the whole civilised world.' If the prospect of such cultural imperialism sent shivers up any English spines it was not the occasion to declare them, with Leitner going on to assert that whatever treasures his countrymen might find among other nations 'they will in our estimation . . . be necessarily always subordinate to the giant form and overwhelming genius of William Shakespeare', who, with Goethe, was 'the most perfect embodiment of the highest aspirations of Saxon poetry' (pp. 189–91). In his reply as mayor Flower expressed pleasure and satisfaction at 'this proof of the love of the German nation for a kindred race' assuring its donors that 'the document will be deposited in Shakespeare's house, and there religiously preserved' (pp. 191–2).

The next day, being Sunday, was devoted to the religious dimension of the occasion, with two sermons being delivered in Holy Trinity Church as official parts of the programme. The first preacher was Richard Chenevix Trench, installed at the beginning of that year as Archbishop of Dublin, but as his biographer (J. Bromley, 1959) aptly put it *The Man of Ten Talents*, being a poet, translator of Spanish literature especially Calderón, and a highly respected philologist (his *On the Study of Words* was repeatedly reprinted) who played a key role in the creation of the *Oxford English*

Dictionary. Trench's text was 'Every good gift and every perfect gift is from above, and cometh down from the Father of lights' (James 1, 17) (see Foulkes, 2001). In contrast to Trench's appropriation of Shakespeare for the established church, in *Father and Son* Edmund Gosse described the hostility voiced at a meeting of Plymouth Brethren in London in April 1864 at which 'Brother-So-and-So', 'an elderly man, fat and greasy, with a voice like a bassoon', denounced the spread of idolatry: 'At this very moment . . . there is proceeding, unreproved, a blasphemous celebration of the birth of Shakespeare, a soul now suffering for his sins in hell' (Gosse, 1907, p. 322). Trench was intent, not on reproving Shakespeare, but on extolling his virtues, which he asserted, in opposition to the evolutionists, were 'the gift of God'; he affirmed Shakespeare as a poet on whose part 'there is no paltering with everlasting ordinances on which the moral estate of man's life reposes, no challenging of the fitness of these, no summoning of God to answer for Himself at the bar of man for the world he has created' (Trench, 1864, p. 9).

The Congregationalist minister R. W. Dale, preaching on 'Genius The Gift of God' at the Independent Chapel in Stratford, proclaimed 'the genius of a great poet is a more wonderful product of the creative energy than the brightest constellation in the sky' (1864, p. 6) and at the other end of the theological spectrum Cardinal Wiseman asserted that genius was a gift from God like 'the very first germ of a plant' (1865, p. 25). Victor Hugo took up the theme in 'Book II Men of Genius' in *William Shakespeare*:

God manifests himself to us in the first degree through the life of the universe, and in the second through the thought of man. The second manifestation is not less holy than the first. The first is named Nature, the second is named Art. Hence this reality: the poet is priest. (1864, p. 28)

With science challenging the traditional religious account of the creation of the universe, the 'second manifestation' – 'God creates art by man' (p. 29) – held obvious attractions for churchmen and the devout, who seized upon the Shakespeare tercentenary as a God-given opportunity to use that argument to counter the recent tide of evolutionism, exemplified by Charles Darwin's *The Origin of Species* (1859).

Though in his rebuttal of evolutionary ideas Trench shared common ground with other denominations and nations, elsewhere in his sermon he spoke forthrightly as a leader of the Church of England. Shakespeare's greatness was inextricable from his Englishness and could quicken 'the mighty heart of a people . . . to heroic enterprise and worthiest endeavour' (1864, p. 8). Carlyle had posed the question which will you give up 'your Indian Empire or your Shakespeare' (1946, p. 148); Trench asked his congregation 'to imagine this England of ours without her Shakespeare . . . the foremost poet whom the world has seen, we are almost bold to prophesy, it will ever see' (1864, p. 16). In bestowing genius upon Shakespeare God was deemed to have shown his favourable disposition towards England. Such a view was by no means exclusive to conservatives like Trench, whose Cambridge contemporary the Revd F. D. Maurice, the founder of Christian socialism, propounded in his 'Introductory Lecture' (1840) as Professor of English Literature and History at King's College, London his inclination 'to think that we shall find the study of words and constructions, the very link between literature and history' and through such studies 'we may interpret the purposes of God to our land' (in Bacon ed., 1998, pp. 66 and 73).

Trench's successor in the Holy Trinity pulpit was Charles Wordsworth, Bishop of St Andrews and nephew of the Lakeland poet, who took as his text: 'All Thy Works Praise Thee, O Lord' (Psalms 145, 10). Wordsworth's *On Shakspeare's Knowledge and Use of the Bible* was published in 1864.

By way of transition to the secular world of the theatre the highlight of Monday 25 April was *The Messiah*, with exhibitions (twenty-eight portraits of Shakespeare) and excursions as added diversions. After all its tribulations with the acting profession, the Stratford committee succeeded in having three plays performed in the Pavilion. J. B. Buckstone, who had been a wise counsellor, brought his Haymarket company in *Twelfth Night* (on 26 April). At the sound of Buckstone's 'genial, familiar voice' as Sir Toby 'never was heard such applause as was then sent up . . . perhaps . . . as much out of a feeling of satisfaction that Mr. Buckstone, in the midst of defection, had remained true, as out of his talents as an actor' (*Morning Post*, 28 April 1864). The warm reception accorded to Stella Colas the following evening was largely a tribute to her loyalty, the programme alluding darkly to 'Mr Fechter, after his repeated pledges . . . at the eleventh hour, withdraw[ing] from his engagement', but by the end of her performance as Juliet 'everybody was convulsed with suppressed tittering though making formal complimentary noises with their hands' (*Standard*, 29 April 1864). The final play was *As You Like It*, specially produced for the occasion by William Creswick (1889, pp. 72–3), with Mrs Vezin playing Rosalind 'with an archness and intelligence that quickly won the hearts of the spectators' (*Daily Telegraph*, 30 April 1864). Generally regarded as Shakespeare's quintessentially Warwickshire play (Arden for Ardennes), *As You Like It* was an apt choice for what in effect was the first play by Shakespeare to be produced in his home town and Mrs Hermann Vezin (who as Mrs Charles Young had enjoyed great success in Australia) became the first in a succession of actresses – Mary Anderson and Ada Rehan soon followed – for whom success as Rosalind was inseparable from performing her in Stratford.

Admission prices for the plays (21*s*, 10*s* 6*d*, and 5*s* unreserved) and the other events in the Pavilion effectively excluded ordinary working people, whose only opportunity to share the celebrations was 'A Grand Display of Fireworks by Mr Darby, the celebrated Pyrotechnist' on the night of 23 April. Resentment against this exclusive provision for what Bellew had called 'the select few' surfaced amongst 'the people' of Stratford, as it was to do amongst their metropolitan counterparts. On the Ides of April a boldly printed handbill appeared on the streets of Stratford:

TIME! SHAKESPEARE THE POET OF THE PEOPLE
People of Stratford! Where are the seats reserved for you at the forthcoming festival? What part or lot have you who originated it, in the coming celebration? None! But you will be permitted to see the Fireworks, because they cannot be set off in the Pavilion; and you are promised something for yourself *after the swells have dined*. Only wait till the next week, and see the dainty mess that shall be BREWED for you out of the cold 'wittles'. PEOPLE OF STRATFORD, who would not see your town disgraced on such an occasion, your streets empty, or blocked up only by the carriages of *profitless swells*, take counsel without delay!
Call a meeting without delay!
Form your own Committee!!
Hold your own Festival!!!
Look to your own business. Lay out your own money.
Get up your own out-door sports and in-door pastimes, and let your
    watchword be
SHAKESPEARE the POET OF THE PEOPLE
AND HURRAH FOR THE PAGEANT
     Hobbesley Hall
     Kendal Green
     Flowery Land
Ides of April 1864[11]

The pageant, so dearly beloved by the townsfolk, did take place on 2 and 3 May, but although it was mentioned in the 'Complete Programme', in connection with the 'Series of Popular Entertainments in the Pavilion' from 30 April, it was not organised by the Stratford committee. It was a measure of public enthusiasm that the pageant could be funded by a door-to-door canvas and the result was no mere homespun affair. Jean Frederick Ginnett, the circus proprietor, 'very kindly placed his unrivalled Equestrian Troupe of Artistes, Horses and Carriages, properly caparisoned and appointed in Shakespearian Costumes, at the service of the Pageant Committee, free of charge'. The association between the poet and the patron saint, established in 1830, was revived: 'An artiste will take part in the Procession, in full armour, as St. George.'[12] The fact that the town was connected to the railway network was vital to the whole Stratford festival not only for transporting the public, but also the performers, their equipment and scenery. An estimated 30,000 people thronged Stratford on 2 May, many of them travelling there on special excursion trains from surrounding towns.

Excursion trains were also laid on for those attending *Othello* (3 May) and *Much Ado About Nothing* with the 'Trial Scene' from *The Merchant of Venice* (4 May), both of them under Creswick's supervision, in the Pavilion, for which admission was 3*s*, 2*s*, 1*s*. Creswick, who as long-serving manager (with Richard Shepherd) of the Surrey Theatre had ample experience of providing Shakespeare for a popular audience, assembled a talented company including the Vezins, Vandenhoff and 'local tragedian' James Bennett. In *Othello* Creswick played the title role and Bennett Iago 'before a house of 4,000 persons' who responded appreciatively to 'the excellence and esprit' of the whole acting company. Amongst those present were the butler and coachman of the rector of Ilmington, the Revd Julian Charles Young, son of the actor Charles Mayne Young. When Young asked his coachman, 'an honest simple creature', how he had been impressed by the play, he said he liked it 'unaccountable', but, pressed for further details, he related: 'It ran upon sweethearting! Aye that it did. And there were two gennelmen, one was in white, and the other was in black; and, what was more, both o' these gents was sweet on the same gal' (Young, 1871, pp. 292–3). Young was typical of a breed of clergymen who saw the potential of literary readings and talks not only as an improving pastime (rather than the pub), but also as a means of drawing parishioners into church. Young cited the redemptive power of his readings: a villager who, in his wife's words, 'were once r-a-ther given to drink; but since he've heard your lecs [lectures], he seems an altered man, and never takes nothing but tea . . . He never used to go to church. He goes now' (pp. 471–2).

LONDON

In London the National Shakespeare Committee struggled to make any showing and even the events in which it had a hand did not turn out as planned. On 23 April Samuel Phelps planted an oak sapling on Primrose Hill. Much was made of the fact that the queen had given the sapling, her only contribution to the tercentenary apart from lending a painting (Lawrence's portrait of J. P. Kemble as Hamlet) to the exhibition in Stratford. The visit to England that spring of Giuseppe Garibaldi, who had been the key figure in the recent unification of Italy, had caused immense interest amongst all levels of society. He was fêted everywhere – from Eton to the Crystal Palace – ; en route from Dublin to Stratford Trench dined with him and Gladstone. However Garibaldi's unexpected departure from England aboard the Duke of Sutherland's yacht *Undine* on the morning of 23 April was interpreted by some disaffected elements as nothing short of expulsion. The Shakespeare gathering on Primrose Hill was effectively turned into a protest meeting about Garibaldi, a 'large proportion of the members of the Garibaldi Committee (a special Working Men's Committee) are also members of the Shakespeare Committee' reported *The Times* (25 April 1864). The police were present in numbers and for a time confrontation seemed inevitable, but the tension was diffused, though questions were asked in parliament.

This incident was in the spirit of Jack Cade who made a rare appearance in *Henry VI Part 2* at the Surrey Theatre, where James Anderson 'thought this an excellent opportunity to produce his historical play of *Henry VI*, which had never been acted in its integrity since his day' (1902, pp. 271–2). Faced with fifty speaking parts for his small company, Anderson 'doubled, trebled, even quadrupled [them], as I have no doubt they were in Shakespeare's time at the Blackfriars and Globe playhouses', but the 'dresses, armour and weapons were bright, beautiful, and appropriate to the fourteenth century, and the scenery was picturesque and truthful'. Although this combination of Elizabethan acting principles and nineteenth-century antiquarianism 'achieved an immense success', it 'drew no money' and Anderson 'got only twelve nights out of it'. He thought it would have 'run a hundred' at Drury Lane, but 'it flew over the heads of the transpontine playgoers'. Anderson's estimate of the play's likely success at Drury Lane was probably unrealistic and *Henry VI* must have seemed an appropriate choice (with its social diversity and action-packed plot) for a transpontine theatre, but perhaps the canvas was too large for audiences who were happier with familiar plays. The enthusiasm for Shakespeare, which had been so evident at the former minor theatres during the 1850s, had greatly diminished, though at the Britannia the 'especial Festival' originally 'billed for six nights' by Sarah Lane 'ran on for six weeks, and kept on and on, whereas the Tercentenary

Shakespeare shows at Drury Lane, and at the Surrey especially, each with big stars, continued only for a week or two' (Newton, 1927, p. 209).

At Drury Lane Phelps as Falstaff in *Henry IV Part 1* was, as always, in Henry Morley's words 'unquestionably good' (1891, p. 275). Morley, who as a reviewer during the 1850s and 1860s made an important contribution to the rehabilitation of the theatre amongst the educated classes and who was appointed Professor of English Literature at University College, London in 1865, took the opportunity to reflect on the English theatre, which 'is not something apart from English life, but is so intimately connected with it' (p. 273). The theatre was now supported by all except 'a still reluctant section of the educated classes' and a diminishing number of religious bigots: 'An English audience with a thoroughly good English play before it should be one of the worthiest assemblies that the world can show' (p. 274). Ironically the queen herself, who, through her personal enthusiasm and sense of duty, had done so much for the theatre, was noticeably absent from the tercentenary celebrations. The theatre's sense of deprivation is evident in a poetical masque 'The Fairies' Festival in Commemoration of Shakespeare's Birthday', written by Edmund Falconer to conclude Drury Lane performances:

A deputation, consisting of a poet, an actor, an editor and a critic, is introduced by Puck, who explains that it is proposed to celebrate the three hundredth birthday of Shakespeare. The royal pair (Oberon and Titania) willingly promise to patronise the festival. There were in this scene some very feeling and graceful allusions to the sorrow which has clouded our Queen, which were well received by the audience. The festival takes place in a sylvan retreat in Windsor Forest. (*Tallis's Illustrated Life of London*, 30 April 1864)

Although many of the contributors to the Shakespeare tercentenary echoed Carlyle's sentiments, the occasion was singularly lacking in the heroic qualities which he had extolled. The absence of royal patronage was made all the more acute by Queen Victoria's and the late Prince Albert's recent contribution to the theatre's enhanced status. If in nothing else, Hepworth Dixon was right about the importance of 'the ascertained sanction and adhesion of the one august personage who represents the whole country', and without that the celebrations splintered into those for the 'select few' and those for the people. Without an outstanding leader in his prime (as in 1769 Garrick had been) the theatre failed to rise above the rivalries and jealousies with which it was persistently beset. The only leading figure in the tercentenary to emerge with real credit was Stratford's mayor, Edward Fordham Flower and it was largely due to

PUNCH, OR THE LONDON CHARIVARI.—January 30, 1864.

SHAKSPEARE AND THE PIGMIES.

4. Shakespeare and the Pygmies.

his strength of character, upheld as an example by Samuel Smiles in *Duty*, that the small Warwickshire market town emerged as the 'elect place' for bardolaters the world over. By 1879 Stratford, in the face of metropolitan disdain, had its own Shakespeare Memorial Theatre. Otherwise the caption to the *Punch* cartoon of 30 January 1864: 'Shakspeare and the Pigmies' was a sadly apt epitaph for the Shakespeare tercentenary.

4

Made in Manchester: Charles Calvert
and George Rignold

COTTONOPOLIS

London and Stratford-upon-Avon were at opposite ends of the spectrum
of urbanisation, which affected not only Britain but also much of the
world during the nineteenth century. More and more of the population
were living in the expanding industrial cities – Birmingham, Manchester,
Leeds, Glasgow and so on – to the extent that whereas in 1851 the
queen's subjects were 'equally divided between town and city dwellers'
thereafter every census 'showed an increase in the population of urban
dwellers: 61.8 per cent in 1871, 72.05 per cent in 1891, and 80 per cent
in 1911, with the large towns of more than 100,000 population taking
a dominant share of that increase' (Meller, 1976, p. 2). As Asa Briggs
pointed out: 'In distant parts of the Empire . . . far bigger communities
[than Middlesbrough] developed from humble beginnings to become
great cities during Queen Victoria's reign' (1968, p. 277). Briggs cites the
expansion of Toronto from 10,000 in 1834 to over 200,000 by the end
of the century and Melbourne from 23,000 in 1850 to more than half a
million (pp. 277–8). After London the two most populous cities in the
British Empire were in India: Bombay and Calcutta. What was true of
Britain, its Empire and much of Europe was also true of North America,
with the growth of east coast cities and the creation of new ones as the
frontier moved westward.

This large-scale migration of the world's population was possible because of an ever-expanding railway network and faster, safer and more
comfortable vessels, aboard which to traverse the oceans. Hegemony
may have been in the minds of monarchs, ministers and the military, but
for the ordinary man and woman (merchant, manufacturer, mechanic,
medic, farmer, man-of-letters or actor) the over-riding consideration in
becoming part of this pattern was the prospect of securing a better life
for themselves and their families.

The principles of free trade upon which so much of this activity was based were closely associated with Manchester where Richard Cobden and John Bright were amongst the local businessmen who founded their own Anti-Corn Law Association in 1838, followed by the national Anti-Corn Law League in 1839. In Gary Messinger's words: 'As the largest industrial city and the centre of Britain's most prosperous industry, Manchester was the logical home of a movement advocating free trade' (1986, p. 66). It was also, like other recently expanded conurbations, a hotbed of Chartism. In his essay *Chartism* (1839) Thomas Carlyle wrote: 'Disorganic Manchester afflicts us with its Chartism' (1915, p. 234), but took a pragmatic approach to 'the strange phenomenon called "over-population!"', pointing out that although 'this small western rim of Europe' might indeed be crowded, elsewhere there was 'a whole vacant Earth' crowded only with opportunities. Carlyle identified 'two great things... hovering, of late, even on the tongues of not a few... Universal Education is the first great thing we mean; general Emigration is the second' (p. 228):

Let us now observe that Education is not only an eternal duty, but has at length become even a temporary and ephemeral one, which the necessities of the hour will oblige us to look after. These Twenty-four million labouring men, if their affairs remain unregulated, chaotic, will burn ricks and mills; reduce us, themselves, and the world into ashes and ruins. (p. 229)

Such a prospect would not have been unwelcome to another observer of the condition of Britain's labouring men: Frederick Engels, Marx's collaborator with the *Communist Manifesto* of 1848 and author of *The Condition of the Working-Class in England. From Personal Observation and Authentic Sources*, first published in Leipzig in 1845. Engels used Manchester, 'the classic type of modern manufacturing town', as his main example (Marx and Engels, 1975, vol. 4, p. 245). A city 'more an outgrowth of accident than any other city' (p. 349), where 'in these filthy holes a ragged, ill-fed population' (p. 366) existed, indulging in 'intemperance in the enjoyment of intoxicating liquors... [and] sexual licence': 'The bourgeoisie has left the working-class only these two pleasures, while imposing upon it a multitude of labours and hardships' (p. 423). The implied dereliction of social responsibility by the bourgeoisie had resulted in 'two radically dissimilar nations' (p. 420), but the outcome was 'a purely proletarian education, free from all the influences of the bourgeoisie' (p. 527) with Shelley, Byron and Bentham amongst its favourite authors.

This grass-root auto-didacticism, which was manifested in Leicester by Thomas Cooper's Shakespearean Chartist Association (Crump, 1986), was countered by Brougham's and Birkbeck's provision of Mechanics' Institutes of which 'by 1841 there were over 300' (Kelly, 1962, p. 125) and the Working Men's Colleges initiated in 1854 by F. D. Maurice (Harrison, 1954, pp. 10–11). Samuel Smiles, author of the hugely successful *Self-help* (1859), expounded the – free trade – principles of the Manchester School in his gospel of self-reliance in which Shakespeare was held up, alongside Richard Arkwright and James Brindley, as an example of those who overcame humble origins to achieve success (1905, pp. 8–9).

Engels' theme of 'two radically dissimilar nations' was explored in three novels based on Manchester: Disraeli's *Sybil: or The Two Nations* (1845), Dickens's *Hard Times* (1854, as Coketown) and Mrs Gaskell's *North and South* (1855). Whereas in Germany the establishment's response might well have been to build a theatre, in England it was to create an Anglican diocese. The first Bishop of Manchester, James Prince Lee, appointed in 1847, was a rather remote figure, but in 1870 he was succeeded by the outgoing, Broad Church, James Fraser, popularly known as 'Tom Brown in lawn sleeves' (Diggle, 1889, p. 9; Tom Hughes, 1887, was also his biographer). Fraser, whose translation to Manchester coincided with Forster's Education Act, had been a member of two Commissions on Education (Newcastle in 1859 and Taunton in 1865) and strongly promoted the church's educational role in the diocese. In 1877 Fraser took the unusual step of preaching sermons in two of Manchester's theatres. He made complimentary allusions to Macready, Mrs Theodore Martin (Helen Faucit) and the Keans, all of whom he had encountered personally, and recalled that he had attended a London theatre no more than 'half a dozen times in my life . . . the last time I was in one was about thirty-five years ago, when Mr. Macready and Miss Helen Faucit were performing in "Othello"' (Diggle, 1889, p. 81). In this admission the bishop was acknowledging that, in his own words, 'legitimate places of amusement' could 'stand like breakwaters amongst the surging waters of vice' (p. 82). Shakespeare was the foundation of these defences:

And I think no one will say who has seen any well-graced actor playing a part – a leading part – in any of Shakespeare's great tragedies, 'Lear,' or 'Hamlet,' or 'Othello' (though, no doubt, the incidents in the drama here and there verge on difficult and delicate points and the language of the age was somewhat coarse and gross), yet I think no one ever left a theatre where he has seen 'Hamlet' or 'Othello' well performed without in some sense or other feeling his whole nature elevated and strengthened, and, even if not spiritualized, at any rate the waters had been wholesome to him that he had drunk at. (pp. 79–80)

Clearly for the bishop imbibing Shakespeare was preferable to imbibing the intoxicating liquor to which Engels found the labouring classes of Manchester were so partial, but, in contrast to London, where after 1843 a large number of central and suburban theatres could offer fare appropriate to a particular (local or social) clientele, in the larger provincial cities the scope for such discrete provision was much more limited.

Opened under the management of the elder Macready on 29 June 1807, Manchester's Theatre Royal was described by Mrs G. Linnaeus Banks in her novel *The Manchester Man* (1876) as 'a building so capacious – so solidly built – it might not fear comparison with Drury Lane' (1932, p. 188). It met the fate of many a nineteenth-century theatre when it was destroyed by fire in 1844. John Knowles (Knowlson, nd), who, though only in his mid-thirties, was renowned beyond Manchester as the Theatre Royal's colourful manager, commissioned the architects Irwin and Chester to build a handsome replacement in Peter Street at a cost of £23,000 (Shaw, 1894, vol. 3, p. 54). This was of course a purely private, commercial venture, but by the 1850s a sense of civic pride was permeating the city (as it had become in 1853), with its public parks, Free Library, Owen's College, the Free Trade Hall, the Town Hall designed by Alfred Waterhouse, and the City Art Gallery. Most large cities could boast of comparable refinements, but Manchester's higher ambition to what Gary Messinger has termed 'metropolitan status' was evident in 'Two developments, the city's growing patronage of visual art and a similar support of fine music' (1986, p. 121).

The idea for the Art Treasures of the United Kingdom Exhibition originated in Germany with Dr Gustav Waagen, the Director of the Royal Gallery in Berlin, drawing attention to the richness of private and public collections in England. In the decade of exhibitions the idea was taken up in Manchester and received the support of Prince Albert. Over one hundred subscribers ensured that the necessary funds were available and a large specially designed, but temporary, building was erected at Old Trafford, two miles out of the city centre. The Prince Consort visited what *The Times* described as 'an event almost unique in the history of art in England, or perhaps in the world. An Exhibition of Art Treasures, never before equalled for extent [27 acres] and importance' (6 May 1857) and was followed a month later by the queen. With such endorsements and attendances from far and near (special transport was provided for the city's working classes) totalling 1,336,715 by 17 October 1857, when it closed, the Art Treasures of the United Kingdom Exhibition had handsomely realised its organisers' aspirations and raised Manchester's cultural status nationally and internationally. Free trade could no longer be crudely equated with philistinism. Amongst the diversions were concerts by Charles Hallé, born in Westphalia, who consolidated on his success by inaugurating regular weekly programmes at the Free Trade Hall from January 1858. Hallé and (the numerous) other Germans living in Manchester must have reflected on the contrast between that city and their homeland. From the 1860s onwards *Manchestertum* was widely used in Germany (not least by Bismarck), to mean both economic threat and a social/political system in which (by German standards) the state's power was not fully realised. For its progress from ghetto to cultural oasis Manchester had not relied on the state.

CHARLES CALVERT

The spirit of self-reliance was strongly upheld at the Theatre Royal, where Knowles's well-known catchphrase was 'It mun be done' (Belton, 1880, p. 137; Coleman, 1904, vol. 1, p. 432 and Sillard, 1901, p. 163), meaning that whatever was being suggested was out of the question on the grounds of cost. In 1859 Knowles had a new stage manager who, far from being deterred by Knowles's cheese-paring, was determined to triumph over it. This was Charles Calvert (Foulkes, 1992a), who over the next twenty years was to make Manchester a force to be reckoned with in the theatrical world.

When in the autumn of 1859 Calvert set about staging *Hamlet* he was obliged to answer Knowles's parsimony with his own ingenuity. The wardrobe was ransacked, but only for serges, cloths and clinging silks which could be fashioned into Scandinavian-style costumes. The Theatre's scenic designer entered into the spirit of the enterprise by over-painting some Norman interiors with appropriate designs and creating an enclosed rising mound 'down which the funeral procession [of Ophelia] wound slowly in the light of the setting sun' (Mrs Charles Calvert, 1911, p. 59). Music was a feature throughout a widely acclaimed production:

A triumphant success was achieved at this house on Saturday night, by the representation of Shakespeare's tragedy of *Hamlet*, with new scenery, dresses and stage effects. We understand it has been 'got up' by Mr. Charles Calvert, the stage manager, who has evidently bestowed a great amount of care on the production. The dresses are entirely different to those used in any previous representation here, and the scenery is graphic in its slightest details. (*Era*, 20 November 1859)

Coming two years before Fechter's performance in London, Calvert's production (Hamlet in a blonde wig) was a harbinger of the new style. Other Shakespearian successes followed. In June 1860 Calvert and his wife Adelaide, who had recently appeared as Emilia to Ira Aldridge's Othello in Brighton, played the leads in *Romeo and Juliet*, extended to six acts to accommodate 'a spectacular representation of the funeral of Juliet, in which the "celebrated dirge" was sung' (*Era*, 17 June 1860). The same play was the choice for the Shakespeare tercentenary in April 1864, but with Wybert Rousby as Romeo to Adelaide's Juliet, Calvert himself as Friar Laurence and a certain Henry Irving as Mercutio. Irving took a central place in a more distinctive tercentenary event, a series of tableaux, which Calvert devised in aid of the Royal Dramatic College. These included a realisation by Henry Irving of Sir Thomas Lawrence's portrait of J. P. Kemble as Hamlet and the 'performance closed with an allegorical tableau of the statue of Shakespeare crowned by Fame and supported by the Muses of Tragedy, Comedy, Poetry and Painting' (*Manchester Guardian*, 25 April 1864). So successful were the tableaux that they were repeated through May and then in June Irving progressed from posing as another actor as Hamlet to playing the Prince of Denmark himself. With the prospect of his benefit in sight the twenty-six year old Irving wanted at least to clear the expenses, which would be due to 'an inexorable management' (Irving, 1951, p. 116) and add to his own reputation. Laurence Irving tells how his grandfather travelled to Birmingham to consult the veteran actor W. H. Chippendale, who had played Polonius to Edmund Kean's Hamlet, and only then decided upon *Hamlet* for his benefit on 20 June. Irving's first Hamlet was a patchwork affair, with touches of Charles Dillon, Edwin Booth and – courtesy of Chippendale – Kean, but some intimations of what lay ahead at the Lyceum Theatre in October 1874 can be discerned: the vocal limitations, scarcely scaling the poetic heights and rather too offhand in colloquial passages; the tendency to lapse into the physical gait and mien of comedy; but above all the force of a personality, which compelled the attention of the audience. Irving played Hamlet twice more on 25 June and 9 July, but by then the Calverts (Charles had played the Ghost, Adelaide Ophelia) had left the Theatre

Royal for the Prince's Theatre, which was to open with Charles Calvert as manager later that year, on 15 October.

Prior to settling in Manchester, Calvert had been at the – transpontine – Surrey Theatre under the joint management of Richard Shepherd and William Creswick which, in Creswick's words, took 'as an example Mr Phelps's conduct of Sadler's Wells Theatre, and endeavoured to do at the Surrey side what he effected at the north end of the metropolis, by creating a taste for a better kind of amusement than that to which the people had been accustomed' (Creswick, 1889, p. 64). With two managers taking precedence over him Calvert's Shakespearian roles were generally in the supporting ranks, but he added to his experience in stage management and gauging audience taste. Greatly though it had expanded, Manchester could not sustain a theatre, such as the Surrey or Sadler's Wells, catering principally for a popular audience for the classics. The question was whether the Prince's, raised at a cost of £18,000, was a theatre which would welcome them and at which they would feel at home.

In *The Art of the Victorian Stage* (1907) Alfred Darbyshire, the architect and authority on heraldry, described the opening of the Prince's Theatre as 'of vital importance in the history, not only of the local, but of the national stage' (p. 33) and attributed its success to a fruitful 'combination of brains and capital' (p. 34). In fact, as Adelaide Calvert's autobiography reveals (1911) her husband's undeniably impressive achievements at the Prince's over the next decade took place despite fluctuating finances (Foulkes, 1992a, pp. 44–55) and at the cost of his deteriorating health. The Manchester Public Entertainment Company Ltd, described by Adelaide Calvert as 'the small body of speculators' (1911, p. 68) and by Darbyshire as a 'number of cultured gentlemen and capitalists' (1907, p. 33), was a limited liability company. In 'a blue funk' (Calvert, 1911, p. 66) over rising costs the directors scaled down the building, which they saw as a venue for light comedies and burlesques, and were only persuaded to open with Shakespeare because Calvert assured them that *The Tempest* required no costly armour and only five or six rich costumes for the nobles. Another inducement was the inclusion of Arthur Sullivan's settings, which he had begun as his graduation exercise at the Leipzig Conservatory and recently expanded to acclaim at the Crystal Palace (Jacobs, 1986, pp. 27–8). This and the rest of the programme of music were prominent in the playbill, no doubt reflecting Calvert's judgement of his potential audience in a city which enthusiastically supported Charles Hallé.

The opening-night audience, who paid from 6*d* in the gallery to 4*s* in the stalls, found themselves in a charmingly decorated and comfortable theatre with effective heating, lighting and ventilation and an ambiance which was likened to that of a lady's boudoir. With Julia St George giving a tour de force as Ariel, a role she had played for Phelps at Sadler's Wells, *The Tempest* ran successfully until the end of November when it had to make way for the pantomime. The pattern of a major Shakespearian revival each autumn, succeeded by a pantomime, which usually ran until Easter, became established during Calvert's years at the Prince's. In his (no doubt unavoidable) adherence to the continuous run, Calvert was following Charles Kean, as he undoubtedly did in his general approach to staging Shakespeare in which, in Tom Taylor's words, 'all the Muses-of poesy, painting, music, history, oratory, the poetry of motion – are engaged as assistant masters' (*Era*, 10 January 1875). Calvert's greatest debt to Kean was his employment of several scenic-artists (Telbin, the Grieves) from the Princess's, but of the attendant muses this one especially did not come cheap and had implications not just for the number of performances, but also for the composition of the audience. Calvert admired Phelps, who appeared in the Prince's revivals of *Twelfth Night* (1873) and *Henry IV Part 2* (1874), and emulated, in principle at least, his ideals of textual restoration and ensemble acting.

All of the plays given full-scale revivals by Calvert had been staged by Phelps; nine (*) of them by Charles Kean: *The Tempest* (15 October 1864), *Much Ado About Nothing* (13 February 1865), *A Midsummer Night's Dream* (2 September 1865), *Antony and Cleopatra* (10 September 1866), *The Winter's Tale* (8 September 1869), *Richard III* (31 August 1870), *Timon of Athens* (6 March 1871), *The Merchant of Venice* (18 August 1871), *Henry V* (19 September 1872), *Twelfth Night* (8 September 1873), *Henry IV Part 2* (28 September 1874) and at the Theatre Royal *Henry VIII* (29 August 1877). The influence of Phelps is most evident in the choice of *Antony and Cleopatra* of which his production at Sadler's Wells (22 October 1849) was the only recent revival and *Timon of Athens* (15 September 1851), though just about the only attraction of the latter was the opportunity for Calvert to re-use scenery and costumes from *The Winter's Tale*.

Stylistically Calvert's Shakespearian revivals were indebted to both Kean and Phelps, but did his audience correspond most closely to the former's educated classes or the latter's rude bosoms, or did he succeed – in Manchester of all places – in attracting a 'one nation' clientele? The press was generally keener to trumpet the Prince's reputation further afield than to remark upon its local patrons. Beddoes Peacock, who was closely associated with Calvert for much of his management recalled:

My early days of dramatic experience are associated with the beggarly rows of empty stalls at our Theatre Royal. At that time the prejudice existing amongst a large class of people of the highest social grades against theatrical entertainments rendered it an apparently insuperable barrier to a competent manager doing as much as he might have desired to uphold or elevate the character of the stage. Mr. Calvert, in my opinion, solved the problem. From the opening night of the Prince's Theatre, from the first play of Shakspere's works (to be ever fresh in the memory of those present from the charming impersonation of Miss Julia St. George as Ariel) the receipts of the stalls and circle were always a most important factor in the dividend accounts. To my personal knowledge gentlemen of the highest social position in Manchester and neighbourhood were induced for the nonce to cast aside those antipathies which until middle life had prevented them from having ever previously entered a theatre.[1]

Clearly such an approach was consistent with Calvert's intent, evident in his determination to inaugurate his management with Shakespeare, to elevate the status of his theatre and his awareness that the directors expected a financial return. It is apparent from Mrs Calvert's memoirs that her husband liked to mix with the elite of Manchester (Hallé, Mr and Mrs Alexander Ireland, A. W. Ward of Owen's College and so on) whom he no doubt wished to patronise his theatre. However Mrs Calvert also relates that during the opening season at the Prince's Calvert introduced 'Early Doors' to enable galleryites to enter in the afternoon rather than have to queue outside, an action which reflects the appeal of the Prince's gallery and Calvert's concern for those who occupied it. Calvert personally reaped the reward of £400 his share (a fourth) of the first season's profits.

Calvert's choice of *Antony and Cleopatra* for his fourth revival, following his lacklustre, under-financed *A Midsummer Night's Dream*, was courageous and he marshalled all the 'attendant Muses' on a scale hitherto unprecedented in Manchester. The *Manchester Guardian*, sensing that the city was being put to the test, concluded its review: 'These are reasons [the play's remote setting, classical allusions etc.] which influence against the frequent production of "Antony and Cleopatra", and it will be to the taste of our Manchester public, as it will undoubtedly be to their intense gratification, if they crowd the Prince's Theatre to witness a dramatic event at once the boldest and most beautiful in the country' (12 September 1866). The idea that at a theatre in their city they could see a production, unrivalled elsewhere in the kingdom, spurred Mancunians into filling the Prince's for six weeks.

Theatrical fortunes are notoriously fleeting and by the next summer Calvert had left the Prince's, with such untoward results for the company that it went into liquidation; in April 1868 the Prince's Theatre Company Ltd, whose directors included printer and bookseller John Heywood and hotelier George Harrie 'Boston' Brown, acquired the premises; Calvert returned and a major renovation was undertaken. According to Alfred Darbyshire 'the policy pursued by Calvert' had become 'so popular, that the little Prince's Theatre was found inadequate to accommodate the increasing audiences' (1907, p. 40). The original architect, Edward Salomons, whose buildings included the Free Trade Hall and the Prince of Wales Theatre in Liverpool (Glasstone, 1975, pp. 42–3), having declined the commission it passed to Alfred Darbyshire, who 'was called in to devise a scheme by which the house should be stretched to its utmost capacity . . . The alterations were very extensive, and somewhat difficult to attain . . . I was instructed to provide an additional circle without raising the roof, and to construct a new proscenium' (1907, p. 40). The *Builder* cast its approving eye over the result. Essentially what Darbyshire had done was to extend the existing upper circle, which had only two rows of seats, back into the gallery and by raising the ceiling (but not the roof) eight feet a new gallery had been constructed over the upper circle: 'By this means three hundred additional seats are gained' (14 August 1869). To invest capital in providing (a lot) more cheap seats, the company must have felt confident that there was demand for them and that the influx of less well-to-do theatre-goers would not deter or discomfort the occupants of the stalls, whose prejudices against the theatre Calvert had succeeded in overcoming and whose patronage could not be jeopardised.

The decorative changes were as significant as the structural changes. Darbyshire was 'allowed *carte-blanche* in the decoration; but the scheme was to be in accordance with the Shakespearean idea of the management' (1907, pp. 40–1). The front of the dress circle was decorated with 'a series of panels illustrative of Shakespeare's principal plays, consisting of a head of the principal character within a circle in the centre of the panel, the rest of the space being filled up on one side by a scene from the play, painted on a small scale, and on the other side by the name in a label surrounded with scroll-work in keeping with the assumed date of the play' (*Builder*, 14 August 1869). At the top of each column was a medallion containing the initials 'WS'. This work was undertaken by William Philips, but Darbyshire commissioned H. Stacy Marks R. A. 'to paint a proscenium frieze, the subject being Shakespeare enthroned between Tragedy and Comedy, and attended on either side by representative figures from the principal plays' (1907, p. 41). The artist, who had recently executed a similar commission at the Gaiety Theatre in London, observed wryly that: 'The upper part of a proscenium is an absurd place for a decoration: no body can see it properly but the "gods", and they don't care to look at it' (Marks, 1894, p. 207). Whether they chose to do so or not, the 'gods' were undoubtedly best placed to admire Marks's frieze, but there was no denying the congruity of the two main features of Darbyshire's renovation: more cheap seats and a Shakespearian ambiance.

No doubt the prospect of seeing the refurbished theatre added to the appeal of *The Winter's Tale*, which opened in September. Amongst the visitors were 'some of our greatest living celebrities', Helen Faucit, Theodore Martin and Madame Titiens (*Manchester Guardian*, 30 October 1869) and happily when Benjamin Webster, the veteran lessee of the Adelphi Theatre in London, attended a local reporter observed the house as a whole:

As became a 'Shakspere night,' it was a first-class house in numbers, and in better than numbers. Pit, stalls, circles – all were quite full. If we might judge from occasional remonstrances in the higher though not always serener regions, the galleries appeared to be crowded to the exclusion of good manners – provided, indeed, it be necessarily a breach of the code to be not quite content to let everybody else see 'A Winter's Tale' better than oneself. (*Examiner and Times*, 29 September 1869)

This evidence of an enthusiastic and acceptably unruly 'gods' audience at the Prince's indicates that, though he recognised that the stalls and circle patrons were essential, Calvert could also fill the expanded gallery. He had succeeded in attracting Manchester's 'two nations' to Shakespeare. Calvert took his benefit on the penultimate night of the eight-week run of *The Winter's Tale*. Every seat in the house was taken and at the end the manager addressed his audience. He pointed out that had the revival not succeeded 'the loss would indeed have been very heavy, and to me, I confess, the disappointment would have been painfully dispiriting', but, to his 'intense gratification', 'upwards of 80,000 visitors have already witnessed this production', with attendance in the last week 'the greatest of all', and 'no single play ever drew so largely in the same time in the provinces since the English nation possessed a drama. What a fallacy, then, to say that the taste for Shakspere is declining' (*Manchester Guardian*, 30 October 1869). In extending his own achievements in Manchester to the blanket rejection of the 'fallacy . . . that the taste for Shakespeare is declining', Calvert was disregarding the generally depleted and lacklustre

5. *The Winter's Tale* at the Prince's Theatre, Manchester.

state of Shakespearian production (especially in the capital) to which the Prince's was such an outstanding exception. Calvert attributed his success to public approval of his production methods and concluded:

Ladies and gentlemen, Manchester has already inaugurated more than one great reform, and it will add to her laurels as the city of progress, if this splendid event (for such it really is) should prove the harbinger of better days for our national drama.

Calvert's formula of scenery to match Kean's at the Princess's and acting depth equal to Phelps's at Sadler's Wells was fully realised in *The Winter's Tale* with scenic artists Thomas Grieve, George Gordon and others delighting the eye with such visions as 'Theatre at Syracuse. Etna in the Distance. – The Queen's Trial'[2] and a company headed by himself as Leontes, Adelaide Calvert as Hermione, Julia Seaman as Paulina and Frank Archer as Polixines.

Reviewing *Richard III* the next year the *Manchester Guardian* (2 September 1870) harked back to the triumph of *The Winter's Tale* and reflected that in Charles Hallé and Charles Calvert Manchester possessed 'two individuals, eminent in their respective vocations' who had 'educated the public' who now attended the former's concerts and the latter's Shakespeare revivals in a way that would have been unthinkable twenty years earlier. The use of 'educated' was significant, since there was no significant pandering to the lower reaches of public taste. In *Richard III* Calvert discarded Cibber and if 'the Eminent Danseuse, Rita Sangalli, And a Full Corps de Ballet' did seem to figure large in *Timon of Athens*, the play's lack of intrinsic appeal was sufficient mitigation.

In *Henry V*, his most successful revival (critically and financially), Calvert drew a fine line between meeting the popular audience's expectations and developing his own original interpretation. A man of strong religious conviction, Calvert was deeply affected by the Franco-Prussian war and, as Darbyshire, who was a Quaker, recalled, 'conceived the idea of a series of Stage Tableaux or living pictures, which should illustrate the horrors of war and the blessings of peace' (1907, p. 50). The tableaux were staged at the Prince's Theatre in February 1871 and raised over £300 for the War Victims' Fund; similar tableaux were staged at the Theatre Royal, Dublin later that month (Meisel, 1983, p. 48).

When Calvert staged *Henry V* in September 1872 he eschewed the blatant militarism, which traditionally dominated (Foulkes, 1989). There was even a touch of pity for the traitors and concern for the fate of the citizens of Harfleur if they did not surrender. On the eve of Agincourt

'Mr Calvert portrayed the pensive king to perfection' (*Salford Weekly News*, 28 September 1872) and the battle itself was presented as 'an elaborate tableau', 'a picture in still life' rather than a 'swaggering attempt to represent the dealing of actual blows' (*Examiner and Times*, 18 September 1872). The 'Historical Episode of Harry's return to London', though derived from Kean, was invested with the direct quality, which Phelps achieved at Sadler's Wells. There was a sensitive blend of rejoicing and sorrow with 'the introduction of groups of anxious women' (*Salford Weekly News*, 21 September 1872) anxiously scanning the faces of the returning soldiers for sight of 'a husband, son or brother'. The French were not guyed, though the Dauphin was seen revelling on the eve of Agincourt, but without the excesses which in John Coleman's revival four years later 'provoked a storm of disapproval' (Knight, 1893, p. 147). J. D. Stoyle, 'a capital Fluellen', and Wyke Moore 'an excellent Pistol', did full justice to the leek-eating scene (*Salford Chronicle*, 21 September 1872) and such female interest as the play possesses was well served by two French actresses as Princess Catherine and her attendant, with Henry's wooing transposed to the last act and the production concluding with their wedding in Troyes Cathedral, magnificently realised by Grieves. Mrs Calvert, in the footsteps of Mrs Kean, appeared as Chorus. Calvert succeeded in carrying his audience on his own terms: 'The house was crowded in every part, and the applause was continuous and enthusiastic throughout the evening' (*Evening News*, 17 September 1872). One critic (*Salford Weekly News*, 21 September 1872) speculated what Shakespeare might think of this style of staging his plays and defended it as a means of popularising 'the great poet' and 'bringing him down to the masses'. The 'down' was unnecessary; Calvert and his company were ably 'discharging that duty which the iron age owes to the golden, talent to genius, matter to mind'.

Calvert's plan to stage *Coriolanus* as the annual revival for 1873 had to be abandoned because of his own poor health and *Twelfth Night* (with Phelps as Malvolio) was substituted. Calvert's condition probably accounted for the impression that at its first night *Twelfth Night* was not quite up to the usual Prince's standard. For one thing it was inordinately long, a common problem in scenic Shakespeare from Charles Kean to Beerbohm Tree, but in Calvert's case it evidently presented serious transport problems for his clientele from the satellite towns around Manchester. *Era* hailed Calvert's 'gorgeous illustrations of the Shakespearian drama' as 'an oasis' in 'the midst of the intellectual desert of burlesque and opera-bouffe that encompasses the theatricals of the present day'. The 'multitudes of visitors who flock to these representations' came 'from all parts of the

great district of which Manchester is the centre' in such numbers that
for this Shakespearian revival the run had been extended – for a total of
twelve weeks – until Christmas 'a period sufficiently long for a constant
succession of well-filled houses to reimburse the treasury for a very large
outlay' (14 September 1873). When *Era* returned the following week it
found that the 'noble production' had begun 'to take a more homoge-
neous form' and 'was over an hour earlier than before' (21 September
1873).

By then Calvert had a substantial financial stake in the Prince's and
in 'Boston' Brown he had a partner 'whose means, liberality and good
taste beautified the house' (Warde, 1920, p. 64). The inference from this
observation (by actor Frederick Warde who was a member of Calvert's
company), that Brown did not apply a strictly commercial approach to
improvements to the building, is borne out by 'the great alterations in
the interior of the house' (*Critic*, 11 April 1874) undertaken in 1874 with
Darbyshire again in charge. This time the flat ceiling over the auditorium was replaced by a beautifully decorated dome which incorporated
a sun-light burner. Features of the 1869 renovation were extended (the
supporting columns in the circle were continued up into the gallery)
and restored (the layers of dust and dirt were removed from Marks's
Shakespearian frieze). The whole of 'the upholstery of the theatre' was
renewed, but most significantly the pit was enlarged backwards with
the side walls (panels, mirrors and lights) and ceiling handsomely fin-
ished: 'The pit is a great institution in a theatre, and we congratulate the
management on the consideration thus shown to its frequenters.' As in
1869, when the upper circle and gallery were extended, the Prince's had
increased capacity for the less well off.

The 1874 revival of *Henry IV Part 2*, with Phelps doubling Henry IV
and Justice Shallow and the young Johnston Forbes-Robertson as 'a
rather lackadaisical Prince' (*Era*, 30 September 1874), was a somewhat
sombre affair. Calvert, who had not completely recovered his health,
was responsible for the production, though he did not appear in it, but
his mind was probably travelling further afield, with the prospect of
exporting his production of *Henry V* to America.

NEW YORK

Previously – in March 1871 – Calvert had sent the New York managers
Jarrett and Palmer a magnificent volume containing his printed acting
version of *Richard III* with sixty-five photographs of the Prince's cast

'as a token of my sincere esteem for you personally and my admiration of your intention to do justice to Shakespeare's Richard, by presenting it in a form, that will (I presume) be as new to *your* country, as it has proved to be to *our* public here'.[3] Jarrett and Palmer had bought the Prince's production of *Richard III* for either £1,000 (Belton, 1880) or £1,200 (Peacock); Beddoes Peacock placed this sum in the overall context of the production which cost £1,800 to mount, £2,000 in salaries and £640 in 'fixed expenses', but brought in £4,800 (at £600 a week for 8 weeks): a healthy profit of £1,560, sufficient to 'satisfy the most enthusiastic philo-Shaksperean with the most sanguine investor in theatrical property'.[4]

Unfortunately Jarrett and Palmer did not reap such rewards in New York. The sets, costume and armour, painstakingly researched by Alfred Thompson and Alfred Darbyshire, were installed on the stage of Niblo's Theatre by its resident stage staff, but the cast, headed by James Bennett, was not of course directed by Calvert himself. The opening night lasted from 8 pm to 1 am the next day. The *New York Times* observed resignedly: 'We shall be sorry if a long run of the piece does not reward good intentions and hard labours. We shall not, however be surprised if the recompense is rather inadequate to their merits' (13 April 1871). Not only did New Yorkers prefer Colley Cibber to Shakespeare, but so did the leading actor: 'It was evident that he had been accustomed to the Colley Cibber version, and therefore felt hampered by the text of the original' (*New York Daily Tribune*, 11 April 1871).

Happily Calvert was not deterred by this experience, nor were Jarrett and Palmer. The New York managers did, however, attach to their 'liberal offer . . . the proviso that my husband go over and produce it, which was acceded to' (Mrs Calvert, 1911, p. 146). Prior to his departure for New York Calvert was accorded (as became customary) a farewell banquet, presided over by Tom Taylor with about seventy gentlemen, most of them literary or theatrical, present. Taylor spoke of the recognition Calvert enjoyed beyond Manchester, his 'great educational services' to the city, which had been acknowledged by its 'wise and large-minded Bishop'. Observing that 'it was often said that small are the profits of management' he expressed his preference for saying 'that we have here to-night a very rare "prophet of management," "a prophet who has honour in his own country" – (Applause)'.[5] Calvert used the opportunity to summarise the principles through which he had secured Shakespeare's place in the 'English Household' at Manchester. He rejected the possibility that Shakespeare's plays were unattractive on the stage or that there were insufficient good actors – though he deprecated individual actors who sought disproportionate prominence, he placed his faith in the people ('the *vox populi* is rarely, if ever, wrong') and described his ambition to give:

A just interpretation of the play, – perfectly natural acting, – correctnesss to the minutest detail in those cognate arts that constitute the illusion of a theatre, – the period in which his play were cast by his own selection, reproduced as perfectly as art can do it, – be it old Rome, old Venice, or old England, with the manners, customs, ceremonies, music, habits, that belonged to the times . . . acting that imitates humanity – that shall never . . . overstep the modesty of nature; acting that shall be too conscientious to care for applause . . . acting without stilts – acting after the manner of man.

Calvert went on to make a striking comparison between 'old Venice' and Manchester:

It would seem that history is reproducing itself. That art and commerce (never antagonistic except to dull eyes), are to go hand in hand together – the one aiding and adorning the other – as they did in a past age, when art was most flourishing. The merchant princes of Manchester will take the lead in this respect and worthily rival the old magnificoes of Genoa and Venice.

The home of free trade had shown that it could produce art, music and theatre of world class and Calvert's achievements were poised to add to his, Manchester's and Shakespeare's 'honour among foreign nations'.

Adelaide Calvert accompanied her husband to America, where she was to repeat her role as Chorus for a salary of $100 a week. It was not her first Atlantic crossing; that had been in 1854 aboard the *Sumter*, a small barque of five hundred tons, and had taken six weeks. Adelaide's father James Biddles managed the minor theatre, the Bower Saloon, situated over the river near Westminster Bridge Road. Amongst the audience one night in June 1854 was Thomas Barry, the manager of the new Boston Theatre, who had been dispatched to Europe to engage actors and acquire 'a considerable assortment of theatrical equipment' (Hughes, 1951, p. 211). On 23 June 1854 Barry wrote home that as there was 'the prospect of securing the services of one of the three pretty girls on the London stage I may be induced to remain until the 8th or 15 [July]'.[6] Barry was successful and Biddles, his second wife and six daughters uprooted themselves for Boston, where Adelaide played Lady Anne to Edwin Forrest's Richard III and Lady Percy to James Bennett's Hotspur with James Hackett as Falstaff. Theatre in Boston (Clapp, 1853), which had had to surmount strong puritan hostility, was predominantly English in its origin and outlook, but the young Adelaide witnessed a scene which demonstrates the extent to which the stage was a cultural battlefield for European nations. At the end of her performance as Virginie, the fabled French actress Rachel chanted the *Marseillaise*, at first faintly, but rising to a crescendo she snatched a huge tricolor from the socket in which it had been placed on the stage and raised it proudly as she cried: 'Aux armes! Aux armes!' (Mrs Calvert, 1911, p. 37).

Adelaide Biddles returned to England to marry Charles Calvert; her younger sister Clara married Barry – forty years her senior – and remained in Boston. The sisters were reunited whilst Charles Calvert immersed himself in the intensive preparation for the first night of *Henry V* at Booth's Theatre. Booth's Theatre had been built by America's greatest Shakespearian actor to date, who during 1864–5 at the Winter Garden Theatre, New York achieved the rare distinction of one hundred (consecutive) performances as Hamlet, the role with which he is enduringly associated (Shattuck, 1969). The exterior of Booth's Theatre was an imposing combination of Italian and French styles, but the auditorium proclaimed its dedication to Shakespeare: 'At the front and center of the proscenium arch was the Shakespeare family coat of arms, above that a statue of Shakespeare in the act of composition, and at either side of him portrait busts of famous actors' (Shattuck, 1976, pp. 131–7). Estimates of the total cost were as high as $1,200,000. Inevitably Booth opened his theatre (3 January 1869) with Shakespeare, *Romeo and Juliet* with his second wife Mary McVicker as his Juliet, but, as usual on such occasions, the audience's attention was directed more at their surroundings than the play. On stage the sets stole the show, those for 'the early acts were the most marvellous specimens of stage production ever witnessed here', though even with innovative stage machinery the waits 'led the performance into the most advanced stillnesses of the night' (*New York Times*, 4 February 1869). Booth's Theatre was a business venture; 'Booth was a poor businessman' (Shattuck, 1976, p. 137), but by the time he was forced to surrender his theatre in 1872 Booth had mounted eight major Shakespeare productions, ending rather ignominiously with Cibber's version of *Richard III*.

Calvert threw himself into getting *Henry V* ready for the opening night with his customary zeal. In 'A talk with Mr Calvert, the Shakespearean Revivalist',[7] the English visitor was asked: 'How does the stage machinery compare?' At Booth's Theatre the 'method of scene-changing with the rise and sink method' was 'revolutionary in design and purpose' (Shattuck, 1971, p. 171), but Calvert was evidently most impressed by the 'superior intelligence [of] the skilled workmen' to whom he owed 'everything' and without whom 'it would have been impossible . . . to get this thing ready in time . . . I had only six days'. Calvert was fortunate. As actors toured with complete productions, rather than as Macready had done as a visiting star, their dependence on host stage staff increased commensurately with the complexity of the sets. As for the cast, apart from Adelaide Calvert as Chorus, there were 'very superb (physically superb) leading men from England, in the persons of Fred Warde [as Williams] and Rignold [Henry V]' (Odell, 1937, vol. ix, p. 529). Presumably not qualifying as 'physically superb', Frederick Thorne as Fluellen was a key member of the cast which 'embraced the best of Booth's Theatre company', plus the now customary French actress (Mdlle Berthe Giradin) as the princess. Odell's emphasis on the English actors' physique was particularly applicable to George Rignold (known as 'Handsome George'), whose only major Shakespearian credential at the age of thirty-seven was playing Romeo to the Juliet of Adelaide Neilson at the Queen's Theatre, Long Acre in September 1872, two months before the English actress made her American debut in the same role at Booth's Theatre, laying the foundation of her sensational success in America. Rignold became the heart-throb of every susceptible girl: 'There was a Rignold cult. He was pursued as if he had been Paderewski . . . He was called the handsomest actor. His portraits were everywhere' (*Cosmopolitan*, May 1899). The fashionable New York photographer Sarony produced photographs of Rignold in various poses to satisfy the huge demand.

RIGNOLD AS HENRY V

Rignold's Henry V was the antithesis of Calvert's. Where the reflective Calvert had excelled Rignold was found wanting: 'he failed . . . in the philosophical scenes, the finer parts of the play' (*New York Herald*, 9 February 1875), but his was a much more martial Henry. At what was the end (Shakespeare's 2.2) of the first act in Calvert's acting version Rignold's delivery of 'Now, lords, for France . . . ' elicited enthusiastic applause, though under Calvert's watchful eye Rignold did not yet introduce the encore, which featured in his later performances.[8] Rignold made 'a second hit' with 'Once more unto the breach, dear friends, once more'; though his voice was 'scarcely loud enough' he compensated for that 'by the spirit and energy with which he infused the address' (*Evening Post New York*, 9 February 1875) and at the concluding line of the speech ('Cry, "God for Harry, England, and Saint George!"')

the stage resounded in music, shouts, cannon and explosives. According to one reviewer of the New York first night, 'Once more unto the
breach . . . ' was 'repeated in the fourth scene [of Calvert's second act],
showing the siege of Harfleur and the surrender of the town' (*New York
Herald*, 9 February 1875).[9] Reviewers were unanimous in their praise of
the 'Historical Episode' of Henry's entry into London, highlighting 'the
bevy of dancing girls clothed in white' (*Daily Graphic New York*, 9 February
1875) and the resounding singing of an English anthem, but with no
mention of the groups of anxious women who had been such a feature
of the scene in Manchester. Not surprisingly handsome George was at
his best in the wooing of the princess and, as at Manchester, the wedding
in the cathedral of Troyes was a triumphant conclusion. Also as in Manchester, Fluellen was to the fore, with Frederick Thorne elevating him into 'what, next to Mr. Rignold, was the success of the evening – an artistic,
admirable performance, a revelation in its way, as showing the capacities
of the Welsh character for comedy' (*New York Herald*, 9 February 1875).

The question of why what the same reviewer called 'a thoroughly
English play, written for an English audience. Its subject . . . the exaltation
of the English name' should be so enthusiastically received in New York
(and elsewhere) inevitably arises. It had the appeal of the unfamiliar, never
having figured significantly in the American Shakespeare repertoire. The
sheer scale and details of the production exceeded American experience;
never before had the 'attendant Muses' been so sumptuously decked
forth. Compared with Manchester there had been a significant shift of
emphasis 'Messrs. Jarrett and Palmer have produced it with a view to the
spectacular and dramatic points than to the subtle philosophy of the text'
(*New York Herald*, 9 February 1875). Back in 1872 Calvert had given a play,
not greatly endowed with 'subtle philosophy', a reflective quality, but that
owed much to his own personality as Henry and the shared consciousness
of recent European conflict. Three years on in New York, the *zeitgeist* had
changed. Since Carlyle had advocated emigration, tens of thousands of
immigrants had settled in America. By 1875 there was a reverse traffic
of the wealthy visiting Europe, but though it was no doubt true, as the
Evening Post (9 February 1875) observed, that the throne in the middle
of 'The Throne Room in the Palace of Westminster' would be 'familiar
to all who have visited Westminster Abbey', such theatre-goers cannot
have been a high proportion of the total. One Anglophile formed 'a very
charming impression' of Rignold and approved the 'scenic splendours'
(Henry James in Wade ed. 1948, pp. 26–7). For others (originating from
Wales, Scotland and Ireland) the inclusion of their countrymen in the

play was probably an attraction. (In contrast the French, who – except for Katharine – were undercast, fared less well than in Manchester.) J. S. Bratton has observed: 'The "happy few" were deliberately given their due . . . and their importance as elements of the English race stressed' (1991, p. 14).

AUSTRALIA

Rignold was shrewd enough to capitalise on the success of *Henry V* and by the end of the decade the production originally conceived by Calvert in Manchester had toured the length and breadth of the United States (Cincinnati,[10] Salt Lake City, San Francisco) and Canada, then Australia and New Zealand. Rignold first appeared as Henry in the country in which he was to settle for the rest of his life at the Theatre Royal, Sydney on 28 August 1876 and was well-received personally for his performance ('possesses many physical advantages', *Sydney Morning Herald*, 30 August 1876), but he had been less successful as a director of 'the company of the theatre' who were 'not at home in a piece of this description'. By then Australian theatregoers in the major cities had had considerable experience of Shakespeare (Golder and Madelaine eds., 2001) by which to judge Rignold's efforts. Indeed for all the local factors from distance and climate to the effects of the gold rush, there was considerable convergence between Shakespeare's fortunes in Australia and England. From the mid-1850s a succession of English actors was drawn to Australia in pursuit of fame and fortune, amongst them G. V. Brooke, Charles Dillon, Barry Sullivan, James Anderson, Daniel Bandmann, William Hoskins, J. B. Howe and so on. Whatever their status at home, in Australia, with the benefit of impresario George Coppin's (Bagot, 1965) promotional skills, they were transformed into the stars which he considered to be essential for the success of Shakespeare down-under (Love ed., 1984, p. 64).

G. V. Brooke, accompanied by his wife, three other actors and two servants, arrived in Australia after a voyage of eighty-five days, prolonged by the repeated breaking of the connecting rods of the paddlewheels on the new steamship *Pacific*. Although English actors did not transport scenery to Australia, they brought with them the latest trends from London. Thus although the playbill of the Queen's Theatre, Melbourne announcing the first night on 26 February 1855 'of the Great Actor, Mr. G. V. Brooke', asserted that 'his extraordinary powers are universally acknowledged to have no compeer since the days of the elder Kean', the 'new and costly Wardrobe and Properties . . . with entirely new Scenery' was more indebted to the production values of Charles Kean (Lawrence, 1892, p. 158). This was most marked when Brooke appeared as Leontes at the Theatre Royal, Melbourne in a production of *The Winter's Tale* in which the 'Theatre at Syracuse' had been selected for 'the ceremony of the trial of Queen Hermione' and Bithinia was substituted for Bohemia (Love ed., 1984, p. 59).

When Coppin succeeded in securing the Keans themselves, their influence, if not always acknowledged, had preceded them. Arriving after an eighty-day voyage the Keans found themselves embroiled in rivalry with Barry Sullivan, who, having made his debut in the country – as Hamlet at the Theatre Royal, Melbourne – on 9 August 1862 and subsequently (7 March 1863) become its lessee, felt that his territory was being invaded (Sillard, 1901, vol. 2, chapters XIX and XX). The Shakespeare tercentenary found the Keans in Melbourne 'where we perform *four* different acts of his plays' (Mrs Kean in Hardwick, 1954, p. 162). The American actor Joseph Jefferson, who was also in Australia at the time (his countryman Edwin Booth had preceded him), reported that the Keans were 'welcomed with great warmth' by the 'old Londoners' who had seen them at the Princess's (Downer ed., 1964, p. 196), but the experience drained Charles Kean's strength, though he succeeded in his objective of returning home a wealthier man by £3,950 (Bagot, 1965, p. 267) despite the cost and duration of the journey.

Like the Keans, and most visiting actors to Australia, Rignold went on to New Zealand, arriving there 'with a grand flourish towards the end of 1878' bringing with him not only the now much-travelled *Henry V* scenery, but also 'a complete company' specially engaged 'from the Theatres Royal, Melbourne and the chief theatres in New Zealand' (Downes, 1975, p. 76). Over twenty years later in 1897 Rignold was back in New Zealand with his indefatigable *Henry V* (Thomson, 1993, p. 83). By then, like other products made in Manchester, *Henry V* had journeyed back from the circumference of the Empire to its hub, London.

Rignold opened at Drury Lane, which he had sub-leased from Augustus Harris, on 1 November 1879. During the preceding decade his unsuccessful attempts to stage Shakespeare at the former patent theatre had brought its manager, F. B. Chatterton, to the conclusion that 'Shakespeare spells ruin, and Byron bankruptcy' (Odell, 1966, vol. 2, p. 258). In June 1879 Charles Calvert had finally fallen victim to his failing health, the streets of Manchester were lined by 50,000 people for his funeral and in October his friends and associates staged the Calvert

Memorial Performance (*As You Like It*) to raise funds for his widow. One former protégé was otherwise engaged: Henry Irving at the Lyceum Theatre of which he had become manager in 1878 and where his revival of *The Merchant of Venice* opened on the same night as Rignold's *Henry V*. The two productions provided a 'striking contrast' (Knight, 1893, p. 306): the old style of Shakespeare in a debased form as against the new style at a still innovative stage. *The Times* (6 November 1879) characterised the difference:

Shakespeare at Drury Lane bears a very different aspect from Shakespeare at the Lyceum. At the latter house the furnishing and adornment of the stage – complete and handsome as it is – is but a complement of the poet's nobler art; at the former this mechanical part is all in all, and the poet itself is little more than a vehicle for the crafts of the scene painter, the carpenter, and the dressmaker.

Though perceived as opposites, Irving and Rignold were both indebted to Calvert, whose influence is evident – with different emphasis – in their careers as it is in those of Forbes-Robertson; Richard Mansfield, whose *Henry V* in New York (17 September 1900) was closely modelled on Calvert's (Winter, 1910, vol. 2, pp. 145–8 and Wilstach, 1908, pp. 348–59); Frederick Warde, whose revival of *Timon of Athens* 'following Mr Calvert's example' (Warde, 1920, pp. 299–302) was staged at the Fulton Opera House on 3 October 1910; and his five sons, of whom Louis made a distinguished contribution to the theatre on both sides of the Atlantic.

5

The fashionable tragedian: Henry Irving

INNOVATOR

On Monday 2 November 1874, *The Times* reported that: 'The great event that has been expected by the whole theatrical world for many months came off on Saturday evening.' Three years after his sensational success as Mathias in *The Bells*, Henry Irving had persuaded the Lyceum Theatre's manager, American H. L. Bateman, to let him essay the role by which theatrical reputations were most commonly judged: Hamlet. The *Era* (1 November 1874) painted a picture of this 'great and stirring enthusiasm' with attention to social detail worthy of a canvas by William Frith. The scene outside the Lyceum was more akin to *Derby Day* (1858), in which all levels of society are united in their common enjoyment of a great national event, than to the social exclusivity depicted in *The Private View* (1883). The entrances to the pit and gallery were thronged with people: 'They waited there patiently for hours, barristers and clerks, and the pick of every form of society, determined to show by their presence, how thoroughly they wished a hearty success to Mr Bateman's venture.' Once the audience was seated it was possible to see:

of what good stuff the house was composed. In stalls and boxes the flower of literary and artistic intelligence; in pit and gallery the good old backbone of intelligence, which, alas! has for some time not been constantly found at our Theatres.

Austin Brereton testified to the calibre and influence of the pit: 'In those days, the occupants of the pit, apart from the professional critics, were the real judges of dramatic art, and their verdict on a first night was a vital moment to the success of an actor or a play' (1908, vol. 1, p. 169). The occupants of the pit received Irving warmly on his first entrance, but they were 'inclined to be reserved in their judgment' and were taken aback by his unconventional appearance as Hamlet and his unorthodox playing of the role. The first two acts were received in silence, then in the 'nunnery scene' with Ophelia (Isabel Bateman), Irving sensed that the audience understood what he was doing and until the curtain finally fell at a quarter to one on Sunday morning he held them in his power. Irving's Hamlet was meditative (metaphysical even), intellectual, tender, fidgety and colloquial, but above all: 'We see Hamlet think. We do not merely hear him speak, we positively watch his mind. We feel and know the man overburdened with this crushing sorrow, with his mind unhinged' (*Era*, 1 November 1874). In an article ('An Actor's Notes on Shakespeare No. 2, Hamlet and Ophelia Act III Scene 1') published in the *Nineteenth Century* (May 1877) Irving analysed the scene in which he had won over his first-night audience: 'the excitability of his [Hamlet's] temperament', 'the high pressure of a forcible mind', 'wild exultation', his aim being to express: 'the motive and variety of passion which it is as necessary to unite in a credible and vivid personality as to bring out boldly and distinctly in separate relief'.

Irving did not approach Shakespeare as the exclusive domain of that rarefied breed the classical actor. He brought to Hamlet the same nervous and mental energy that he had to Mathias in *The Bells*. This was a challenge even for his devotees, but they, like the actor, persevered. Not everyone was persuaded. The loudest dissenting voices came from Scotland, where, playing in Edinburgh in 1877, Irving 'became embroiled in public controversy' (L. Irving, 1951, p. 290) arising from the publication of a slim (twenty-four pages) pamphlet *The Fashionable Tragedian* by three young Edinburgh men, Robert Lowe, George Halkett and William Archer. It scorned Irving (the 'indiscriminately belauded . . . interpreter of Shakespeare to the multitude' – Archer and Lowe, 1877, p. 3) for the qualities for which his admirers praised him: his intellectuality, his originality, his picturesqueness, his psychological subtlety, his attention to detail and his good taste. Despite the authors' intended irony their description of 'every elevation of the eyebrows, every protrusion of the lower jaw, being carefully studied and contributing towards a defined end' in fact encapsulated one of Irving's most effective qualities: his picturesque ability to project character through facial and bodily movements, which his detractors would say were often extraneous to the author's intention. The pamphlet also attacked Irving's generally awkward locomotion around the stage and his idiosyncratic speech, which transmuted 'blood' into 'ber-a-lud' (p. 8). Archer used the pamphlet to advocate a scheme to which he was to remain committed for the rest of his life: the founding of the National Theatre. The fact that this proposal was combined with an attack on Irving no doubt contributed to a wariness about such an institution not only on his part, but also amongst actor–managers generally. After his Hamlet debut, Irving certainly had no cause to feel threatened as the run continued for a total of 200 nights. He prevailed upon the widowed Mrs Bateman to let him play Macbeth and Othello, but in neither role did he enjoy comparable success and when he took over the management of the Lyceum Theatre he opened with *Hamlet* (30 December 1878) with Ellen Terry, his new leading lady, as Ophelia. Irving went on to mount revivals of eleven other Shakespeare plays (Hughes, 1981). As the dramatist Henry Arthur Jones observed, echoing Edmund's 'Brave word, "legitimate"', in 'the [Victorian] pantheon of the "legitimate" sat enthroned Shakespeare' (1931, p. 47), with a few other 'stragglers' and imitators, and for any actor who aspired to a place in the pantheon of his profession some engagement with Shakespeare's works was a virtual necessity. What was apparent to Irving, with his success soon became apparent to other London managers.

Irving was not only the cause of Shakespeare being staged at the Lyceum, but also at other theatres. Archer observed that 'almost simultaneously there arose a revived interest in Shakespeare, the New Shakespeare Society being one of its symptoms' (1883, p. 104). The formation in 1873 of the New Shakespeare Society by F. J. Furnivall (see Benzie, 1983) had preceded the Lyceum *Hamlet*, but Irving's success undoubtedly encouraged other managers. As Brereton pointed out, by the hundredth performance of Irving's *Hamlet* a change had taken place 'in the public taste, and, consequently, in the programmes of several theatres' (Brereton, 1908, vol. 1, pp. 174–5) where Shakespeare was staged in preference to the accustomed fare: *A Midsummer Night's Dream* with Phelps as Bottom at the Gaiety, *As You Like It* with Mr and Mrs Kendal at the Opera Comique, and *The Merchant of Venice* at both the – normally equestrian – Holborn Amphitheatre and the Prince of Wales's Theatre, 'the dainty home of Robertsonian comedy'.

Of these the most significant was *The Merchant of Venice* at the Prince of Wales's for which a visit to Venice had been an inspiration to the Bancrofts and their scene painter George Gordon as they aspired to 'soar to Shakespeare' with 'an elaborate as well as an artistic production of "The Merchant of Venice"' (Pemberton, 1902, p. 142). The detailed sets of Venice were the product not only of Gordon's location sketches and skill in the studio, but also of the architect E. W. Godwin who 'lent his valuable archaeological knowledge' (Mr and Mrs Bancroft, 1889,

p. 209). The impact of the scenery, which the *Era* considered 'beyond praise', was felt far beyond the disappointing run of thirty-six nights, not least on Godwin's then three-year-old son Edward Gordon Craig, whose mother Ellen Terry 'fairly charmed everybody' (18 April 1875) as Portia. The role had been offered to Madge Kendal, who declined it because her husband 'did not see his way to play Bassanio' (1933, p. 117). The Bancrofts' good fortune with their alternative Portia did not extend to the casting of Shylock: Charles Coghlan. Tom Taylor, who thought 'Portia perfect' and 'the mounting of the play . . . the best I ever saw', described Charles Coghlan's Shylock as 'the most hopeless thing I ever saw' to Frank Archer, formerly a long-serving member of Calvert's company, who was Antonio at the Prince of Wales's (F. Archer, 1912, p. 180).

MAGNIFICENT HOSPITALITY

Within a few months of Irving assuming the management of the Lyceum Theatre, which he proceeded to make a National Theatre in all but name, London theatre-goers had the opportunity of experiencing another model . . . the institutionalised theatre receiving financial support from the state. The visit of the Comédie-Française to London's Gaiety Theatre in the summer of 1879 was, as John Hollingshead the manager put it, on a 'purely commercial' basis (1898, p. 360). Henry James for one felt that the company had lost its 'sanctity . . . [and been] vulgarised, reduced to the level of ordinary commercial ventures, departing from its traditions and compromising with its ideal' (Wade ed., 1948, p. 127). The idols of the French and English theatre were represented at the inaugural ceremony: 'The curtain drew up on the assembled troupe. Near the busts of Shakespeare and Molière stood M. Got, who recited an address . . . having on his right and left Mdlle. Sarah Bernhardt and Mdlle. Croizette' (*Illustrated London News*, 7 June 1879). Although it was presumably intended to convey harmony between two rival traditions, the scene inevitably reopened the old debate. *Punch* (14 June 1879) by way of asserting Shakespeare's superiority compared his 'living men and women' with Molière's 'abstractions' and postulated:

An ideal 'House of Shakspeare' wherein those men and women should be embodied with an Art as consummate as that of the Actors of *La Comédie Française* would be as much grander a thing than any possible 'House of Molière' as Versailles is grander than Buckingham Palace.

If any members of the fashionable first night audience, which included Princess Mary, Duchess of Teck and the Duke and Duchess of Connaught, were interested in what would be involved in creating such an institution they could attend the talk on 'The Comédie Française' given by the critic, Francisque Sarcey, whom Hollingshead described as one of 'the hangers-on of the theatre' who 'seemed to be imbued with the Voltaireian idea that England was a half-civilized nation of Shakespearian barbarians' (1898, p. 363). Hollingshead's description of Sarcey as a 'hanger-on' was as significant as his allusion to Voltaire, reflecting as it did the English suspicion of institutionalised bureaucracy in state-funded theatres. Those who listened to or read (*Nineteenth Century*, July 1879) Sarcey's unstinting account of the history, organisation and fluctuating fortunes of the Comédie-Française may well have sympathised with Hollingshead. The next issue of the *Nineteenth Century* (August 1879) carried Matthew Arnold's celebrated essay 'The French Play in London' in which he claimed that 'the performances of the French company show us plainly . . . what is to be gained by organising the theatre'. Others were disinclined to adopt such a reverential approach, arguing that 'Free trade is good in the long run whatever people may say' and it was more appropriate to receive the visitors as 'our equals' than as 'our superiors' (*Era*, 8 June 1879).

Henry Irving, assuming the role of host, which he was to play with mounting assurance to a succession of foreign visitors over the next twenty-five years, sent a bouquet to greet Sarah Bernhardt at her London residence in Chester Square (Aston, 1989, p. 17). Whatever the long-term effects of the Comédie-Française's visit might be on the English theatre, it had an immediate effect on Sarah Bernhardt. The acclaim of the press, the patronage of the Prince and Princess of Wales, the admiration of Mr Gladstone, Frederick Leighton and many more luminaries of London life were all testimonials to Bernhardt's success, but more eloquent to Hollingshead, and ultimately to the actress, was the box office which showed that performances (eighteen) in which she appeared averaged £534, the others (twenty-five) £350. In the manager's words 'these facts and figures taught Madame Bernhardt her commercial value' (1898, p. 371); she resigned from the company (1984, pp. 321–2) and set out on her trajectory as an international star. Over the next three decades Bernhardt performed literally around the world (South America, Australia – Fraser, 1998) adding Hamlet (Taranow, 1996), Lady Macbeth and her own version of Cleopatra to her repertoire. Like Rachel before her she had outgrown the Comédie-Française to become the model for other divas of the lyric stage from Helena Modjeska to Henry James's Miriam Rooth in *The Tragic Muse*.

The Polish actress Helena Modjeska found a bouquet of white flowers from Henry Irving awaiting her at the Court Theatre, where she appeared in *Heartsease*, a version of *La Dame aux Camélias* on 1 May 1880. Of all the foreign actors who converged on London in the 1880s, none had surmounted more barriers than Modjeska. Born in Cracow in 1840, Modjeska's worship of Shakespeare began when she saw Fritz Devrient (nephew of Emil) perform Hamlet there. Her first husband (Gustav Modrzejewski) tracked down what few Polish translations of Shakespeare there were and organised her stage debut, but died the same year (1861). For the next fifteen years Modjeska pursued her career in the Polish theatre, though doing so was inseparable from the political struggle in which the Poles were attempting to wrest their own identity from the competing forces of Russian and German domination. By the time she and her second husband Count Bozenta, succumbing to political pressure, left Poland for California in 1877, Modjeska was a highly accomplished actress with Juliet, Ophelia and Desdemona amongst her successes, but in order to establish herself she had to learn English, as she had been encouraged to do by American actor Maurice Neville (born Grossman), who acted Shakespeare in Warsaw with a Polish supporting company. With the support of John McCullough and Henry Longfellow, Modjeska gained in confidence until she felt ready to take the latter's advice: 'Play in London and play Shakespeare!' (Modjeska, 1910, p. 381). Although eventually she was to include fourteen Shakespearian roles in her repertoire (of thirty-five; Coleman, 1969, p. 879), Modjeska was hesitant about making her English debut as Juliet.

This she did in the relative obscurity of the remote fishing village of Cadgewith in Cornwall, where she and Johnston Forbes-Robertson performed some scenes from *Romeo and Juliet* in aid of St Ruan's church: 'The lighting came from screened oil lamps and the lucky help of a full moon. No stage balcony scene was ever so beautiful. It was full of mystery and charm, and Modjeska seemed to be inspired by the beauty and novelty of the surroundings' (Forbes-Robertson, 1925, p. 99). Walter Sickert attended the performance, news of which reached Lady Archibald Campbell inspiring her own staging of *As You Like It* in the grounds of Coombe House. Her Cornish success brought Modjeska a letter of congratulation from Longfellow mentioning such fashionable contacts as Lord Houghton and Lord Rosebery, but though, like Bernhardt, after *Heartsease* the Polish actress was fêted by London society, including the Prince of Wales, she approached her London Shakespearian debut purposefully, albeit under the conflicting tutelage of John Ryder and Mrs Stirling.

Modjeska had been on the brink of agreeing to play Juliet to the Romeo of Frank Benson (1930, p. 147), who was only just down from the University of Oxford where his performance as Clytemnestra in Aeschylus's *Agamemnon* had impressed even Irving and Ellen Terry, when Wilson Barrett, her manager, decided to stage *Romeo and Juliet* at the Court Theatre with Forbes-Robertson as Romeo. Jan McDonald (1971) has charted Modjeska's progress as Juliet from scene to scene showing that she had her (somewhat contradictory) critics, but the *Era* (2 April 1881) concluded that, despite her age and acting in a foreign tongue:

The balance of the advantages, then, was on the side of the actress and they enabled her to achieve a triumph which cannot fail to add to her already great reputation, to add to the laurels she has won since she came amongst us, and to largely increase the ever-swelling list of the ardent admirers of her brilliant talents.

If, as one might suppose, Henry Irving was one such, the sentiment was not completely reciprocated. Of his Shylock Modjeska wrote: 'the extravagant way of accentuation, the artificial gestures and gait, his breathless voice, and altogether the lack of simplicity made me wonder why the English public admired this man', but, as the performance continued, she came under Irving's power: 'all those deficiencies disappeared and I saw only the Jew Shylock . . . Such is Irving' (1910, p. 405).

As John Stokes has observed, Modjeska's Polish origins added to her allure for the so-called 'Marlborough House Set',[1] but in that summer of 1881 London Society's theatregoing took on a truly international aspect with the capital's stages playing host to leading American actors Edwin Booth and John McCullough and the Duke of Saxe-Meiningen's Company, all of them in Shakespeare.

EDWIN BOOTH

Edwin Booth had made a successful tour of Britain in 1861–2. Laurence Irving describes the experience of performing with him in Manchester as inspirational for Henry Irving, who supported the American star as Laertes, Cassio and Malcolm. The young Irving was impressed by Booth's intellectual approach to characters, his avoidance of meretricious tricks, his graceful bearing and flexible voice (1951, p. 109). When he returned to London in 1880, the passing years had exacted a heavy toll: his brother John Wilkes Booth's assassination of President Lincoln; the unstable behaviour of his second wife, Mary McVicker and changes in theatrical fashion. Booth's engagement at the Princess's Theatre met with a disheartening response. His style was now regarded as dated and stagy and he personally as too mature for Hamlet. Whereas other foreign actors – Fechter and Booth himself two decades earlier – had challenged insular British tradition, now 'that reverence for tradition has affected injuriously Mr. Booth's Othello. For the stage Othello, even though he comes to us from the other side of the Atlantic, has not yet attained complete emancipation from the tradition, the points, it may even be said the tricks of Edmund Kean' (Dutton Cook, quoted in Mullin, 1985, p. 71). The American colony in London turned out in force and eventually the Prince of Wales attended a performance, principally it seemed to consult the American actor about 'Mrs Langtry's chances of success as an actress in America' (Ruggles, 1953, p. 219). Booth's complaints that the London audiences were cold and the critics were damning him with faint praise reached receptive ears at home and sections of the American press indicated that if, or rather when, Henry Irving came to America he could expect the same treatment. When the Princess's season closed after one hundred and nineteen nights on 26 March 1881, Booth's self-esteem and financial expectations were both greatly diminished, to the extent that he approached Irving about giving some matinée performances at the Lyceum. Irving agreed and then had a much better idea: he invited Booth to alternate Othello and Iago with him in a freshly mounted production of *Othello*. Booth, naturally, accepted.

Whether one sees this as an act of gratitude, diplomacy or self-interest on Irving's part, it was a brilliant theatrical coup. Bram Stoker denounced 'busybodies who tried always to make mischief between Americans and English', pointing to Irving's willingness to accommodate Booth's preferences and the American actor's rediscovered enthusiasm for rehearsals (1906, vol. 1, p. 89). Seat prices in the stalls and dress circle were 'altered' (Stoker's word) from 10*s* to 21*s* and 6*s* to 10*s* respectively, though Irving, prudently sensitive to 'the good old backbone of intelligence', kept the ordinary prices for the amphitheatre, pit, upper-circle and gallery. Joseph Hatton described the audience for the first night:

The gallery seemed crowded unto overflowing, the front being packed with human beings. In the upper circles, between the pit and the gallery, were many of the distinguished people you expect to find in the stalls; but the prices had been doubled, and they therefore occupied seats which it is not considered *infra dig* to occupy at the Italian opera. The stalls and boxes were full of well-known people, including all the leading critics, many of the usual habitués of the house, and some eminent citizens of the United States. (in Winter 1893, p. 112)

Irving had already played Othello at the Lyceum under Mrs Bateman's management (14 February 1876) and had not impressed even his ad-mirers, so he opted to open as Iago. *Era* reported that the crowded house cheered 'the entrance respectively of Mr Irving, Mr Booth, and Miss Terry, and at every possible opportunity, and with even the slightest of excuses, these cheers were repeated' (7 May 1881), but this show of even-handedness could not disguise the fact that:

Interest, we need hardly say, was directed to the Iago of Mr Henry Irving, for this was to be the novelty of the evening. Let it be said at once that the artist achieved a brilliant triumph, and that henceforth his Iago will be numbered amongst his most successful impersonations.

Although Booth's Othello 'in what is called the business of the part . . . at the Lyceum differs little from that presented at the Princess's; yet must it be pronounced more successful'. Thus added to the faint praise with which he was again damned was the condescending suggestion that the hapless Booth's slight improvement was because he had 'profited by the hints that had been offered him – your truly great actor is never above learning, and never thinks himself above criticism – or that he was moved to greater efforts by his associates and surroundings in this memorable event'. Even when roles were reversed Booth could fare no better. Irving's Othello was a lost cause, so critics concentrated on Booth's Iago, but though he was better received than as Othello he was still Irving's inferior in the role. Ellen Terry contrasted her two Othellos: with Booth she emerged without a trace of his make-up thanks to his skilful deployment of 'a corner' of his 'drapery' whereas with Irving 'I was nearly as black as he' (Craig and St John eds., 1933, p. 160). Ellen Terry, who saw her two leading men at closer quarters than did anyone else, observed: 'I cannot be sure that Booth's pride was not more hurt by this magnificent hospitality than it ever could have been by disaster. It is always more difficult to *receive* than to *give*' (p. 159). However it must be remembered that at the time Mary Booth's London doctors were in despair over her worsening condition (Ruggles, 1953, p. 222) and that Booth himself described his 'engagement with Irving' as 'one of the most agreeable' in his life and wrote 'I wish I could do as much for Henry Irving, in America, as he has done here for me' (Winter, 1893, pp. 115–16).

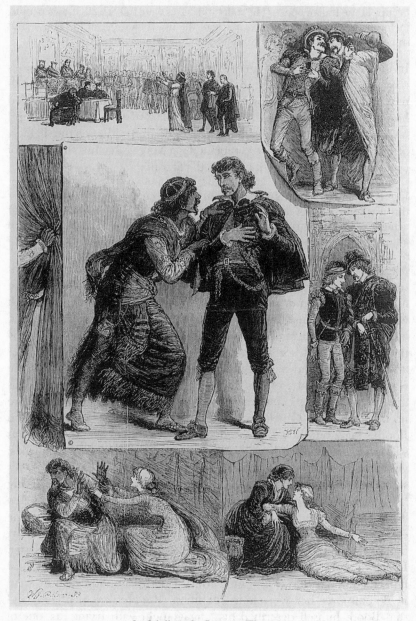

6. *Othello* at the Lyceum Theatre.

In autumn 1882, after his wife's death, Booth returned to tour the English provinces, then early the next year he took up a longstanding invitation to appear in Germany at the Residenz Theatre, Berlin. Booth performed in English with a German-speaking company, something of which he already had experience from playing opposite Fanny Janauschek in *Macbeth* at the Boston Theatre in 1868: 'It was the general opinion that Mr Booth never played Macbeth in so masterly a manner' and such was the force of Mme Janauschek's 'facial expression and . . . artistic gesticulation that the meaning of her utterances were almost as comprehensive as if given in English' (*Boston Post*, 4 November 1868). From Berlin Booth wrote to William Winter on 29 January 1883: 'tho' I have not acquired a word of the language I seem to think it and comprehend it while I am acting with Germans' (Watermeier ed., 1971, p. 230). Booth's technique was 'mentally to recite in English what the Germans are saying, in order to make the speeches fit' (Grossman, 1894, p. 242) and for *Hamlet* he also prepared a special promptbook in which 'Hamlet's speeches . . . are pasted on blank sheets opposite the German text' (Lockridge, 1932, p. 284).

Booth's entirely Shakespearian repertoire was warmly received (eighteen curtain calls as Lear) with the patronage of Crown Prince and Princess (Vicky) until the death of Prince Karl, the Kaiser's brother, when court mourning was enforced. Booth's daughter Edwina was no doubt echoing her father when she wrote to Winter: 'How different are they [Berlin audiences] from the English, who are so slow to accept any ideas save their own! The Germans appear to me, less narrow, and certainly more Shakespearian, and I am proud to have Papa win their approval so readily' (Watermeir ed., 1971, p. 232). Edwina Booth understandably relished the Berliners' admiration for her father, reports of which reached London: 'The papers are unanimous in placing Booth in front of Salvini and Rossi (both favoured in Berlin)' (*Era*, 27 January 1883). Three years later Booth appeared with one of his rivals when he played Iago to Salvini's Othello (in Italian), enabling New York audiences to experience 'the elegance, subtlety, and intellectual force of the English-speaking ancient' alongside 'the barbaric grandeur of the Italian Moor' (*New York Times*, 27 April 1886).

THE PRINCE OF WALES AS PATRON

The navigation lanes and railroads of the western world seemed to be devoted to transporting rival Othellos and Iagos from one theatre to another. Concurrently with Booth's appearance with Irving at the Lyceum his fellow American John McCullough was appearing at Drury Lane as Othello with – American-born – Herman Vezin as Iago. Although it judged McCullough's 'rendering of the character' as belonging 'to the old-fashioned order', being 'particularly distinguished by its power and declamatory force', the *Era* declared its preference for it over 'any that has recently been seen upon the London stage' (21 May 1881). As was expected of them, Americans in London rallied to McCullough as did society, led by the Duke of Manchester who arranged a grand reception attended by the Prince and Princess of Wales (Clark, 1914, p. 137). Whether the Prince seized the opportunity to enquire about Mrs Langtry's prospects on the American stage is not recorded. When Mrs Langtry appeared as Rosalind the following year in London and subsequently in New York, the attraction of seeing the future king's mistress in the revealing garb of Ganymede might be regarded as a form of royal theatrical patronage. Her American manager Henry Abbey was under no illusion: 'he saw that sex, sin and sensation were what playgoers really wanted, even if you had to cover it up behind Shakespeare and the classics' (Dudley, 1958, p. 77). In the view of some New Yorkers, as Ganymede Mrs Langtry was insufficiently clad, the actress having abandoned the traditional high boots and trunks for – more revealing – cross-gartered tights.

The Prince of Wales expressed his attitude towards theatre patronage to Helena Modjeska at a supper where she was 'seated next to the prince and had vis-à-vis the most beautiful Mrs Langtry', whose early interest in the theatre the Polish actress had fostered, as she was no doubt intended to do:

It was during that supper that the prince spoke to me about the drama. He said that dramatic art was not yet in its full development in England. I suggested the founding of an endowed national theatre, such as all other countries in Europe possess. His answer was discouraging: 'Do you think there is enough love for art in the Anglo-Saxon race to make the theatre a state affair?' There was no answer to that. I was nonplussed, and did not know what to say next. (Modjeska, 1910, pp. 424–5)

In his speech at the Shakespeare tercentenary Professor Leitner had outlined the common Anglo-Saxon origins of England and Germany and claimed Shakespeare as a heritage shared by the two countries. Germany, as the prince fully knew, had a long tradition of court theatres which his father had emulated at Windsor and which his sister (as Crown Princess)

7. Mrs Langtry as Rosalind.

patronised. It was England that was the exception. The Prince of Wales did not let his reservations about funding the theatre as 'a state affair' stand in his way when state-subsidised companies visited London. The prince and his wife were part of 'a very exceptional audience' at Drury Lane on 1 May 1881 'to give the first welcome to our visitors', the Duke of Saxe-Meiningen's Company in *Julius Caesar*. Also present were the King of Sweden and his suite, numerous German princes, 'a learned array of talent and first night notabilities' (*Stage*, 3 June 1881) and, whereas English residents in Germany could not be relied upon to turn out for English actors, their German counterparts in London were present in force, indeed 'the majority of the public present . . . consisted of elements of that nationality, who watched the performance with the deepest interest and occasionally broke out into loud and enthusiastic applause, in which, however, the English portion of the population heartily joined' (*Era*, 4 June 1881).

The Prince of Wales 'was helpful to his cousin, the Duke of Meiningen' in a number of ways especially by 'agreeing to be named as official sponsor to the tour' and 'using his influence with the press to secure publicity' (Osborne, 1988, p. 80) in the form of an article in *The Times* (27 May 1881) and the striking full-page picture of the Forum scene in the *Illustrated London News* (4 June 1881). The *Era* published a lengthy account of the origins of the company, Duke George's devotion to his court theatre since becoming Duke in 1866, the role of 'Herr Intendant' – currently Chronegk – and its emphasis on *ensemble* acting and 'cleverly conceived and artistically elaborated *mise en scène* . . . [of] strict . . . historical accuracy' combined to create 'dramatically animated pictures' (25 May 1881). An older theatregoer, Theodore Martin, could trace the 'excess of scenic illustration' (*Blackwood's Magazine*, August 1881) back to Macready and J. P. Kemble and the influence of Charles Kean (Byrne, 1964) has been noted as that of Phelps's visit to Berlin should be. Nevertheless the impact of the Saxe-Meiningen productions was immense, especially perhaps on younger actor–managers-to-be such as Frank Benson and Herbert Beerbohm Tree whose work bore the influence of the Saxe-Meiningen method for decades to come.

In 1881 the leader of the theatrical profession was indisputably Henry Irving and where the Prince of Wales led he would not be far behind. T. H. S. Escott in *Society in London by A Foreign Resident* described 'London society', with the Prince of Wales at its head setting the example, as 'in a sense, stage-struck' (1885, p. 296) and Irving as 'the most prodigal and magnificent of theatrical hosts' (p. 303). A particular target for Irving's hospitality was Ludwig Barnay who, though he played Mark

Antony, was not a permanent member of the company in London. Barnay and Chronegk were not only entertained in the Beefsteak Room at the Lyceum, but also together with Alma Tadema, American actor Lawrence Barrett and William Terriss, at a banquet which began on Sunday 17 July but 'did not break up till six o'clock A. M.' (Stoker, 1906, vol. 2, p. 153). At a supper given by J. L. Toole at the Adelphi Hotel on 1 July the discussion had turned to subsidy. Barnay, whose turn to speak came last, referred to subsidised theatre in France, Germany and Austria and went on to bring the proceedings to an electrifying conclusion:

'But' – and here his eyes flashed, his nostrils quivered, and his face was lit with enthusiasm – 'Your English freedom is worth them all!' Then, springing to his feet, he raised his glass and cried in a voice that rang a trumpet: 'Freiheit!' (p. 154)

Irving did not perform in Germany, but he made a visit in 1885 in preparation for his production of *Faust*, in which the Saxe-Meiningen influence was discernible, as it was in his much more scenically elaborate Shakespeare revivals from *Romeo and Juliet* (8 March 1882) onwards. Barnay returned Irving's hospitality by giving special performances of *Julius Caesar* and *The Merchant of Venice* at his Berliner Theater. In 1888 Barnay, in correspondence with Bram Stoker, acknowledged 'your kind letter and the book of The Merchant of Venice', but requested 'some details about the costumes . . . drawings or photographs [or] one or two of the principal dresses itselves'.[2] Irving also continued to cultivate his connection with the Duke of Saxe-Meiningen, who upgraded the order, which he had bestowed on him in 1881, and was entertained by Sir Henry, as he had become in 1895, at the Beefsteak Room on 25 May 1897 (Stoker, 1906, vol. 2, p. 155). The duke maintained his interest in the English theatre, attending Lady Archibald Campbell's pastoral performance of *As You Like It*, under the direction of E. W. Godwin (Stokes, 1972, pp. 47–50), in the grounds of Coombe House, as part of an audience which included the Prince and Princess of Wales, numerous German princes, ambassadors of Persia and other countries 'as well as some five hundred men and women representative of leisure, rank, and culture' (*Illustrated London News*, 6 June 1885).

THE ITALIAN TRAGEDIANS

During the first half of the 1880s theatregoing almost threatened the leisured classes with a full-time occupation. When Adelaide Ristori appeared as Lady Macbeth at Drury Lane on 3 July 1882, the *Era* observed the customary 'large and fashionable audience assembled to give the eminent artist cordial and enthusiastic greeting' (8 July 1882). Although it had been nine years since her last London appearance, the Italian actress had a long association with the city in which she had first performed in 1857 and from which she had gone on to 'create a furore in Spain', invade Russia and Constantinople and conduct 'many triumphant campaigns, not only in the United States, but also in the remotest Republics of South America' (*Illustrated London News*, 8 July 1882). In these far-flung engagements Ristori acted in Italian, as at the French Theatre, New York where as Lady Macbeth 'her study of the part is noticeable in every word that she utters and every attitude that she takes' (*New York Times*, 20 October 1866), though the reviewer considered her impersonation 'gaunt, unfeminine, harsh and overbearing'. Madame Ristori's careful 'study of the part' is evident in her analysis published in her memoirs (1907, Chapter III). Earlier (p. 107), Ristori wrote of 'the anxiety and emotion', which she experienced 'on the night of July 3, 1882', the reason for which was that she was playing the entire role of Lady Macbeth in English for the first time (with William Rignold, George's brother, as her thane). In 1873 Ristori had performed the sleep-walking scene in English to great acclaim, though a good deal of her effect was achieved non-verbally through 'her glazed and fixed expression, her marvellous attitudes' (*Era*, 13 July 1873). The question in the minds of 'a rather exacting audience' was whether her mastery of English was sufficient to the task:

Madame Ristori answered the question plainly enough in her impersonation, for her English was not only wonderfully perfect, but she acted in a manner that showed how thoroughly she comprehended every word. It is, however, in the intensity of her manner that Madame Ristori seems to shine; her facial expression and gesticulation, without showing the slightest exaggeration, seeming always in keeping with the dialogue she utters. (*Echo*, 4 July 1882)

The core of Ristori's performance was 'the intensity of her manner', to which the substitution of English for Italian was almost incidental, as the substitution of standard English for his idiosyncratic utterance would have been in Henry Irving's performances.

Ristori was followed by the two other Italian actors on the international stage: Ernesto Rossi played Lear at Drury Lane in the week of 12 June 1882 and Tommaso Salvini was at Covent Garden (Othello, King Lear and Macbeth) during February and March 1884 (Carlson, 1985, Appendix). Although Italy discovered Shakespeare rather late (mid-eighteenth century) and indirectly (via France) and had a comparatively weak dramatic tradition of its own, as Carlson claims (p. 11), 'most of the honors of this era of international touring' were carried off by Italian players: Ristori, Salvini, Rossi and rather later Duse. The Italian settings of many of Shakespeare's plays may often have been an inspiration, certainly for Duse who played Juliet in Verona at the age of fourteen (Rheinhardt, 1930, p. 23). There was also the suggestion that so well had Shakespeare captured the Italian temperament that Italian actors were best suited to certain roles.

Salvini made his first appearance as Othello in Vicenza in June 1856 and added other Shakespearian roles (Hamlet, Lear, Macbeth and Coriolanus) to his repertoire before he tested himself against English audiences in London in 1875. Reports of Salvini preceded him. One in the *Athenaeum* (30 January 1864) was by M. C. C. from Genoa, who revealed she was 'an Englishwoman' for whom 'it was a glorious privilege . . . to witness this unequivocal homage to the dramatic genius of one whose noble productions are true to universal nature'. M. C. C. described Salvini's 'noble person and handsome features', his 'natural, unforced voice', the passion which, as Iago's venom took effect, transformed him into 'some Eastern animal' and the sensational climax clasping Desdemona's head 'within his arms, and smothering it against his breast'. Italians experienced none of the queasiness to which the French were so susceptible.

Salvini's arrival in London in April 1875, barely six months after Irving's sensational Hamlet, inevitably occasioned gossip about rivalry, with accusations that Irving had been negligent in his courtesies to the foreign visitor. These, according to Percy Fitzgerald, Irving refuted and Salvini became the first of the succession of visiting fellow-professionals who experienced 'not merely the lavish hospitality of the Lyceum manager, but a series of thoughtful kindnesses and services' (1893, p. 86). Salvini's Othello (Mason, 1890) caused great controversy. The veteran critic G. H. Lewes admired his 'noble bearing, and the subtle music of his varied declamation' (1875, p. 224) and considered he 'surpassed' Edmund Kean in his treatment of Iago in Act 3 Scene 3, but: 'In the fifth act my admiration ceased' (p. 227). Lewes did not object, as many did, that Salvini cut his throat – amidst much gurgling and loss of blood – with a scimitar instead of a dagger, but because 'it is underfelt and overacted', an excess of effects had replaced the one 'massive effect' needed. In London Salvini was supported by an Italian company as he customarily was in America, though when he performed there 'with an English company he made £10,000', compared with 'only £2,000' with his compatriots (F. Archer, 1912, p. 176).

Salvini's contract with manager John Mapleson included Hamlet, which would obviously invite comparison with Irving whom the Italian actor saw in the role. In the audience at the performance of a play in a language he did not understand Salvini experienced a role reversal, but had no difficulty in following Irving whose 'mobile face mirrored his thoughts' (1893, p. 165). In the ['nunnery'] scene with Ophelia Irving 'was deserving of the highest praise' (p. 166), 'further on it was not so', the English actor seemed 'lacking in power' and resorting to mannerisms. Salvini resolved: 'I too can do *Hamlet*, and I will try it.' Lewes found that the play had been 'cut down to suit Italian tastes', 'the scene with Ophelia was a revelation' with its pervading tenderness, the graveside scene was 'dull beyond all precedent' but: 'The close was magnificent. No more pathetic death has been seen on the stage' (1875, p. 231). When *The Fashionable Tragedian* was published the authors had the advantage of being able to compare the two actors as Othello:

Comparison between Salvini and Mr Irving was, of course, unavoidable but it was at the time impossible. To compare the noble dignity of the great Italian with the physical and intellectual feebleness of Mr Irving is to compare the sublime and the ridiculous. Mr Irving's failure in Othello would have been equally pronounced if Salvini had never been heard of. (Archer and Lowe, 1877, p. 18)

Salvini's countryman Ernesto Rossi was a serious student of Shakespeare, learning some English before travelling to London to watch Charles Kean (Collison-Morley, 1916, p. 155) and contributing thoughtful essays on Hamlet to the *Theatre* (April and October 1884), but though he had admirers of his Italianite Hamlet in 1876, 'the upper-crust did not take to him; he did not become the fashion' (Anderson, 1902, p. 328). The 'fashionable tragedian' did not concern himself greatly with Signor Rossi.

Irving skilfully used the visits to London by foreign actors to secure his position as the head of his profession and to advance it and himself in society. He ensured that his approval became an essential part of the imprimatur, which these players were seeking for their Shakespearian performances. In doing so he placed upon himself the expectation of Shakespearian pre-eminence as actor and producer. In marked contrast to Macready, Charles Kean, Helen Faucit and Samuel Phelps, Irving – publicly at any rate – was never discountenanced by unfavourable comparisons with visiting actors. Salvini described Irving as 'an accomplished gentleman in society ... loved and respected by his fellow-citizens, who justly look upon him as a glory to their country' (1893, pp. 167). Modjeska and Edwin Booth agreed:

that Irving is a 'great man.' 'Not a great actor – but a great man,' said Edwin Booth. 'His knowledge of human nature – and his fibs are equally great.' (1910, p. 500)

It was commonly remarked that Irving would have become the leader of whatever profession he had joined. William Archer characteristically made fun of Irving's penchant for mixing with those whom he considered to be his peers:

The intelligent foreigner is there as a matter of course, and the non-intelligent foreigner, the Prince of Crim Tartary or the Ambassador from Cariboo is taken to the Lyceum as to the House of Lords or Madame Tussaud's. (1883, p. 30)

One such was the Chinese Ambassador, the Marquis Tseng attending *Hamlet* on 18 January 1879, who though he had not read the play, seemed, with the assistance of Sir Halliday Macartney, 'to be absolutely correct on the human side' (Stoker, 1906, vol. 2, p. 78). Irving, having perfected his performance as genial host, assumed the role of ambassador extraordinary to the United States.

AMBASSADOR TO AMERICA

Irving's departure for the United States was preceded by a series of ceremonies, which raised his personal status and public awareness of his forthcoming venture. The first was the traditional end-of-season speech from the Lyceum stage. Irving naturally dwelt on his forthcoming tour, which was to last for six months and cover 'some forty cities', though in the event it was a dozen, but his concluding 'Good-bye' was followed by a scene which Austin Brereton found 'words . . . almost useless to describe':

The band played 'Auld Lang Syne,' and the curtain was again raised disclosing the entire Lyceum company on the stage, a sight which caused the great audience to burst into an extraordinary tumult of enthusiasm. (1908, vol. 1, p. 371)

Shortly after this enthusiastic demonstration of loyalty and affection from the Lyceum audience, on 4 July 1883 Irving was guest of honour at a banquet in St James's Hall with the Lord Chief Justice (Coleridge) in the chair and a galaxy of eminent guests, most notably the

American ambassador the Hon. J. Russell Lowell. Next came a banquet at the Garrick Club, arranged for the profession by Squire Bancroft (Mr and Mrs Bancroft, 1889, pp. 357–60), at which speakers included Pierre Berton for the French stage and Lawrence Barrett for the American. Irving then set off on a progress through Scotland and the north of England. He and Ellen Terry sailed from Liverpool on 11 October aboard the *Britannic*, with Oscar Wilde and Lillie Langtry amongst the numerous wellwishers seeing them off (Craig and St John, 1933, p. 198); the rest of the company was already en route aboard the *City of Rome*, a slower vessel.

The presence at these functions of the American ambassador was particularly apt in the case of J. Russell Lowell, who was not only the representative of the country which Irving was about to visit, but also a Shakespearian author. In *Among My Books* (1870) Lowell begins his essay 'Shakespeare Once More' by extolling Shakespeare's unique qualities as the common heritage of 'the English-speaking nations' (p. 145) and proceeds to give an authoritative account of his reception in Europe and beyond. As Professor Ashley Thorndike observed in his British Academy lecture *Shakespeare in America* though '[Washington] Irving, [Fenimore] Cooper, [Nathaniel] Hawthorne, [Henry David] Thoreau, [Ralph Waldo] Emerson, and others [Henry Longfellow and Walt Whitman] were creating a new literature', 'this literary movement which . . . was so impressive and so creditable to the aesthetic and spiritual aspirations of the new nation, found little companionship in music or painting or any other of the fine arts, but in the theatre it had Shakespeare' (1927, p. 11). The view that its own new literature and Shakespeare constituted the high ground of American culture in the second half of the nineteenth century invites the question whether they were equally pervasive across that vast country. Thorndike was in no doubt that in the creation of 'a united civilization . . . Shakespeare had been a symbol of unity, a moving force, almost a directing deity' (p. 10). In the East he was enshrined in libraries and theatre; in the West actors on a Mississippi showboat 'became his emissaries and evangelicals . . . no other writer was so quickly assimilated in the wilderness'. Shakespeare provided 'so unifying an element in our culture' that 'Reverence for him became the symbol, the mark of culture, which united the frontiersman with Lowell and Emerson.'

The example of Edwin Forrest reflects the complexity of the relationship between America and Shakespeare (see also Bristol, 1990), but the style of acting, which John Forster had denigrated for its coarse appeal to the gallery, helped to ensure the English dramatist's place on American stages. Estimates of the number of these vary: William Winter (1913, p. 23) calculated that in 1880 there were 5,000 (in 3,500 towns); Joseph Hatton gives 1,800 (1884, vol. 1, p. 246). Different definitions of what actually constituted a theatre probably account for the considerable disparity, but even at the lower figure the extent of theatrical activity in America was remarkable. This was not organised theatre in Matthew Arnold's sense of being government-sponsored, though much of it (the more prestigious theatres and companies) certainly operated on a well-regulated system, dominated by the Theatrical Syndicate and later the Shubert Brothers. Nevertheless there was scope for the likes of George C. Miln, who later extended his activities to Australia, and Frederick Warde, formerly a member of Charles Calvert's company in Manchester. Between mid-October 1882 and January 1883 George C. Miln and his company gave 'some seventy performances' of 'three Shakespeare plays [*Hamlet*, *Othello* and *Macbeth*] in nearly forty cities, twenty-five of which were one-night stands'. Chicago, Minneapolis and St Paul were the only major cities and 'only in Chicago did they play a full week'. In 1883–4 Miln gave 254 performances in 107 towns/cities and in 1884–5 258 in seventy-two (Woods, 1977–9, p. 140). Frederick Warde, whose revival at the Fulton Opera House of *Timon of Athens* in the mode of his mentor lay a quarter of a century in the future (Warde, 1920, p. 298), shuttled along the railroads with a predominantly Shakespearian repertoire, albeit that the 'tragedies were presented in heavily cut versions which transformed them into the same romantic mold [as the contemporary plays]' (Woods, 1977, p. 336). At the time of Irving's first visit to the United States, Miln and Warde were at their zenith, whereas Augustin Daly, who between 1869 and 1877 had produced thirteen Shakespeare plays, was in 'a six-year hiatus . . . before his next production, a presentation of *The Merry Wives of Windsor* on January 14, 1886' (Felheim, 1956, p. 228). This was followed by ten sumptuous revivals centred on Ada Rehan (Winter, 1898), several of which were seen in London, where Daly opened the theatre bearing his name (Forbes-Winslow, 1943) on 12 March 1893 with *The Taming of the Shrew*. In 1890, Daly's production of *As You Like It* played at the Lyceum with Ada Rehan as Rosalind, a favourite role of another American actress Mary Anderson, who occupied the Lyceum at the beginning of Irving's first American tour, being succeeded by Lawrence Barrett, under the management of Henry Abbey who was presenting Irving in the United States (Wilson, 1952, p. 135).

Abbey ensured that the arrival of London's fashionable tragedian in New York was as dramatic as any of his stage entrances. On his first (of eight) North American tour Irving was accompanied by the journalist Joseph Hatton, whose *Henry Irving's Impressions of America* comprises a first-hand – if not exactly disinterested – chronicle. The *Britannic* reached New York on the morning of 21 October 1883. Soon alongside was the *Blackbird* complete with Abbey himself and a band of thirty Italian musicians, which in due course – inevitably – burst into 'Hail to the Chief'. Irving was brought ashore by the luxury yacht, the *Yosemite*, on which reporters from Boston, Chicago and St Louis as well as New York vied with each other to interview the eminent visitor.

Although English actors had been frequent visitors (and emigrants) none had ever brought such an entourage with them. The acting company and other personnel numbered between sixty and seventy and then there was the scenery, properties, costumes and so on. Irving was determined that American audiences should not be at a disadvantage compared with those at the Lyceum. Ellen Terry was emphatic:

What I want to make clear is that in 1883 there was no living American drama . . . that such productions of romantic plays and Shakespeare as Henry Irving brought over from England were unknown, and that the extraordinary success of our first tours would be impossible now. We were the first and we were pioneers, and we were *new*. To be new is everything in America. (Craig and St John, 1933, p. 201)

The subject of greatest interest to the reporters aboard the *Yosemite* was William Shakespeare. Irving was asked when New York would see his Hamlet, replying that he was keeping it back until the spring to ensure some novelty for his second visit to the city. In an exchange about Edwin Booth, Irving was careful to impose his own version of events:

'You played in "Othello" with Mr. Booth in London, you say?'
'I produced "Othello" especially for Mr. Booth, and played Iago for the first time on that occasion. We afterwards alternated parts.' (Hatton, vol. 1, 1884, p. 64)

Irving identified *Hamlet* as Shakespeare's most popular play in England, followed by *Othello*, not as in America by *Julius Caesar*. Irving's personal subtext runs through his reply: 'Salvini's Othello, for instance, suffered because the Iago was weak' (p. 65). Irving effectively presented the greatest Othello of the day as an object of pity, whilst implying Booth's good fortune and the superiority of his own Iago, though – needless to say – skating over his own ill-received Othello, which Americans were certainly not going to see. As for *Julius Caesar*, Irving remarked on 'the difficulty in filling worthily the three leading parts', but he was hardly likely to stage a play with three leading parts. Irving described his approach to Shakespeare as 'giving him the same advantage that I would give to any modern author' and proclaimed – proprietorially – Shakespeare's popularity 'in my own dear land' (p. 108).

Shakespeare was central to Irving's impact and prestige in the new world. The dramatist's name was invoked at the never-ending sequence of receptions, banquets and testimonials arranged to greet the English actor. In Philadelphia Irving was presented with Edwin Forrest's watch, a symbolic gesture of reconciliation, and Edwin Booth paid his debt of hospitality with a breakfast, though not until shortly before Irving's homeward departure. On the *Yosemite* Irving had regaled the reporters with an anecdote about a friend who, when told by the actor of his forthcoming appearance as Charles I (in W. G. Wills's play) enquired: 'Do you mean Shakespeare's Charles I?' (Hatton, vol. 1, p. 109). Irving, one suspects, would have been relieved had the American public been gullible enough to accept some of the modern plays in his repertoire as from the bard's pen. As Charles Shattuck has observed, Shakespeare was not what Irving played 'most often, nor was it what he was really best equipped for. When he presented himself to America in 1883, meaning surely to put his best foot forward, it was not so much the Shakespearean that he showed us, but the specialist in contemporary melodrama' (1987, p. 158).

Thus it was; during the opening four weeks in New York Shylock was Irving's only Shakespearian role with Ellen Terry as Portia, repeating her success at the Prince of Wales's Theatre in 1875. Though it did not escape controversy his innovatively sympathetic Shylock did not expose Irving to the level of critical rigour that Hamlet inevitably would. When this happened in Philadelphia Hatton protested at what he described as 'the influences of London', by which he meant the reaction typified by *The Fashionable Tragedian*, in some notices which Irving himself considered 'were in opposition to the verdict of the audience' (Hatton, 1884, vol. 1, pp. 227–8). Irving, like all English actors, had to adjust to the absence in American theatres of the pit and gallery, which were such a vital part of the Lyceum audience. As at the Lyceum on 2 November 1874 'the audience was puzzled by Irving's interpretation [of Hamlet] because for the first two acts he did not observe the points and artificialities to which they were used' (Rood, 1982, p. 20), but, as at that historic first night, Irving persevered and succeeded to the extent that he said of that Philadelphia audience: 'I never played it to an audience that entered more fully into the spirit of my work' and a veteran playgoer testified that he had never seen a Philadelphia audience respond so enthusiastically

(Hatton, 1884, vol. 1, p. 227). During his second (1884–5) American tour Irving discoursed on 'The American Audience', identifying 'impartiality' as their 'dominant characteristic' (in Richards ed., 1994, p. 119), having by then experienced the disapproval of the Lyceum's 'good old backbone of intelligence' for *Twelfth Night* on 8 July 1884.

On the first tour Boston was treated to Hamlet and Shylock. It appreciated Irving's unstagy delivery of Hamlet's familiar lines, but Irving himself thought that American audiences were accustomed to 'the part of Shylock strongly declaimed' (p. 263) and Hatton noted that Irving's delivery was a little more vigorous than in London. In his review the Boston critic Henry Clapp attacked Irving on the same grounds as the authors of *The Fashionable Tragedian* had: 'his ungracefulness . . . his atrocious enunciation . . . lingua-matricide . . . his oddities of utterance . . . Irving *patois* . . . declamation [which is] weak and ineffectual . . . exceedingly flexible eyebrows . . . thin jaw . . . large, deep-set, darkly-luminous eyes', all features belonging to 'a most striking and impressive personality' (1902, pp. 200–5). Clapp conceded that onstage 'the injury [of this catalogue of faults] is much less than anyone, upon a merely theoretic consideration of Mr. Irving's art, would believe to be possible'; they were outweighed by Irving's 'prime distinctions . . . intensity . . . and intellect', 'the dramatic consequences of such a high intensity' were 'obviously great, but the value of the quality in holding the attention of audiences is inestimable' (pp. 208–9).

In the 'Prairie City' of Chicago, where Irving was anxious about the absence of artistic appreciation, his Shylock was hailed for its Zola-esque modernity; in Cincinnati, with its large German population, it was judged the equal of Theodor Doring; in Washington President Chester Arthur attended performances and received Irving at the White House; and by the time Irving exposed his Hamlet and *Much Ado About Nothing* to the scrutiny of New York his triumph was assured. Irving had brought the Lyceum Theatre company to America and it was the theatre's coffers, rather than his own, that were swelled by the profit of £11,700. He returned seven times, but the only further Shakespearian roles he took with him were Malvolio, Wolsey and Macbeth. Shylock was most durable of all, surviving to the final tour in 1903 (Winter, 1911, p. 53). By then Irving had left the Lyceum and Ellen Terry had moved on, but she long recalled:

'No actor or actress who doesn't play in the "classics" – in Shakespeare or old comedy – will be heard of long,' was one of Henry Irving's sayings, by the way, and he was right. (Craig and St. John, 1933, p. 128)

Not only to be remembered, but to lead his profession, to walk with princes, to reach out to all sections of society, to preside over visiting actors, to represent his country abroad . . . for all these aspirations Irving needed Shakespeare. As critics from Archer to Clapp and fellow-actors from Modjeska to Salvini knew, Irving was not by conventional standards a great actor, but he was a remarkable man and by the sheer force of his extraordinary personality he transfixed audiences with his compelling realisations of Shakespeare.

6

The imperial stage: Beerbohm Tree and Benson

A CAPITAL THEATRE

As the twentieth century opened Henry Irving's name appeared, as president, at the head of a 'Preliminary Circular'[1] for the British Empire Shakespeare Society. The vice-presidents were George Alexander and Johnston Forbes-Robertson from the profession and the Bishop of Ripon, William Boyd Carpenter long known for his sympathy towards the theatre when many clergy were hostile to it. The patrons included other actors and clerics, a few members of the nobility, men of letters (Edmund Gosse, J. H. Newbolt) and leading Shakespearian scholars (Edward Dowden, F. J. Furnivall, Sidney Lee).

The objects for which BESS had been founded were fourfold:

1 To promote greater familiarity with Shakespeare's work among all classes throughout the British Empire.
2 To help the rising generation not only to study Shakespeare's works, but to love them.
3 To form Shakespeare Clubs and Reading Societies (or help those existing in London) and in the large provincial towns and in the Colonies.
4 To encourage the study of Shakespeare by Prizes given yearly for the best reading, recitation, acting scenes from his plays, or essay on Shakespeare by Members or Associates of the Society.

Although its first director Acton Bond was considered 'a fine Shakespeare actor' (Newton, 1927, pp. 189–90) and established actors were occasionally involved in its activities, BESS was fundamentally amateur and literary. The growth of Shakespeare Reading Societies reflected the influence of academics such as Sidney Lee whom Robert Graves recalled as one of the distinguished members of such a group, which met at his parents' house for years (1961, p. 9). The BESS societies spread across the country and beyond, providing improving recreation for those with the leisure to indulge in it. Some of the more energetic members performed at the annual festival, for instance Mrs Archibald Flower as Viola in Stratford in 1910. By then the society had royal patronage with H. H. Princess Marie Louise of Schleswig-Holstein as its president (*Windsor Magazine*, November 1910). The princess, a grand-daughter of Queen Victoria, returned to England in 1900 after the annulment of her marriage to Prince Albert of Anhalt and immersed herself in charitable and artistic causes, of which the theatre was particularly close to her heart, with H. B. Irving, his wife Dorothea Baird and Mary Anderson amongst her personal friends (Marie Louise, Princess, 1956).

The society's membership increased and in November 1913 the *Thespian* reported that it amounted to 'some 10,000', but there were those for whom Shakespeare's proper place was on the – professional – stage and there was one London theatre where the regular weekly attendance at its sumptuous Shakespearian revivals exceeded BESS's total membership: His Majesty's, presided over as it had been since its opening as Her Majesty's in 1897 by Herbert Beerbohm Tree, was a theatre worthy of a great empire.

As Hesketh Pearson noted, 'Herbert Beerbohm Tree had German, Slavonic and English forbears' (1956, p. 5), a combination which served Tree, his profession and his country well during a period in which Britain's imperial and European ambitions reached new heights. As an actor Tree was even less of a natural Shakespearian than Henry Irving, but, perhaps out of a sense of rivalry with the man whose successor in so many respects he was, Tree outdid Irving by reviving sixteen (four more) Shakespeare plays and in 1905 establishing an Annual Shakespeare Festival at His Majesty's. In the first decade of his acting career Tree had performed only three Shakespeare roles, though he could claim to have shown unusual range: Sir Andrew Aguecheek and Falstaff, plus King John. During his nine years (1887–96) as actor–manager of the Haymarket Theatre, Tree revived four plays from the canon, but, although he had to abandon his plan to open His Majesty's Theatre with *Julius Caesar* 'because time and the particular cast on which he had set his heart were lacking' (Beerbohm, 1920, p. 106), in 1898 that was the first of the grandiose revivals which continued (almost annually) until 1913.

Designed by the prolific theatre architect Charles Phipps, Her Majesty's was the most impressive of the many theatres that rose in London during the 1890s (Maguire, 1992). Shaw devoted much of his review of the opening performance to the theatre itself, praising the interior decoration by Romaine-Walker as a perfect complement to Phipps's elegant and imposing exterior, all in the French style: 'you feel that you are in a place where high scenes are to be enacted and dignified things to be done' (1932, vol. 3, p. 117). Tree spared no effort to reinforce that impression on the opening night. The Prince of Wales was present, as was republican Henry Labouchere; Maud Tree, Herbert's actress-wife, delivered an ode written for the occasion by the poet laureate Alfred Austin and Clara Butt sang 'God save the Queen'. The – apparently unavoidable – absence of Shakespeare from the stage notwithstanding, the occasion was conducted in a manner that would scarcely have been inadequate for a National Theatre and Tree's perception of Her Majesty's as the closest Britain was likely to get to such an institution was to be a powerful factor in debates on that subject over the next two decades.

Shaw calculated that for such a theatre 'in some Continental cities, where the theatre rivals the parliament house, or the cathedral as a public building, the cost is over £300 a head', but 'in England we have achieved the commercial triumph of getting the cost down to £7':

Under these circumstances the fact that Her Majesty's is no £7 commercial affair, but quite the handsomest theatre in London, must go altogether to the credit of Mr Tree's public spirit and artistic conscience. (p. 117)

Shaw reflected on the impression created by this splendid ambiance:

Nobody can say of Her Majesty's that it proclaims itself a place built by a snob for the entertainment of snobs, with snobbish plays. It rises spaciously and brilliantly to the dignity of art . . . (p. 118)

Shaw had a suggestion to make about the theatre's highest vantage point: the gallery. The stage being flat instead of sloping, 'the view of the stage from the back rows of the gallery at Her Majesty's is as foreshortened as that from the operatic altitudes of Covent Garden'.

He understood that the gallery would 'not always be used', but proposed that 'rather than wasting it on ordinary occasions':

to set it [the gallery] apart at a charge of sixpence or even less for such faithful supporters of high art as the working-man with a taste for serious drama – especially Shakespear – and the impecunious student, male and female, who will go to the stalls or balcony later in life. (p. 119)

Shaw pointed out that although 'the working-men connoisseurs' constituted 'a very small percentage of their class' because that class was so large they were more numerous than might be expected. Shaw and Tree may have disagreed profoundly about its taste, but they were at one on the desirability of a large and socially diverse audience for Shakespeare.

Tree's essay 'The Living Shakespeare' was his catechism. He proclaimed the huge audiences for his Shakespeare revivals: 242,000 for *Julius Caesar*, over 170,000 for *King John* and nearly 220,000 for *A Midsummer Night's Dream* – 'in all a grand total of six hundred and thirty-two thousand visitors to these three productions' (1913, p. 46). He naturally interpreted these figures as an indication 'that public taste . . . lies in the direction of the method in which Shakespeare has been presented of late years by the chief metropolitan managers'. This method was what Tree, whose 'earliest theatrical recollection was of the Bancrofts' (p. 44) production of *The Merchant of Venice*, termed 'complete illusion' (p. 59), the detailed recreation on stage of the locations in which Shakespeare set his plays, in defence of which Tree repeated the familiar argument, citing the Chorus in *Henry V*, that 'Shakespeare regretted the deficiencies of the stage of his day' (p. 60). Tree acknowledged that there was an alternative approach, that of 'frank convention', but could not 'admit a compromise between them' (p. 59), by which he presumably meant that though he accepted the neo-Elizabethan style of William Poel, he rejected Harley Granville Barker. Once adopted, the 'complete illusion' method had its own unassailable logic (Mazer, 1981). It required: lengthy preparation and careful rehearsal; considerable rearrangement and cutting of the text; an 'all-round cast of a high level' (p. 52) – at his theatre anyway, where the production would not be a vehicle for a single star – ; a long run; and therefore large numbers of people from all social classes to fill all parts of the theatre. Tree was in no doubt that 'it is better to draw multitudes by doing Shakespeare in the way the public prefers than to keep the theatre empty by only presenting them "adequately"' (p. 50).

In his annual Shakespeare Festivals from 1905 to 1913, Tree accommodated productions by other managers, some of them in the opposing 'frank convention' school, such as William Poel's *The Two Gentlemen of Verona* in 1910 (Speaight, 1954, p. 121). In contrast to the usual long run, there was a daily change of programme (six days, six plays), but even then, as George Rowell (1975) has shown, Tree made a profit with an average 'take' in the first two years of £373 10s 4d, not much under the £400 represented by a full house. Hosting the Shakespeare Festivals was part of Tree's strategy for establishing himself and his theatre as being pre-eminent in the production of the national playwright, an important claim as the debate about a National Theatre intensified. Tree's determination to identify his theatre with the national interest is evident in his designation of the 1911 Shakespeare Festival as the Coronation Festival, lasting from 9 May to 15 July and incorporating the Coronation Gala performance.

Perhaps his own background gave Tree a heightened awareness of English history, the traditions of the monarchy and the *zeitgeist* of the country. In 1896 at the Haymarket Theatre he played Falstaff at a matinée performance of *Henry IV Part 2* of which the *Daily Courier* wrote: 'The psychological moment of "Henry IV" has arrived. It is only the other month that Mr Louis Calvert mounted the masterpiece in Manchester' (9 May 1896). As William Archer's review indicated Louis Calvert had been as adroit as his father in matching a Shakespeare play to the mood of the moment: 'A spasm of patriotism ... is at present agitating the empire on which the sun never sets', this 'incomparable heirloom' had been too long neglected until the present 'crisis [gave] it positive actuality' (1897, p. 31). Archer's 'outburst of literary jingoism', as he called it, was presumably prompted by events in southern Africa where 1896 had opened with the defeat of Jameson's raid by the Boers and Cecil Rhodes's resignation as premier of Cape Colony.

The nearest Tree got to Shakespeare in the year (1897) of Queen Victoria's diamond jubilee was Garrick's *Katherine and Petruchio*, with which 'elegant tomfoolery' William Archer observed 'the audience ... were highly amused' (1898, p. 314). The following year for *Julius Caesar* Tree enlisted Louis Calvert, who in Kate Terry Gielgud's words was 'looked upon as an authority where Shakespearean productions are concerned' (1980, p. 70). Calvert took particular responsibility for the crowd, especially in the celebrated Forum scene and the promptbook[2] reveals that it was divided into units of which each member was individualised in the tradition of the Saxe-Meiningen company which both Tree and Calvert had seen in 1881 (Calvert, 1919, pp. 39–40). One example was a man, absorbed in doing up his shoelace, growing 'rapt in the great speech [Mark Antony's]' (Cran, 1907, p. 53). The production's appeal was not confined to its antiquarian accuracy and stagecraft. It partook of that immediacy evident in Charles Calvert's *Henry V*, with its anxious women. Madeleine Bingham has drawn a parallel between Imperial Rome and Britain: 'the Roman mother saw her sons leaving for the frontiers of Gaul or Britain, the British matron saw her sons leaving for the North-West frontier, or darkest Africa' (1978, p. 98); and Ralph Berry has likened the Roman/British analogue drawn in Tree's programme to 'veiled social criticism', referring as it does to Rome as 'the pleasaunce of the aristocracy ... [with] their boundless wealth and indescribable extravagance . . . a hot-bed of profligacy and corruption. It was Caesar's aim to reform it altogether' (Berry, 1986, pp. 155–6).

In September 1899 Tree staged *King John*, again with Calvert's assistance. In addition to its scope for historically accurate scenic display (as in Kemble's, Kean's and Macready's revivals) the play, with its forthright assertion of English nationalism, had a timely appeal to a population preoccupied with the Boer war and the interpolated tableau, the Signing of Magna Carta (held for a full minute), celebrated prized freedoms. Two other actor–managers, Frank Benson and Lewis Waller, chose *Henry V*, both at the Lyceum Theatre (15 February and 22 December 1900), in response to the moment.

The end of the Boer War on 31 May 1902 should have been followed by the coronation of Edward VII a month later on 26 June. Tree's choice of *The Merry Wives of Windsor*, apt for any coronation, was particularly so for that of Edward VII. Tree (Falstaff) had also pulled off the remarkable coup of securing Ellen Terry as Mistress Page and Mrs Kendal ('By the Courtesy of Mr. W. H. Kendal')[3] as Mistress Ford. When the production opened in May it was presented as Tree's dutiful response to a national occasion: 'Mr Tree had not forgotten that this is Coronation year, and that something worthy of the occasion is expected from him'. Tree, having observed that Shakespeare was not represented at any other West End theatre, resolved 'to save London from the stinging reproach' that the absence of Shakespeare from the nation's capital in a coronation year would incur (*Daily Telegraph*, 23 May 1902). The new monarch insisted that despite the postponement (caused by his operation for perityphlitis) of the coronation to 9 August, all functions of hospitality to overseas guests should take place as arranged. Earlier in the year Irving had enquired of the Lord Chamberlain if it would be in accordance with the king's wishes for the stage to contribute to the forthcoming ceremony. The king commanded that such an occasion should be included in 'the official list of "informal" formalities' (Stoker, vol. 1, p. 334). On 3 July, within forty minutes of the end of a performance of *Faust*, the Lyceum stage was ready for a glittering reception for a thousand guests 'from every part of the world and of every race under the sun' (p. 339). India was well represented and: 'Many who were at both functions said that it [the Lyceum's] was even finer than the reception at the India Office, which was a spectacle to remember' (p. 341). Irving did not enjoy exclusive rights to represent the theatre on the '"informal" formalities'. Tree (on 2 July) and George Alexander (on 4 July with *Paolo and Francesca* at the St James's) shared the honours. In terms of professional rivalry the advantage probably lay with Tree. He had lured Ellen Terry away from the Lyceum and (unlike Irving of late) cast her brilliantly in a Shakespearian role to which she was ideally suited. Those coronation visitors (from Canada, Australia, Ceylon, the West Indies) who attended Her Majesty's saw Shakespeare performed in the empire's capital city and at the reception afterwards: 'Mr Tree received his visitors in the forest scene of Shakespeare's playful comedy, thus securing a pleasantly unconventional environment for the occasion' (*Daily Telegraph*, 3 July 1902). King Lewanika, Paramount Chief of the Barotse Kingdom cannot have been alone in 'marvel[ling] greatly at the ingenious and elaborate stage arrangements' (*Daily Chronicle*, 5 July 1902). When Tree brought the season to an end in mid-August, *The Merry Wives of Windsor* had played to audiences totalling 94,000 to 95,000 at fifty-six performances (*Era*, 16 August 1902).

The theatre's contribution to the coronation did not bring the honours to which a few aspired for themselves and others felt were due to the profession. Tree did not receive his by then very long-awaited knighthood until 1909, by which time he, like other leading actor–managers, had performed at one or more royal residence, in a revival of the court drama which had begun towards the end of Queen Victoria's reign.[4] With his customary sense of timing, Tree contrived to play Malvolio ('some have greatness thrust upon them') on the night his knighthood was announced.

BERLIN

The most conspicuous service which Tree had by then done for his sovereign was to take his company and a repertoire of five Shakespeare plays (*King Richard II, Twelfth Night, The Merry Wives of Windsor, Hamlet* and *Antony and Cleopatra*) plus *Trilby* to perform before the German emperor (Edward VII's nephew) at the New Royal Opera House in Berlin.[5]

Tree had been preceded in 1898 by Johnston Forbes-Robertson and a company of forty including Mrs Patrick Campbell and J. H. Barnes. Forbes-Robertson found that the best way to counter the 'petty tyrannies' (1925, p. 174) of the German railway officials was to assume complete ignorance of the language and Mrs Campbell's strategy of introducing Forbes-Robertson to everyone as ''Amlet the Dine' was extraordinarily effective. Forbes-Robertson described Berlin as 'a showy and tawdry-looking town, with here and there some imposing though florid-looking buildings' (p. 175) and Barnes, writing in 1914, recalled 'the ever-present militarism' from the students whose faces were 'slit and cut about by

8. Souvenir programme for Tree's visit to Berlin.

duelling swords' to 'the rolling stock of all the railways bearing the Government mark of its capacity for carrying men, horses, and provisions in time of war' (1914, p. 221). Though they had a week in which to prepare for the first performance, the English actors encountered frustrating delays, the source of which was identified as the intendant of the New Opera House (previously known as Krolls Opera House) whom he soon discovered was 'a very deft and complete liar' (1925, p. 175). Once inside the theatre it was clear that it was 'admirably conducted, with all the latest contrivances for simplifying the moving of the scenery and properties'. Evidently the visitors were using local sets for their performances. As the theatre was the Kaiser's own, Forbes-Robertson 'was allowed to employ soldiers as supers'; he found them 'very attentive and willing, though sometimes a little slow in their movements' (p. 176).

In contrast to London, where the late arrival of the royal party could be an untoward distraction, in Berlin the curtain went up immediately the emperor was seated in the royal box in the middle of the dress circle, with the result that Forbes-Robertson and his stage-hands had to scatter quickly on the first night of *Hamlet* (Peters, 1985, p. 163). The Kaiser had found *Hamlet* so long that when he attended *Macbeth*, in which Forbes-Robertson and Mrs Patrick Campbell were playing the leads for the first time, he came prepared with his own chef. During the hour-long interval, in which the royal family fortified themselves, the Kaiser summoned Forbes-Robertson and Mrs Campbell to his presence and gave him a scarf pin and her a bracelet. The German emperor impressed Forbes-Robertson with his fluent English and his knowledge of 'the Drama in general, and *Macbeth* in particular' (1925, p. 178) and, although he told her that he would like her to teach German actors not to shout, Mrs Patrick Campbell was struck by her host's 'powerful voice . . . piercing steel blue eyes' and 'the impression of intellectual force' (1922, p. 125). Barnes wrote that 'it would be quite impossible to overstate his indefatigability' (1914, p. 222). In marked contrast was the Dowager Empress, whose marriage ceremonies had occasioned the ill-fated performance of *Macbeth* in London and Samuel Phelps's visit to Berlin. In widowhood the empress, like her mother, did not go to the theatre, but was not even well enough to attend the private performance, which the English players were to have given for her. She did however send for Forbes-Robertson:

She was indeed a gracious and charming lady, with a strong look of her mother, Queen Victoria. Before I had spoken to her five minutes she had noticed a scarf-pin I was wearing that the Queen had given me on the occasion when I played before her as a member of Sir John Hare's company at Balmoral. Her face beamed with pleasure when I said, 'Yes, my Queen gave me that.' The Empress impressed me as one being clouded over with an unutterable sorrow. It seemed to me the saddest face I had ever looked upon. (1925, pp. 178–9)

Sharing a great love for the theatre, as they did less happily early widowhood and an uneasy relationship with their eldest son, Queen Victoria and the Empress Frederick died within a few months of each other in 1901. Forbes-Robertson's visit to Berlin had been part of a commercial tour extending to Hanover, Hamburg and Holland, but it had also functioned at a diplomatic level as Lady Emma Cavendish, sister of the British ambassador, wrote to Mrs Patrick Campbell, the 'Emperor has just been with my brother. He is loud in his praises of you and Mr. Forbes-Robertson' (Mrs Patrick Campbell, 1922, p. 126).

The diplomatic aspect of such a visit was clearly to the forefront of Herbert Beerbohm Tree's mind when in January 1907 he wrote to his young admirer and friend Olivia Truman:

I told you I would come one night, and tonight should have been the night, but something very important has been happening to-day – you will probably read about it in the newspapers to-morrow. The German Emperor has sent me an invitation to go to Berlin and I have to see all sorts of important people to-night and tomorrow morning. Is it not a great coup? You see it is more than a mere personal compliment to me – it has an international aspect and I am sure you will rejoice for me. (Truman, 1984, p. 70)

Tree's was a simplified account of the events leading up to his Berlin visit, which actually came about as a result of negotiations involving J. T. Grein, the Dutch-born founder of the Independent Theatre (a London counterpart to Antoine's Théâtre Libre), and the German ambassador, Count Wolff Metternich (Orme, 1936, pp. 180–1). When the visit was under discussion Tree had recently opened his grandiose revival of *Antony and Cleopatra*, rarely seen in London since Mrs Langtry had embodied the serpent of old Nile in 1890 (see Lamb, 1980). The axis of Tree's production was tilted heavily towards the Orient with Constance Collier's dusky Cleopatra in a series of ravishing costumes (Hodgson, 1998, pp. 91–2) and sets worthy of mention in Baedeker. Though it was not really one of his great successes Tree's willingness to suspend the run of *Antony and Cleopatra* was presented as another example of his selfless sense of duty.

What had become the customary preliminaries to an overseas tour by a leading actor–manager were duly observed, this time at the Hotel

Cecil, with the Lord Mayor of London presiding over a gathering at which Germans and Englishmen presented at least the appearance of unalloyed conviviality. Both national anthems having been played, the Lord Mayor spoke of the honour conferred on Tree by the German Emperor and Herr von Stumm, the German Chargé d'Affairs, speaking on behalf of the ambassador, reassured Tree of 'a warm reception in Germany', protesting – a shade too much – that there was 'no ill-feeling against this country among the large masses of German people, and he hoped that Mr. Tree's visit would reap most beneficial results in creating better feelings between the two nations' (*Era*, 13 April 1907). Tree, lacing his speech with German words and phrases, must have felt that this was his hour of destiny, for which his German ancestry and education and his English birth and affiliation had uniquely equipped him. In a parody of the grand titles of German theatre officials he claimed that his stage manager Henry Dana now called himself 'Herr Kaiserlich, Königlicher, Hof Ober Regisseur and Geheimer Haupt unter Flisser' and looked forward to what he believed would be 'a joyous pilgrimage':

Art knows no jealousy and no Chauvinism. All nations meet on the common ground of Art – that blessed spot of neutral territory – that land of cordial content. It is in this sense that His Imperial Majesty the Kaiser has said that the Art of the Drama is a mediator between nations.

Henry Dana had produced an impressive programme of the 'pilgrimage', but from the beginning all did not go well. The scene at Hanover station, as described by Nigel Playfair, borders on farce with the reception party from the Royal Hanover Schauspielhaus amounting to 'a dejected looking low life comedian, an elderly and even more dejected looking leading lady, and perhaps three others equally depressed' and Tree's toast, in fluent German, to the aforementioned playhouse being curtailed by the abrupt movement of the train (1930, p. 150).

Like Forbes-Robertson, Tree and his company were to perform at the Kaiser's own theatre, the New Royal Opera House, which, belying its name, was 'a quaint old theatre, picturesquely situated in the midst of the Tiergarten Park of 600 acres' (*Standard*, 13 April 1907), with 'the worst possible' acoustics and a stage 'so constructed that only the centre is visible to the entire audience'. The Kaiser took the theatre, and other arts, seriously and left no stone 'unchiselled, no dramatist, musician or philosopher unhonoured, whose honour would add to the lustre of the Court of Wilhelm II' (*Tribune*, 13 April 1907). Thus Berlin had received a succession of artistes from the rest of Europe and America, but had 'grown weary of the patronage of art' with dissatisfied Junkers pouring 'vials of... scorn' on the Kaiser's 'Theaterpolitick'. Wilhelm II's determination to make his court a showcase for visiting artistes contrasted with his refusal to patronise the arts elsewhere in his own country. Ernst Stern pointed out that: 'None of the Berlin Theatres, with the exception of the Royal Opera House and Theatre Royal (Königlisches Schauspielhaus) had ever been honoured with the Royal Presence' (1951, p. 110). The Crown Prince and his brothers attended Reinhardt's Deutsches Theater, but were 'unable to persuade their father to visit a Reinhardt performance. The Kaiser is credited with the witty observation that as he was a theatre-owner, it would be bad business on his part to take his custom to his competitors.'

The Kaiser's policy was in marked contrast to that of his nephew who, as Prince of Wales and king, extended his patronage and the benefits flowing from it to many theatres. With the debate about a National Theatre intensifying in England, German practice was looked at with great interest. Exponent of commercial Shakespeare that he was, by taking his company to the Kaiser's state theatre, Tree was intimating some comparable national status for His Majesty's. In fact, as the journalists' reports indicated, the court theatre was hardly a thriving affair. Two years later in an article on 'Shakespeare and the Modern German Stage', 'Eulenspiegel' dismissed 'the Prussian Royal theatres' with their large subsidies and conscripted audiences, turning instead 'to a more reliable source, the independent theatres. Here the popularity of Shakespeare strikes home at once' (*Contemporary Review*, June 1909). Two years after that in his article 'Two German Theatres', Harley Granville Barker, the arch exponent of subsidised theatre, categorised the Deutsches Theater as 'private enterprise' (*Fortnightly Review*, 1911, p. 60). This it certainly was, Reinhardt having – unusually for a manager – bought the theatre in 1906. Reinhardt's classical revivals, especially of Shakespeare, were a revelation to audiences which had been brought up to regard the theatre as 'an educational and cultural institution', sitting there 'humbly' like a congregation listening to a sermon 'to the good of their souls' (Stern, 1951, p. 73). Though to Reinhardt a long run meant keeping *A Midsummer Night's Dream* in the repertoire for years over which hundreds of performances were given (rather than consecutively), he shared the same populist zeal as Tree. Ironically Ludwig Barnay, who as a member of the Saxe-Meiningen company in London in 1881 had memorably proclaimed 'Freiheit', now 'had some official position in the State Theatre'

(Collier, 1929, p. 189), but he and Reinhardt led the hospitality for the English players.

The atmosphere at the New Royal Opera House was not so harmonious. The rest of his company, apart from Mrs Lyn Harding and music director Adolf Schmid who were German, did not share Tree's understanding of the native tongue. Neither did the German supers have much grasp of English. As Robert Atkins recalled, Tree had at his disposal 'a crack infantry regiment', but on the morning of the first performance (*Richard II* on 12 April) 'they were not present, they had been marched away to Hanover' (Rowell ed., 1994, p. 54). Thanks to J. T. Grein and Max Hecht the soldiers were back in time to appear (as ordinary citizens) that evening, though they were 'utterly worn out' (Gill, 1948, p. 32) and went soundly to sleep in the wings between their entrances. There were difficulties with the female supers too, as they were 'too large for our costumes' (p. 61). As with all casts made up of different nationalities there were language problems, which were more acute with casual than with leading players. Constance Collier described how 'our English stage manager ... invented a kind of Esperanto' finding 'the equivalent sound in the German language' for each cue. Unfortunately at full rehearsal it was discovered that the cue words often occurred 'several times in the speeches, and the crowd dashed on regardless' (1929, p. 190). Tree had brought his own key staff with him (e.g. consulting electrical engineer Mr Digby), who then had to work with the theatre's own employees.

The opening performance of *Richard II* went smoothly, though the 'beautiful horses' most generously provided by the army became nervous in the 'unfamiliar surroundings' (Gill, 1948, p. 37) – as too were the cast at the prospect of performing in front of 'Little Willie' as Robert Atkins called the Kaiser. According to Atkins, who had replaced Fred Lewis as the Gardener at short notice, there was 'no applause unless the Kaiser's hands dictated' (Rowell ed., 1974, p. 54) and when, after the fall of the curtain on the garden scene, it came it brought with it immense relief. Reports in the English press suggested a more spontaneous response: 'a marked exception was made, enthusiastic applause breaking forth from every part of the crowded house after many of the scenes' (*Era*, 20 April 1907), but the *Tribune* (15 April 1907) observed that at *Twelfth Night* (which the Kaiser did not attend) on 12 April the 'audience was freer from restrictions and more determined to enjoy whatever was set before them'. *Tribune* also reported that the German 'critics hardly [had] a good word to say of *Richard II*. According to Ernst Stern the 'most reactionary band of all were the theatre critics', who behaved like despots defending 'the nation's literary traditions and treasures' (1951, p. 73). In reality Tree's 'joyous pilgrimage' was a pilgrim's progress from snare to snare. Like Macready on his last visit to the United States, Tree was beset by national, political and personal rivalries. Relations between Germany and England veered uneasily between fraternity and rivalry; in Germany there were powerful elements (the critics, described by Playfair as 'vitriolic', 1930, p. 152) determined to assert the supremacy of their own culture and disinclined to praise anyone else's and others (the Junkers) who despised the whole business of 'Theaterpolitick'.

Trilby and *The Merry Wives of Windsor* were well received by the German audiences. The Kaiser returned for *Hamlet*, in the title role of which Tree's reading was (in his own words) 'inclined to be Germanic in tone'. Tree admitted that he would like to 'play Hamlet in the German language' and had studied the part with that in mind (*Daily Mail*, 21 March 1907), but he did not seize the opportunity of doing so in Berlin. Nigel Playfair, who was suddenly promoted from Second Gravedigger to First, went on without rehearsal and without Yorick's skull, which had been 'smashed to pieces' (Collier, 1929, p. 191) by antagonistic stage hands. The set for *Hamlet* was by Tree's standards very simple and attracted Reinhardt's particular interest, though he doubted if the 'sans-scenery' style would ever 'go beyond the experimental stage' (*Standard*, 6 April 1907). It was unusual for Tree to be perceived as an experimenter, but his experience two nights later when *Antony and Cleopatra*, the play the Kaiser had particularly asked to see, was performed, probably dampened his enthusiasm for elaborate scenery.

Tree's production of *Antony and Cleopatra* comprised ten scenes, which at His Majesty's were changed swiftly and silently by stage staff, who were accustomed to the task. In Berlin the same smoothness could hardly be expected for a single gala-performance, but the problem was aggravated by the truculence of the local crew. Tree, already tense, was irritated by the desultory way in which a stagehand was looking for somewhere to put his beer and gave the man 'a slight push to hurry him up', the beer was spilt and the rest of the staff, regarding this 'as an international incident' (Collier, 1929, p. 191) walked out. In Constance Collier's ring-side account: an hour elapsed; the German Emperor, unaware of the circumstances, was becoming impatient; it was decided to finish the play on the existing set for the market-place; at the end of the performance

Wilhelm sent for the English actors, presented Tree with a decoration and Viola Tree and Constance Collier with bracelets (of diamonds and sapphires); there were ominous noises from the auditorium where students were breaking up benches; the Kaiser led Tree and Collier into the royal box; 'in deference to their Emperor's express desire' (p. 193) his riotous subjects were subdued and issued 'a great cheer'.

Tree still went on to entertain over two hundred guests at the Hotel Bristol and he and his daughter were received at the British embassy (*Era*, 20 April 1907), but the visit had been closer to a disaster than a diplomatic triumph. Rarely an object of sympathy (except for his deformed arm), the Kaiser was in an awkward predicament, knowing, as Robert Atkins put it, that 'Edward VII had one eye cocked upon the nature of the German's reception of his leading actor manager' (Rowell ed., 1994, p. 55).

Such was the drama surrounding Tree's visit that any attempt to assess what happened on the stage was and remains secondary. No more of a natural Shakespearian actor than Irving, who on his first American tour skilfully judged how many Shakespeare roles to play and where and when to play them, Tree took on five major roles with only Svengali from the modern repertoire. No doubt Tree felt that, given Germany's known interest in Shakespeare, this was appropriate, but he may – inadvertently – have fed some sense that a challenge was being mounted, but in any case he was not an actor of sufficient calibre to dominate the stage before such an audience. Tree's company acquitted themselves well, but were not outstanding. That left the productions. The Germans took exception to: the interpolated scenes (Richard II and Bolingbroke still progressed through the streets of London as in Charles Kean's day), the ravages of the text, the underplaying of the comedy – but the straining after melodramatic effects elsewhere – and the incidental music. Tree was unlucky to arrive in Berlin when Reinhardt had succeeded in accommodating Shakespeare's timeless insights into human nature in a style which combined atmospheric (symbolist) use of colour and modern techniques (the revolving stage) in a manner appropriate to the individual play. With Reinhardt experimentation and popular appeal went hand in hand and he created 'what many thought to be the characteristic style of Shakespearian performance for the twentieth century' (Styan, 1982, p. 52). Nevertheless there was no denying the scale of Tree's achievement in transporting and staging five Shakespeare productions (plus *Trilby*) and furthermore doing so on a commercial basis. As Robert Atkins observed: 'The German press was appreciative but guarded, the

main wonder being that one man could do so much and so well without
state aid' (Rowell ed., 1974, p. 55).

For Tree, publicly at least, the visit to Berlin was never anything less than a
triumph. That it probably helped him secure a knighthood, which he had
every reason to expect anyway, reflects the potency of the honours system
as a form of (or alternative to) state patronage, especially at a time when
leading actors zealously prized their profession's enhanced social status.
When Edward VII died, Tree said of the invitation which he received
to the funeral: 'I don't care a rap about the invitation, but I should have
been damned angry if they hadn't sent it' (Pearson, 1956, p. 222). The funeral of one monarch meant the coronation of another and fortunate
was the actor–manager who had two such occasions within a decade.
Charles Lander had made 'the following suggestion' that 'Henry VIII
would be an excellent play for that great character actor your husband [as
Wolsey]' to Maud Tree in November 1908.[6] Edward VII died on 6 May
1910. Tree's production of *King Henry VIII* (Booth, 1981, pp. 127–60)
opened on 1 September, late enough to show respect for the deceased
king, but in time to catch the growing excitement about his successor's
forthcoming coronation (22 June 1911) and achieve an eventual run of
252 performances and a profit of £19,282 6s 1d.[7] Arthur Bourchier grew
a – much publicised – beard to play Henry VIII giving such a successful
performance that Reinhardt, who had come to London principally to
see Granville Barker's production of *The Winter's Tale*, was so impressed
'that in all seriousness he suggested that Bourchier should learn German
and come to Berlin to play him' (Stern, 1951, p. 101). Amongst the first
night audience at His Majesty's, at a time of year when many members of society were otherwise engaged on the grouse moors, *Vanity Fair*
(10 September 1910) noticed the Ranee of Sarawak, Sir Arthur and Lady
Conan Doyle and Prince Francis of Teck, brother of the new queen.

As Princess May of Teck, Queen Mary had been an enthusiastic playgoer, celebrating her birthday one year at the Lyceum Theatre, where
Irving had the Beefsteak Room decorated in the 'pink and white of May'
and presented her with 'an exquisite little set of *Shakespeare* specially bound
in white vellum by Zaehndorf, with markers in blush-rose silk' (Stoker,
1906, vol. 1, p. 311). On 17 May 1911 King George V and Queen Mary
attended a command performance of Bulwer Lytton's 1840 *Money* at
Drury Lane, with the Kaiser amongst their guests. According to Arthur

Bourchier, an old Etonian who had taken the lead in the formation of the Oxford University Dramatic Society in 1885 (Carpenter, 1985), the 'original suggestion' for the Coronation Gala came from 'the late Prince Francis of Teck, whose devotion to the English stage was quite remarkable' (*Daily Telegraph*, 17 June 1911). The prince 'undertook to bring the matter to the notice of His Majesty', who gave it his approval and 'the next step' was 'to see Sir Herbert Tree to whom as the leader of the theatrical profession further measures would naturally be entrusted'. Bourchier went on to express the hope that 'in the Gala Performance and in the recognition it involves of the English stage by the King and Queen, may be detected a foreshadowing of that National Theatre for the establishment of which so many of us are working heart and soul'.

Amongst the many 'working heart and soul' for a National Theatre there was a marked divergence of view between the traditionalists and the progressives, but though the former dominated the Executive Committee and the General Committee constituted to organise the gala, the latter were represented. The centrepiece of the programme, which included a prologue, the letter scene from *The Merry Wives of Windsor*, Act 2 of T. W. Robertson's *David Garrick*, Jonson's masque *A Vision of Delight*, and scenes from Sheridan's *The Critic*, was the Forum scene from *Julius Caesar*, produced by Granville Barker with Tree as Mark Antony and a crowd peopled by all the leading actors of the day. Tree's tone towards Granville Barker suggests aloofness spiced with mockery:

For once I step aside and play second fiddle in my own theatre, and every one of us passes into the puissant hands of Mr Granville Barker, and, to give you some idea of that gentleman's amazing thoroughness, he has got out a book of stage directions for the Forum Scene, which runs to 24 closely printed pages. In the scene of 'Julius Caesar' there are to be 300 people on at one time. Everyone of that number has a 'part' however slight and each man's 'business' is differentiated from another. (*Standard*, 20 June 1911)

Befitting such an occasion, just before 8.30 pm on 27 June 'The King and Queen' arrived at His Majesty's Theatre 'in the State carriage, with an accompanying escort of the Life Guards' and inside the auditorium 'burly Beefeaters, armed with their pikes, were stationed at the line which divided these stalls [occupied by guests] from those occupied by the general public' (*Era*, 29 June 1911). Amongst the guests were the Crown Prince and Princess of Germany, though they were no doubt occupying a more elevated position. Tree paid a high price for these prestigious occasions. The 1911 Coronation (Shakespeare) Festival, including the gala performance, resulted in 'a loss of £3,173 11*s* 5*d*' (Rowell, 1975, p. 79). The theatre could be said to be subsidising the monarchy.

Many of those present at His Majesty's Theatre that night had attended the Shakespeare Ball in the Albert Hall on 20 June. The moving force behind the ball was Mrs George Cornwallis-West (Winston Churchill's American-born mother), who was chairman of the ten-strong (all female) committee, all but three of whom were titled, by virtue of being married either to an aristocrat or to a knighted actor. The purpose of the ball was to raise money for the Shakespeare Memorial National Theatre, a cause in which – after much wrangling – the foundation of a National Theatre was intrinsically linked with Shakespeare's name. Seeking consolation from the death of her first husband, Lord Randolph Churchill, the future Mrs Cornwallis-West had set up the *Anglo-Saxon Review* through which she met William Archer who recruited her for his National Theatre campaign, in aid of which she even wrote a play, *His Borrowed Plumes* (Bryan, 1974) thereby setting a precedent for Shaw's *The Dark Lady of the Sonnets* (1910).

For most of those who attended it the Shakespeare Ball was principally a glittering social event, but it succeeded in raising £10,000 for the Shakespeare Memorial National Theatre, of which Lord Lytton wrote:

If the desire to erect a memorial is in itself an expression of the universal instinct in man for worship, the form which the Memorial is to take is evidence of the prevailing opinion that the plays of Shakespeare can best be studied and appreciated on the stage for which they were written. So long as the production of these plays is left to the private enterprise of individual managers the public will be without the means of paying constant homage to the greatest of English dramatists. (Cornwallis-West ed., 1912, p. 23)

Lytton had identified the one irrefutable advantage, which an endowed and/or subsidised theatre had over private enterprise: it was 'constant'. However effective actor–managers might be at staging Shakespeare, and during the past seventy-five years they had overall been immensely successful, there was no assurance of continuous provision. This a National Theatre would ensure. Lytton's use of 'studied and appreciated' was indicative of the fact that such a theatre would be 'an educational and cultural institution', to use Stern's description of the pre-Reinhardt German stage, rather than a place of popular entertainment.

Mrs Cornwallis-West produced a magnificent *Shakespeare Memorial Souvenir of the Shakespeare Ball*, in which articles by G. B. Shaw,

G. K. Chesterton and Israel Gollancz are interwoven with portraits of the aristocratic participants, such as that of Mrs Cornwallis-West herself as Olivia by John Lavery. The centrepiece of the ball was a great procession, arranged by Tree's pageant-master Louis Napoleon Parker, of Queen Elizabeth and her court in which forty lineal descendants took part. There was also a series of quadrilles on Shakespearian plays or groups of characters. Lady Tree was in charge of the 'Quadrille of Shakespeare's Lovers', which included Hamlet (F. E. Smith), the Dark Lady of the Sonnets (Lillah McCarthy), Oberon (Viola Tree) and Shakespeare himself (the Duke of Marlborough). Although King George V declined an invitation, over seventy royal guests attended, headed by the German Crown Prince and Crown Princess. The prominence of the Shakespeare ball in the 1911 coronation festivities indicated that Shakespeare had reached the heart of the British establishment, of which the theatre was at last a part with the prospect of institutionalised membership in sight. With so many dignitaries from overseas present, the ball was also an exultation of Shakespeare 'for our honour among foreign nations'.

Buoyed up by her triumph at the ball, Mrs Cornwallis-West went on to mount an exposition called Shakespeare's England (O'Connor, 1987) at Earl's Court the next year, a commercial venture the profits of which were destined for the Shakespeare Memorial National Theatre. The two principal features, both of them free standing, were reconstructions of the first Globe Theatre and of Plymouth harbour complete with the *Revenge*. The latter served as the background for the visit by the king and queen on Armada day (20 July) 1912 and a speech by Winston Churchill, for whom, as First Sea Lord, the present German navy was a greater preoccupation than the Spanish armada. For Louis Napoleon Parker (1928, pp. 239–40) a visit on the same day as the Empress Eugénie was – in view of his middle name – a happy augury for his forthcoming pageant drama *Drake* with Tree at His Majesty's.

The Globe Theatre, designed by Edwin Lutyens, who had been responsible for the decorations in the Albert Hall for the Shakespeare ball, failed to win much professional or popular support. Patrick Kirwan, an Irish-born actor–manager whose Idyllic Players specialised in outdoor performances, provided half-hour-long performances of extracts from plays by Shakespeare and a few contemporaries, but the whole venture was received with contempt by William Poel, the doyen of Elizabethans, who observed 'several errors' in the reconstruction and wrote of the excerpt 'The Tricking of Malvolio': 'it is impossible that so many mistakes could have been crammed into a single scene of "Twelfth Night"'

(1913, pp. 14–15). Far from making a surplus, Shakespeare's England was sinking deep into financial trouble. Mrs Cornwallis-West called in C. B. Cochran, described by W. Bridges Adams, who was one of Kirwan's company at Earl's Court, as 'a splendid tough' (Speaight ed., 1971, p. 92). 'Cockie', as he was known, was a showman, whose successes included Reinhardt's *The Miracle* with Lady Diana Manners at Olympia; faced with the challenge of filling the huge Empress Hall, Cochran, undeterred by the absence of any discernible connection with Shakespeare's England, imported a circus consisting mainly of continental acts. The crowds flocked in but left 'the Britain of the Bard comparatively deserted' (Heppner, 1969, p. 69).

The indifference which the crowds displayed for a piece of fabricated national heritage created, not entirely disinterestedly, by a leading member of society for the foundation of a state institution, reflected a fissure in the nation. Beneath the conspicuous display 'of Imperial England, beribboned, bestarred and splendid' (Dangerfield, 1936, p. 378) social and political tensions were mounting. The challenge to the power of the House of Lords preceded the accession of King George V. The suffragette movement was growing in strength and the Irish situation remained intractable. Lloyd George's 1911 National Insurance Act coincided with a rapid increase in trades union membership (from 2,369,067 to 3,918,809 between 1910 and 1914). The dispute in the coalmines during the early months of 1912 was followed by unrest in other industries and by 1914 the Triple Alliance (miners, railwaymen and transport workers) threatened what was tantamount to a general strike. Even without the intervention of an assassin in Sarajevo, change was inevitable.

IMPERIAL PREFERENCE

Within months of his coronation in London the King–Emperor enacted another imperial pageant at the Delhi durbar on 12 December 1911. George V's announcement that the seat of government was to be transferred from Calcutta to Delhi (another opportunity for Lutyens) might be seen as an indication that imperial power could be exercised more effectively away from its centre. Calcutta had always been the theatrical centre of colonial India, though British actors who travelled that far naturally played in other cities too. Sushil Kumar Mukerjee writes that: 'When the English came to Calcutta they brought with them the plays of William Shakespeare' (1982, p. 3). Constructed in 1813, the elegant Chowringhee Theatre played host to visiting English actors, Mrs Esther

Leach 'The Indian Siddons' being the most favoured, until it was burnt down and the new Sans Souci took its place (Mrs Leach again) in 1841. There in August 1848 'something as yet unheard-of happened'; the manager James Barry, desperate to find an attraction, cast the young Bengali Baboo Bustomchurn Addy as Othello with Mrs Anderson (Mrs Leach's daughter) as Desdemona (Chatterjee and Singh, 1999, p. 75). The *Bengal Hukaru* (19 August) hailed 'Shakespeare, exiled from the country he honours so much, seek[ing] asylum on the Calcutta boards' and reported a 'hearty welcome' from a large audience which included 'influential members of the civil service', evidence that Macaulay's 'Minute of 2 February 1835' on Indian Education was taking effect:

English is better worth knowing than Sanscrit or Arabic . . . We must at present do our best to form a class, who may be interpreters between us and the millions whom we govern: a class of persons, Indian in blood and colour, but English in taste, in opinions, in morals and intellect. (Young ed., 1952, p. 729)

When William Archer visited India he concluded 'in that we have succeeded' (1917, p. 246).

Indian universities placed Shakespeare on their syllabuses long before most of their English counterparts, at the University of Calcutta from its inauguration in 1857. If students were the most enthusiastic patrons of Shakespeare, Indian maharajahs and the British viceroy were the most influential. Daniel Bandmann, the German-born actor, who entitled his memoirs *An Actor's Tour or Seventy Thousand Miles with Shakespeare* recorded the request from the Marchioness of Ripon, the vicereine, to repeat *Hamlet* (1885, p. 127) and the Maharajah of Darbungha's splendid edition of Knight's Shakespeare on the table before them as they chatted about Shylock (p. 130). It was through Maurice E. Bandmann, whom he described as 'the son of an old German tragedian' (Holloway, 1979, p. 133) that John Holloway and Matheson Lang visited India at the time of the Delhi durbar. Though as Holloway realised there was 'no possibility of a Command performance . . . the royal presence did not hinder theatre-going' (p. 142). The English actors had to contend with difficult local conditions. They had brought full sets and costumes, but resolved to simplify the former and replace the latter with lighter versions made locally. Make-up ran, which was particularly difficult for Lang when he played Othello, but 'it was only the Shakespearean plays that attracted the native population. Whenever *Hamlet, Romeo and Juliet* or *The Merchant of Venice* was in the bill, the theatre was besieged by Indians, mostly young students from the Universities' (Lang, 1940, p. 99).

Also drawn to India to play a season 'coinciding with the visit of their Majesties' (Wilkie, nd, p. 112) was Alan Wilkie,[8] who claimed that his was 'the first fully-equipped Shakespearean company to tour east of Suez' though such equipment ('eighty tons of scenery') made heavy demands on transportation, but once this was dealt with and Wilkie and his company examined the Calcutta Grand Opera House 'we were not a little surprised to find a building fit to stand beside the majority of our own West End theatres' (*Thespian*, October 1913). What was true of the theatre was true in part of the audience:

the theatre presented the appearance of a fashionable audience in the West End... except that the gallery was filled with native students, and amongst the glistening shirt fronts and evening dresses of the Anglo-Indian in the stalls and circle could be seen a number of Rajahs in their turbans and silken and bejewelled costumes together with the Bengali magnates in their white Dhotis. The whole effect was a striking contrast to the last audience before which I had played only a few weeks earlier in England where the theatre was filled with beshawled and clogged Lancashire lasses and the men in their rough working garb. (Wilkie, nd, p. 119)

Another example of the diversity of audiences before whom an itinerant Shakespearian actor played came when Wilkie appeared (on Sunday evenings) 'at the Koh-I-Noor Theatre in the native quarter, to an audience comprised entirely of Bengalis' (p. 121). Shakespeare's direct emotional force and thrilling story line transcended barriers of time, culture, race and language. During 'the more pathetic and moving scenes of *Othello*, (whose colour doubtless added to their sympathies)', the audience wept 'openly and unashamed' and in *Macbeth* 'the realistic combat between Macbeth and Macduff aroused them to such a frenzy of excitement and panic that many of them dived under their seats and others made a mad rush for the door' (p. 121).

Both Lang and Wilkie proceeded eastwards, the latter progressing from India to Ceylon (Sri Lanka), Singapore, Hong Kong, Shanghai, China, Japan (with its magnificent new western-style Imperial Theatre). Such was the lure of the orient to British actors that *The Stage Year Book* published an article 'Theatrical Touring in the Far East by one who has tried it', giving useful information about the theatres, the length of the journeys, health and clothing: 'a topee is required... wear underclothing... you will be more cooler in the end' (1917, p. 43). Wilkie and his company travelled 30,000 miles in twenty months 'staging Shakespeare in many places for the first time and frequently to alien races whose enthusiastic appreciation testified once more that not only is Shakespeare for all time but for all people' (Wilkie, nd, p. 197). Wilkie's greatest distinction, for which he was awarded the CBE, was staging Shakespeare in Australia, where his Australian Shakespearian Company, launched on 20 September 1920, produced twenty-seven of the plays in ten years.

Wilkie succeeded in establishing an Australian-based Shakespearian company in a country which had continued to rely on visiting actors. Oscar Asche, the most celebrated Australian-born (in Geelong in 1872) actor pursued his career in England with Benson and Tree and eventually in management with his wife Lily Brayton, with whom he scored a great success in *The Taming of the Shrew*. According to Elisabeth Fagan, Asche 'always intended . . . to return to Australia in triumph' (1923, p. 53). This he succeeded in doing in 1909 with 'a full company, scenery, properties, and costumes' (Asche, 1929, p. 124) for seven plays, five of them by Shakespeare. *The Taming of the Shrew* played consistently to full houses, but in both Sydney and Melbourne *Othello* caused considerable agitation in audiences unfamiliar with it. As in India attendance by the monarch's representative was highly prized, with 'the Governor-General, Lord Dudley, and the State-Governor, Lord Chelmsford' attending the same performance of *The Taming of the Shrew* in Sydney. The Asches returned to Australia in 1912–13, soon after appearing in the Coronation Gala, with the addition of *The Merry Wives of Windsor* and *Kismet* to their repertoire. Asche's revival of *Antony and Cleopatra*, which took place at the Theatre Royal, Melbourne, was specifically designed to make maximum use of the great depth of the stage, but his debt to Tree's house-style is evident in the acknowledgements for scenery 'by Joseph and Phil Harker and the costumes by Percy Anderson', albeit 'carried out by B. J. Simmons' (Asche, 1929, p. 142). Another distinguished visitor from England operated on a more modest scale: Ellen Terry arrived in Melbourne towards the end of April 1914 and was still touring Australia with her Shakespeare lectures when war broke out in August. She wrote home: 'All engagements are being cancelled . . . Yet all professional folk are acting "for the war", or for various charities, "for love" ' (Craig and St. John, 1933, p. 291).

Lang, Wilkie and Asche were amongst the numerous English actors who stopped in South Africa en route to and/or from more distant destinations. The voyage to South Africa was usually enjoyable (far pleasanter than the Atlantic crossing), but fortunes in southern Africa depended very much on time and place. In 1892 Genevieve Ward toured successfully for nine months with twenty-six plays, even giving six Shakespeare plays in Johannesburg 'till then a thing unknown' (Ward, 1918, p. 172). Less fortunate was W. J. Holloway, who began his tour with *Othello* in Johannesburg on Boxing Day 1895 (Holloway, 1979, pp. 70–1). When Wilson Barrett reached Cape Town in May 1902 there were, in Lillah McCarthy's words, 'British soldiers eager to adore us – any of us' (1933, p. 48) and in 1906 Mrs Langtry's first visitor was 'Sir Starr Jameson, at that time Premier of the Union of South Africa' (1925, p. 254). Hayden Coffin was in a company whose arrival in South Africa coincided with the opening of 'the first Union parliament' (1930, p. 164) by the Duke of Connaught. The creation of the Union of South Africa did not eradicate the hostility between the British and Africkaan communities, which had resulted in the Boer War. Indeed as another war loomed in Europe, loyalties in South Africa were divided.

On 13 September 1913 Cedric Hardwicke sailed on the *Garth Castle* for South Africa as a member (ironically) of Frank Benson's 'North Company' – 'thirteen men...thirteen plays' (1961, p. 75) – opening in Capetown on 13 October and Johannesburg on 13 November, where they had recently been preceded by Asche and Lewis Waller, also in Shakespeare. The appetite for Shakespeare even amongst the English communities seemed to be satiated and audiences dwindled. At the end of the official Benson tour Henry Herbert, 'who did not relish sailing home quite so close to poverty', enlisted Hardwicke and others to 'play Shakespeare on the veldt' (p. 80), which, with their 'scenery loaded on to an ox wagon', they did with great success: 'No matter what the conditions were Shakespeare triumphed' (p. 80). They 'presented *Hamlet* in its entirety' (p. 81), lasting from 6 pm to 11 pm, and *As You Like* in the grounds of a hotel, near the Victoria Falls, where 'although the audience was small it enabled us to draw our money' (Hardwicke, 1932, p. 89). With the outbreak of war:

Shakespeare paled somewhat as a dramatist, in comparison with the spectacle that the generals were putting on, a mere two weeks' sailing away. The Wars of the Roses, as related by the Great William, could not hold an audience the way the big German victory at Tannenbaum did, and our revenues rapidly dwindled to vanishing point. But we struggled along until we reached the Orange Free State, where the inhabitants of the dorps were almost exclusively Boers. Then, as now, most of them had little love for Britain. Memories of the South African War still rankled. (Hardwicke, 1961, p. 84)

With vociferous 'pro-German elements in our audience' making the performances unrewarding as well as unprofitable, Hardwicke and his fellow players left for England, where all the men enlisted.

Concurrently with his North Company's tour of South Africa, Benson, whom Hardwicke described as 'an actor–manager with a mission . . . to present the classics, notably Shakespeare, in the provinces and the farthest corners of the British Empire, wherever there was the promise of an audience' (p. 71), was personally leading the Stratford-upon-Avon Players on a tour of North America with an entirely Shakespearian repertoire of nine plays (Trewin, 1960, pp. 276–7). The tour set a precedent being under the aegis of the Shakespeare Memorial Theatre, Stratford-upon-Avon, which had opened in 1879 (Beauman, 1982) and at which Benson had presented the annual festivals since 1886. The programme at His Majesty's Theatre, Montreal announced: 'This is the only endowed theatre among nations speaking the English tongue.'[9] Benson opened with one of his established successes, *Richard II*, in which his own performance in the title role had drawn forth a eulogy from C. E. Montague in the *Manchester Guardian* (4 December 1899; in Wells ed., 1997, pp. 165–70). The Montreal press was respectful, though hardly enthusiastic. The version of *Richard II* was 'admirably condensed'; the simplicity of the sets was noted (*Montreal Star*, 10 October 1913) and Benson's Richard was commended as 'a striking study in psychology' (*Montreal Telegraph*, 10 October 1913). In Toronto the tone was similar, but in Chicago, the Prairie city of which Irving had been so apprehensive and which was known to have a large anti-British element, the gloves were off. Benson's decision to avoid New York had caused comment, the *New York Times* concluding ironically that the Shakespeare Memorial Theatre had 'forbidden' its players to appear there 'because the stage of this city had fallen so low' (10 October 1913). If the strategy was to avoid the full rigour of American theatrical criticism, it failed. The *Daily News Chicago* (6 November 1913) derided Benson in *Richard II* as 'an impossible old gentleman . . . without any technical command of [his] art' and the *Record and Herald* (6 November 1913) dismissed his performance as 'hard, wooden, loud, graceless'. The same newspaper (9 November 1913) had no sympathy for 'a feeling in certain sensitive breasts that some sacred law of hospitality was broken by newspapers which printed the facts concerning Mr Benson's attempts last week to enact various important and exacting characters in the plays of Shakespeare'. Any expectation that an English actor appearing in Shakespeare was entitled to be loved by 'everybody born under the Union Jack and the Stars and Stripes' was rebuffed. Syracuse was tough, but St Louis and Baltimore kinder as was New Orleans where Archibald D. Flower, chairman of the Stratford governors, spoke of the significance of their visit:

We look upon Shakespeare as the greatest link for peace between the English-speaking nations of the world. His works are a world force. Shakespeare is universal. But to the English-speaking people he holds out the link which connects us all, no matter where the sun finds us. (*New Orleans Times Democracy*, March 1914)

In Edmonton Benson himself was reported as saying 'Canadians are never thought of but as loyal at home' and looking forward to the time when 'Great Britain and India and the United States shall be one [and] ... This vast empire imbued with inspiration of art, ready for responsibilities, will take the place it has deserved as mother of all races ... '[10] Benson's evocation of the Carlylean ideal of 'Saxondom', though no doubt genuinely felt, had an air of expediency, tinged with desperation, about it.

The Stratford-upon-Avon Players were not the only English troupe visiting Canada that winter. John Martin-Harvey also undertook an extensive tour with a sizeable repertoire in which Shakespeare was substantially represented. Martin-Harvey had come to Canada under the aegis of 'The British Canadian Theatrical Organisation Company' whose function he described as 'largely patriotic' (Martin-Harvey, 1933, p. 419). The long-term aim of this syndicate, which was 'sponsored by Mr. Francis Pryor and Carl Leyer', was eventually to organise a chain of theatres so that 'British theatrical companies' could undertake an 'all red' tour, so-called because of the colour in which the British empire was traditionally marked on maps. However in Canada, where the scheme was initiated, an immediate goal was to counteract 'secession from the British Empire [which] was seriously considered in certain provinces of the Dominion' (p. 423). Martin-Harvey had crossed the Atlantic on the *Empress of Ireland*, but exchanged his return passage with Laurence Irving and his wife Mabel Hackney who perished when she sank in the St Laurence Seaway on 29 May 1914. The Irvings had just completed a tour (under the same auspices as Martin-Harvey) of Canada (Brereton, 1922, p. 220).

In the three years between the coronation of King George V in June 1911 and the outbreak of war in August 1914, British actors toured the empire in unprecedented numbers, most of them performing at least some Shakespeare. With the Coronation Gala the theatre had enjoyed greater prominence than ever before at such a national event and actors who travelled to India and other parts of the empire may have felt that they were furthering that association, as well as earning a living. That in 1913 Benson should concurrently mount two tours to parts of the English-speaking world which were not entirely secure members of Saxondom, having previously only sent one troupe to the West Indies in 1904–5 and that in response to an offer of backing from a firm of banana importers, might with hindsight be seen as prescient, especially alongside Martin-Harvey and Laurence Irving also visiting Canada. It was certainly a timely rehearsal for the role the theatre was to be called upon to play during the Great War. Meanwhile in London the traditionalists and progressives were competing for control over the proposed Shakespeare Memorial National Theatre.

CHAPTER 7

The national arena: Granville Barker, Louis Calvert and Annie Horniman

THE SCHEME FOR A NATIONAL THEATRE

The foundation of a National Theatre provided the subtext and the pre-text for much that happened during and on the imperial stage. From the abolition of the patent theatres' monopoly in 1843 onwards the actor–managers who dominated the English stage adopted an ambivalent position towards a National Theatre, perceiving it as both a status symbol for their profession and a threat to their own position.

The early advocates for a National Theatre tended to be literary men of one sort and another. Bulwer Lytton, the driving force behind the 1832 Select Committee, the principal recommendation of which was to abolish a monopoly in the interests of free trade, nevertheless opposed the Benthamite view that people would always find money for their amusements and argued for 'the patronage of the state' (1833, vol. 1, p. 176). W. J. Fox, the politician, preacher and journalist with whom Sarah Adams Flower lived after her father Benjamin's death, had eulogised Macready's Shakespearian revivals at Covent Garden and Drury Lane, but argued:

When the process needs resources ordinarily beyond the reach of individuals, that collective power we term the State should interpose ... So far as the very conception of a national theatre exists in the public mind it is the suggestion of Mr Macready's management ... (in Garnett and Garnett, 1910, p. 250).

In 1848 bookseller and publisher, Effington Wilson, a supporter of Mechanics' Institutes, proposed a National Theatre and other advocates included Tom Taylor (1871), George Godwin (1878) and in 1879 William Gladstone before (in an open letter to the *Theatre*, 13 March 1879), and Matthew Arnold after, the London visit of the Comédie-Française, but J. R. Planché thought it was 'hopeless to expect government subsidy as in France' (1879, p. 4) as did Henry Irving who wrote to Godwin saying he had 'little, if any, doubt' about the desirability of a National Theatre, but thought it would be 'at present unadvisable to touch upon the subject of State subsidy with reference to the British Stage' (Godwin, 1878, pp. 26–8). The notion of setting up a National Theatre by endowment rather than state finance prevailed well into the twentieth century.

With the Lyceum Theatre increasingly regarded as the equivalent of a National Theatre, Irving was disinclined to see that designation applied elsewhere. For Irving the fact that William Archer, one of the authors of *The Fashionable Tragedian*, was a leading campaigner for a National Theatre can hardly have endeared the scheme to him. In 1907, two years after Irving's death and thirty after the publication of the offensive pamphlet, William Archer joined with Harley Granville Barker to produce *A National Theatre: Scheme and Estimates*. The fraternity of leading actor–managers, with Irving's son Harry alongside Bancroft, Hare and Tree, was suspicious and defensive, but, with the likes of Winston Churchill, with whose mother Archer had formed a literary attachment, expressing support, outright opposition was not a shrewd tactic. In their preface Archer and Barker used much of the familiar rhetoric: 'The acted drama ought to be, and indeed is, one of the great bonds of union between all the Anglo-Saxon peoples' (1907, p. ix); they proposed 'a National Theatre, worthy of the metropolis of the Empire', but though it would break away from 'the profit-seeking stage' in 'its ample, dignified, and liberal existence':

It must not even have the air of appealing to a specially literary and cultured class. It must be visibly and unmistakably a popular institution, making a large appeal to the whole community. (p. x)

The National Theatre then, like Irving's Lyceum and Tree's His Majesty's, would embrace the full social range, but of course it would differ from them in other fundamentals not least the replacement of the long run by the repertoire. This distinction was particularly significant for Shakespeare, whose plays attracted the huge attendances of which Tree was so proud. In the 'Schedule of Repertory', the – hypothetical – first season opened on 15 September with *King Richard II*, followed by *King Henry IV Part 1* on 17th, *King Henry IV Part 2* on 18th and *King Henry V* on 20th (p. 46). Benson, if no other manager, had achieved comparable feats, most famously at the Shakespeare Memorial Theatre, Stratford-upon-Avon in April 1901 when W. B. Yeats, for one, saw six history plays in a week. Part of the thinking behind opening with a cycle of four plays was that it would 'render almost imperative from the first the observance of a just standard of dignified moderation', whereas 'opening with a single Shakespearean production, the management might not unnaturally be tempted to aim at a degree of scenic luxury – as opposed to appropriateness – inconsistent with the idea of the Theatre' (p. 38). In other words it was part of the strategy for excluding the traditionalist from the National Theatre. In addition to the cycle there were to be five other Shakespeare plays: *The Tempest* 'as a beautiful poem, much neglected of late years', *The Taming of the Shrew* 'as a popular farce, showing the more prosaic and commonplace side of the poet's genius; and *Romeo and Juliet, Hamlet* and *As You Like It*, simply as immortal masterpieces which no English theatre can make too great haste to establish in its repertory' (p. 38). The 'Schedule of Repertory' for the first season (15 September to 1 August) listed thirty-four plays in all, a total of 363 performances of which 124 were of the nine Shakespeare plays (pp. 46–7). The number of performances per play was variable. There were to be twelve of *King Henry IV Part 1*, but only five of *King Henry IV Part 2*, which opened on the following night, raising the question why only half as many people would want to see *Part 2* as *Part 1*. *The Tempest,* though it did not start until 12 December had completed thirty-one performances when it brought the season to an end on 1 August. With such a huge repertoire, 'dignified moderation' would have been necessary for all the plays, even the 'Modern English Plays (since 1870)', which had been written for a very different type of theatre from Shakespeare's.

Allowing for the need to get the repertoire established, the number of plays in the first season would have been larger than subsequently. 'Certain plays' would be carried forward 'as belonging to the permanent substratum of the repertory – what is called in France the *répertoire courant*' (p. 39). In the case of Shakespeare, six plays 'on an average' would be revived each year and 'the whole list (save one) would be gone through once in four years'. This could be achieved because the canon (of thirty-seven plays) had been reduced to 'twenty-five plays, which ought never to be suffered for long to drop out of the repertory of an English National Theatre' (p. 39). *Titus Andronicus* was 'wholly unpresentable on the modern stage'; *Troilus and Cressida,Timon of Athens, Pericles* and the three parts of *Henry VI* were only capable of performance 'with doubtful advantage, after heroic manipulation', they could not 'possibly take a permanent place in the repertory of any theatre' though they might get an occasional revival 'at long intervals', as might '*The Two Gentlemen of Verona, The Comedy of Errors,* and *Love's Labour's Lost,* as immature productions'. There remained '*All's Well that Ends Well,* as likewise immature (in spite of retouching), and unacceptable in theme; and *Henry VIII*, as a formless pageant play, which has very little claim to rank as Shakespeare's' (p. 39). To exclude over one third of Shakespeare's plays from its repertoire (except for the occasional token performance of some of them) was a surprising policy for a National Theatre. True its repertoire would be much larger than Irving's or Tree's (remembering though the six plays in six days at Tree's Shakespeare Festivals), but would fall far short of Phelps and Benson. William Poel had staged some of the proscribed plays in the Elizabethan style for the Independent Theatre Society, the Elizabethan Stage Society (founded in 1895), summer schools at the Universities of Oxford and Cambridge and other organisations (Speaight, 1954, pp. 279–85). Even with so many less well-known plays discarded, there would be insufficient performances of the rest to cater for a popular audience. It would take the National Theatre a very long time to draw as many people to see Shakespeare as Tree did in one of his long runs at His Majesty's.

In the debate between the traditionalists and the progressives over the production of Shakespeare, the *Scheme and Estimates* was unequivocally on the side of the latter, but within the National Theatre campaign as a whole there were two rival camps competing for control of the movement and the supremacy of their Shakespearian principles. The complex and convoluted history of the National Theatre has been recounted by Geoffrey Whitworth (1951) and John Elsom and Nicholas Tomalin (1978). In addition to the National Theatre movement, the idea of a Shakespeare monument in London, which dated back to the 1864 National Shakespeare Committee, had been revived. The Shakespeare Memorial Committee was formed at a meeting in the Mansion House on 28 February 1905 and on 6 July of the six schemes under consideration it was decided to give priority to that for a statue, but 'the committee recommended that the idea that a small theatre for the furtherance of dramatic art and literature, and the performance of Elizabethan and other plays, be erected on land adjoining might be borne in mind', but such an edifice was to be modest and the committee did not adopt the scheme for a National Theatre, principally because of the very large sum of money involved (Whitworth, 1951, p. 46). According to William Poel the 'subsidiary project' for 'the erection of a building in which Shakespeare's plays could be acted without scenery . . . met with strong opposition from some members of the committee, and Sir Herbert Beerbohm Tree, as representing the dramatic profession, declared that he could not, and would not, countenance it' (1913, p. 231). The actor–managers were happier with a statue, which would in no way challenge their own position; a theatre, especially one devoted to the rival Elizabethan style of producing Shakespeare, was another matter.

On 19 May 1908 a public meeting at the Lyceum Theatre passed a resolution in favour of a National Theatre as a memorial to Shakespeare and steps were taken to amalgamate the Shakespeare Memorial Committee and the National Theatre Committee. The two general committees met at the Mansion House with the Lord Mayor presiding on 23 July and agreed to produce a prospectus, which was presented at a meeting of the (new, unified) General Committee at the Mansion House on 28 March 1909.

That 'Illustrated Handbook' for the Shakespeare Memorial National Theatre[1] listed the membership (nearly forty strong) of the Executive Committee under the chairmanship of the Rt Hon. The Lord Mayor of London, with the aristocracy (the Earl of Lytton whose ancestor Edward Bulwer Lytton had led theatrical reform, the Rt Hon. Alfred Lyttleton), the church (Bishop Boyd Carpenter), the stage (Tree, Bourchier, Forbes-Robertson, Martin-Harvey and Ellen Terry), dramatists (Pinero and Shaw), academics (Sidney Lee, Israel Gollancz as Hon. Sec.), philanthropists (Sir Carl Meyer Bt, who donated £70,000) and Archer and Granville Barker. Inevitably the handbook drew on *Scheme and Estimates*, but with the integration of Shakespeare in the National Theatre the patriotic tone was very much more pronounced with the bard being described as 'the supreme intellectual glory of our race' and Britain's 'greatest son' (p. 3). The first object was 'to keep the plays of Shakespeare in the repertory', and (less specific than Archer and Barker) 'all the poet's plays, with very few exceptions, would be frequently passed in review. No actable play would ever be left unacted (as is now frequently the case) for twenty or thirty years at a stretch' (p. 10). The prospects of some of the lesser plays still did not look too promising and, with the statutes binding the management 'to give (on an average) at least one Shakespearian performance a week', the annual tally might be on a truly modest scale.

The handbook contained illustrations of the Théâtre-Français, the Royal Playhouse in Berlin and comparable establishments in other countries, whose citizens 'are amazed to find in London no permanent home of Shakespearian drama' (p. 9), but at last 'Shakespeare, in short, would receive in his own country the constant and assiduous homage which he now receives in Germany' (p. 10). The words 'constant homage' were to be reprised by the Earl of Lytton for the Shakespeare Ball and though in that context he diplomatically forbore mention of Germany, comparison and competition with that country's record of Shakespearian productions was undoubtedly a major spur to the foundation of a National Theatre in Britain. As to whether the British National Theatre should resemble its European counterparts architecturally, the handbook was not specific except in its insistence that it should be imposing:

the Shakespeare National Theatre should be a building wholly different in character and aspect from any existing building . . . It ought to be one of the great public edifices of the Metropolis, bearing unmistakable testimony to the nation's reverence for its greatest poet and respect for the art to which his life and genius were devoted . . . It is a great reproach to England that it contains no theatre that can for a moment compare with the palaces devoted to drama in almost every foreign capital . . . (pp. 13–14)

London though was more than a nation's capital, it was the centre of a great empire and of English-speaking peoples in the larger Saxondom. In the section headed 'Government' the handbook declared: 'In order that the whole nation and the Empire at large may share in the ultimate control of the Theatre, it has been decided that the Governing Body shall be a large and widely-representative one' (p. 16). The full list of governors was earnest of this intent with representatives of six universities, the Royal Academy, the British Academy, the Workers' Educational Association, nine provincial cities and the Chairman of the Shakespeare Memorial Association, Stratford-upon-Avon. These nominations clearly reflected a determination that the National Theatre should belong to the whole nation, geographically and socially. The additional members betokened the larger stage on which a British National Theatre would operate: the High Commissioners for Canada, Australia and 'for any other federated Colonies' and 'the Ambassador of the United States' (pp. 23–4), 'that great English-speaking nation which justly claims its share in the heritage of Shakespeare's renown' (p. 16). The benefits of a National Theatre would flow forth from London: 'But the final and most substantial benefit the Shakespeare National Theatre would confer would lie in its pervasive influence on theatrical enterprise throughout the three kingdoms and the Empire' (p. 19). This was no doubt intended to encourage the millions of potential donors outside London to contribute to the appeal. This was made up of: £100,000 for the site; £150,000 for the building and equipment; £250,000 for endowment and a general category, which could be allocated 'at the discretion of the Committee' (p. 20).

The length of time which it would take to raise this amount did not discourage immediate speculation about the first director. Whereas Archer and Barker in their *Scheme and Estimates* had been dogmatic that the director of the National Theatre should not be an actor, the handbook was prepared to entertain the possibility, but required that 'the Director, if an actor, should in no case practise his art for fee or reward during his term of office' (p. 25). Without any history of state funding the British theatre did not have and was mistrustful of the administrative and directorial structure of its European counterparts: the Intendant in Germany and the General Administrator in France. Cary Mazer has unearthed the evidence of Tree's attempts 'to commandeer the SMNT to his own purposes during the pre-war period' (1983, p. 23), not only through overt strategies such as his Annual Shakespeare Festival and his response (a hugely successful revival of that 'formless pageant play' *Henry VIII* and the gala) to the 1911 coronation, but through committee-room politics culminating in the offer to 'sell his own playhouse and management to the SMNT' (p. 21).

GRANVILLE BARKER

The chief contender to run the Shakespeare Memorial National Theatre was Granville Barker, whose career had included acting Richard II and Marlowe's Edward II under William Poel's direction; creating many Shavian characters, notably Marchbanks in *Candida*; producing with J. E. Vedrenne three seasons of 'uncommercial drama' at the Court Theatre; writing a handful of plays; and in 1910 running a repertory season at the Duke of York's Theatre with the American impresario Charles Frohman, a leading member of the New York Theatrical Syndicate. What Barker had not done was to produce Shakespeare and Tree had some justification for thinking (Pearson, 1956, p. 159) that his rival's decision to do so was partly to add a vital credential to his qualifications for the post as director of the Shakespeare Memorial National Theatre.

Barker (Salmon, 1983; Kennedy, 1989) had to operate within the commercial theatre, but succeeded in securing the patronage of Lord Lucas 'who had recently sold his pig-farm' (Greif, 1980, p. 1) and Lord Howard de Walden, who had sponsored other managers, notably Herbert Trench at the Haymarket Theatre where his revival of *King Lear*, with scenery by Charles Ricketts, was greeted by Max Beerbohm as 'excellent high courage' (1970, p. 483). Although Barker and his (first) wife Lillah McCarthy had worked with Poel, he was not a thoroughgoing

Elizabethan, saying of *Twelfth Night* 'We shall not save our souls by being Elizabethan' (in Dymkowski, 1986, p. 29). Instead he reworked Elizabethan principles in a contemporary style. Thus the stage for his first production at the Savoy Theatre, *The Winter's Tale* (21 September 1912), was divided into three acting areas: 'the platform constructed over the orchestra pit . . . struck the most obviously Elizabethan note', behind it lay the main proscenium stage at the back of which – four steps up – was 'the inset stage' (Bartholomeusz, 1982, p. 146). A three-sided frame of white classical columns, with green-gold curtains hung between them, served for Sicilia and the shepherd's cottage in Bohemia was likened by one critic to 'a modern bungalow from the Ideal Homes exhibition' (in Trewin, 1964, p. 53). The extravagant costumes, in bold tones of emerald, magenta, lemon and scarlet, belonged to no particular place or period. The lighting was bright throughout (footlights had been abolished). The text (only six lines were cut) was spoken swiftly and naturally, but with due attention to the verse structure. As J. L. Styan put it 'nothing touched reality'. Various influences and attributions were suggested – Art Nouveau, Max Reinhardt, Post-Impressionism – but, whatever else it may have been Barker's Shakespeare was indisputably a rejection of traditional scenic (actor–manager) Shakespeare. Instead of swamping the audience with weltering detail, Barker tried to release the imagination into ' a world of artifice' (Styan, 1983, p. 86). Such success as *The Winter's Tale* had enjoyed in the nineteenth century had been due, as with Charles Kean and Charles Calvert, to the attraction of elaborate antiquarian scenery; in 1912 it was a little-known play with, it turned out, little appeal. Barker's production was withdrawn after six weeks, but even so it had achieved more performances than would any single Shakespeare play in a year under his *Scheme and Estimates for a National Theatre*.

Barker's next choice, *Twelfth Night*, was much more familiar, indeed it was encrusted with tradition and business. He stripped all of that away and let Shakespeare 'be spoken as he wrote . . . and I do not believe that three hours of such unmeasured enjoyment are to be spent in any theatre in London' (*Nation*, 23 November 1912; in Evans ed., 1968, pp. 114–15). The public concurred and Barker was rewarded with a run of 137 performances, more than the combined total for the nine Shakespeare plays in the proposed repertoire for the first season of the National Theatre. Another indicator of the success of Barker's *Twelfth Night* was the production by the Hong-Kong Mummers 'In the New Way: Barker Shakespeare in Hong-Kong', which virtually replicated the Savoy sets (*Sketch*, 24 December 1913). There was a gap of over a year before

Barker's next Shakespearian revival at the Savoy Theatre: *A Midsummer Night's Dream* on 6 February 1914. The wood, so beloved of Victorian scene and costume designers, was a green velvet mound overhung with a vast terra-cotta wreath flickering with fireflies and glow-worms, the habitat of 'ormolu fairies, looking as though they had been detached from some fantastic, bristling old clock' (Desmond MacCarthy in Trewin, 1964, p. 57). Barker's *A Midsummer Night's Dream* ran for ninety-nine performances. These three productions, which Dennis Kennedy describes as synthesising 'the reforming modes of stagecraft that had appeared since 1890' (1993, p. 77), would have been worthy and durable additions to the *répertoire courant* of a National Theatre.

His three Shakespeare productions undoubtedly enhanced Barker's candidature for the directorship of the Shakespeare Memorial National Theatre, but Lillah McCarthy did not confine her efforts on her husband's behalf to the stage, where she appeared as Hermione, Viola and Helena. Having secured Carl Mayer's donation of £70,000 for the National Theatre, McCarthy, 'the princess of promoters' (Kennedy, 1989, p. 194), no doubt felt that such a handsome contribution should weigh in Barker's favour. McCarthy was every bit as aware as Tree of the importance of royal patronage:

I wished very much that Their Majesties, the King and Queen, should see the play, and therefore wrote to a friend at Court. He replied telling me that he shared my wish, that he held the opinion that the Sovereign of a country should be associated with what is best in art and there could be no two opinions about the beauty of 'A Midsummer Night's Dream.' He ended up by saying that he would do his best. He did, and was successful. Their Majesties came and I have reason to believe were pleased with the play. (1933, p. 175)

THE NEW THEATRE, NEW YORK

Barker had already received an offer to run what was conceived as the equivalent to a national theatre. Amongst the playhouses illustrated in the handbook for the Shakespeare Memorial National Theatre was the New Theatre, New York. That it did not look out of place amongst its European counterparts was attributable in some measure at least to the influence of Heinrich Conried, a German immigrant, who had been elected managing director of the Metropolitan Opera House in 1903. When William Archer made a (return) visit to the United States in 1907 he detected that 'the preponderance [in the theatre] of power had quite decidedly shifted from the foreign to the American' (*McClure's*

Magazine, November 1909). Although the New Theatre was an expression of American national identity and pride, it was beholden to European models not just for its architecture. Archer and Barker had produced an American edition of *Scheme and Estimates for a National Theatre* with a new 'Preface for America':

The Repertory set forth in Section IV is naturally not in the least like that we should have sketched had we had an American theatre in view... The tendency to be guarded against in America – if I may venture to say so – is too great hospitality towards foreign works, and a lack of reasonable discrimination in favour of native authors...

It would, of course, be quite inappropriate to open an American theatre with Shakespeare's four great histories. Every effort should be made, it seems to me, to secure a drama of American history adequate to the occasion; but if no good play of the type were forthcoming... the obvious course would be to fall back upon *Hamlet*, or *Julius Caesar*, or *A Winter's Tale*, and let Shakespeare the world-genius, as distinct from Shakespeare the Briton, consecrate the new Temple of Art. (1908, pp. iv–v)

There can have been little doubt in anyone's mind that 'the new Temple of Art' was the New Theatre, popularly known as the 'Millionaires' Theatre' because of its thirty wealthy benefactors. It also had the endorsement of Theodore Roosevelt who sent his presidential good wishes to the ceremony for which Richard Watson Gilder had composed his poem 'Shakespeare's New Home', subtitled 'For the Laying of the Corner-Stone of the National (or New) Theater'.[2] The prospectus proclaimed that the New Theatre was devoted to:

The cause of art only, and not in any way the cause of profit... The classical repertoire as well as modern plays shall be performed by a Stock Company, in a manner worthy of the best traditions of the stage.[3]

Conceived on an operatic scale, 'Shakespeare's New Home', was 'a palatial building... to rival in magnificence Vienna Theater, or the Paris Opera House' (Shattuck, 1987, p. 276), with a stage 102 feet wide and 66 feet deep (incorporating a revolve) and a proscenium opening $41\frac{1}{2}$ feet wide by 40 feet high. The ornate auditorium accommodated 2,200 spectators.

Early in 1908 Granville Barker was invited to inspect the rising edifice with a view to becoming its director. Realising that the New Theatre lacked the intimacy which he prized, Barker declined (*Town and Country*, 25 January 1908). Had he assumed the directorship of this or any other national theatre, Barker was clear how he saw his role: 'The director of the theatre should be an autocrat, and that his autocracy may be effective it must be strictly limited' (1922, p. 182). It seems unlikely that the man who did take the job on fitted this mould. Winthrop Ames, a patrician Harvard graduate, had run the Castle Theatre, Boston, but was otherwise thin in practical experience. A frequent visitor to Europe, between November 1907 and January 1908 (before being appointed to the New Theatre) Ames inspected eighty-eight theatres and seven concert halls, attending sixty-seven dramatic and five musical performances. He saw *As You Like It* (Oscar Asche and Lily Brayton) at His Majesty's Theatre in London, *A Midsummer Night's Dream* and *Twelfth Night* at the Deutsches Theater in Berlin and *Measure for Measure* at the Schiller Theater in Dusseldorf.[4] Like Thomas Barry over three-score years earlier, Ames also secured plays and actors. He postulated a season on 'The Development of the English Drama' with a stock company with traditional types 'Heavy and Poetic Lead', 'Ingenue Lead' and 'Character Lead and Grande Dame'. Prior to a visit to London he speculated to William Archer whether Robert Loraine, Oscar Asche, C. Aubrey Smith, Henry Ainley and Violet Vanbrugh might be persuaded to take up engagements at the New Theatre.[5]

The flowering of social and society drama (made up of give-and-take short speeches) in the 1890s had brought a new generation of players and a new style of playing to the fore in England and America. When this generation turned to Shakespeare the result could range from the revelational (Barker) to the unfortunate (Janet Achurch's Cleopatra opposite Louis Calvert's Antony in 1897). Partly in response to this (and no doubt partly to enhance his own status) in 1904 Tree had founded the Academy of Dramatic Art, initially at His Majesty's Theatre and then in its own Gower Street premises, with Kenneth Barnes (Violet Vanbrugh's brother) becoming its principal in 1909. Of the situation in America Archer wrote: 'The American stage . . . had fallen behind. For instance, the Shakespearian tradition was in danger of extinction' (*McClure's Magazine*, November 1909) and Henry Austen Clapp bemoaned the want of 'technical training' and the tendency of even Richard Mansfield in his celebrated performance of Henry V to 'misplace and misproportion his emphasis' (1902, p. 75). Clearly if the New Theatre was going to be 'Shakespeare's New Home', it needed expertise and that was most likely to be found in Shakespeare's homeland.

Ames appointed two stage-managers to take charge of producing 'Shakespearian and classical performances' and 'modern dramas' respectively.[6] The appointees were Louis Calvert, son of Charles, and George Foster Platt. Calvert's credentials were impressive, embracing as they did lavish productions with Tree and Richard Flanagan (in Manchester) and more innovative work such as *Richard II* 'performed without scenery, thus reproducing the conditions of the Elizabethan stage' for the Manchester Committee of the Independent Theatre in February 1895 (Foulkes, 1992b). Calvert had also created Shaw's Broadbent in *John Bull's Other Island* and Undershaft in *Major Barbara*. Prior to his departure for New York Calvert was accorded dinners at the Hotel Metropole and the Garrick Club, the latter attended by Arthur Bourchier, Robert Loraine, William Archer and Austin Brereton, with Tree as host (*New York Dramatic Mirror*, 24 July 1909).

The situation in which Calvert found himself at the New Theatre was fraught with difficulties. A 'drama of American history adequate to the occasion' not having been forthcoming, the New Theatre opened on 8 November 1909 with a work of Shakespeare's 'world-genius' classification: *Antony and Cleopatra*. This was of course a play which Calvert knew well both as an actor and director, but it was clear that its selection had been determined by the casting of E. H. Sothern (son of E. A., celebrated as Lord Dundreary in Tom Taylor's *Our American Cousin*) and his English-born wife, Julia Marlowe. Their weekly salaries of $2,800 each dwarfed Calvert's $379[7] and reflected their status. Miss Marlowe, who was in the habit of preparing an elaborate promptbook complete with detailed business (not only for herself), soon challenged Calvert's authority:

The stage manager had been brought from England, where he was of much renown, but he was quite unacquainted with American ways, unaware of the magnitude of his task, unprepared either mentally or by experience with the ideas of Miss Marlowe and Mr Sothern as to Shakespeare. (Russell, 1926, p. 469)

When it came to 'open rupture' with the stars, for such they were, declaring that they could not go on, Calvert was relieved of his duties for the production. Whether he could have saved the day is doubtful. With a budget of $41,309,[8] the elaborate scenery had been constructed by Ernest Albert from colour drawings by Jules Guérin. The opening night lasted from 8.30 pm to 12.55 am, the endurance of the audience being further tried by the theatre's dire acoustics and the deficiencies of the leading players, who did not complete their contracts for the rest of the season.

Calvert resumed his duties with *Twelfth Night* (21 January 1910) in which he also played Sir Toby indulging like most of the cast in strained business and forced hilarity, but with *The Winter's Tale* on 28 March Shakespeare was fittingly housed in his 'New Home'. The production was a collaborative undertaking, with Winthrop Ames in overall command and E. Hamilton Bell designing the set and décor, which was the concept of the literary director, John Corbin, author of *An American in Oxford* (1902) and *A New Portrait of Shakespeare* (1903). The staging (budget $13,172) shared significant features with Barker's, which it pre-dated by two years: 'a platform, or apron, that extended over the footlights and orchestra pit, and an inner stage curtained with tapestries and surmounted by a balcony extending on three sides of a square' (*New York Times*, 29 March 1910). The costumes were Elizabethan. Calvert was responsible for the performances, drawing praise for 'his group-ing... the dance of the shepherds and shepherdesses... keep[ing] the players well to the front of the stage – which has been built over the orchestra pit at the New Theater, a great aid to acoustics – and he keeps well to the front also the primary motive of this revival, the swift, il-lusive, poetic narration of Shakespeare's romantic fable' (Eaton, 1910, pp. 85–6). Calvert had created 'one of those rarely enjoyable ensemble companies' (*New York Dramatic Mirror*, 9 April 1910) with an American and English (Edith Wynne Mathison as Hermione and Rose Coghlan, who had been in Charles Calvert's Manchester company, as Paulina) cast. Despite Calvert's success with *The Winter's Tale*, his contribution to *The Merry Wives of Windsor* (14 November 1910), which was produced by Platt, was limited to playing Falstaff, a role in which he had many ad-mirers (including James Agate), but this time the fat knight eluded him. Though it survived longer as a building, the New Theatre's pretensions to being a national theatre expired within two years. Calvert spent most of the remainder of his career in America and his manual *Problems of the Actor* was published in New York (1918) before London (1919).

In what respects the British National Theatre, had it been built at the same period, would have resembled the New Theatre can only be guessed at. Granville Barker's influence after the merger of the National Theatre Committee with the Shakespeare Memorial Committee declined and, though he personally would not have favoured such a grandiose building, the photographs in the handbook and the section on architecture suggest that there were many who did. The inherent disinclination of wealthy Englishmen to sponsor the theatre may have saved the country from a long-to-be-regretted architectural mistake.

ANNIE HORNIMAN

There were exceptions to this rule and it has been remarked that such benefaction as the British Theatre enjoyed was derived from the two basic commodities of tea and milk, as represented respectively by Miss Horniman and Barry Jackson (Maypole Dairies). In funding the Irish National Theatre Society Ltd to set up at the Abbey Theatre in Dublin, Miss Horniman was supporting a movement which was intent upon using drama to help create a sense of national identity. Traditionally Dublin had been an important date on the touring circuit (Barton, nd,), but amongst the visiting stars Ireland's own Barry Sullivan was a special favourite, not least of the youthful George Bernard Shaw, who recalled that: 'His stage fights in Richard III and Macbeth appealed irresistibly to a boy spectator like myself' (St John ed., 1952, p. xxi). The subtler style of Henry Irving also had its admirers in Dublin, where his visit in August 1867 marked the beginning of his long association with Bram Stoker, who was a student at Trinity College (Ludlam, 1977, p. 15). On his return in 1876 Irving's already celebrated Hamlet impressed Edward Dowden, Professor of English Literature at Trinity College whose *Shakespeare: A Critical Study of his Mind and Art* had been published the previous year, and his friend J. B. Yeats, who took with him his young son William Butler (Allison, 1997, p. 116). In his celebrated essay 'At Stratford-on-Avon', Yeats refers to Dowden's idealisation of England ('for, as we say, "cows beyond the water have long horns"'; Jeffares ed., 1964, p. 99) and the crescendo of 'imperialistic enthusiasm' for Henry V. When Yeats visited Stratford in April 1901 to see Benson's company in the sequence of six history plays (*King John, Richard II, Henry IV Part 2, Henry V, Henry VI Part 2* and *Richard III*) the Boer War was at its height, but far from being alienated by the exhibition of English history, Yeats could regard Shakespeare as 'a kind of honorary Irishman' and draw strength and encouragement from him for his own Cuchulain cycle (Nevo, 1991, p. 183). Indeed, as Philip Edwards (1979) has argued, there were significant similarities between the England of Shakespeare and the Ireland of Yeats and the function of drama at the threshold of nationhood. This separation of Shakespeare from British imperialism was adopted by other literary Irishmen of nationalist persuasion such as Darrell Figgis and Douglas Hyde. For his visit to Dublin in July 1903 King Edward VII included a royal command, but it was cancelled 'in consequence of the lamentable death of his Holiness the Pope' (*Era*, 25 July 1903). Ironically it was the Abbey Theatre's failure to show the same respect at the time of the king's death that provoked Miss Horniman's telegrams to Lady Gregory, Lennox Robinson and the business secretary Henderson: 'Opening last Saturday was a disgrace. Performance on day of funeral would stop subsidy automatically' (in Gooddie, 1990, p. 139). The telegram arrived too late (Fay, 1958, p. 139), but Miss Horniman was already disenchanted with Ireland and was directing her attention and money elsewhere to Manchester.

THE BIRTH OF REPERTORY

Manchester still enjoyed the position of provincial pre-eminence which Charles Calvert had achieved. Only there – in 1893 – did J. T. Grein succeed in establishing a branch of the Independent Theatre (Schoonderwoerd, 1963, p. 113) for which Louis Calvert staged *Richard II* in the Elizabethan style at the Gentlemen's Concert Hall in 1895. Calvert also catered for devotees of spectacular Shakespeare with his sumptuous *Antony and Cleopatra* at the Queen's Theatre in March 1897, Shaw's review of which, after generous measures of his caustic wit, concluded:

Considering that the performance requires an efficient orchestra and chorus, plenty of supernumeraries, ten or eleven distinct scenes, and a cast of twenty-four persons, including parts of the first magnitude; that the highest price charged is three shillings; and that the run is limited to eight weeks, the production must be considered a triumph of management. There is not the slightest reason to suppose that any London manager could have made a revival of Antony and Cleopatra more interesting. Certainly none of them would have planned that unforgettable statue death for Cleopatra, for which I suppose all Miss Achurch's sins against Shakespear will be forgiven her. (1932, vol. 3, pp. 82–3)

Shaw was again showing his acuity about the economics of the theatre and the importance of popular appeal.

When Louis Calvert was not available to cater for the popular Shakespeare audience in Manchester, there were two other managers well equipped to do so: Robert Courtneidge and Richard Flanagan. In 1901 Courtneidge produced *A Midsummer Night's Dream* with his eight-year-old daughter Cicely as Peaseblossom in her 'first speaking part' (1950, p. 11). He followed this (at Calvert's old theatre the Prince's) with *As You Like It*, the main attraction of which in the industrial conurbations was its picture of rural England from which most members of the audience were a generation or more removed. Thus reviews of Courtneidge's revival waxed lyrical about 'the beautiful scenery' (*Manchester Evening News*, 17 September 1902). Act 1 Scene 1 was 'Orchard of Oliver's House' and Scene 2 was 'Lawn before the Duke's Palace', with half a dozen different forest locations (one by Conrad Tritschler; two by Hawes Craven) to come.[9] The wood was impressively 'thick, the trees look like monarchs

9. The Forest of Arden by Conrad Tritschler at the Prince's Theatre, Manchester.

of the wood', the foliage was 'admirably executed' and of Craven's two contributions:

one [is] a clough, with a winding way which contrives to lose itself in a distant valley near the setting sun; the other a rich pastoral bit, thickly spread with green grass. On the same scale of beauty is another forest scene by Mr R. M'Cleery. All the pictures are masterpieces, transporting us into the open air, where they fleet the time carelessly. (*Manchester Evening News*, 17 September 1902)

Poignancy and pride mingle in the reviewer's approval of the production 'as the most perfect that had been seen on the London or provincial stage', a sense of gratitude that through the marvels of the stage Mancunians could be transported back into the golden age and even they for a few hours at least could 'fleet the time carelessly'. The production was seen further afield. O. B. Clarence, who played old Adam, recalled touring 'the north country towns, Liverpool, Bradford, Newcastle-on-Tyne, etc.' (1943, p. 80), bringing the playgoers of those industrial cities a glimpse of Arden made in Manchester. Then Courtneidge sold his productions of *A Midsummer Night's Dream* and *As You Like It* to 'George Musgrove for reproduction in Australia' (1930, p. 181). Courtneidge went out to Melbourne 'with the company I had selected' and found theatrical business in 'a woeful state', but audiences (hungry with nostalgia) flocked to his realisation of rural England. *A Midsummer Night's Dream* ran for eleven weeks, only being taken off 'so that I might produce *As You Like It* before I left' (p. 182). The plays enjoyed comparable success in Sydney.

In 1908 Richard Flanagan staged *As You Like It* at the Queen's Theatre as his thirteenth Shakespeare revival. These productions were 'essentially of the popular kind' with the audience 'bent on showing how appreciative they could be on the slightest pretext' and rather carrying some of the players 'off their feet by the extreme cordiality of the reception'. Margaret Halstan as Rosalind and Harcourt Williams as Orlando were particular favourites and their 'mock love-making was capitally done' to the extent that:

Considering the high-pitched enthusiasm of the audience it was not remarkable that a section of them deliberately tried to get one scene between the lovers enacted all over again, and there were even loud cries of 'encore' at the close of the famous 'Seven Ages' speech by Jaques. Mr Clifton Anderson's performance of the arch cynic was among the best things of the evening. (*Manchester Evening News*, 13 January 1908)

The actors were not the only objects of this enthusiasm:

here was a real brook which made a real noise that sometimes drowned the actors' voices, and (we were convinced) had fishes in it; and when three beautiful deer had been carefully herded across a space of what looked like real vegetable matter a real Mr. Flanagan was compelled to respond to our plaudits. (*Manchester Guardian*, 13 January 1908)

Flanagan revived his production of *As You Like It* as an early contribution to the Shakespeare tercentenary in January 1916 – the commercial theatre's own form of *répertoire courant*.

A green velvet mound might be enough to represent a wood near Athens for Barker's sophisticates at the Savoy, but in Manchester who would gainsay the appetite for real rusticity on the stage. The answer of course was Annie Horniman. Prompted by a letter by B. Iden Payne which appeared in several Manchester newspapers on 11 July 1907 (Pogson, 1952, p. 22) the city nerved itself for the prospect of a repertory theatre sponsored by Miss Horniman with Payne as its manager. Payne had suggested Manchester for the reasons which had encouraged and underpinned Charles Calvert's regime: it was 'recognized as a cultural center . . . the only provincial city that supported a symphony orchestra' and it was 'centrally located among many subsidiary towns' (1977, p. 79).

Strong encouragement was forthcoming from the *Manchester Guardian* in its leader of 16 August 1907:

So far has this loss of balance gone that in a city like Manchester the theatre can be virtually abandoned by the majority of those playgoers who, in a German town of similar rank would be the main guard of the chief theatres. Our theatre is thus left almost in undisputed possession of those who in the German town would count as somewhat half-baked and hobble-de-hoyish playgoers.

The patrons whom Miss Horniman sought were of the same ilk as those who had supported the Manchester branch of the Independent Theatre, which had succeeded between 1893 and 1898 in staging in addition to *Richard II* the even less well-known *Love's Labour's Lost* and *The Two Gentlemen of Verona*, five Ibsen plays and four other rarities (Pogson, 1952, p. 43). In her prospectus Miss Horniman wrote of affording 'regular playgoers an opportunity of witnessing the finest dramatic works . . . [and] drawing back to regular theatre-going all those who have lost the habit'.[10] In a talk to the Manchester Statistical Society on 14 December 1910 Miss Horniman referred to the tendency towards bad behaviour in the pit, which she attributed to the influence of musical comedy, and continued: 'Good taste must be cultivated, so that in time the minds of the people may be opened to what is better . . . it is our duty to educate public opinion and to uphold the best in the Drama'.[11]

The Gaiety Theatre, which Miss Horniman had acquired for her venture, was thoroughly spring-cleaned and its capacity reduced by one third. In the re-arranged auditorium the pit stalls (2s 6d) and the pit (1s) had numbered seats which could be reserved in advance, which proved to be so successful that a second box office had to be opened. Only the upper circle (2s 6d) and the gallery (6d) were unreserved. The ambiance was distinctly red-plush and refined.

It was inevitable that Miss Horniman's repertory theatre would open with Shakespeare, but the choice of producer, William Poel, preceded the choice of play, *Measure for Measure*. Best known as the founder (in 1895) of the Elizabethan Stage Society, between 1881 and 1885 Poel had been general manager of Emma Cons' Royal Victoria Coffee Hall (the Old Vic) and in 1904 under the aegis of Stewart Headlam (Bettany, 1926, p. 197) London Continuation Schools had toured *Much Ado About Nothing* to Shoreditch, Bow, New Cross, Hammersmith, St Pancras and Bermondsey setting up a simple platform stage in the town halls. In the programme Poel told readers that they were 'not obliged to read the educational matter' in it nor 'obliged to regard the entertainment as educational, but you may laugh your fill at what we may presume to be an Elizabethan rendering of the character of Benedick . . . at a full-bloodied Beatrice, and a fine ripe Dogberry'.[12]

The choice of *Measure for Measure* and Poel's treatment of it were not conducive to a full-bodied or ripe experience. Through his ruthless pruning Poel transformed a 'Play Unpleasant' into a 'Play for Puritans' to the extent that 'Mistress Overdone's Profession' may have remained obscure to many. References to Juliet's pregnancy were toned down: 'He hath got his friend with child' becoming 'He is like to be a father' (1.4.28).[13] Although (a Poel convention) the cast was meant to remain anonymous, he was the preachy Angelo, Sarah Allgood an emotional Isabella and Edward Lander, in preference to Lewis Casson, the Duke. Basil Dean, as Claudio, 'was given strenuous daily instruction' on verse speaking by Poel (1970, p. 53). Poel took little interest in the prose scenes (apart from cutting them) and Iden Payne as Lucio evidently caught something of the Elizabethan spirit, drawing laughter and cheers as 'a roistering, swash-buckling, free-liver, with a cock of the hat, a swirl of the moustache, and a swagger' (*Courier*, 13 April 1908). Overall the production was dismally lacking in interaction between the actors and the audience. Poel had reconstructed an Elizabethan theatre on the Gaiety stage, but in the antiquarian spirit in which Tree realised the Forum in Rome. C. E. Montague, the distinguished critic on the *Manchester Guardian*, opined:

Mr. Poel did wonders, but he could not get rid of the proscenium arch. What he gave us was not an Elizabethan stage as it was to Elizabethan playgoers, but a picture of an Elizabethan stage seen through the frame of a modern proscenium. So we gained a good visual idea of a Shakspearean stage, but not the Elizabethan sensation of having an actor come forward to the edge of a platform in the midst of ourselves . . . (1941, p. 240)

There was more of that genuine Elizabethan interchange in the cries of 'encore' from Flanagan's audience at the Queen's Theatre than in Poel's asceticism at Miss Horniman's Gaiety Theatre.

Encouraged by Miss Horniman's example others rallied to the repertory movement: Glasgow in 1909, Liverpool in 1911 and Birmingham in 1913. Basil Dean took his experience of Manchester with him to Liverpool, but Shakespeare did not feature in the repertoire until Christmas 1913 when a decline in support was halted and reversed by a production of *Twelfth Night* 'which eventually became very popular and ran for thirty-two performances' (Goldie, 1935, p. 90). However, as George Rowell has observed, 'Shakespeare was much better represented on the Birmingham bills than at Glasgow or Liverpool' (Rowell and Jackson, 1984, p. 50), principally because Barry Jackson, who ran the Birmingham Repertory Theatre, was an enthusiast with the means to indulge his own taste. Clare Cochrane has chronicled the developments from the first production of the (amateur) Pilgrim Players in *The Two Gentlemen of Verona* at the Edgbaston Assembly Rooms in April 1908 to the opening of the purpose-built Repertory Theatre in Station Street with *Twelfth Night* on 15 February 1913 (Trewin, 1963, pp. 19–20). Occurring when and where it did Jackson's *Twelfth Night* invited comparison with Barker's productions and it is clear that they had much in common: virtually uncut texts, swift playing, suggestive rather than elaborate scenery and ensemble playing (Cochrane, 1993, p. 7). Eleven Shakespeare plays were performed between February 1913 and June 1918 (Matthews, 1924, p. 210). Allan Wilkie, home briefly from his labours in the empire, stood out as a rather old-fashioned Falstaff in a production of *Henry IV Part 1* (11 October 1913), mounted, as was all Birmingham Rep. Shakespeare, according 'to the same comparatively austere formula' (Cochrane, 1993, p. 49). That of course, in revolt at scenic excess, was the hallmark of the movement.

The 'Illustrated Handbook' upheld the Shakespeare Memorial National Theatre as 'a model for repertory theatres in all the great centres of population, and as an incentive to their establishment' (p. 15) and as the repertory movement flourished it regarded the foundation of a National Theatre as its apex. Neither paid any attention to the Shakespeare Memorial Theatre in Stratford-upon-Avon, which since its opening in 1879 (Beauman, 1982 and Pringle, 1994) had mounted an annual spring, and often a summer, festival (Ellis, 1948). With its simple auditorium, likened to 'a non-conformist chapel' (Bott, 1974, p. 9), and its art gallery and library, the Memorial Theatre was sustained by the generosity of the Flower family (beer rather than milk or tea) and the indefatigable enthusiasm of Frank Benson. Whereas in 1864 Stratford, David to the metropolis's Goliath, had upstaged London, in the early twentieth century, as the idea of a National Theatre rather belatedly took hold, there was no doubt that its place was in the capital with such satellites as it might have in the major industrial centres to the benefit of their large populations. Laurence Senelick (ed., 1991) has assembled extensive documentary material on the National Theatres of northern and eastern Europe and Lauren Kruger (1992) has analysed the arguments and issues in England, France and America, but the country which set the pace at the time was of course Germany.

In 1908 Edward Gordon Craig wrote 'if you ask me where the Theatre is most active, I reply it is in Germany. The German activity is not only impulsive, but systematic, and this combination is going to bring the German Theatre in twenty years to the foremost position in Europe' (1911, p. 125). Many would have said that Germany already enjoyed that precedence, though it was of course in Moscow in 1912–13 that Stanislavski enabled Craig to realise his concept of *Hamlet*, using 'simple convex screens which could be placed on the stage in endless combinations' (1967, p. 471), which Isadora Duncan and Herbert Beerbohm Tree found 'beautiful but the actors not quite good' (Senelick, 1982, p. 182). In 1912 Huntly Carter published his *The New Spirit of Drama and Art*, complete with a 'List of Art Theatres' including the Moscow Art Theatre, four in Paris, fifteen in German-speaking Europe, one in Poland and (provisionally) the Abbey Theatre in Dublin. Britain could probably have surveyed the arts theatres, the municipal (seventy) and state (twenty-seven) theatres in Germany (Lee, 1906, p. 134) with equanimity had it not been for the fact that one particular dramatist was far better represented there than in the land of his birth: William Shakespeare.

THE PARLIAMENTARY DEBATE

Shakespeare's place in the repertoire of German theatres was a recurrent theme in the House of Commons debate on 23 April 1913 on the resolution:

That in the opinion of this House there shall be established a National Theatre, to be vested in trustees and assisted by the State for the performance of plays by Shakespeare and other dramas of recognized merit. (*Parliamentary Debates*, 1913, p. 454)

The resolution, put forward by Halford John Mackinder, an economic geographer and Unionist MP for Glasgow (Camlachie), represented a significant development on the endowed scheme by calling for state assistance.

Mackinder looked ahead three years to the forthcoming tercentenary in 1916 of Shakespeare's death and the prospect of a 'celebration throughout a large part of the civilised world . . . [which] may be utilised for the purpose of peace in the world'. Until he had begun preparing his speech Mackinder had had 'no idea of the depth and breadth of the influence of

Shakespeare, and therefore of our country, in the literature in which the German youth is brought up' (pp. 454–5). He held in his hand advance sheets of the forthcoming issue of *Shakespeare Jahrbuch*:

I find that in Germany 'Hamlet' was performed in the year 1912, 148 times by no fewer than fifty-two theatrical companies, an average of about three times for each company; 'The Merchant of Venice,' 124 times by fifty-seven companies; 'A Midsummer Night's Dream,' 124 times by thirty-eight companies; 'Othello,' 119 times by fifty-nine companies, and so on. The total may be summarised thus: There were 178 separate theatrical companies who performed twenty-one of Shakespeare's plays on 1,156 occasions.

Mackinder remarked, with justifiable pride, on 'the enormous influence of our poet in Germany' and, with something approaching shame, that 'we have nothing in this land of Shakespeare which is comparable in the very least degree to the facts indicated by these figures' (p. 455). He then gave an account of the National Theatre campaign from Matthew Arnold to the present; its importance 'with increasing leisure on the part of the vast masses' (p. 459); its 'central position as a National and Imperial Theatre . . . in London . . . which might be visited and would be visited by the vast mass of Americans or Provincials, or of the men from the Dominions who visit this country' (p. 460) and concluded with an appeal for 'an annual subvention' such as those given to universities (p. 464).

Of the other speakers Mr Neilson said that rather than be comparable with the playhouses in Stuttgart and Wiesbaden: 'Let it be a British House . . . that will speak to Canada, South Africa, and the Antipodes' (p. 468) and Mr Lynch warned against 'this desire to Prussianise our institutions. The Schauspielhaus is one of the innumerable ways of glorifying that stupendous Prussian system' and questioned whether if there had been a National Theatre in Shakespeare's day 'he would have had a chance of being represented' (p. 471). Lynch voiced not only a prevalent attitude towards Germany, but also a fundamental difference in the role of the state in the two countries. Whereas under Bismarck and Kaiser Wilhelm II the German state had been systematically aggrandised, the British way was for the state to refrain from intervening in activities which were functioning without it. That was a defensible position, even though the lack of a National Theatre could be seen as a corollary of it.

Although when the House divided the Ayes numbered 162 to the 32 Noes, 'Mr Speaker declared that the Question was not decided in the affirmative, because it was not supported by the majority presented by

Standing Order No. 27' (p. 495). Despite this technical defeat the positive view prevailing in the House of Commons must have heartened the advocates of a National Theatre and encouraged them to press forward. Herbert Asquith, who was a personal friend of the Beerbohm Trees and Lillah McCarthy, did not take part in the debate, though in him the nation possessed one of the most cultured holders of the office of prime minister in its history (Jenkins, 1964). Indeed within days of the Coronation Gala, King George V and Queen Mary visited 10, Downing Street where they watched the third act of *John Bull's Other Island* and J. M. Barrie's *The Twelve-Pound Look*. Lillah McCarthy exulted that 'the revolutionary Bernard Shaw was at last to be played before his King and Queen' (1933, p. 148). The tastes of this artistic coterie were far removed from those of the population at large, which all too soon would be plunged into a conflict of unprecedented magnitude.

8

The theatre of war: the 1916 tercentenary

THE OLD VIC

In his House of Commons speech supporting a National Theatre H. J. Mackinder drew an analogy between the mixed economy that government support for a National Theatre would create and that which already existed in the dockyards:

That you place the State in competition with private enterprise is nothing new. You already build some of your battle-ships in Government dockyards, and a greater number in private dockyards. You exchange even your constructors between the national dockyards and private dockyards. And so it might be with your actors.

(*The Parliamentary Debates*, 1913, p. 464)

Though Shakespeare was to take his place in the nation's armoury alongside the battle-ships constructed in government and private dockyards, theatre remained an entirely private function. Jay Winter's opening sentence in his essay 'Popular culture in wartime Britain' reads: 'In terms of domestic – though not imperial – institutions, the British state was perhaps the weakest in Europe' (1999, p. 330). The situation with the Shakespeare Memorial National Theatre exemplifies this. In Britain the political and economic traditions of libertarianism and free trade militated against centralisation of power in the state. As Winter implies, the demands of a vast empire absorbed much of the capacity for governing. The King–Emperor's edict that the capital of India should be moved from Calcutta to Delhi contrasted with his and his government's inability to resolve complex political and social problems in Britain. When war finally broke out in August 1914, one feature of Germany against which most sectors of British society could unite was the overweening power of the state. Ironically in order to fight a system which she abhorred, Britain had to imitate it. In a sense the war was being waged in defence of a way of life in which the state did not appropriate functions, of which the provision of theatre might be regarded as one, which could be provided by other means. The problem, as the war went on, was that in the commercial theatre supply and demand combined to produce unrelentingly lightweight fare. Popular taste elsewhere in Europe was not markedly different, but, in Prague for instance, though in 'the more popular theatres . . . Shakespeare was often replaced by operettas, then at the peak of their popularity', 'the center of dramatic life was the National Theater, built by the nineteenth-century nationalist movement as a symbol of Czech cultural revival', where fifteen Shakespeare plays could be seen during March and April 1916 (Nolte, 1999, pp. 169–70). With so many plays being performed in such a short time the National Theatre was inevitably appealing to a relatively small clientele.

No such bastion had been created in London and the outbreak of war coincided with a low ebb in Shakespeare production in the capital. In November 1914 Tree revived *Henry IV Part 1*, but it ran for a mere thirty performances (Trewin, 1964, p. 78) and on Boxing Day Benson brought his *Henry V* to the Shaftesbury Theatre. The next year was a Shakespearian void until December when Matheson Lang's *The Merchant of Venice* arrived at the St James's, Benson's company played *A Midsummer Night's Dream* at the Court and Miss Horniman's *The Comedy of Errors* appeared at the Duke of York's. The first four months of the tercentenary year itself produced only Oscar Asche and Lily Brayton in *The Taming of the Shrew* at the Apollo. The argument that only a National Theatre could ensure 'constant' provision of Shakespeare's plays could not have been illustrated more clearly or made at such a cruelly inopportune time. Benson kept the bard alive in Stratford-upon-Avon and in the provinces, but in London the task fell to a shabby transpontine theatre presided over by an eccentric spinster: the Old Vic.

In his history of the Old Vic George Rowell entitled the chapter beginning in 1914 'Seeking Shakespeare' (1993, pp. 97–120). Since its transformation by Emma Cons on Boxing Day 1880 from 'the gaff of a permanent bottle party' to 'the grimly re-christened Royal Victoria Coffee Music Hall' (Trewin, 1964, p. 70), the Old Vic had been devoted to a range of improving activities – from opera to the adult education programme provided by Morley College (Richards, 1958) – but Shakespeare had not been among them. In April 1914 Lilian Baylis, who had assumed control of the Vic following her aunt's death in 1912, had admitted Miss Rosina Filippi's company to play a short, principally Shakespearian season. Miss Filippi, as an advocate of People's Theatre, had common ideals with Miss Baylis, but neither her tenure nor that of Mr Shakespeare Stewart lasted long. Then Miss Baylis, whose direct line to God was well known, dreamt of Shakespeare who asked her why she allowed his 'beautiful words to be so murdered' and instructed her to 'run the plays yourself as you do the operas' (Findlater, 1975, p. 107). Such unequivocal directions from the bard himself could not be ignored and on 9 September 1914, barely a month after Britain had declared war on Germany and the very day on which the British army crossed the Marne, the following advertisement appeared in the *Era*:

Wanted: Experienced Shakespeare Actors for special performance at Royal Victoria Hall, Waterloo Road, certain of being in London till end of October. Apply by letters only to the Manager, Box 7, 194.

Encouraged by Estelle Stead (daughter of the pioneering journalist W. T. Stead), who sat on a committee with Mrs Alfred Lyttleton (wife of the leading National Theatre campaigner) and Miss Baylis, the call was answered by Matheson Lang and his wife Hutin Briton, who staged and appeared in *Hamlet, The Merchant of Venice* and *The Taming of the Shrew* (Lang, 1940, p. 119). The wandering Langs did not remain at the Old Vic, but their scenery and costumes did, being recognised for years to come as old friends often put to unaccustomed uses: 'That's the Hamlet throne.' Miss Baylis was now a thoroughgoing Shakespearian and the Old Vic became a cut-price home for the bard, with admission from 2*d* in the gallery to 2*s* in the orchestra stalls.

With such modest box-office income, even with full houses, a tight regime was inevitable and in Philip Ben Greet Miss Baylis, again with Estelle Stead's help, found a director who was no stranger to economy. Greet's particular forte was the pastoral performance. His companies (Pastoral, Woodland) performed in parks, botanical gardens, private homes and college grounds. Sybil Thorndike, having attended Greet's Academy, spent the summer of 1904 appearing with the Pastoral Players in such settings as Worcester College, Oxford and Downing College, Cambridge, her father Canon Thorndike having already consented to his twenty-one year old daughter touring America with Greet in the autumn (Morley, 1977, p. 149). The young actress regaled her parents about her exploits in a succession of breathless letters: 'We saw New York early this morning' (Thorndike, 1929, p. 131); 'We're in Chicago' (p. 139); 'We are staying in Berkeley' (p. 147) and 'Here we are in San Francisco' (p. 150). In addition to the excitement of travel, Sybil Thorndike was gaining experience with roles ranging from Lucianus and Ceres to Viola, Rosalind and Ophelia. The theatre offered a unique opportunity to young women from genteel families who felt reassured of their well-being in Greet's company. Socially Greet aimed for prestigious venues such as the gardens of Sir Arthur Hodgson's Clopton House (Isaac, 1951, p. 35) and Harvard University (pp. 86–7), but his was a Micawberish way of life, as reflected in this letter:

We are simply starving here for people . . . The company is a very large one, and it is simply impossible to keep it on unless we can get the intelligent classes to support it.

I don't want to have to seek shelter for our Company at the Poor House, but it looks very like.[1]

Thus although Greet was used to mixing in rather different social circles from the denizens of 'The Cut' he was no stranger to straitened circumstances.

As with all People's Theatres (Sadler's Wells, the Surrey) performing the classics, the question arises as to the actual composition of the audience. Winifred Isaacs maintained that: 'As the years went by, Ben Greet's productions of Shakespeare's plays . . . attracted the educated people of the middle classes' (1951, p. 127) and Huntly Carter considered that 'it [the Old Vic] is only a "People's" theatre in the sense that it is situated in a quarter mainly populated by costers, some of whom it attracts' (1925, p. 72), but was heavily dependent on other support:

From 1914 to 1919 the 'Old Vic' was kept alive by an annual grant from the City Parochial Foundation, from the Carnegie United Kingdom Trust in 1918 and on, by large helpings of Miss Lilian Baylis's private purse, by sympathisers, public subscriptions, and other charitable bequests. Of course, help of some kind was required to give the public Shakespeare at twopence. (p. 73)

The output of Shakespeare at the Old Vic during the First World War amounted to twenty-five plays, amongst them a few of those which Archer and Barker had relegated from the repertoire. Each play ran (initially anyway) for one week. Performed on a night of enemy bombing, *King John* gave the Old Vic its motto, literally hung over the proscenium arch, for the duration of the war:

FAULCONBRIDGE This England never did, nor never shall
Lie at the proud foot of a conqueror.

Lilian Baylis, ever alert to the hand of providence, observed: 'We might have chosen it on purpose' (Hamilton and Baylis, 1926, p. 211).

Inevitably the staging and costumes were very basic and as the supply of able-bodied actors diminished actresses stepped into the breach and breeches, Sybil Thorndike playing Hal and Ferdinand as well as Puck and the Fool in 1917–18. Greet, already a devotee of clear diction (important *al fresco*), insisted upon it for the benefit of playgoers unfamiliar with Shakespeare. Informative programmes clarified the plot.

The mainstay of the Old Vic's wartime activities was the schools matinée. This initiative came from the Revd Stewart Headlam, Etonian socialist and founder of the Church and Stage Guild, who, following his estrangement from the Anglican hierarchy, had devoted himself to education as a member of the London School Board from 1888 to 1904. Between them Headlam, Greet and Sir Robert Blair, the Education Officer of the London County Council, launched the Shakespeare matinée scheme, which expanded rapidly. Packed houses of pupils occupied the Vic's benches, which were no more comfortable than those at school and the stage was little more highly decorated than a classroom, but 'Attendance at the playhouse is officially counted as an attendance at school' (Trewin, 1964, p. 75). Average weekly attendance was 1,700 and in one week 4,000 children saw *As You Like It*. There can be no doubt that, as Winifred Isaac said: '*It was this weekly influx of the children which saved The Old Vic financially*' (1951, p. 132). There were benefits for all concerned: the children and the teachers no doubt preferred Shakespeare at the Old Vic to an afternoon in the classroom; Greet and Miss Baylis secured audiences en bloc; and the authorities could console themselves that at least one section of the population was having its dose of wartime Shakespeare. The real issue, of whether there was a mass audience for Shakespeare at this time of national crisis and – if there was – whether the Old Vic was providing what was wanted, passed by unanswered.

ON THE OFFENSIVE

If the schools provided the conscript Shakespearian army at home, what of Kitchener's volunteer army on the Western front? Amongst the first in the profession to respond to the cause were husband and wife Seymour Hicks and Ellaline Terriss. They supported fund-raising performances at home (Collins, 1998, p. 53), but their main objective was to organise entertainment for the troops in France. Kitchener offered to pay 'half of whatever it costs' (Terriss, 1928, p. 213) and at the end of December 1914 Hicks 'took out the first concert party to the front' (1939, p. 222), where playbills proclaimed them as 'The National Theatre at "The Front"'

(Terriss, 1955, p. 219). Hicks had assembled a troupe (Gladys Cooper, Ivy St Helier, Ben Davies, Willie Frame, Will van Allen) drawn from the legitimate stage and music hall, as he was well qualified to do since he had 'produced for Sir Oswald Stoll, a condensed version of Richard III' though modestly he would 'not say whether I was good or not as the Crookback' (p. 214). Better, one hopes, than an American actor by the name of O'Connor whom Hicks saw play the Crookback in Chicago behind a net which protected him from the avalanche of vegetables, which 'with the true commercial spirit of all great artists' (1939, p. 59) O'Connor subsequently sold. A similar fate overtook the dauntless Frank Benson, who also played, sometimes with his wife Constance, Shakespearian scenes in music halls where the response was usually tepid, except in Barrow where 'the audience rallied enough [to Macbeth's meeting with the witches] to throw cabbages' (Trewin, 1960, p. 220). Mary Anderson fared better with her appearances (twice a day for a week) as Juliet in the balcony scene, with Basil Gill as Romeo, at the Stoll, succeeding in Sir Oswald's opinion in arousing 'a new interest in Shakespeare amongst thousands who might otherwise have given him little thought [furthermore it had] prove[d] financially successful even in these times' (Anderson, 1936, p. 154). On balance trying to popularise Shakespeare by infiltrating him into music hall bills and other popular entertainments was at best an uncertain strategy.[2]

Neither in the view of Lena Ashwell was it what the typical 'Tommy' wanted. As well as enjoying a successful career in the West End, including appearances at the Lyceum Theatre with Irving, Ashwell was active in radical and suffragette circles to the extent of leading a deputation of the Actresses' Franchise League to see Asquith at 10 Downing Street in June 1910 (Holledge, 1981, pp. 73–4). In 1914 Lena Ashwell 'saw the war as an opportunity to show what women could do' (Whitelaw, 1990, p. 151), which in her case was to organise entertainment for the troops. Through influential contacts (Lady Rodney and Her Highness Princess Helena Victoria), Ashwell got approval for and assistance with her plans for 'the men at the Base camps who, after difficult fighting, were being given rest and training' (1936, p. 195). Lena Ashwell described how:

He [Tommy] shocked the serious French troops with his frivolity, but what he asked of us was not current Jazz or rag-time, syncopated Negroid melody, but the finest music and Shakespearian plays. After the performance of 'Macbeth' in the old Municipal Theatre in Rouen a sergeant was so enthusiastic that he tried to tell me what he felt, but could not get beyond: 'It was just great, Miss.' So I asked him what they thought about the play in the sergeants' mess, and he answered: 'Well there, Miss, I ain't 'eard no complaints.' (p. 209)

Miss Ashwell was insistent that amongst all categories of men in all camps it was 'always the deeper, not the shallower dramas' that drew 'the largest and most appreciative audiences' (1926, p. 15). Often using a small core of professional actors augmented by suitable military personnel, Lena Ashwell set up in Rouen (Mary Barton as producer), Abbeville (Cicely Hamilton, see Whitelaw, 1990, pp. 153–7) and Paris always under the auspices of the YMCA. Ironically British actors were at last appearing in state-run theatres, but in doing so became all the more aware of their own country's deficiency in that respect. In the colliery town of Lille, the theatre had actually been built by Kaiser Wilhelm II and the 'old Théâtre Municipal' in Rouen was 'where Corneille appeared as an actor' (Ashwell, 1929, pp. 83–4):

In short, every country in the continent of Europe has recognised the importance of music and the drama by giving them State and municipal support. So far from limiting the scope of national composers and dramatists in all these countries, they include in their repertory the creations of great foreign masters and notably of Shakespeare. We rather plumed ourselves upon the Old Vic, our one and only theatre which rendered Shakespeare's plays during the War, while our more accessible theatres were content with 'Chu Chin Chow' and 'A Little Bit of Fluff'. (p. 84)

One of those European countries where Shakespeare's plays were (still) to be seen in the repertoire was Germany.

The prospect of a Shakespeare Memorial National Theatre in London had certainly not discouraged German Shakespearians, on the contrary it may well have spurred them on. The publication in 1911 of what Werner Habicht has described as 'Friedrich Gundolf's cult book *Shakespeare und der deutsche Geist*' reinforced the association between the discovery of Shakespeare and German nationhood (1996, p. 87). Then in April 1914, two years ahead of the commemoration on which English eyes were focused, at Weimar, the city of Goethe and Schiller where such celebrations customarily took place, Shakespeare's 350th birthday was celebrated in conjunction with the fiftieth anniversary of the *Deutsche Shakespeare-Gesellschaft*. The Kaiser was already a member, but Franz Josef I of Austria and Hungary and King George V joined (Engler, 1992).

In response to the outbreak of war over ninety 'academics, artists and writers . . . signed the famous manifesto of 1914 pledging support for the national war effort' (Styan, 1982, p. 7). Michael Patterson has argued that whereas in England radical young artistes were left to their own devices (however outlandish), 'their German counterparts were forced [by the Kaiser's attitude to culture] to take things more seriously' and they welcomed the war, imagining 'that the mighty upheavals of war and its heroic idealism would usher in a new civilization' (1981, p. 14). Gerhart Hauptmann, whose *The Weavers* the Kaiser considered to be 'dangerous socialistic propaganda' (Styan, 1982, p. 6), patriotically proclaimed: 'Although he [Shakespeare] was born and buried in England, Germany is the country where he truly lives' (Habicht, 1983, p. 153). Similarly Max Reinhardt, who was irretrievably tainted in the Kaiser's eyes by his youthful connection with Otto Brahm's production of *The Weavers*, participated actively in what was essentially a wartime form of 'Theaterpolitick', as Ernst Stern recalled:

Hohenzollern Germany in the first [world war] was very anxious to remind the neutrals that she was a country of eminent cultural attainments, and to this end the Government subsidized operatic and theatrical companies to tour neutral countries. Our company was one of them. We went to Scandinavia, and our programme included Goethe's 'Faust', a number of Strindberg's plays and several Shakespearian productions. In this way, in particular, the world was to learn that Great Britain's enemy honoured Great Britain's poet despite the war. (1951, pp. 144–5)

In the season at the Royal Opera House, Stockholm in November 1915 three Shakespeare plays (*Twelfth Night, A Midsummer Night's Dream* and *Macbeth*) were performed and in April 1916 *Twelfth Night* and *Macbeth* were performed at the Grosses Schauspielhaus in Rotterdam, in the Hague and at the Stadttheater, Amsterdam. In January 1917 Reinhardt's repertoire in Zurich, Bern, Basle, St Gallen, Davos and Lucerne included *A Midsummer Night's Dream* and in May *Othello* was performed in Stockholm (Styan, 1982, pp. 140–3), where Reinhardt declared: 'art is a truly neutral country whose goods ought to be exchanged at all times irrespective of nationality' (in Hortmann, 1998, p. 43).

Although a special portable revolving stage was constructed and transported with 'a shipload of props' (Stern, 1951, p. 143) to these venues, Berlin remained the centre for Reinhardt's most important work. Shakespeare appeared regularly at the Volksbühne and the Deutsches Theater, with *Much Ado About Nothing* (25 January) and *Romeo and Juliet* (20 April) at the former and *Macbeth* (29 February) at the latter early in the tercentenary year. Reinhardt's production of *Macbeth* was remarkable not just for its historical context. Ernst Stern's atmospheric sets of heath and battlements silhouetted against brooding skies and those skies visible between ox-blood drapes in the banquet scene (Stern and Herald,

1920, pp. 9–17) and Paul Wegener's gentlemanly Macbeth, attempting to conceal his anxieties behind a warrior's mask (Melchinger, 1968). In *Shakespeare and Germany* the British dramatist H. A. Jones wrote: 'One soldier [Macbeth], indeed, Shakespeare had drawn in whom Germans may behold the true and dreadful image of themselves' (1916, p. 21). Did audiences detect in Wegener's thoughtful interpretation any traces of their Emperor, whose parents' marriage had been marked by an unfortunate performance of the Scottish play?

TRANSATLANTIC

The English actor who suffered the greatest personal setback from the outbreak of war between Britain and Germany was Herbert Beerbohm Tree, who had so enthusiastically embraced 'Theaterpolitick'. As his chauffeur Sam Wordingham recounted, Tree was in fact in Germany – en route to Marienbad – when at Frankfurt the situation became so threatening that he reluctantly agreed to return to England, but at Cologne they had to abandon the car and take a train (Beerbohm, 1920, pp. 155–60). Back at the Garrick Club Tree joked with Seymour Hicks about sending a telegram to the Kaiser: 'You gave me a third-rate order for acting in Berlin – I've left you a fourth-rate motor car for acting just as badly!' (Hicks, 1949, p. 71). At heart Tree, a 'fervent anti-militarist' (W. Knight, 1964, p. 201), was stricken, as Constance Collier realised as she saw him after nightfall in the Haymarket 'leaning against the railings':

> His face was ashen... His whole manner was a shock to me. It was my first realization of the seriousness of it all. I never forgot the expression in his eyes. They were filled with the horror of the tragedy that was upon the world... He looked a broken man. (1929, p. 228)

In an article entitled 'The Most Impressive Sight I Ever Saw', Tree described witnessing as a fourteen-year old schoolboy the Battle of Langensalza on 27 June 1866 in the Austro-Prussian war and the personal sorrow which he felt for the '1400 of those gallant Prussians' who were 'killed or wounded' but had set out 'so light-heartedly', chanting an 'old battle-hymn'.[3]

The flair which Tree had so often shown to respond to the national mood faltered. He revived *Drake* with some success, but *Henry IV Part 1* survived for barely a month and though its replacement *David Copperfield* enjoyed a reasonable run, it was succeeded by two flops. His Majesty's subsequently housed the great wartime hit, Oscar Asche's escapist *Chu Chin Chow*, but that did not open until 31 August 1916 and long before then Tree accepted an offer to film *Macbeth* in Hollywood. The exact circumstances and mood in which Tree left Britain remain mysterious. His German background was no longer the asset it had been. Unlike Germany, Britain did not formally direct, let alone fund, theatre as part of its propaganda offensive, but Tree and his wife were personal friends of Prime Minister Asquith and many leading politicians, so the possibility of encouragement from that quarter cannot be ruled out.

Tree was no stranger to filming Shakespeare, his production of *King Henry VIII* having been filmed at Ealing where Will G. Barker had constructed four special sets based on the originals at His Majesty's, declaring: 'We are not attempting to produce a Kinematograph film of *King Henry VIII* but to place Sir Herbert's great production on record in a living picture form' (*Kinematograph and Lantern Weekly*, 17 November 1910), but for all his efforts (four hours of filming for 25 minutes viewing) and good intentions Barker's film has not survived. Contradictory though it seems, filming Shakespeare was a large-scale, international business. Silent film instantly removed all language barriers. The strong storylines, full of incident, made exciting watching. No longer confined to the stage, scenes could take place in appropriate locations. The unities were banished utterly. There was also a potential new audience, those who were not theatre-goers, but who were attracted by the novelty of film. Although Tree's *Henry VIII* has not survived, several examples of silent Shakespeare have, including the first attempt (*King John* in 1899), Benson in *Richard III* and Forbes-Robertson in *Hamlet*.[4]

According to Roger Manvell (1971, p. 19), Tree received £1,000 for *Henry VIII* from which he reimbursed the cast (under £20 each); in Hollywood he signed a contract with Triangle 'for remuneration in excess of $100,000 to make pictures under the supervision of David Wark Griffith' (Ball, 1968, p. 229). Taking his daughter Iris, who at Tree's request had been warned by her mother that she would be meeting a natural son of his in America, for company, Tree soon settled in California which attracted numerous English expatriates including Charlie Chaplin and Constance Collier. Constance Collier was cast opposite Tree in *Macbeth*, the choice of Griffith and John Emerson, who wrote the screenplay and directed the picture. Emerson had thought carefully about the suitability of *Macbeth* for the silent screen as he revealed in a press interview. He found 'Shakespeare's dramatic

structure . . . more near in form to that of the film than the modern play
or novel', *Macbeth* being 'aside from its psychological aspects . . . a rat-
tling good melodrama'. In the tradition beloved by the gallery, Wilfred
Lucas as Macduff fought courageously on though 'maddened with
pain' by a broken wrist (*New York City Sun*, 14 June 1916). In addition
Emerson promised the fight between Macbeth and Cawdor, the execution of Cawdor, Macbeth's coronation and Birnam Wood actually on
the move. Scenery could be found in California, which was 'almost
identical with that of Scotland', but the camera was not limited by
natural terrain: the witches, the visionary dagger and Banquo's ghost
could all be conjured up as far more convincing manifestations of
the supernatural than was ever possible on the stage (in Ball, 1968,
pp. 229–30). More conventionally the studio librarian undertook extensive research in order to provide an authentically eleventh-century
setting and Griffith himself supervised rehearsals, but then (occupied
with *Intolerance*) he handed over to Emerson. Tree seems to have taken
to film as a form, apart from anything else he was spared the repetition,
which he found so boring in the theatre. He still 'insisted on speaking every word' (Collier, 1929, p. 245), though often (unknowingly) to
a dummy camera and he was equally unaware that an acrobatic double was shooting some horseback sequences, but he did recognise the
necessity of scaling his performance to the camera. Tree's 'facial expressions' were judged 'exceptionally good' (*New York Herald*, 5 June 1916)
and the supernatural effects were admired, but although the film was
received respectfully in New York and London, where it was shown at
Her Majesty's, it achieved neither popularity nor permanence, except in
the form of numerous legendary tales about its making.

Tree's own account ('Impressions of America') did not appear in *The
Times* until September 1916 and was followed by further articles there
and in the *Daily Chronicle* (Beerbohm, 1920, Appendix III). These show
Tree's alertness to the political climate in America:

Although there is a considerable section of the community which is pro-dollar,
the vast majority in the East are enthusiastically pro-Ally; and this whole-hearted
sympathy is reflected in the Press. The measures taken towards the Irish rebels
did much at the time to alienate the sympathy of many Americans from the
British cause. In the Middle West and in the West the pro-Ally sentiment is
less pronounced . . . This neutral tepidness [in the press] may be in no small
measure due to the remarkable efficiency of German propaganda. (*The Times*
8 September 1916)

Though Tree's observations may have been valuable to Britain, the actor had to sustain his presence in the United States on a commercial basis. Had his contract with Triangle gone according to plan, Tree's war effort would have been personally lucrative, but this was not the case. Tree set about raising money for his tercentenary theatre season in New York, in association with Marc Klaw and A. L. Erlanger, founder members of the Theatrical Syndicate, which was dissolved in 1916. A letter to Tree indicates that the three of them invested $10,000 each and three other 'contributors to the fund' put in $5,000 each, making $45,000 in all. Any surplus was divided two-thirds to Tree and 'one third to the other participants'.[5] As usual with Tree 'Shakespeare is no losing investment' (*Louisville Kentucky Herald* 14 May 1916) and he personally made substantial contributions to charity, being particularly concerned 'to stand well with the public'.[6]

Tree's production of *Henry VIII* opened at the New Amsterdam Theatre in New York on 14 March 1916 with Lyn Harding as Henry, Edith Wynne Matheson as Queen Katharine and himself as Wolsey. The 'scenery, costumes and effects . . . [were] entirely as they were in Merrie England', the Prime Minister of which had sent a much-publicised telegram: 'Warmest wishes for the success of your Shakespeare Festival. Asquith' (*New York Evening Journal,* 15 March 1916). As with Benson's 1913–14 North American tour, the tone of much of the criticism was distinctly acerbic. George S. Kaufman suggested that:

If Sir Herbert Tree had chosen to turn his attention to politics, instead of the theatre, this war would probably be over now, with Britain triumphant . . . mutilate the text though he does, strip it of so much of its poetic beauty swathe it and smother it in costumes and scenery – no account of a Tree is complete without adding that the method is successful. (*New York City Tribune,* 14 May 1916)

Successful maybe for a little longer, but *The Winter's Tale* at the New Theatre and Barker's *A Midsummer Night's Dream* 'free from all cumbersome trapping' (*New York Times,* 17 February 1915) at Wallack's Theatre had shown the more discerning New York Shakespearians that there was an alternative method. Tree followed *Henry VIII* with *The Merchant of Venice* for just two weeks, then his other (earlier) coronation piece *The Merry Wives of Windsor* in which he even attracted some favourable personal reviews for his Falstaff.

Intrepid as ever, Tree immersed himself in New York's own tercentenary commemorations. Early in April, as guest of honour, he ventured together with Iris, Mrs Patrick Campbell and Sir Cecil Spring-Rice – the British ambassador – to the Lafayette Theatre where, it being a Sunday evening, a full-scale dramatic performance was not permissible, but Mr Wilbur Wright 'spoke the lines of Othello, Desdemona, Iago and the other characters'. When his opinion was sought, Tree showed himself still master of the diplomatic skills he had displayed in Berlin: 'All I can do is praise' (*New York City World*, 3 April 1916). On Easter Sunday, which fell on 23 April, there was a commemorative service arranged by the Actors' Church Alliance at the Cathedral of St John the Divine, with Miss Margaret Wilson, the daughter of President Wilson, amongst the congregation. Frederick Warde read a lesson and Britain was represented by two actor-knights: Forbes-Robertson and Tree. In his address Tree declared:

Today our two countries are united as one to honor the memory of the greatest man who ever spoke our common language. On this Easter day two books stand side by side – the Bible and Shakespeare. (*New York Herald*, 24 April 1916)

The church service was followed by wreath laying at the statue of Shakespeare in Central Park. The American actor James K. Hackett, limping along with the aid of crutches, pointed to the statue's legs and said 'those are my father's legs you see', explaining that when his father, James. H. Hackett first saw the statue – erected for the 1864 tercentenary – he had berated the sculptor 'Why don't you give Shakespeare a decent pair of legs?' (*New York City Telegraph*, 24 April 1916). Tree, aiming rather higher, placed 'a British flag over the bust of the statue . . . and an American flag was placed beside' it (*New York Herald*, 24 April 1916). The next day Tree, with 'many players of note' including Laurette Taylor, appeared as Malvolio, Falstaff, Richard II and Macbeth at a special matinée, which raised $3,500 for the Red Cross (*New York Times*, 25 April 1916).

James Keteltas Hackett, having recently inherited a million dollars, had seized on the tercentenary to transform himself from a matinee idol into a Shakespearian actor. He engaged Joseph Urban, recently arrived from Vienna, to design the sets for *Macbeth*, *Othello* and *The Merry Wives of Windsor*. The verdict on *Macbeth* was that it was 'magnificently mounted', but 'inadequately acted' (Shattuck, 1987, p. 300). Hackett's illness obliged him to withdraw from that and *The Merry Wives of Windsor* in which Falstaff (his father's most celebrated role) was taken over by Thomas Wise, a popular comedian, who had not previously played Shakespeare. *Othello* was abandoned. In spite of Hackett's setbacks New York rose to the occasion as William Lyon Phelps of Yale University observed: 'Although Shakespeare is not acted in New York nearly so often as he ought to be, the tercentenary year 1916 is memorable. One hundred and thirty-nine performances of Shakespeare were given in the metropolis' (1918, p. 103). Of these the most notable was *The Tempest* with Louis Calvert as Prospero at the Century (formerly New) Theatre.

For Professor Phelps one of his dreams had been realised 'tickets were sold to children at reduced prices' and he would never forget the delight of 'several hundred small boys and girls' at the matinée he attended (p. 104). Under the auspices of the Drama Society of New York, which was committed to 'Shakspere at Popular Prices [ten cents for students]'[7] the production reunited Calvert and John Corbin, with Walter Hampden as Caliban. The play was performed complete on a permanent Jacobean-style set by Thomas Benrimo, an experiment which caught on with the public and achieved the unusual distinction of full houses for Shakespeare at the Century/New Theatre. Calvert was praised for his 'robust, imperious, genuinely benevolent Prospero' (*New York Times*, 24 April 1916), though offstage his (belated) application for American citizenship seemed curiously timed (*New York Times*, 16 April 1916). The programme for *The Tempest* pointed out a happier juxtaposition:

By a fortunate coincidence, the Community Masque which Mr. Percy Mackaye is to present in May, represents an imaginary incident in the life of 'The Tempest'. The Drama Society revival will thus afford, to the thousands who will act in the Masque or see it, a lively understanding of the materials from which Mr. Mackaye has drawn his inspiration.

Caliban by the Yellow Sands was an enormously ambitious undertaking by its author/director Percy Mackaye. Having failed to secure Central Park as the venue, Mackaye created a huge outdoor theatre at the Lewisohn [athletic] Stadium with seats for 20,000 spectators and a stage, not just for the forty-seven professional actors, but also dancers, singers and other community performers of which there were 1,500 in all. Mackaye himself acknowledged that in those conditions many, probably most, of the audience would not hear the words, but he rejected the 'total elimination of speech . . . [advocated by] artists as eminent and constructive in ideas as Gordon Craig', though it had to be made 'relatively non-essential in case it should *not* be heard' (Mackaye, 1916, pp. xxiv–xxv). Thus despite the thematic links between the Corbin–Calvert production of *The Tempest* and Mackaye's masque they represented stylistic extremes.

Mackaye's text repaid the effort of those who managed to hear and/or chose to read it. In his preface Mackaye wrote of the opportunity 'to create new splendid symbols for peace through harmonious international expression' (p. xiii). Interludes based on different dramatic periods punctuated the main sequence, which was broken up by 'inner scenes', of which the tenth was King Henry V before Agincourt concluding:

Cry, 'God for Harry, England, and Saint George!'
    THE SOLDIERS
    [With a great shout.]
Ho, God for Harry, England, and Saint George!
    [As they leap forward, to the blare of trumpets, and begin to scale the ladders,
    THE CLOUDY CURTAINS CLOSE]   (p. 138)

In the epilogue the great actors and dramatists of the world passed in review before Prospero, with 'the modest figure of Shakespeare' emerging from amongst his contemporaries (p. 144) and assuming Prospero's cloak and place. Caliban, identified throughout with evil – accompanied by the spirits of war, death and lust – now 'crouches at Shakespeare's feet, gazing up in his face, which looks on him with tenderness' (p. 145). Charles Shattuck justifiably categorises Mackaye's masque as 'banal allegory' (1987, p. 307), but it was an attempt to rework (rather than revive) a Shakespeare play with reference to the current conflict and in a manner which reflected the multiple national backgrounds of which the United States was comprised. The series of tercentenary supplements published in the *New York Times* took up this international theme: 'He Conquered France But Slowly'; 'He Has Become "Part and Parcel" of the Intellectual Equipment of Every German'; 'And Through Him Russia Has Found Herself' (16 April 1916).

At Harvard University links with the English Theatre had been cultivated for some years by Professor George Pierce Baker, a Shakespearian scholar as well as the director of the renowned playwriting course, which numbered Eugene O'Neill amongst its alumni. Visiting England in 1901–2 Baker had seen William Poel's production of *Henry V* and was emboldened to ask Johnston Forbes-Robertson to perform *Hamlet* in the Elizabethan style at Harvard. Since his debut as the Dane at the Lyceum Theatre in 1897, Forbes-Robertson had been the definitive – graceful, thoughtful and beautifully spoken – Hamlet of his day, though he had not, as he now agreed to do, appeared in such a staging. On 5 and 6 April 1904 Forbes-Robertson played *Hamlet* at the Sanders Theatre with Gertrude

Elliott – his American-born wife – as Ophelia and C. Aubrey Smith as the Ghost.[8] In an article published in *Shakespeare Jahrbuch*, Baker wrote of his division of the stage into three parts: upper, front and inner stage. The Ghost's appearance on the upper stage had been particularly effective: 'he seemed only a face' as his costume of mail merged with the 'grey-brown background of painted cloth . . . the effect was incomparably better than any Ghost with lime-light or electric bulb' (in Kinne, 1954, p. 64). Forbes-Robertson had played his farewell London season at Drury Lane in 1913, the year in which he was knighted, but his last American tour stretched into 1916. In concluding it at Harvard Forbes-Robertson was assured of a particularly warm response. The Elizabethan stage was reconstructed and students disported themselves as orange-sellers in 'the pew-like respectability of the Sanders Theatre' (*Boston Transcript*, 25 April 1916), which was customarily used for lectures. At the end of the performance the audience rose enthusiastically, handed large laurel wreaths on to the stage and called 'speech', remaining standing as the actor responded. In bidding farewell to the stage after over forty years Forbes-Robertson seized the opportunity to alert his audience – and the American public – of the critical situation in Europe:

I am returning on Saturday to England, my stricken country. I have just one message for the American people. Do not live in a fool's paradise, as England did for years. Prepare yourselves against national attack. In the next few years I look for a closer relationship among the nations of the English-speaking people. I hope for some working agreement among them, for they have done more for civilization than any other people. Let them combine for better and greater work for humanity. (*Boston Traveller*, 27 April 1916)

THE HOME FRONT

Of the two actor-knights, both born in 1853, who spent the tercentenary in America, Tree did not survive until the end of the first world war, Forbes-Robertson lived to within two years of the second. In their absence a prominent part in the English tercentenary planning was taken by literary and academic figures. With the foundation of the British Academy in 1901, the world of letters had acquired an institutional equivalent to the Académie Française, whilst the theatre's aspirations remained unrealised. Israel Gollancz (knighted in 1919) was a founder, original fellow and long-serving (1902–30) secretary of the British Academy whose first Annual Shakespeare Lecture had been given by J. J. Jusserand, author of *Shakespeare in France under the Ancien Régime* and French ambassador to the United States, on 'What to Expect from Shakespeare' (1913). The third Annual Shakespeare Lecture had been presented on 1 July 1913 by Professor Alois Brandl of Berlin University and president of the German Shakespeare Society on the subject of 'Shakespeare and Germany'. Brandl followed his – fairly conventional – account of the development of Germany's love of Shakespeare with recent examples of notable Shakespeare enthusiasts: Bismarck whose favourite character was Prince Harry (1913, p. 8) and 'His Majesty the German Emperor, who is well known as a warm admirer especially of Shakespeare's *Histories*' (p. 9) and moved to his stirring conclusion:

If, on April 23, 1916, the world's homage to the poet of Hamlet and Lear will be rendered, as is hoped, here, in the capital of his country, the scene of his literary activity, it will demonstrate the empire of Shakespeare of which Carlyle perhaps spoke in even too modest terms, and it will help us to realise that, after all, humanity is larger than nationality. *Au revoir* till Shakespeare Day, in 1916 (p. 14)

When Gollancz came to compile *A Book of Homage to Shakespeare* he did his best to ensure that, with the inevitable exception of Germany, it was as representative of humanity at large as possible. The basis on which Gollancz worked was to invite prominent writers, several statesmen, some actors and other eminent individuals to contribute a poem or some other form of eulogy on the subject of Shakespeare. Russia, Burma, India, Iceland and the English-speaking nations of the world were represented. Individuals included Thomas Hardy, Robert Bridges, Wilfred Blunt, Laurence Binyon, W. H. Davies, John Drinkwater, Douglas Hyde and Soloman Tshekisho Plaatje from South Africa. Sol Plaatje, who in 1916 was in London 'petitioning the British government to intervene in South Africa against racist legislation passed by the Union government' (Johnson, 1996, p. 74), recalled how seeing *Hamlet* in the Kimberley Theatre in 1896 had made him 'curious to know more about Shakespeare and his works'. Then when he met his future wife not only did their situation resemble *Romeo and Juliet*, but Shakespeare also provided them with a common language ('the language of educated people – the language which Shakespeare wrote'). Plaatje's original conclusion, which was not published, ran as follows:

Being an Imperialist and subject of an Empire which is four fifths black, I am convinced that if our Othellos were given an opportunity in front as well as at

the rear, they would serve this empire as nobly as Toussaint L'Ouverture served
his West Indian State and as faithfully as Enver Bey and the other Beys served
Germany at Gallipoli.[9]

Plaatje saw the British Empire as a safeguard against his national government, a view at total variance with the contribution of Douglas Hyde,
who, like W. B. Yeats before him, could only respond to Shakespeare
(and Stratford-upon-Avon) by divorcing him from British imperialism.
An outstanding linguist (Latin, Greek, Hebrew, French and German),
Hyde was elected president of the Gaelic League at its formation in
1893, remaining in office through its years of expansion (550 branches
in 1905), but resigning in 1915 when his repudiation of any political
aim aroused impatience among the younger member. Not surprisingly
Hyde, who became the first president of Eire, wrote his contribution in
Gaelic supplying his own English translation. Gollancz requested several
changes, notably in stanza xxv, which originally ran:

> O Albion, deceitful sinful guileful
> Hypocritical destructive lying slippery,
> If an enemy knock at thy door
> – Take him to Stratford on the Avon.[10]

Hyde responded to Gollancz good-naturedly:

Yes of course I'll change v. 25, as it might as you say, be wrenched from its
context, would this do you 'O Albion who destroyedst my ancestors, O Albion
of the smooth words' – and goodness knows that's letting 'la perfide' down
easily![11]

In the end the verse was reduced to:

> O Albion,
> If an enemy knock at thy door,
> Take him to Stratford on the Avon.

However, with the Gaelic version appearing in full, it was apparent
that something was missing. Hyde's separation of his admiration for
Shakespeare from an abhorrence of all (other) things English, was symptomatic of his insistence that the Gaelic League should be non-political, a
policy which younger members increasingly opposed. The ground-swell
of discontent came to a head with the Easter Rising, Easter day 1916 also
being St George's Day and Shakespeare's birthday.

On Saturday 22 April the *Irish Times* published a short piece headed 'Shakespeare's Day':

April 23rd is always for Englishmen a special day. It is St. George's Day – not quite all that St. Patrick's Day is to Irishmen, but becoming every year more nearly so. It is also certainly the date of Shakespeare's death, and very probably also his birthday. April 23 is still more this year. It is Easter day; and it is the three hundredth anniversary of Shakespeare's death.

Largely because of the circumstances attending Sir Roger Casement's return from negotiations in Germany, the rising originally planned for 22 April did not take place until two days later, but it was still consecutive with a date so laden with significance for England as to make it peculiarly appropriate for such an act of defiance against British rule. W. J. Lawrence, the theatrical scholar and biographer of the actor G. V. Brooke, described the 1,000–1,500 participants as 'a small but resolute band of political malcontents [who] began the celebrations prematurely with a vivid pyrotechnic display'.[12] As far as Lawrence was concerned, the most distressing aspect of the Easter Rising seemed to be that it had 'incontinently knocked on the head our poor little supplement', the *Irish Times* having cancelled the special tercentenary section – on Shakespeare on the Irish stage, most of it written by him – which had been prepared for Monday 24 April. None of the theatres in Dublin had a Shakespeare production planned, but with the introduction of martial law on 25 April 'the inhabitants are required to be indoors at 7.30 each evening' (*Era*, 10 May 1916).

The official Shakespeare tercentenary had been deferred to avoid clashing with Easter day, but this meant that when it did take place an unhelpful new element had been introduced into the diplomatic offensive, directed mainly at America, which the British government was poised to wage. The Shakespeare Tercentenary Committee was imbued with the full authority of the state with 'Their Majesties the King and Queen' as its Patrons, Prime Minister Herbert Asquith as its Honorary President, Lord Plymouth as Chairman, the Lord Mayor of London as Honorary Treasurer and Professor Israel Gollancz of the British Academy as Honorary Secretary. Sunday 30 April was designated Shakespeare Sunday with Bishop Boyd Carpenter preaching the Shakespeare sermon in Westminster Abbey setting the example for all denominations across the land. On 1 May the Lord Mayor presided over a memorial meeting at the Mansion House; on 2 May the tercentenary performance of *Julius Caesar* took place at Drury Lane;

and 3 May was designated Shakespeare Day to be observed in schools and colleges, together with the British Academy Annual Shakespeare Lecture (Dr J. W. Mackail on 'Shakespeare after Three Hundred Years') in the evening. Also incorporated in the programme were exhibitions, performances (Stratford-upon-Avon, the Old Vic and Martin-Harvey at His Majesty's), a concert and even 'Shakespeare Rambles'.

The Mansion House meeting was a major diplomatic occasion, marred somewhat by the absence of Asquith and Balfour who with the situation in Ireland added to the ongoing conduct of the war – the second German attack on Verdun was imminent – had more pressing concerns. Lord Crewe (Milnes-Crewe), a former viceroy of Ireland who was president of the Board of Education, represented the government and amongst those attending were the American ambassador, the High Commissioners of the Empire and Belgian, Swiss, Greek and other Ministers. With the Duke of Alba present, Lord Crewe dwelt at some length on Cervantes, the tercentenary of whose death also fell in 1916, and the prospect of establishing a Chair of Spanish Literature at the University of London. Germany having declared war on Portugal on 11 March, Spain's neutrality was an obvious subtext to the occasion, as of course was the neutrality of the United States. Spain and the United States had both been affected by the recent sinking of the Folkestone-Dieppe ferry the *Sussex* with the Spanish composer Enrique Granados and two American citizens amongst the victims. Five days later, on 28 March, the Reichstag had voted in favour of unrestricted submarine warfare. President Wilson, for whom the forthcoming (in November) presidential election was an inescapable consideration, instructed his ambassador in Berlin to protest against the sinking of the *Sussex*, which he did with such force and frequency that the Allies speculated that America might enter the war (Gilbert, 1997, vol. 1, pp. 399–400). In his speech at the Mansion House Mr Page, the American ambassador to Britain, avoided giving rise to any speculation of a political nature, concluding his carefully judged speech by saying that he had 'the honour to bring the heartiest loyalty of the whole American people in their homage to the great poet of the English-speaking world' (*The Times*, 2 May 1916).

The next day the theatrical profession joined together to pay its homage to Shakespeare at Drury Lane Theatre with a matinée performance consisting of *Julius Caesar* and a Shakespeare Pageant comprising scenes from eight other plays. The choice of *Julius Caesar* inevitably recalled the staging of the Forum scene in the 1911 Coronation Gala at His Majesty's. Tree, although absent in America, was Honorary

President of the Actors' Committee for the tercentenary performance, with Sir George Alexander as its Honorary Chairman and Organiser. The programme included a list of members of the Actors' Association who were appearing. Founded a quarter of a century earlier, largely thanks to Robert Courtneidge, the Association, of which the Abbey Theatre's W. G. Fay was the current chairman, had responded for the profession to the imposition of Entertainment Tax in the 1916 budget (Macleod, 1981, pp. 114–16). The government's main target was the booming light entertainment industry, but there was evidently no thought of applying some of the income to encouraging performances of more serious fare. The tercentenary performance itself was fund-raising and state patronage took the form of attendance by the king and queen, Queen Alexandra and other members of the royal family including the Schleswig-Holstein branch. The principal attraction of *Julius Caesar* for such an occasion was its range of male characters, rather than any thematic appositeness, especially as Julius Caesar was being played by that best-loved of actors Frank Benson, who furthermore was 'knighted in a theatre, in theatrical costume and with a theatrical sword' (*The Times*, 3 May 1916). This was of course extremely newsworthy at the time and has gone into the annals of an occasion which otherwise is best memorialised by the fifty illustrations on Shakespearian themes which were reproduced in *The Memorial Volume*, amongst them Briton Riviere's timely interpretation of Casca's 'Against the Capitol I met a lion' and Byam Shaw's time-spanning diptych 'It is the Prince of Wales'.[13]

King George V exchanged telegrams celebrating the tercentenary with other heads of state including the King of Spain and the President of France. In his survey of Shakespeare productions in Europe during the period Huntly Carter (1925, pp. 279–80) reported that in France, at the Comédie-Française anyway: 'There was no sign of Shakespeare', but in 1917 Jacques Copeau's acclaimed production of *Twelfth Night*, originally staged at the Vieux Colombier on 15 May 1914 (Speaight, 1973, p. 186), was seen in New York (Kennedy, 1993, p. 81). Czecho-Slovakia, Poland, Hungary, Austria all made creditable returns, but in Germany such was the volume of activity: 'It is impossible to give figures' (1925, p. 280).

In Britain, as *The Stage Year Book* put it, the 'war has stayed the project of the Shakespeare National Theatre' (1917, p. 22), though with £100,000 raised it was not an impecunious presence on the scene. The *Pall Mall Gazette* (10 June 1916) took the Shakespeare Memorial Theatre to task for its 'unwise and unmasterly inaction' and proposed that, instead of 'waiting for people to subscribe to a prospective mausoleum on a forlorn site in

Ich dien

"It is the Prince of Wales"   *I Henry IV., Act V., Scene IV*

BYAM SHAW, A. R. W. S.

10. 'It is the Prince of Wales' by Byam Shaw.

Bloomsbury', it should take Drury Lane and turn it into a Shakespearian theatre for the duration. Such a bold use of its funds, though it would have depleted them, might have demonstrated the case for a National Theatre more effectively than any prospectus. Instead the Shakespeare Memorial National Theatre committee spent a substantial part of its capital on the Shakespeare YMCA Hut, which occupied over an acre of land (in Keppel Street) providing a canteen, a dormitory and leisure activities including 'a delightful little theatre' which Johnston Forbes-Robertson inaugurated with an address on Shakespeare in December 1916 (*Morning Post*, 8 December 1916). What in retrospect appears to be a curious (mis-)use of resources probably reflects the prevailing attitude about directing public money towards the theatre which in any form was regarded as little more than a diversion from the serious business of war.

John Martin-Harvey, the one actor who was determined to use the tercentenary to keep some momentum behind the National Theatre scheme, would have been a worthy recipient of financial support. At a lunch of the City Livery Club at De Keyser's Hotel, Martin-Harvey contrasted the situation in Britain with that in Germany where 'Shakespeare Commemorations' were taking place 'throughout the length and breadth of the land' (*The Times*, 2 May 1916). Prior to the outbreak of war, Martin-Harvey had worked with Max Reinhardt, appearing in the title role of *Oedipus Rex* under his direction with designs by Ernst Stern at Drury Lane in January 1912 (Disher, 1948, pp. 204–7) and showing considerable indebtedness to Reinhardt in his own productions. Martin-Harvey, whose most celebrated role was Sydney Carton in *The Only Way* (an adaptation of Dickens's *A Tale of Two Cities*), was a romantic actor who could draw a non-specialist audience to Shakespeare.

Martin-Harvey had hoped to organise a sequence of existing Shakespeare productions playing a week each at a London theatre, but, when this proved to be unattainable, he went ahead with a five-week season of his own at His Majesty's Theatre; their 'Most Gracious Majesties the King and Queen allowed their names to be associated with the season as Patrons' (Martin-Harvey, 1933, p. 461). Martin-Harvey opened with *Hamlet* on 8 May, a production in which he admitted adopting Reinhardt's device of 'a huge semi-circular concave erection of white plaster which stood in the theatre permanently, and upon which the various lights were operated' (p. 462) and which proved to be particularly effective for the battlement and graveyard scenes. There was 'a rush of seats at once to see this *Hamlet*' (p. 465), but Martin-Harvey continued as planned with *The Taming of the Shrew*, played on a single stylised set of a fifteenth-century garden, and his more traditional *Richard III* with Genevieve Ward as Queen Margaret. All three were existing productions, but Martin-Harvey added a fresh revival of *Henry V*, not an unpredictable choice, but approached in a novel way, based on Irish nationalist author Darrell Figgis's interpretation of the Elizabethan stage in his *Shakespeare* (1911). The stage was split into two parts by a false proscenium arch and the scene was indicated by the use of one of the two sets of curtains: the first across the false proscenium and the second at the back of the stage (revealed when the first set was drawn back). Although this method was very different from the long-established Calvert style, it could still produce powerful effects, as with the revelation of the English fleet at Southampton, which moved the audience to applause. It was, however, 'the only play not to show a profit!' (p. 467). A stranger to discouragement, Martin-Harvey continued to tour the country, giving his 'War Lectures' in addition to the plays. Even in Dublin at the end of the performance, he would appeal to 'the youngsters present to join up', drawing the response 'We're not going, Harvey' (p. 359). He ceased his visits to Dublin, where for many years he, like many other English actors, had been accustomed to a warm welcome, after 1916. According to Constance Benson, her husband's delivery of Henry V's 'stirring words . . . to his troops before Agincourt', at the Shaftesbury Theatre in December 1914, 'made so deep an impression on the audience, that some three hundred (we were told) before our short season was over, had given in their names for enlistment' (1926, pp. 281–2).

The tercentenary found Benson in Stratford-upon-Avon for a two-week season from 24 April to 6 May. Benson had absented himself for the Drury Lane performance on 2 May and that evening news of his knighthood was enthusiastically received by the Stratford audience at the end of *A Midsummer Night's Dream*. On Friday 5 May a special 'Tercentenary Commemoration Performance Under the Patronage of His Majesty The King and Her Majesty The Queen'[14] was given in the Shakespeare Memorial Theatre. Their majesties did not journey to Stratford, but amongst the performers, who did so to appear in a scene in one of the nine plays, which made up the programme, was Gladys Cooper, as Hero in *Much Ado About Nothing*:

May 4 Tomorrow I make my debut in Shakespeare. I am very nervous about it. We go to Stratford-on-Avon and get back to play in Town in the evening . . . All the 'nuts' of the stage in it such as Ellen Terry, George Alexander, Irene Vanbrugh and Gladys Cooper. (Cooper, 1931, p. 137)

During that one afternoon the little Warwickshire stage was crowded with more London luminaries than in all the years since its inauguration by Helen Faucit and Barry Sullivan in *Much Ado About Nothing* in 1879. Not all the performers rushed back 'to Town', Ellen Terry, Genevieve Ward and Mary Anderson remained to appear with Benson in his *Homage to Shakespeare* the next afternoon (Trewin, 1960, p. 218). Nine years later, Dame Ellen Terry returned to Stratford to lead the homage to those Bensonians who had been killed in the war by unveiling the Benson Memorial Window.

In a sense that swift departure of the fashionable young actress to appear in one of the light confections which predominated on the wartime London stage, leaving behind the older generation of actresses whose careers had been substantially devoted to Shakespeare, was a sign of the times. Perhaps if Gladys Cooper and some of the younger 'nuts' had taken to Shakespeare the story might have been different. As it was Francis Colmer in *Shakespeare in Time of War* observed: 'How small the interest in Shakespeare and his works really is becomes apparent when we consider that many of his plays are so rarely enacted – some, indeed never at all' (1916, p. xviii). The rhetoric of Carlyle lived on as in S. P. B. Mais's 'Our Greatest Privilege and Achievement':

It is the greatest privilege that we enjoy as Englishmen that this man was of our blood, an Englishman for the English. It is by far the greatest achievement that we as a nation have yet wrought that we have produced Shakespeare. (*Nineteenth Century*, April 1916)

Just as the state had recognised the importance of Shakespeare for 'our honour among foreign nations', he was less a part of 'our English household' than he had been for three-quarters of a century or more.

In conclusion

For most of the period under review Shakespeare's plays held their place on the stage not only in Britain, but also across the English-speaking world and much of continental Europe. For the most part this was achieved on a commercial basis without state subvention. And yet Shakespeare flourished. In Britain the government's role was confined to enabling legislation and the royal family's to patronage on a decidedly modest scale compared with most other European states. Clearly there were factors working in Shakespeare's favour: the demand for entertainment in the new industrial conurbations and the expansion of British power and influence across the world. There were also disadvantages: Shakespeare wrote for a theatre very different from the Victorian model, but such was the inventiveness and confidence of the age that actors, managers, designers and the rest refashioned the plays and harnessed them to the tastes and techniques of the day. However fundamentally they diverged from many of the characteristics of Shakespeare's theatre, the Victorians were generally true to that of a broad popular appeal.

It has long been fashionable to decry Victorian Shakespeare as bowdlerised and overblown and to hail the reaction against it as a new dawn. However it is all too apparent that in the years leading up to the First World War Shakespeare ceased to be a genuinely popular dramatist. No doubt there were several reasons for this: the naturalistic school of playwriting which swept Europe and North America in the wake of Ibsen brought with it a new generation of actors unaccustomed and often unsuited to performing in Shakespeare; the blurring of the distinction between the legitimate and the illegitimate, which had resulted in audiences following favourite actors from melodrama to Shakespeare, no longer pertained; and new forms of entertainment such as music hall, musical comedy and cinema siphoned off sections of the former audience. Over and above these factors was the schism between the traditionalists and the progressives and the increasing association between Shakespeare and education. Shakespeare traditionalists, working on commercial lines, had basically served public taste, though often giving it a nudge and a jolt in the process. Since their production methods were costly they necessarily sought to attract large and socially diverse audiences for long runs. The progressives, opting for simpler staging, set their sights on the more discerning playgoers, who could appreciate the artistic merit of what they saw. Alongside this process Shakespeare was being absorbed in all levels of education, which although it was not necessarily inimical to the theatre tended to regard it as an adjunct to itself. In the minds of many Shakespeare had become an unapproachable icon, associated with high culture and erudition rather the fount of popular entertainment.

This situation was already discernible in the First World War, when it became apparent that Britain had neither the popular commercial base nor the state-supported institutions to commemorate the tercentenary in 1916 of Shakespeare's death adequately. It took another world war and the prospect of another Shakespeare centenary (the quatercentenary in 1964) to bring the Royal Shakespeare Company and the (Royal) National Theatre into being. It is as inappropriate to judge these institutions by Victorian standards as it is to apply strictly twentieth/twenty-first century assumptions to Victorian Shakespeare. Yet the same themes arise: the distinctive position of British culture *vis à vis* Europe and the English-speaking world and the involvement of the population at large with its cultural heritage, Shakespeare in particular. Only in the realms of fantasy can a Victorian deliver judgement on the twentieth century, but if we trespass there awhile might we not reach a concord that each age should treat 'the abstract and brief chronicles of the [other's] time' with due regard to its 'own honour and dignity'?

Notes

1 THE HERO AS ACTOR: WILLIAM CHARLES MACREADY

1 For the full text of Macready's petition see Pollock, 1876, pp. 537–8.
2 Playbill in the Theatre Museum, London.
3 Unidentified newspaper cutting in the Surrey Theatre file in the Theatre Museum, London.
4 Unidentified newspaper cutting in the Surrey Theatre file in the Theatre Museum, London.
5 Letter of 27 August 1843 from Carlyle to John Greig y.c. 464(2) in the Folger Shakespeare Library.

2 EQUERRIES AND EQUESTRIANS: PHELPS, KEAN AND ASTLEY'S

1 Mark Twain, *The Adventures of Huckleberry Finn* (chapter 21), published in 1885, set in the 'Early Nineteenth Century'. Twain drew on his own *Life on the Mississippi*, see S. J. Berret, *Mark Twain and Shakespeare*, 1993.
2 Corbould's 'Sketchbook containing rough drawings of designs of costumes (mostly with colour notes), settings, backcloths and stage properties for the theatrical productions of Charles Kean' in the Department of Prints and Drawings at the Victoria and Albert Museum.
3 Letter 11 March 1853 from Corbould to Kean y.c. 618(2) in the Folger Shakespeare Library.
4 As above, 28 March 1857 y.c. 618(3).
5 As above, 29 March 1857 y.c. 618(4).
6 See R. Derek Wood, *The Calotype Patent Lawsuit of Talbot v. Laroche 1854*, 1975.
7 In the Royal Archives (RA PP/VIC/2/25/8128), Windsor Castle.

8 'Theatrical Album' in the Royal Photographic Collection, Windsor Castle.
9 'Theatrical and Musical Portraits 80, vol. 1 ... Collected and Arranged ... as far as Page 43 ... by HRH The Prince Consort' in the Royal Photographic Collection, Windsor Castle. For other examples of photographic theatrical montage see Laurence Senelick, 'Face Cards' in *History of Photography*, vol. 8, no. 1., January 1984, pp. 43–6.
10 Letter of 31 December 1860 from Donne to Fanny Kemble w.b. 598 'Kemble Correspondence', vol. III, p. 311 in the Folger Shakespeare Library.
11 As above, 17 May 1861, p. 327.
12 Playbills in the Standard Theatre file in the Theatre Museum, London.
13 W. J. Lawrence, 'Some Women Players of Hamlet', in the *Illustrated London News*, 17 July 1899. Lawrence was prompted by Sarah Bernhardt's appearance as Hamlet at the Adelphi Theatre, London on 12 June 1899.
14 In 'Reward Applied to Art and Science' Bentham wrote 'they are useful only to those who take pleasure in them, and only in proportion as they are pleased'. Bentham dismissed the idea of (elected or self-appointed) arbiters 'purifying the public taste ... There is no taste which deserves the epithet *good*' (Bowring ed., vol. 2, pp. 253–4).
15 M. Wilson Disher, *The Greatest Show on Earth*, 1937, p. 219 and *Fairs, Circuses and Music Halls*, 1942, p. 34 refers to Queen Victoria attending a performance of *Richard III*, as does A. H. Saxon in 'Shakespeare and Circuses' (*Theatre Survey*, 78, p. 64), reproducing the (composite) illustration which seems to depict a royal visit (p. 66). However Rowell (*Queen Victoria Goes to the Theatre*) does not record such a visit.
16 Astley's playbills in the Harvard Theatre Collection.
17 Unidentified newspaper cutting in the Astley's Theatre file in the Theatre Museum, London.
18 Playbill for *Richard III* in the Harvard Theatre collection.
19 Unidentified newspaper cutting in the Astley's Theatre file at the Theatre Museum, London.

3 A BABEL OF BARDOLATERS:
THE 1864 TERCENTENARY

1 In Shakespeariana 'The Jubilee Scrapbook' in the Folger Shakespeare Library.

2 Dewey Ganzel in *Fortune and Men's Eyes*, 1982, sifts the evidence and concludes that Collier was probably not guilty of the charges of forgery and that his accusers knew he was innocent.

3 Tercentenary correspondence in the Shakespeare Birthplace Trust Record Office, Stratford-upon-Avon.

4 Letter 12 December 1863 in the Shakespeare Centre Library, Stratford-upon-Avon.

5 Letter 28 December 1863 in the Shakespeare Centre Library.

6 Letter 21 January 1864 in the Shakespeare Centre Library.

7 Letter 30 March 1864 in the Shakespeare Centre Library.

8 Letter of 18 April 1864 in the Shakespeare Centre Library.

9 Poem in the Flower scrapbook vol. 1, p. 27 in the Shakespeare Centre Library. See also *The National Shakespeare Committee and The Late Mr. Thackeray Signed by the Lounger in the Clubs*, 1864.

10 This and other information about the Stratford celebrations from *Complete Programme of the Tercentenary of the Birth of Shakespeare to be held at Stratford-upon-Avon* in the Shakespeare Centre Library.

11 In the Shakespeare Centre Library.

12 Details also from *Complete Programme*.

4 MADE IN MANCHESTER: CHARLES CALVERT AND GEORGE RIGNOLD

1 Undated newspaper cutting from the *Manchester City News* in the Local History Library, Manchester Central Library.

2 Playbill in the Arts Library, Manchester City Library.

3 Red leather volume (*Richard III*, fo. 3) in the Folger Shakespeare Library.

4 Unidentified newspaper cutting in the Local History Library, Manchester Central Library.

5 Unidentified newspaper cutting in the Local History Library, Manchester Central Library.

6 Calvert envelope in the Harvard Theatre Collection.

7 Manuscript letter in the Harvard Theatre Collection.

8 Shattuck, 1965, lists nine Calvert promptbooks for *Henry V* (nos. 19–27). No. 20 has the following handwritten direction at the end of Act 1: 'King on platform – shouts and curtain. For encore all the Lords and Archers form around stage with spears and swords up and shouting until curtain then Act Curtain.'

9 This is the only evidence I have found.

10 Amongst the audience in Cincinnati was the Shakespearian scholar Joseph Crosby (see Velz and Teague eds., 1986), who reported: 'a very enjoyable treat... Rignold – exceedingly well supported... it is a grand pageant, very well done indeed... a capital Pistol and a splendid Fluellen, and Rignold is a host in himself'. Letter to Joseph Parker Norris, y.c. 1372(102) in the Folger Shakespeare Library.

5 THE FASHIONABLE TRAGEDIAN: HENRY IRVING

1 I am grateful to John Stokes for a copy of his paper 'Helena Modjeska in England' as published in *Women and Theatre*, Occasional Papers 1, 1992, pp. 19–37.
2 Letter from Ludwig Barnay to Bram Stoker y.c. 86(i.a) in the Folger Shakespeare Library.

6 THE IMPERIAL STAGE: BEERBOHM TREE AND BENSON

1 In the Birthplace Trust Record Office, Stratford-upon-Avon.
2 The Tree promptbooks listed by Charles Shattuck in *The Shakespeare Promptbooks*, 1965 (*Julius Caesar* nos. 56–60 and 62–6) are in the University of Bristol Theatre Collection.
3 Theatre programme in the University of Bristol Theatre Collection.
4 John Parker ed., *Who's Who in the Theatre*, 1947, pp. 1791–2 lists these occasions.
5 I am indebted to Anthony Meredith for a copy of the programme from his personal collection and for other information about Tree.
6 In Maud (Lady) Tree's letters in the University of Bristol Theatre Collection.
7 From Tree's 'Analysis of Treasury Payments and Estimated Weekly Trading Accounts' in the University of Bristol Theatre Collection.
8 Allan Wilkie's unpublished 'All the World My Stage. The Reminiscences of a Shakespearean Actor–Manager in Five Continents', copy in the Theatre Museum, London. See also Lisa J. V. Warrington, 'Allan Wilkie in Australia. The Work of a Shakespearian Actor–Manager', unpublished thesis, University of Tasmania, 1981.
9 Volume B44 of Benson papers in the Shakespeare Centre Library, Stratford-upon-Avon.
10 Unidentified newspaper cutting in Volume B44 as above.

7 THE NATIONAL ARENA: GRANVILLE BARKER, LOUIS CALVERT
AND ANNIE HORNIMAN

1 *The Proposed Shakespeare Memorial National Theatre An Illustrated Handbook Issued by the Executive Committee.*
2 George Foster Platt's papers (volume 2) in the Shubert Archive, New York.
3 Prospectus in the Harvard Theatre Collection.
4 Theatre Notes of C. H. Blackhall 'From notes by Winthrop Ames' in the Harvard Theatre Collection.
5 George Foster Platt's papers (volume 2) in the Shubert Archive.
6 Ibid.
7 Details in the Shubert Archive. I have assumed the amounts are weekly, but that is not specified.
8 This and other budget figures from the Shubert Archive.
9 Programme in the Arts Library, Manchester Central Library.
10 *Miss Horniman's Company and the Gaiety Theatre, Manchester,* undated (*c.* 1908) booklet in the Arts Library, Manchester Central Library.
11 *A Talk about the Drama by Miss A. E. F. Horniman M.A., read December 14 1910,* Manchester Statistical Society.
12 The Poel Dossier, compiled by Sir Barry Jackson in the Shakespeare Centre, Stratford-upon-Avon.
13 Poel promptbooks in the Theatre Museum, London. Charles Shattuck, *The Shakespeare Promptbooks,* 1964, *Measure for Measure* nos. 17 and 18.

8 THE THEATRE OF WAR: THE 1916 TERCENTENARY

1 Letter 3 January (no year) to C. M. Pratt y.c. 1097(2b) in the Folger Shakespeare Library.
2 *Era,* 3 May 1916 carried an article 'Shakespeare in the Halls'. See Constance Benson, *Mainly Players; Bensonian Memories,* 1926, p. 301 regarding music hall appearances in 1917.
3 Tree ephemera in the University of Bristol Theatre Collection.
4 See British Film Institute videotape *Silent Shakespeare* (nd, *c.* 1999).
5 Tree ephemera in the University of Bristol Theatre Collection.
6 Ibid.
7 Programme in the Harvard Theatre Collection.
8 Programmes for 1904 and 1916 in the Harvard Theatre Collection.
9 Folder of 'Book of Homage to Shakespeare' y.d. 85(58) in the Folger Shakespeare Library.

10　As above y.d. 85(30).

11　Gollancz correspondence concerning *The Book of Homage* w.a. 79(62) in the Folger Shakespeare Library. See also at the Folger Shakespeare Library w.b. 260 Sir Sidney Lee's leather-bound, gold-embossed and jewelled *Songs and Sonnets by William Shakespeare Tributes of Three Centuries written by Sir Sidney Lee on the Tercentenary of his death April 23 1916*.

12　As above w.a. 80(6).

13　*Shakespeare Tercentenary Commemoration Performance The Memorial Volume*, programme, incorporating illustrations.

14　Programme in the Shakespeare Centre Library, Stratford-upon-Avon.

References

Allen, Shirley. 1971. *Samuel Phelps and the Sadler's Wells Theatre*, Middletown, Conn.

Allison, Jonathan. 1997. W. B. Yeats and the Shakespearean Character. In Thornton and Wray eds. 1997, pp. 109–21.

Anderson, James. 1902. *An Actor's Life*, London and Newcastle.

Anderson, Mary. 1936. *A Few More Memories*, London.

Appleton, William. 1974. *Madame Vestris and the London Stage*, London.

Archer, Frank. 1912. *An Actor's Notebooks*, London.

Archer, William. 1883. *Henry Irving Actor and Manager A Critical Study*, London.

1890. *William Charles Macready*, London.

1897. *The Theatrical World of 1896*, London.

1917. *India and the Future*, London.

Archer, William and Barker, Harley Granville. 1907. *Scheme and Estimates for a National Theatre*, London.

1908. *Scheme and Estimates for a National Theatre*, New York.

Archer, William and Lowe, R. W. 1877. *The Fashionable Tragedian*, London.

Archer, William and Lowe, Robert W. eds. 1896. *Dramatic Essays by John Forster and George Henry Lewes*, London.

Arnold, Matthew. 1879. The French Play in London. In *Nineteenth Century*, August 1879, pp. 228–43.

Arundell, Dennis. 1965. *The Story of the Sadler's Wells Theatre 1683–1964*, London.

Asche, Oscar. 1929. *Oscar Asche By Himself*, London.

Ashwell, Lena. 1926. *Reflections from Shakespeare*, London.

1929. *The Stage*, London.

1936. *Myself A Player*, London.

Aston, Elaine. 1989. *Sarah Bernhardt A French Actress on the English Stage*, Oxford.

Bacon, Alan ed. 1998. *The Nineteenth-Century History of English Studies*, Aldershot.

Bagot, Alec. 1965. *Coppin the Great Father of the Australian Theatre*, Melbourne.

Ball, J. Hamilton. 1968. *Shakespeare and the Silent Film A Strange Eventful History*, London.

Bancroft, Mr and Mrs. 1889. *Mr and Mrs Bancroft On and Off the Stage*, London.

Bandmann, Daniel E. 1885. *An Actor's Tour or Seventy Thousand Miles with Shakespeare*, Boston.

Banks, Mrs G. Linnaeus. 1932. *The Manchester Man*, London.

Barker, Clive. 1971. A Theatre for the People. In Richards and Thomson eds. 1971, pp. 3–24.

Barker, Harley Granville. 1911. Two German Theatres. In *Fortnightly Review*, vol. 89, pp. 60–70.

1922. *The Exemplary Theatre*, London.

Barnes, J. H. 1914. *Forty Years on the Stage*.

Barrett, Lawrence. 1881. *Edwin Forrest*, New York.

1889. *Charlotte Cushman A Lecture*, New York.

Bartholomeusz, Denis. 1982. *The Winter's Tale in Performance in England and America 1611–1976*, Cambridge.

Barton, Sir D. Plunket. Nd. *Links between Shakespeare and Ireland*, Dublin.

Bate, Jonathan. 1989. *Shakespearean Constitutions: Politics, Theatre, Criticism 1730–1830*, Oxford.

1997. *The Genius of Shakespeare*, London.

Bate, Jonathan and Jackson, Russell eds. 1996. *Shakespeare An Illustrated Stage History*, Oxford.

Beauman, Sally. 1982. *The Royal Shakespeare Company A History of Ten Decades*, Oxford.

Beerbohm, Max. 1920. *Herbert Beerbohm Tree Some Memories of Him and His Art*, London.

1970. *Last Theatres*, London.

Bell, Edward ed. 1890. *Selected Prose Works of G. E. Lessing*, London.

Bellew, J. C. M. 1863. *Shakespeare's House at New Place*, London.

Belton, Frederick. 1880. *Random Recollections of An Old Actor*, London.

Benson, Constance. 1926. *Mainly Players Bensonian Memoirs*, London.

Benson, Frank. 1930. *My Memoirs*, London.

Benzie, William. 1983. *Dr F. J. Furnivall Christian Socialist*, Norman, Okla.

Bernhardt, Sarah. 1984. *My Double Life*, London.

Berret, S. J. 1993. *Mark Twain and Shakespeare*, Lanham, Maryland.

Berry, Ralph. 1986. The Imperial Theme. In Foulkes ed. 1986, pp. 153–62.

Bettany. F. G. 1926. *Stewart Headlam: A Biography*, London.

Bevan, Ian. 1954. *Royal Performance The Story of Royal Theatregoing*, London.

Bingham, Madeleine. 1978. *The Great Lover, The Life and Art of Herbert Beerbohm Tree*, London.

Booth, Michael. 1981. *Victorian Spectacular Theatre 1850–1910*, London.

1987. Touring the Empire. In *Essays in Theatre*, vol. 6, no. 1, pp. 50–60.

Borgeroff, J-L. 1913. *Le Théâtre Anglais à Paris sous la Restauration*, Paris.

Bott, John. 1974. *The Figure of the House*, Stratford-upon-Avon.

Bowring, John. ed. 1962. *The Works of Jeremy Bentham*, 11 vols., London and New York.

Brandl, Alois. 1913. *Shakespeare and Germany*, Oxford.

Bratton, J. S. and Cave, Richard Allen eds. 1991. *Acts of Supremacy The British Empire and the Stage*, Manchester.

Brereton, Austin. 1908. *The Life of Henry Irving*, 2 vols., London.

1922. *"H. B." and Laurence Irving*, London.

Briggs, Asa. 1968. *Victorian Cities*, Harmondsworth.

Bristol, Michael D. 1990. *Shakespeare's America, America's Shakespeare*, London and New York.

British Parliamentary Paper, Stage and Theatre 1, 1968, Shannon.

Broadbent, R. J. 1901. *Stage Whispers*, London.

Bromley, J. 1959. *A Man of Ten Talents: Richard Chenevix Trench*, London.

Brown, Eluned ed. 1966. *The London Theatre 1811–1866 Selections from the Diary of Henry Crabb Robinson*, London.

Bryan, George B. 1974. Dear Winston's Clever Mother... Lady Randolph Churchill and the National Theatre. In *Theatre Survey*, vol. 15, pp. 143–70.

Bulwer Lytton, Edward. 1833. *England and the English*, 2 vols., London.

Bunn, Alfred. 1940. *The Stage Before and Behind the Curtain*, 2 vols., London.

Byrne, Muriel St Clare. 1964. Charles Kean and the Meininger Myth. In *Theatre Research*, vol. 6, pp. 137–53.

Calvert, Mrs Charles. 1911. *Sixty-Eight Years on the Stage*, London.

Calvert, Louis. 1919. *Problems of the Actor*, London.

Campbell, Mrs Patrick. 1922. *My Life and Some Letters*, London.

Carlisle, Carol Jones. 2000. *Helen Faucit Fire and Ice on the Victorian Stage*, London.

Carlson, Marvin. 1985. *The Italian Shakespearians Performances by Ristori, Salvini and Rossi in England and America*, Washington.

Carlyle, Thomas. 1946. *On Heroes, Hero-worship and the Heroic in History*, Oxford.
1915. *Chartism*, London.

Carpenter, Humphrey. 1985. *OUDS A Centenary History of the Oxford University Dramatic Society*, Oxford.

Carson, William G. B. 1945. *Letters of Mr and Mrs Charles Kean Relating to their American Tour*, Saint Louis.

Carter, Huntly. 1912. *The New Spirit of Drama and Art*, London.
1925. *The New Spirit in the European Theatre 1914–24*, London.

Chapman, John. 1849. *The Court Theatre and Royal Dramatic Record*, London.

Chatterjee, Sudipto and Singh, Jyotsna G. 1999. Moor or Less. The surveillance of *Othello*, Calcutta 1845. In Desmet and Sawyer eds. 1999, pp. 65–82.

Clapp, Henry Austin. 1902. *Reminiscences of a Dramatic Critic with an Essay on the Art of Henry Irving*, Boston and New York.

Clapp, William W. 1853. *A Record of the Boston Stage*, Boston.

Clarence. O. B. 1943. *No Complaints*, London.

Clark, Susie C. 1914. *John McCullough As Man, Actor and Spirit*, 1914.

Cochrane, Claire. 1993. *Shakespeare and the Birmingham Repertory Theatre 1913–1929*, London.

Coffin, Hayden. 1930. *Hayden Coffin's Book Packed with Acts and Facts*, London.

Cole, J. W. 1859. *The Life and Theatrical Times of Charles Kean FSA*, 2 vols., London.

Coleman, John. 1886. *Memoirs of Samuel Phelps*, London.
1904. *Fifty Years of An Actor's Life*, 2 vols., London.

Coleman, Marion Moore. 1969. *Fair Rosalind The American Career of Helena Modjeska*, Cheshire, Conn.

Collier, Constance. 1929. *Harlequinade*, London.

Collison-Morley, Lacy. 1916. *Shakespeare in Italy*, Stratford-upon-Avon.

Colmer, Francis. 1916. *Shakespeare in Time of War*, London.

Cooper, Gladys. 1931. *Gladys Cooper*, London.

Cornwallis-West, Mrs George. 1912. *Shakespeare Memorial Souvenir of the Shakespeare Ball, 20 June 1911*, London.

Courtneidge, Cicely. 1950. *Cicely*, London.

Courtneidge, Robert. 1930. *I was an Actor Once*, London.

Craig, Edith and St John, Christopher, eds. 1933. *Ellen Terry's Memoirs*, London.

Craig, Edward Gordon. 1911. *On the Art of the Theatre*, London.

Cran, Mrs George. 1907. *Herbert Beerbohm Tree*, London.

Creswick, William. 1889. *An Autobiography*, London.

Crump, Jeremy. 1986. The Popular Audience for Shakespeare in Nineteenth-Century Leicester. In Foulkes ed. 1986, pp. 271–82.

Dale, R. W. 1864. *Genius The Gift of God A sermon on the Tercentenary of the Birth of William Shakespeare*, London.

Dangerfield, George. 1936. *The Strange Death of Liberal England*, London.

Darbyshire, Alfred. 1907. *The Art of the Victorian Stage*, London.

Davies, James A. 1983. *John Forster: A Literary Life*, Leicester and New Jersey.

Davis, Jim ed. 1992. *The Britannia Diaries of Frederick Wilton*, London.

Dean, Basil. 1970. *Seven Ages An Autobiography*, London.

Deelman, Christian. 1964. *The Great Shakespeare Jubilee*, London.

Desmet, Christy and Sawyer, Robert eds. 1999. *Shakespeare and Appropriation*, London.

Dickens, Charles. 1842. *American Notes*, London.

1843–4. *Martin Chuzzlewit*, London.

1854. *Hard Times*, London.

Diggle, John W. 1889. *The Lancashire Life of Bishop Fraser*, London.

Dimond, Frances and Taylor, Roger. 1987. *Crown and Camera*, London.

Disher, Maurice Wilson. 1937. *Greatest Show on Earth*, London.

1942. *Fairs, Circuses and Music Halls*, London.

1948. *The Last Romantic The Authorised Biography of Sir John Martin-Harvey*, London.

Disraeli, Benjamin. 1845. *Sybil: or The Two Nations*, London.

Dobson, Michael. 1992. *The Making of a National Poet: Shakespeare Adaptation and Authorship 1660–1769*, Oxford.

Donohue, Joseph W. ed. 1971. *The Theatrical Manager in England and America*, Princeton.

Dowden, Edward. 1875. *Shakespeare A Critical Study of His Mind and Art*, London.

Downer, Alan S. 1946. Players and the Painted Stage. In *PMLA*, vol. 41, pp. 522–76.

1966. *The Eminent Tragedian William Charles Macready*, London and Cambridge, Mass.

Downer, Alan S. ed. 1964. *The Autobiography of Joseph Jefferson*, Cambridge, Mass.

Downes, Peter. 1975. *Shadows of the Stage Theatre in New Zealand – in the First 70 Years*, Dunedin.

Dudley, Ernest. 1958. *The Gilded Lily The Life and Loves of the Fabulous Lillie Langtry*, London 1958.

Dymkowski, Christine. 1986. *Harley Granville Barker A Preface to Modern Shakespeare*, Washington.

Eaton, Walter Pritchard. 1910. *At the New Theatre and others. The American Stage: Its Problems and Performances 1908–1910*, Boston.

Eddison, Robert. 1955. Souvenirs de Théâtre Anglais à Paris 1827. In *Theatre Notebook*, vol. 9, no. 4, pp. 99–103.

Edgett, Edwin Francis. 1901. *Edward Loomis Davenport A Biography*, New York.

Edwards, Philip. 1979. *Threshold of a Nation A Study of English and Irish Drama*, Cambridge.

Eksteins, Modris and Hammerschmidt, Hildegard eds. 1983. *Nineteenth-Century Germany*, Tubingen.

Ellis, Ruth. 1948. *The Shakespeare Memorial Theatre*, London.

Elsom, John and Tomalin, Nicholas. 1978. *The History of the National Theatre*, London.

Emerson, Ralph Waldo. 1850. *Representative Men: Seven Lectures*. Boston.

Engle, Ronald G. and Watermeier, Daniel J. 1972. Phelps and his German Critics. In *Educational Theatre Journal*, no. 24, pp. 237–47.

Engler, Balz. 1992. Shakespeare in the Trenches. In *Shakespeare Survey 44*, pp. 105–11.

Escott, T. H. S. 1885. *Society in London by A Foreign Resident*, London.

Esher, Viscount, ed. 1912. *The Girlhood of Queen Victoria*, 2 vols., London.

Eulenspiegel. 1909. Shakespeare and the Modern German Stage. In *Contemporary Review*, No. 522, June 1909, pp. 726–37.

Evans, Gareth Lloyd ed. 1968. *Shakespeare in the Limelight An Anthology of Theatre Criticism*, Glasgow and London.

Ewbank, Inga-Stina. 1996. European Cross-Currents: Ibsen and Brecht. In Bate and Jackson eds. 1996. *Shakespeare An Illustrated Stage History*, Oxford, pp. 128–38.

Fagan, Elizabeth. 1922. *From the Wings by 'The Stage Cat'*.

Fairbrother, Sydney. 1939. *Through an Old Stage Door*, London.

Fay, Gerard. 1958. *The Abbey Theatre Cradle of Genius*, Dublin.

Felheim, Marvin. 1956. *The Theater of Augustin Daly*, Cambridge, Mass.

Field, Kate. 1882. *Charles Albert Fechter*, New York.

Figgis, Darrell. 1911. *Shakespeare*, London.

Filon, August. 1897. *The English Stage*, London.

Findlater, Richard. 1975. *Lilian Baylis: The Lady of the Old Vic*, London.

Fitzgerald, Percy. 1893. *Henry Irving A Record of Twenty Years at the Lyceum*, London.

Flower, Sarah. 1964. *Great Aunt Sarah's Diary*, Stratford-upon-Avon.

Forbes-Robertson, Johnston. 1925. *A Player Under Three Reigns*, London.

Forbes-Winslow, D. 1943. *Daly's The Biography of a Theatre*, London.

Foulkes, Richard. 1984. *The Shakespeare Tercentenary of 1864*, London.

    1985. The Royal Dramatic College. In *Nineteenth Century Theatre Research*, vol. 13, no. 2, pp. 63–85.

1989. Charles Calvert's *Henry V*. In *Shakespeare Survey*, 41, pp. 23–34.

1992a.*The Calverts Actors of Some Importance.*

1992b. Louis Calvert: a Shakespearian in the Nineties. In Foulkes ed. 1992, pp. 165–83.

2001.'Every Good Gift from Above' Archbishop Trench's Tercentenary Sermon. In *Shakespeare Survey 54*, pp. 80–8

Foulkes, Richard ed. 1986. *Shakespeare and the Victorian Stage*, Cambridge.

1992. *British Drama in the 1890s Essays on Drama and the Stage*, Cambridge.

Fraser, Corille. 1998. *Come to Dazzle Sarah Bernhardt's Australian Tour*, Sydney.

Fulford, Roger ed. 1977. *Dearest Child Private Correspondence of Queen Victoria and the Princess Royal*, London.

Ganzel, Dewey. 1982. *Fortune and Men's Eyes The Career of John Payne Collier*, Oxford.

Garnett, Richard and Garnett, Edward. 1910. *Life of W. J. Fox*, London.

Gaskell, Mrs. 1855. *North and South*, London.

Gielgud, Kate Terry. 1980. *A Victorian Playgoer*, London.

Gilbert, Martin. 1997. *A History of the Twentieth Century*, 3 vols. London.

Gill, Maud. 1948. *Mainly Players*, Birmingham.

Glasstone, Victor. 1975. *Victorian and Edwardian Theatres*, London.

Godwin, George. 1878. *On the Desirability of obtaining a National Theatre*, London.

Golder, John and Madelaine, Richard, eds. 2001. *O Brave New World Two Centuries of Shakespeare on the Australian Stage*, Sydney.

Goldie, Grace Wyndham. 1935. *The Liverpool Repertory Theatre 1911–1934*, London.

Gollancz, Israel. 1916. *A Book of Homage to Shakespeare*, London.

Goodie, Sheila. 1990. *Annie Horniman A Pioneer in the Theatre*, London.

Gosse, Edmund. 1907. *Father and Son*, London.

Graves, Robert. 1960. *Goodbye to All That*, Harmondsworth.

Greif, Karen. 1980. 'If this were play'd upon a stage': Harley Granville Barker's Shakespeare Productions at the Savoy Theatre, 1912–1914. In *Harvard Library Bulletin*, vol. 28, no. 2, pp. 117–45.

Grossman, Edwina Booth. 1894. *Edwin Booth Recollections by his daughter Edwina Booth Grossman and Letters to her and his Friends*, London.

Guizot, M. 1852. *Shakespeare and his Times*, London.

Habicht, Werner. 1983. Shakespeare in Nineteenth-Century Germany. The Making of a Myth. In Eksteins and Hammerschmidt eds. 1983, pp. 141–57.

1996. Shakespeare and the German Imagination: Cult, Controversy and Performance. In Kerr, Eaden and Mitton eds. 1996, pp. 87–101.

2000. Shakespeare und die Grunder. In *Shakespeare Jahrbuch*, Band 136, pp. 74–89.

Hamilton, Cicely and Bayliss, Lilian. 1926. *The Old Vic*, London.

Hardwick, J. M. D. ed. 1954. *Emigrant in Motley*, London.

Hardwicke, Cedric. 1932. *Let's Pretend Recollections and Reflections of a Lucky Actor*, London.

1961. *A Victorian in Orbit*, London.

Harrison, J. F. C. 1954. *A History of the Working Men's Colleges*, London.

Hatton, Joseph. 1884. *Henry Irving's Impressions of America*, 2 vols. London.

Hemmings, F. W. J. 1994. *Theatre and State in France 1760–1905*, Cambridge.

Heppner, Sam. 1969. *'Cockie'*, London.

Heylen, Romy. 1993. *Translations, Poetics and the Stage Six French Hamlets*, London.

Hicks, Seymour. 1939. *Me and My Missus: Fifty Years on the Stage*, London.

1949. *Hail Fellow Well Met*, London.

Hill, Erroll. 1984. *Shakespeare in Sable: A History of Black Shakespearean Actors*, Amherst, Mass.

Hodgson, Barbara. 1998. *The Shakespeare Trade Performances and Appropriations*, Philadelphia.

Holledge, Julie. 1981. *Innocent Flowers: Women in the Edwardian Theatre*, London.

Hollingshead, John. 1898. *Gaiety Chronicles*, London.

Holloway, David. 1979, *Playing the Empire*, London.

Hortmann, Wilhelm. 1998. *Shakespeare on the German Stage: The Twentieth Century*, Cambridge.

Howard, Jean E. and O'Connor, Marion F. eds. 1987. *Shakespeare Reproduced: The Text in History and Ideology*, New York and London.

Howe, J. B. 1888. *A Cosmopolitan Actor*, London.

Hughes, Alan. 1981. *Henry Irving, Shakespearean*, Cambridge.

Hughes, Glenn. 1951. *A History of the American Theatre 1700–1950*, New York.

Hughes, Thomas. 1887. *James Fraser Second Bishop of Manchester*, London.

Hunter, Robert. 1864. *Shakespeare and Stratford-upon-Avon Together With a Full Report of the Tercentenary Celebration*, London.

Irving, Henry. 1877. An Actor's Notes on Shakespeare No. 2, Hamlet and Ophelia Act III Sc. I. In *Nineteenth Century*, May 1877, pp. 524–30.

1885. The American Audience. In Richards, Jeffrey, ed. 1994, pp. 116–20.

Irving, Laurence. 1951. *Henry Irving The Actor and his World*, London.

1971. *The Precarious Crust*, London.

Isaac, Winifred F. E. C. 1964. *Ben Greet and The Old Vic A Biography of Sir Philip Ben Greet*, London.

Jacobs, Arthur. 1986. *Arthur Sullivan: A Victorian Musician*, Oxford.

Jackson, Russell ed. 1999. *Shakespeare in the London Theatre 1855–58*, London.

James, Henry. 1890. *The Tragic Muse*, London.

Jeaffreson, J. Cordy. 1894. *A Book of Recollections*, 2 vols., London.

Jeffares, Norman A. ed. 1964. *Yeats Selected Criticism*, London.

Jenkins, Roy. 1964. *Asquith*, London.

Jeremiah, John. 1876. *Notes on Shakespeare and Memorials of the Urban Club*, London.

Johnson, David. 1996. *Shakespeare and South Africa*, Oxford.

Johnson, Edgar and Eleanor eds. 1964. *The Dickens Theatrical Reader*, 1964.

Jones, Edmund D. ed. 1956. *English Critical Essays (Nineteenth Century)*, Oxford.

Jones, Henry Arthur. 1916. *Shakespeare and Germany Written During the Battle of Verdun*, London.

1931. *The Shadow of Henry Irving*, London.

Juden, B. et Richer, J. 1962-3. L'entente cordiale au théâtre Macready et Hamlet à Paris en 1844. In *La Revue des Lettres Modernes*, nos. 74–5, pp. 3–71.

Jusserand, J. J. 1899. *Shakespeare in France under the Ancien Régime*, London.

Kelly, Thomas. 1962. *The History of Adult Education in Great Britain*, Liverpool.

Kemble, Frances [Fanny]. 1878. *Records of a Girlhood*, 3 vols., London.

Kendal, Dame Madge. 1933. *Dame Madge Kendal by Herself*, London.

Kennedy, Dennis. 1989. *Granville Barker and the Dream of Theatre*, Cambridge.

1993. *Looking at Shakespeare*, Cambridge.

Kerr, Heather; Eaden, Robin; and Mitton, Madge eds. 1996. *Shakespeare: World View*, Newark and London.

Kinne, Wisner Payne. 1954. *George Pierce Baker and the American Theatre*, Cambridge, Mass.

Knight, G. Wilson. 1964. *Shakespearian Production*, London.

Knight, Joseph. 1893. *Theatrical Notes*, London.

Knight, William G. 1997. *A Major London 'Minor' The Surrey Theatre 1805–65*, London.

Knowlson, Joyce. nd. *Red Plush and Gilt: The Heyday of Manchester Theatre*, Manchester.

Koller, Ann Marie. 1984. *The Theatre Duke Georg II of Saxe-Meiningen and the German Stage*, Stanford, Calif.

Kruger, Loren. 1992. *The National Stage: Theatre and Cultural Legitimation in England, France and America*, Chicago and London.

Lamb, Margaret. 1980. *'Antony and Cleopatra' on the English Stage*, London.

Lane, R. J. ed. 1870. *Charles Kemble's Shakespeare Readings*, 3 vols., London.

Lang, Matheson. 1940. *Mr Wu Looks Back*, London.

Langtry, Lillie. 1925. *The Days I Knew*, New York.

Lawrence, W. J. 1892. *The Life of Gustavus Vaughan Brooke*, Belfast.

1899. Some Women Players of Shakespeare. In *Illustrated London News* 17 July 1899.

Leach, Joseph. 1970. *Bright Particular Star The Life and Time of Charlotte Cushman*, New Haven and London.

Leather, Victor. 1959. *British Entertainers in France*, Toronto.

Lee, Sidney. 1898. *A Life of William Shakespeare*, London.

1902. *Queen Victoria A Biography*, London.

1906. *Shakespeare and the Modern Stage with other Essays*, London.

1925–7. *King Edward VII A Biography*, 2 vols., London.

Lehman, B. H. 1966. *Carlyle's Theory of the Hero*, New York.

Levine, Lawrence W. 1988. *Highbrow/Lighbrow The Emergence of Cultural Hierarchy in America*, Cambridge, Mass. and London.

Lewes, G. H. 1875. *On Actors and the Art of Acting*, London.

Le Winter, Oswald ed. 1976. *Shakespeare in Europe*, Harmondsworth.

Lockridge, Richard. 1932. *Darling of the Gods Edwin Booth: 1833–1893*, London.

Lounger in the Clubs. 1864. *The National Shakespeare Committee and the Late Mr Thackeray Signed The Lounger in the Clubs*, London.

Lounsbury, Thomas R. 1902. *Shakespeare and Voltaire*, New York.

Love, Harold, ed. 1984. *The Australian Stage: A Documentary History*, Kensington, NSW.

Lowell, James Russell. 1870. *Among My Books*, London.

Ludlum, Harry. 1977. *A Biography of Bram Stoker Creator of Dracula*, London.

Mackaye, Percy. 1916. *Caliban by the Yellow Sands*, New York.

Macleod, Joseph. 1981. *The Actor's Right to Act*, London.

Maguire, Hugh. 1992. The Architectural Response. In Foulkes ed. 1992, pp. 149–64.

Mais, S. P. B. 1916. Our Greatest Privilege and Greatest Achievement. In *Nineteenth Century*, April 1916, pp. 813–31.

Mankowitz, Wolf. 1982. *Mazeppa The Lives, Loves and Legends of Ada Isaacs Menken*, London.

Manvell, Roger. 1971. *Shakespeare and the Film*, London.

Marie Louise, Her Highness Princess. 1956. *My Memories of Six Reigns*, London.

Marks, H. Stacy. 1894. *Pen and Pencil Sketches*, London.

Marshall, Herbert and Stock, Mildred. 1958. *Ira Aldridge The Negro Tragedian*, London.

Marston, Westland. 1890. *Our Recent Actors*, London.

Martin, Theodore. 1880. An Eye-Witness of John Kemble. In *Nineteenth Century*, February 1880, pp. 276–96.

  1881. The Meiningen Company and the London Stage. In *Blackwood's Magazine*, August 1881, pp. 248–63.

  1882. *Life of the Prince Consort*, 2 vols., London.

  1890. *Helena Faucit (Lady Martin)*, London and Edinburgh.

  1906. *Monographs Garrick, Rachel and Lord Stockmar*, London.

Martin-Harvey, John. 1933. *The Autobiography of Sir John Martin-Harvey*, London.

Marvin, F. S. ed. 1908, *Reports on Elementary Schools 1852–82 by Matthew Arnold*, London.

Marx, Karl and Engels, Frederick. 1975. *Collected Works*, London.

Mason, Edward Tuckerman. 1890. *The Othello of Tommaso Salvini*, New York and London.

Mathews, Mrs A. 1838. *Memoirs of Charles Mathews*, 3 vols., London.

Mazer, Cary M. 1981. *Shakespeare Refashioned Elizabethan Plays on Edwardian Stages*, Ann Arbor, Michigan.

  1983. Treasons, Stratagems, and Spoils: Edwardian Actor–Managers and the Shakespeare Memorial National Theatre. In *Theatre Survey*, vol. 24, pp. 1–33.

McCarthy, Lillah. 1933. *Myself and My Friends*, London.

McDonald, Jan. 1971a. *The Taming of the Shrew* at the Haymarket Theatre, 1844 and 1847. In Richards and Thomson eds., 1971, pp. 157–70.

  1971b. Helena Modjeska's Season at the Court Theatre, London, 1880–1881. In *Theatre Research*, vol. 11, nos. 2 and 3, pp. 141–53.

McIntyre, Ian. 1999. *Garrick*, London.

Meisel, Martin. 1983. *Realisations*, Princeton.

Melchinger, Siegfried. 1968. *Max Reinhardt – Sein Theater in Bildern*, Hanover and Vienna.

Meller, J. E. 1976. *Leisure and the Changing City*, London.

Messinger, Gary S. 1985. *Manchester in the Victorian Age: The Half-Known City*, Manchester.

Modjeska, Helena. 1910. *Memories and Impressions of Helena Modjeska An Autobiography*, New York.

Montague, C. E. 1941. *Dramatic Values*, London.

Moody, Jane. 1994. Writing for the Metropolis: Illegitimate Performances in Early Nineteenth-Century London. In *Shakespeare Survey* 47, pp. 61–9.

2000. *Illegitimate Theatres in London 1770–1840*, Cambridge.

Moody, Richard. 1958. *Astor Place Riot*, Bloomington, Ind.

Morley, Henry. 1891. *The Journal of a London Playgoer*. London.

Morley, Sheridan. 1979. *Sybil Thorndike. A Life in the Theatre*, London.

Mortimer, Owen. 1995. *Speak of me as I am The Story of Ira Aldridge*, Wangaratta, Australia.

1996. *Ira Aldridge and Poland*, Wangaratta, Australia.

Mukherjee, Sushil Kumar. 1982. *The Story of the Calcutta Theatre*, Calcutta and New Delhi.

Mullin, Donald ed. 1983. *Victorian Actors and Actresses in Review*, Westport, Conn.

Nevo, Ruth. 1991. Yeats, Shakespeare and Ireland. In Newey and Thompson, eds. 1991, pp. 182–7.

Newey, Vincent and Thompson, Ann eds. 1991. *Literature and Nationalism*, Liverpool.

Newton, H. Chance. 1927. *Cues and Curtain Calls*, London.

Nicholson, Watson. 1906. *The Struggle for a Free Stage in London*, Boston and New York.

Nodier, Charles. 1801. *Pensées de Shakespeare extraites de ses Ouvrages*.

Nolte, Claire. 1999. Ambivalent Patriots: Czech Culture in the Great War. In Roshwald and Stites eds. 1999, pp. 162–75.

Norton, Charles Eliot ed. 1883. *The Correspondence of Thomas Carlyle and Ralph Waldo Emerson*, 2 vols., London.

ed. 1887. *Correspondence Between Goethe and Carlyle*, London.

O'Connor, Marion F. 1987. Theatre of the Empire: 'Shakespeare's England' at Earl's Court, 1912. In Howard and O'Connor eds. 1987, pp. 68–97.

Odell, George C. D. 1920. *Shakespeare from Betterton to Irving*, 2 vols., New York.

1927–49. *Annals of the New York Stage*, vol. 9, 1937, New York.

Orme, Michael. 1936. *J. T. Grein The Story of a Pioneer 1862–1935*, London.

Osborne, John. 1988. *The Meiningen Court Theatre 1861–1890*, Cambridge.

Pakula, Hannah. 1996. *An Uncommon Woman The Empress Frederick*, London.

Palmer. David. 1965. *The Rise of English Studies*, Oxford.

Parker, John ed. 1947. *Who's Who in the Theatre*, London.

The Parliamentary Debates (Official Report) Third Volume of Session 1913, 5th Series, Vol. 81, London.

Patterson, M. 1981. *The Revolution in the German Theatre 1900–1933*, London.

Payne, Ben Iden. 1977. *A Life in a Wooden O*, New Haven.

Peters, Margot. 1985. *Mrs Pat The Life of Mrs Patrick Campbell*, London.

Pearson, Hesketh. 1956. *Beerbohm Tree His Life and Laughter*, London.

Pemberton, T. Edgar. 1902. *Ellen Terry and Her Sisters*, London.

Phelps, William Lyon. 1918. *The Twentieth Century Theatre Observations on the Contemporary English and American Stage*, New York.

Phelps, W. May and Forbes-Robertson, Johnston. 1886. *The Life and Life-Work of Samuel Phelps*, London.

Planché, J. R. 1879. *Suggestions for Establishing an English Art Theatre*, London.

1901. *Recollections and Reflections*, London.

Playfair, Nigel. 1930. *Hammersmith Hoy A Book of Minor Revelations*, London.

Poel, William. 1913. *Shakespeare in the Theatre*, London.

Pogson, Rex. 1952. *Miss Horniman and the Gaiety Theatre Manchester.*

Pollock, Sir Frederick ed. 1876. *Macready's Reminiscences*, London.

Pringle, Marian J. 1994. *The Theatres of Stratford-upon-Avon 1875–1992*, Stratford-upon-Avon.

Private Life of Queen Victoria by One of Her Majesty's Servants, The, 1898, London.

Proposed Shakespeare Memorial National Theatre An Illustrated Handbook Issued by the Executive Committee, 1909, London.

Raby, Peter. 1982. *Fair Ophelia: A Life of Harriet Smithson Berlioz*, Cambridge.

Rheinhardt, E. A. 1930. *The Life of Eleanora Duse*, London.

Richards, Denis. 1958. *Offspring of the Vic: A History of Morley College*, London.

Richards, Jeffrey ed. 1994. *Sir Henry Irving Theatre, Culture and Society*, Keele.

Richards, Kenneth. 1971. Samuel Phelps's production of *All's Well that Ends Well*. In Richards and Thomson eds. 1971, pp. 179–95.

Richards, Kenneth and Thomson, Peter, eds. 1971. *Nineteenth Century British Theatre*, London.

Ristori, Adelaide. 1907. *Memoirs and Artistic Studies of Adelaide Ristori*, New York.

Roshwald, A. and Stites, Richard eds. 1999. *European Culture and the Great War*, Cambridge.

Rowell, George. 1975. Tree's Shakespeare Festivals (1905–1913). In *Theatre Notebook*, vol. 29, no. 2, pp. 74–81.

1978. *Queen Victoria Goes to the Theatre*, London.

1993. *The Old Vic A History*, Cambridge.

Rowell, George ed. 1994. *Robert Atkins An Unfinished Autobiography*, London.

Rowell, George and Jackson, Anthony. 1984. *The Repertory Movement A History of Regional Theatre in Britain*, Cambridge.

Ruggles, Eleanor. 1953. *Prince of Players Edwin Booth*, London.

Russell, Charles E. 1926. *Julia Marlowe Her Life and Art*, New York.

Salmon, Eric. 1983. *Granville Barker*, London.

Salvini, Tommaso. 1893. *Leaves from the Autobiography of Tommaso Salvini*, New York.

Sarcey, Francisque. 1879. The Comédie Française. In *Nineteenth Century*, July 1879, pp. 182–200.

Saxon, A. H. 1966. Shakespeare and Circuses. In *Theatre Survey*, 78, pp. 59–79.

1966. *Enter Foot and Horse A History of Hippodrama in England and France*, London and New Haven.

Scott, Clement. 1899. *The Drama of Yesterday and Today*, 2 vols., London.

Schlegel, William. 1846. *A Course of Lectures on Dramatic Art and Literature*, London.

Schoch, Richard W. 1998. *Shakespeare's Victorian Stage Performing History in the Theatre of Charles Kean*, Cambridge.

Schoonerwoerd, N. 1963. *J. T. Grein*, Netherlands.

Senelick, Laurence. 1982. *Gordon Craig's Moscow Hamlet*, London and Westport, Conn.

1984. Face Cards. In *History of Photography*, vol. 8, no. 1, pp. 43–6.

Senelick, Laurence ed. 1991. *National Theatres in Northern and Eastern Europe, 1746–1900*, Cambridge.

Shakespeare Tercentenary Commemoration Performance The Memorial Volume, 1916, London.

Shattuck, Charles H. 1965. *The Shakespeare Promptbooks*, Urbana and London.

1969. *The Hamlet of Edwin Booth*, Urbana and London.

1971. The Theatrical Management of Edwin Booth. In Donohue ed. 1971, pp. 168–78.

1976. *Shakespeare on the American Stage From the Hallams to Edwin Booth*, Washington.

1987. *Shakespeare on the American Stage From Booth and Barratt to Sothern and Marlowe*, Washington.

Shattuck, Charles H. ed. 1962a. *Mr Macready Produces As You Like It A Prompt-Book Study*, Urbana.

1962b. *William Charles Macready's King John A Facsimile Prompt-Book*, Urbana.

Shaw, G. B. 1910. *The Dark Lady of the Sonnets*, London.

1932. *Our Theatres in the Nineties*, 3 vols., London.

Shaw, William A. 1894. *Manchester Old and New*, 3 vols., London.

Sillard, Robert M. 1901. *Barry Sullivan and His Contemporaries*, 2 vols., London.

Smiles, Samuel. 1880. *Duty*, London.

1905. *Self Help*, London.

Smither, Nelle. 1944. *A History of the English Theatre in New Orleans*, New York.

Speaight, Robert. 1954. *William Poel and the Elizabethan Revival*, London.

1973. *Shakespeare on the Stage*, London.

Speaight, Robert ed. 1971. *A Bridges-Adams Letter Book*, London.

St John, Christopher ed. 1952. *Ellen Terry and Bernard Shaw: A Correspondence*, London.

The Stage Yearbook, 1917, London

Stanislavski, Constantin. 1967. *My Life in Art*, Harmondsworth.

Stavisky, Aron Y. 1969. *Shakespeare and the Victorians*, Oklahoma.

Stendhal. 1962. *Racine and Shakespeare translated by Guy Daniels with a Foreword by André Maurois*, London.

Stern, Ernst. 1951. *My Life My Stage*, London.

Stern, Ernst und Herald, Heinz. 1920. *Reinhardt und seine Bühne*, Berlin.

Stochholm, Johanne M. 1964. *Garrick's Folly. The Stratford Jubilee of 1769*, London.

Stoker, Bram. 1906. *Personal Reminiscences of Henry Irving*, 2 vols., London.

Stokes, John. 1972. *Resistible Theatres*, London.

1992. Helena Modjeska in England. In *Women and Theatre*, Occasional Papers 1, pp. 19–37.

Stoval, Floyd ed. 1964. *The Collected Writings of Walt Whitman*, New York.

Styan, J. L. 1982. *Directors in Perspective Max Reinhardt*, Cambridge.

1983. *The Shakespeare Revolution*, Cambridge.

Tallis's History and Description of the Crystal Place, 1851. 2 vols., London.

Taranow, Gerda. 1996. *The Bernhardt Hamlet Culture and Context*, New York.

Taylor, Gary. 1990. *Reinventing Shakespeare*, London.

Taylor, Tom. 1871. *The Theatre in England Some of its Shortcomings and Possibilities*, London.

Terriss, Ellaline. 1928. *Ellaline Terriss by Herself*, London.

1955. *Just a Little Bit of String*, London.

Thimm, Franz. 1865. *Shakespeariana 1564 to 1864 An Account of the Shakespeare Literature of England, Germany and France during Three Centuries with Bibliographical Introductions*, London.

Thomson, John. 1993. *The New Zealand Stage 1891–1900*, Wellington.

Thorndike, Ashley. 1927. *Shakespeare in America*, Oxford.

Thorndike, Russell. 1929. *Sybil Thorndike*, London.

Thornton, M. and Wray, Romona (eds.) 1997. *Shakespeare and Ireland*, Basingstoke.

Toynbee, William ed. 1912. *The Diaries of William Charles Macready*, 2 vols., London.

Tree, Herbert Beerbohm. 1913. *Thoughts and After-Thoughts*, London.

Trench, Richard Chenevix. 1864. *'Every Good Gift From Above' Being a Sermon Preached in the Parish Church of Stratford-upon-Avon April 24 1864 at the Celebration of Shakespeare's Birth*, London.

Trewin, J. C. 1955. *Mr Macready*, London.

1960. *Benson and the Bensonians*, London.

1963. *The Birmingham Repertory Theatre 1913–1963*, London.

1964. *Shakespeare on the English Stage 1900–1964*, London.

Trollope, Frances. 1832. *Domestic Manners of the Americans*, London.

1836. *Paris and the Parisians*, London.

Truman, Olivia. 1984. *Beerbohm Tree's Olivia*, London.

Turner, Godfrey. 1877. Amusements of the English People. In *Nineteenth Century*, December 1877, pp. 820–30.

Twain, Mark. 1885. *The Adventures of Huckleberry Finn*, New York.

Velz, John M. and Teague, Francis N. eds. 1986. *One Touch of Shakespeare: Letters of Joseph Crosby to Joseph Parker Norris*, Washington.

Voltaire, F-M. 1731. Preface to *Brutus*: Discourse on Tragedy. In Le Winter ed. 1976, pp. 29–43.

Wade, Allan ed. 1957. *Henry James. The Scenic Art*, New York.

Walbrook, H. M. 1926. *A Playgoer's Wanderings*, London.

Ward, Genevieve and Whiteing, Richard. 1918. *Both Sides of the Curtain*, London.

Warde, Frederick. 1920. *Fifty Years of Make-Believe*, New York.

Warwick, Lou. 1974. *Theatre Unroyal*, Northampton.

Watermeier, Daniel ed. 1971. *Between Actor and Critic Selected Letters of Edwin Booth and William Winter*, New Jersey.

Webster, Benjamin. 1849. *The Series of Dramatic Entertainments Performed at Windsor Castle*, London.

Webster, Margaret. 1969. *The Same Only Different*, London.

Wells, Stanley ed. 1997. *Shakespeare in the Theatre An Anthology of Criticism*, Oxford.

Whitelaw, Lis. 1990. *The Life and Rebellious Times of Cicely Hamilton*, London.

Whitworth, Geoffrey. 1952. *The Making of a National Theatre*, London.

Williams, Clifford. 1973. *Madame Vestris – A Theatrical Biography*, London.

Williams, Simon. 1986. The 'Shakespeare Stage' in Nineteenth-Century Germany. In Foulkes ed. 1986, pp. 210–22.

1990. *Shakespeare on the German Stage. Volume 1: 1586–1914*, Cambridge.

Williamson, Jane. 1970. *Charles Kemble, Man of the Theatre*, Lincoln, Nebr.

Wilson, A. E. 1952. *The Lyceum Theatre*.

Wilstach, P. 1908. *Richard Mansfield: The Man and the Actor*, New York.

Winter, Jay. 1999. Popular Culture in Wartime Britain. In Roshwald and Stites eds. 1999, pp. 330–48.

Winter, William. 1893. *Life and Art of Edwin Booth*, London and New York.

1898. *Ada Rehan A Study*, London and New York.

1910. *Life and Art of Richard Mansfield*, 2 vols., New York.

1911. *Shakespeare on the Stage*, New York.

1913. *The Wallet of Time*, New York.

Wiseman, Cardinal. 1865. *A Lecture on Shakespeare*, London.

Wood, R. Derek. 1975. *The Calotype Patent Lawsuit of Talbot v. Laroche*, Bromley.

Woods, Alan. 1977. Frederick B. Warde: America's Forgotten Tragedian. In *Educational Theatre Journal*, no. 29, pp. 333–44.

1977–9. Quality wasn't Expected: the Classical Tours of George C. Miln. In *Theatre Studies*, nos. 24/25, pp. 139–47.

Wordsworth, Charles. 1864. *On Shakespeare's Knowledge and Use of the Bible*, London.

Yates, Edmund. 1884. *Recollections and Experiences*, 2 vols., London.

Young, G. M. ed. 1952. *Macaulay Prose and Poetry*, London.

Young, J. C. 1871. *A Memoir of Charles Mayne Young Tragedian With Extracts from His Son's Journal*, London.

JOURNALS

Athenaeum
Bengal Hukaru
Blackwood's Magazine
Boston Post
Boston Transcript
Boston Traveller
Builder
Contemporary Review
Cosmopolitan
Critic
Daily Chronicle
Daily Graphic, New York
Daily Mail
Daily News, Chicago
Daily Telegraph
Echo
Educational Theatre Journal
Era
Essays in Theatre

Evening Post, New York
Examiner
Examiner and Times
Fortnightly Review
Harvard Library Bulletin
Illustrated London News
Irish Times
Kinematograph and Lantern Weekly
Lloyd's Weekly London Life
Louisville Kentucky Herald
Manchester Evening News
Manchester Guardian
McClure's Magazine
Montreal Telegraph
Morning Post
New Orleans Times Democracy
New York City Sun
New York City Telegraph
New York City Tribune
New York Daily Tribune
New York Dramatic Mirror
New York Evening Journal
New York Herald
New York Times
Nineteenth Century
Nineteenth Century Theatre Research
Pall Mall Magazine
Punch
Record and Herald
Revue des Lettres Modernes
Salford Chronicle
Salford Weekly News
Shakespeare Jahrbuch
Shakespeare Survey
Sketch
Standard
Tallis's Illustrated Life of London
Theatre Notebook
Theatre Research
Theatrical Journal
Thespian
The Times
Town and Country
Tribune
Vanity Fair

Index